continued . . .

"Smart, fast-paced, unique . . . a blend of sophistication and wit that has you laughing out loud."
—Christine Feehan, *New York Times* bestselling author of *Dark Demon*

"Tongue-in-cheek . . . fast pacing and in-your-face action. Give it a try. Kate's a fun character, and keeps you on the edge of your seat."
—*SF Reader*

"Ms. Kenner has a style and delivery all her own . . . fun and innovative . . . [*Carpe Demon*] shouldn't be missed."
—*Fallen Angel Review*

"You're gonna love this book! A terrific summer read with lots of humor and crazy situations and action."
—*Fresh Fiction*

"Kenner scores a direct hit with this offbeat and humorous adventure, which has an engaging cast of characters. Car pools and holy water make an unforgettable mix."
—*Romantic Times*

California Demon

Demon

The Secret Life of a
Demon-Hunting
Soccer Mom

Julie Kenner

BERKLEY BOOKS, NEW YORK

THE BERKLEY PUBLISHING GROUP
Published by the Penguin Group
Penguin Group (USA) Inc.
375 Hudson Street, New York, New York 10014, USA
Penguin Group (Canada), 90 Eglinton Avenue East, Suite 700, Toronto, Ontario M4P 2Y3, Canada
(a division of Pearson Penguin Canada Inc.)
Penguin Books Ltd., 80 Strand, London WC2R 0RL, England
Penguin Group Ireland, 25 St. Stephen's Green, Dublin 2, Ireland (a division of Penguin Books Ltd.)
Penguin Group (Australia), 250 Camberwell Road, Camberwell, Victoria 3124, Australia
(a division of Pearson Australia Group Pty. Ltd.)
Penguin Books India Pvt. Ltd., 11 Community Centre, Panchsheel Park, New Delhi—110 017, India
Penguin Group (NZ), Cnr. Airborne and Rosedale Roads, Albany, Auckland 1310, New Zealand
(a division of Pearson New Zealand Ltd.)
Penguin Books (South Africa) (Pty.) Ltd., 24 Sturdee Avenue, Rosebank, Johannesburg 2196, South Africa

Penguin Books Ltd., Registered Offices: 80 Strand, London WC2R 0RL, England

This is a work of fiction. Names, characters, places, and incidents either are the product of the author's imagination or are used fictitiously, and any resemblance to actual persons, living or dead, business establishments, events, or locales is entirely coincidental. The publisher does not have any control over and does not assume any responsibility for author or third-party websites or their content.

Copyright © 2006 by Julie Kenner.
Cover design by Richard Hasselberger.
Cover illustration by Mark Gerber.
Text design by Stacy Irwin.

First edition: June 2006

Library of Congress Cataloging-in-Publication Data

Kenner, Julie
    California demon / Julie Kenner.— Berkley trade pbk. ed.
        p. cm.
    ISBN 0-425-21043-X
    1. Suburban life—Fiction. 2. Demonology—Fiction. 3. Mothers—Fiction. I. Title.

PS3611.E665C35 2006
813'.6—dc22

                                                                    2006042814

PRINTED IN THE UNITED STATES OF AMERICA

10 9 8 7 6 5 4 3 2 1

California Demon

One

My name is Kate Connor, and I'm a Demon Hunter.

It feels a little odd saying that. For the last fifteen-plus years, I've been a *retired* Demon Hunter, my hunting responsibilities traded for the equally dangerous, if not as dramatically compelling, duties of a stay-at-home mom to my teenager and toddler. And no, I'm not exaggerating the danger factor of mommy-dom. Infiltrating a nest of vampires at dusk might be a tad on the treacherous side, but it's nothing compared to telling a fourteen-year-old that she's not allowed to wear eyeshadow. Trust me. I know of what I speak.

I'd been drawn back into active duty after a demon attacked me in my kitchen, setting off a whole chain of events which (as you can probably guess) pitted the forces of good against the forces of evil in one final, cataclysmic battle. Sounds like a movie ad doesn't it? But it's true. And after the battle was over, I had to admit that I missed being involved in something big. Something important.

Not that cheerleader tryouts and potty training aren't important. But, well, you know what I mean.

At any rate, I agreed to pick up where I left off, and suddenly I found myself with not one, but two full-time jobs: Level Four Demon Hunter and Stay-at-Home Mom.

And I'm here to tell you that those two jobs don't exactly go together like oh, say, peanut butter and jelly. Why? Because the demon-hunting thing is a great big secret. I work for a supersecret arm of the Vatican known as *Forza Scura,* and one of the first rules is utter secrecy. Nobody knows. (Well, nobody except my best friend Laura, but every rule deserves an exception, don't you think?)

Unlike most working moms, I'm cut zero slack by society. If Carla Corporate serves frozen dinners three nights in a row, no one bats an eye. After all, Mommy's got a big presentation coming up.

But me? I'm expected to at least make an effort at cooking. (And I do try, really I do, but I think I lack the haute-cuisine gene. Or even the short-order gene, for that matter.) I don't even get to enjoy any of the perks that might otherwise go along with my demon-hunting career. Like, "Sorry, Officer, I didn't realize I was speeding. But sometimes we Demon Hunters are in a hurry. Safety of mankind. Fate of the world. Good prevailing over the forces of darkness. You understand."

Nope. Doesn't work that way. And in order to make my two lives jibe, I end up telling a lot of little white lies. And sometimes, they backfire on me.

Which goes a long way toward explaining why I was spending a Friday morning in December precariously balanced on an ancient wooden ladder in the media room at Coastal Mists Nursing Home, a few feet of silver garland draped over my shoulders, a staple gun holstered in my back pocket, and my two-year-old playing snooker with the Christmas tree ornaments on the rug below me.

A few months ago, this place was crawling with demons. (Okay, maybe that's a slight exaggeration, but there were at least a half dozen walking around in their geriatric disguises, acting like they owned the place.) Since such a situation was beyond unacceptable, I'd gone in to clean the place up. Not unlike Marshal Dillon, really. Except I didn't have a cool white hat or little silver star.

What I did have was a lovely arsenal of lies (along with the more practical tools like holy water, wooden stakes, and a kick-ass stiletto knife). And I have to say that I did a hell of a job. After only a few short months, Coastal Mists was demon-free. For that matter, many of the administrators and doctors had vanished into the night. Not demons, but human facilitators who'd been seduced by the promise of power, wealth, whatever. A too-common tale, and one that had transformed a run-of-the-mill nursing home into a demon factory.

I, however, had shut that down.

Now the place that had once been a depressing breeding ground for the undead was a pretty cheerful establishment, complete with HBO, Cinemax, and a state-of-the-art plasma television with a sound system that made my husband drool.

But did I get to cross Coastal Mists off my to-do list? Free up a little time for grocery shopping, carpooling, and other miscellaneous family chores? No, I did not. Because in order to infiltrate myself into Coastal Mists in the first place, I'd had to concoct a cover story. And mine was volunteering.

The demons might have been eradicated, but the responsibilities weren't. So in addition to cooking meals for my family, I was now delivering meals to the bedridden. In addition to reading Dr. Seuss to my toddler, I was now reading Zane Grey to men who probably remembered the Wild West. In addition to potty training my kid, I was now—well, you get the idea.

Also—and this was a big "also"—as much of a time drain

as my Coastal Mists activities were, the truth was that I needed to keep a presence there. The nursing home had a high-mortality rate (that's just the nature of nursing homes), which made it the perfect breeding spot for any demonic leader looking to get a toehold in San Diablo.

It had happened once. I didn't intend to let it happen again.

On that particular day, my best friend Laura and I were helping decorate the place for Christmas. We'd brought Timmy with us for three reasons, the first being totally selfish: mommy guilt. Although I'd enrolled Timmy in day care—and although he actually seemed to enjoy it—my guilt level was high enough that I only took him in when absolutely necessary. Like when the Legions of Hell descend on the neighborhood. Or when I need to buy new clothes. Trust me. I'd rather slay fifteen demons with a toddler at my side than take the munchkin shopping for the perfect outfit to wear to one of my husband's politically motivated, deathly dull cocktail parties.

My second reason originated from a more altruistic place: The folks at the nursing home absolutely adored the little bugger. Makes sense. They didn't get that many visitors, and even fewer from the preschool crowd. Besides, as toddlers go, mine was practically perfect. Not that I'm biased or anything.

Finally, I'd brought Timmy along because today was Family Day at my daughter Allie's school. As soon as Laura and I were finished with the decorating, we were going to pack up Timmy, swing by the bakery to pick up the PTA-mandated two dozen cupcakes, and head over to Coronado High School where we would do our best not to embarrass our freshman daughters by mentioning boys, grades, teachers, boys, television, politics, boys, movies, food, or any other potentially disastrous subject.

Laura concentrated on trimming the tree while I stapled

garland to the archway, trying my best to drape it artistically but failing miserably. Martha Stewart, I'm not. Below me, my little boy entertained the elderly by abusing the Christmas ornaments, rummaging in my purse, singing "Jingle Bells," and demonstrating his well-developed skill at blowing raspberries.

I carefully lined up a twist of garland, pulled the trigger on the staple gun, gave the garland a satisfied tug, then checked my watch. Not quite eleven.

"Why don't you go on, honey? I can take care of hanging the rest of that."

The suggestion came from Delia Murdock, who'd just celebrated her ninety-first birthday. She was standing at the base of my ladder, one hand on the frame, ostensibly holding it steady. As a general rule, the woman spent her life listing slightly to the left, and there was no way I was letting her climb a ladder.

"We're not in any hurry," I lied. "Are we, Laura?"

Laura stared at me as if I was insane because, of course, I was. We were due in the school's gymnasium—cupcakes in hand—in exactly one hour and fifteen minutes.

"Five minutes," I said as I descended the ladder, then dragged it to the next archway. "The girls will understand if we're a teensy bit late." Another lie. Allie had reminded me of this command performance at least three times a day for the last two weeks. She'd left reminder notes on my bathroom mirror, on the coffeepot, and on my steering wheel.

Apparently Family Day is a big enough deal at the high school to overcome the typical teenage mortification that comes from having a parent nearby. And I knew that if I arrived late, there would be hell to pay. I deal with hell every day. And believe me, the fire-and-brimstone variety is a lot more palatable than what my fourteen-year-old is capable of dishing out.

Laura looked dubious, but didn't argue, so while Bing Crosby crooned on about White Christmases, I *ker-chunked* the stapler in time with the music, speeding up considerably when Bing faded away and "Jingle Bell Rock" blasted out from the media-room speakers. Behind me, I could hear Timmy counting ("one, two, free, four, six . . .") as Mr. Montgomery burst out with "atta boy," and "smart as a whip, that kid." My heart did a little twisting number. I have great kids, and today my mommy-pride was working overtime.

The tightness in my heart increased, as it so often did when I thought of the kids, especially Allie. Tim has his daddy, but Allie and I lost Eric, my first husband, to a brutal mugging five years ago. And although I'm happily remarried and wouldn't trade Stuart for the world, not a day goes by that I don't feel the loss, like someone had taken a cookie cutter and stolen an Eric-shaped piece of my soul.

The shrill ring of my cell phone jarred me out of my melancholy. I steadied myself on the ladder with one hand, then pulled my phone out of my pocket with the other. *Stuart.* I frowned, fearing I knew what he was calling about.

"Don't tell me you're not coming."

"Are you kidding? Of course I'm coming. Allie's been bugging us about this for weeks."

"Oh," I said, feeling a bit guilty for doubting him. I had cause though. My husband was about to formally announce his candidacy for county attorney, and his days (and nights) had been filled with all manner of schmoozing, politicking, and fund-raising. The kids and I had gotten the short end of the scheduling stick on more than one occasion.

Being a wonderfully supportive wife, I tried not to let it bother me. Some of the time, I even succeeded.

"So," I said, trying again. "What's up?"

"Just reporting in," he said. "And I wanted to see if you needed me to get anything for you. The cupcakes? Eddie? Ibuprofen for a migraine?"

Is he an incredible man or what? I mean, how many husbands actually commit their wife's PTA obligations to memory? Or volunteer to pick up their daughter's pseudo-great-grandfather despite the fact that—truth be told—the two men really don't get along that well? I figure not many, and I'm lucky that one of the few belongs to me.

"Eddie's taking a cab," I said, figuring both Eddie and Stuart would thank me for that one. Eddie's a retired Demon Hunter who'd recently taken up permanent residence in my life and temporary residence in my guest room. Due to a misunderstanding that I never bothered to clear up, my family believes that Eddie is Eric's grandfather. Just one of those little *Forza*-related obfuscations that makes my life so interesting.

The cupcake question required a bit more consideration, but in the end I declined that offer as well. I love my husband, but I don't trust his taste in pastries. I may not be able to cook worth a damn, but I can shop with the best of them. As for the painkillers, I've learned to carry my own supply.

"You're sure?" he asked, when I told him he was off the hook.

"Totally. All you have to do is show up and you'll be golden."

"No problem there," he said. "Clark's got a potential contributor waiting to meet me in his office, but that's the only thing on my plate. After that, I'm heading to the school."

Clark Curtis is my husband's boss. He's also the lame-duck county attorney who favors my husband to step into his shoes. When I'd met Stuart, he'd been slaving away as an underpaid government attorney in the real-estate division with no political aspirations whatsoever.

Clark, however, had seen some potential, and had plucked my husband from relative obscurity and thrust him into the political limelight. Great for Stuart, not so great for me. Selfish, maybe, but I'm not crazy about the trappings of political wife-dom. And I'm *really* not crazy about the sporadic hours that my newly politicized husband has been keeping.

All of which meant that the mention of Clark didn't exactly send ripples of warm, fuzzy confidence racing through my body. The opposite, in fact, and I kept my grip tight on the ladder as I closed my eyes and breathed deep, weighing what to say. Now wasn't the time for a spousal tiff, but at the same time, a tiff would be small potatoes compared to Allie's silent, sulky disappointment if Stuart didn't show. Finally, I settled on diplomacy. "Just don't lose track of time."

"I won't," he said. "I know my priorities."

"Okay," I said, but not entirely comforted. I started to say more, but my attention was grabbed by a rousing chorus of "Na-KED baby! Na-KED baby! Naked baby! Naked baby! Na-ke-ed ba-A-A-A-BEEEEEEE," screeched more or less to the tune of the "Hallelujah Chorus." For this, I have no one to blame but myself, and I twisted around on the ladder with a sense of dread coupled with amusement. Sure enough, my kidlet had managed to strip off his shirt, his pants, and his Pull-Ups.

I said a quick good-bye to my husband. He'd either make it or he wouldn't; and if he didn't, then he'd be getting the cold shoulder from both of the females in his life. In the meantime, I needed to focus on the younger male in my life.

He was marching in a circle, not a care in the world, his little legs pumping in time with the song that was blaring out of his mouth. Mr. Montgomery and the others were laughing so hard that I was tempted to call the nurse; I really didn't want my son to be the catalyst for a spate of coronaries.

I watched for longer than I probably should have—What can I say? He was cute—then put on my stern face and said, "Timmy!"

He clamped his mouth shut, but his eyes were wide and innocent. "I sing, Momma!"

"You certainly do," I said. I glanced over at Laura for support, but her entire face was flush with laughter, and the little Santa ornament that dangled between her fingers trembled with evil glee.

So much for a little help from my friends.

I focused on keeping a firm expression. "The singing is fine, sweetie. But we wear clothes when we're in public."

"Not public. Inside!"

I swear, the kid was going to grow up to be a lawyer. Like father, like son.

"Yes," I said, infinitely patient. "We are inside. But we wear clothes inside, too, don't we? At home and at school and at mass."

"And the mall," he said.

"Exactly," I said, completely proud. "And right now, you're inside and have to put your clothes back on."

My little boy wasn't listening though, too fascinated with his own nakedness. I sighed and moved farther down the ladder, leaving the last bit of garland hanging like a sad tail from the middle of the arch. Apparently, I'd been wrong about the demons having left Coastal Mists. My own little devil was prancing away right there in the media room.

Before I reached the floor, Laura held up a hand, stopping me. "I'll get Timmy dressed. You hurry." She tapped her watch. "Cupcakes, remember?"

Timmy, meanwhile, was racing around the area rug,

launching himself at the residents, who were laughing and egging him on. I had a sneaking suspicion a few had given him some chocolate. They might as well have passed him crystal meth; the effect couldn't have been any more pronounced.

Laura saw where I was looking, and cut me off before I could protest. "He's not even three, Kate. I can handle it. I have one of my own, remember?"

Except hers was now fourteen and dressed herself. Even so, I nodded. I knew better than to argue with Laura; she's the woman who'd successfully returned outfits to Nordstrom despite the huge *75-percent Off, No-Return, Clearance-Final-Sale* signs plastered all over the store.

I watched, impressed, as she gathered up Timmy's clothes, then gathered up Timmy. He started to struggle, but then she flipped him over, holding tight around his waist, as his head bobbed somewhere around her knees. His protests morphed into squeals of delight, and she marched past me toward the ladies' room, shooting me a look of smug triumph as she went.

I turned back to the task at hand, hurrying since we still had to pick up the cupcakes on the way to school, and knowing the extreme wrath that awaited me if we showed up late.

From my ladder-top vantage point, I could see through the wide windows to the cliffs in the distance. I could even see part of the ocean, billowing and churning, the sun's rays sending miniature rainbows flying each time the froth burst against the beach.

I love California. The weather. The beach. Pretty much everything. But as I stapled garland to the thickly painted wood, I realized that I was craving the white Christmas that Bing so convincingly crooned about. I made a mental note to buy hot chocolate, whipping cream, and some fluffy red-and-green throws. We might not be getting a blizzard this year, but at least I could crank up the air conditioner and wheedle Stuart into lighting a fire in our rarely to never used fireplace.

I was trying to justify a crackling fire despite the seventy degree weather, when I noticed that some of the residents who'd been in the media room were heading down the hallway toward the glass doors, where a uniformed man stood with a cardboard sign, a red gimme cap slung low on his head. I couldn't read the sign or hear what he was saying, but since the residents were queuing up, I assumed they were heading out.

"Where are they going?" I asked.

"Hmm? Who, dear?" Delia answered.

I pointed down the hall, almost losing my balance in the process.

"Ah, hmm. I think they're going on that school field trip."

"Which school? The high school?"

"Oh, yes, the high school." Delia frowned. "I never did finish high school. Daddy didn't think an education was fitting for a woman."

While I was pondering that little bit of insight into Delia, Jenny rounded the corner, clipboard in hand and a crease on her brow. Jenny's a candy striper, a little ditzy, and almost as tuned-in to the Coastal Mists gossip as Delia.

"Mrs. Connor!" she said, looking up at me waving wildly. "Wow. You're doing a great job."

I inspected my work, and decided that Jenny's standards were way too low.

I was just about to ask Jenny if the bus really was going to the high school when Nurse Ratched stomped up, took Jenny by the elbow, and pulled her aside. I aimed a comforting smile in Jenny's direction. I'd been on the receiving end of Nurse Ratched's displeasure, and it really wasn't pretty. (In fairness, I should add that Nurse Ratched is really Nurse Baker, and as far as I can tell, she's not the demon-aiding sycophant I originally presumed. But I still don't like her.)

Nurse Ratched has one of those gravelly voices that's almost impossible to ignore. I liked Jenny, though, and it didn't seem polite to bear witness to her dressing-down. So I tried to keep my mind on other things, doing everything short of sticking my fingers in my ears and humming.

Didn't work. No matter how good my intentions, I couldn't help but hear a few snippets. A good thing, too, considering the subject of their conversation. Good in that it clued me in to the possible presence of demons. Bad for the exact same reason.

The conversation I overheard went like this:

"Jenny, I'm tired of having this same discussion with you. You have *got* to concentrate. I can't have you mixing up the patients."

"But—"

"No buts. There is absolutely no way Dermott Sinclair got on that bus. Which means your field trip list is wrong, and we have one resident unaccounted for!"

"No, we don't! It *was* Mr. Sinclair. He even told me to leave him alone!" Jenny's chin quivered and her skin had turned all blotchy, but so far the tears weren't rolling.

Nurse Ratched sighed and put her arm around the girl. "Jenny, *think*. The man had a heart attack. He's been in a coma for three months. He's been conscious for less than two days. So how could he possibly have the strength to have gotten up and walked onto that bus?"

That one seemed to stump Jenny, and I had to bite back the urge to raise my hand and shove it high into the sky.

That's me, the prize pupil. But what could I say? I knew the answer, or, at least, I knew *an* answer. And it wasn't pretty.

Dermott Sinclair was a demon—and he'd just climbed aboard a bus aimed straight toward my daughter's high school.

Two

About two seconds later, my staunch position had withered. True, Dermott Sinclair was *probably* a demon, but he could also be one of the very fortunate few who really did come out of a coma without any side effects, then decided to head out on a field trip. Granted, the odds favored demon, but it's incredibly bad form to go around killing old men.

And I had another reason to hesitate: If Dermott Sinclair really was a demon, he was taking a hell of a chance making himself known while I was on the premises. Was he trying to bait me? Or was there a plot brewing in the demon world? Something big enough that justified the risk of discovery by the town's only active Hunter?

Obviously, I had some investigating to do.

Except, of course, Sinclair was on the bus and I wasn't. Plus, I had a toddler to deal with. Not to mention the promise I'd made to Allie to absolutely not be late for Family Day. (Technically, chasing Dermott Sinclair wouldn't make me late, since the bus was heading for the high school.

But I had a sneaking suspicion that any brownie points I'd earn by being punctual would be offset by the demerits I'd incur if I wrestled an old man to the gymnasium floor in front of the faculty, the students, and the PTA.)

Which left me with only one workable plan of attack: foist my youngest child onto my best friend, and waylay the demon before the bus reached the high school.

That, I could do.

I snatched my purse from where I'd left it on the floor, then raced to the restroom near the front entrance. I could see the parking lot from there, and the bus was still sitting on the asphalt, blocking my car, actually. I didn't see any exhaust, and a few of the residents milled around while Nurse Ratched and Jenny consulted a clipboard.

I said a quick thank-you to Saint Peoni, the patron saint of fools and Demon Hunters. I still had time.

The ladies' room is just off the main lobby behind the reception desk, and I burst through the door, calling out for Timmy and Laura as I did so.

"Mommy, Mommy! I going potty!" My little boy's voice boomed out from one of the many handicapped stalls. (In my opinion, and in Laura's, schlepping a toddler around in public is handicap enough to justify use of the reserved toilet stalls. At least until the powers that be fire the genius who designed the regular stalls to be too small to hold a mom, a kid, a diaper bag, a purse, and a stuffed animal.)

"Great, sweetie," I said automatically. Then, "Laura, emergency. Can you take care of the munchkin?"

"Demons?" she asked.

I winced, but a quick check under the doors of the other stalls revealed no other occupants.

"Roger that."

"Go, then," she said, almost offhandedly. A few months ago, the idea of a demon wandering loose in the world would have completely freaked her out. Now, it was just one of those things. I felt a twinge of guilt for tainting my friend's view of the world, but moved quickly past it. If I didn't get on that bus and head off Mr. Sinclair, Laura's world might be tainted in more than theory.

I tossed my keys onto the bathroom counter. In a perfect world, I'd find Sinclair and steer him back inside, but since the bus was about to leave—and since I didn't know what Sinclair looked like—I figured the odds were good I'd be on that bus. Besides, I'd learned long ago that this wasn't a perfect world. "For the Odyssey," I said, referring to my minivan. "But, um, don't rush getting to Family Day, okay?"

At that, the rattle of the toilet paper dispenser stopped, and Laura's head appeared over the stall door. "You want to explain that?"

"Not really."

She took a deep breath, and I could see the worry in her eyes. "Keep my baby safe."

I nodded, then glanced at the stall door and the little boy chattering softly to himself behind it. "Ditto," I said.

Naturally, Timmy chose that moment to comprehend that Laura's status had changed from temporary companion to full-fledged babysitter, and he announced his displeasure by screaming for me at the top of his lungs. My heart did another flip-flop, but I steeled myself and backed out of the room. He was safe with Laura, and he'd forgive me later. Now, though, my heart hurt. I told myself that saving the world from the forces of darkness benefits everyone, my children included. But damned if those maternal instincts don't always listen to logic.

Timmy's squeals of displeasure were still ringing in my ears as I jogged across the parking lot to the bus. Everyone was onboard now, and the engine was running. Nurse

Ratched had left, and only Jenny remained, clipboard in hand, a frown on her perky little face.

"Jenny!" I called. "Hold the bus!"

She looked up, her eyes wide with surprise and confusion. "Hey, Mrs. Connor! What's up?"

"I told Nurse Ra—Nurse Baker that I'd go along as a chaperone," I lied. "Since I'm heading that way myself."

"Oh." Her forehead creased. "She didn't say anything to me . . ."

"That's because I just bumped into her." I pointed to my van. "Timmy's sick, so Laura's taking him home, but that leaves me without a way to get to Allie's school. And when I told Nurse Baker, she very kindly suggested that I go on the bus. As a chaperone, of course." I smiled and waited. I was a little afraid that the "kindly" embellishment was going to reveal my story as pure fabrication.

"But we've already got a chaperone," she said. "Marissa Cartright. She's already on the bus."

"Oh." I considered heading back inside right then. Marissa Cartright is, to put not too fine a point on it, a pain in the ass. One of those mothers who lets her demon-child (and I mean that metaphorically, not literally) run wild to torment other children. Like, for example, my kid. Unfortunately, our youngest kids are in the same play group, and Timmy likes the other children. And I like the other moms. So I suck it up and put up with Marissa and little demon-Danielle every other week. That wouldn't be so bad except that Marissa's also a Coastal Mists volunteer *and* on the same PTA committees *and* the president of my Neighborhood Association *and* her daughter (a junior) is on Allie's cheerleading squad.

Honestly, sometimes I'd really rather just deal with the forces of evil.

"Mrs. Connor?"

I waved a hand, shooing away my thoughts. Marissa or not, I needed on that bus. "Nurse Baker thought Marissa might need help."

"Really? Even with Nurse Kelly along, too?"

I just held out my arms and shrugged. "That's what she said."

"Oh. Well, okay," she said, not really caring.

She signaled for the driver to open the door, and as the hydraulic mechanism hissed and moaned, I took the clipboard from her and scanned the names. If Dermott Sinclair wasn't on there, my entire fabrication was for naught. But there he was, a red checkmark confirming his presence.

"Dermott Sinclair," I said, as if I had some vague memory of the name. "Hasn't he been in a coma?"

"Oh, yeah," Jenny said, then leaned closer, a conspiratorial gleam in her usually clueless eyes. "I told Nurse Baker that he'd joined the group, and she didn't believe me. But then she saw him, and she said he couldn't go, and he got all surly with her, but you know Nurse Baker, and she wasn't about to give in."

She sucked in air. I did, too. "Anyway, she said that he wasn't up for traveling, but he said he'd been cleared by his doctor, and she said he hadn't, and he said he had, and—"

"Jenny."

"Right. Anyway, that's why we're running late. She held up the bus while she went and got his chart. And sure enough, his doctor signed off. He's allowed to go on field trips and participate in all activities. No restrictions, it says. Isn't that wild? I mean, from a coma to walking around just like he'd never even been sick. It's almost like a miracle."

"Almost," I said, making a mental note to investigate his doctor.

"Lady, are you getting on the bus or not?" That from the bus driver.

I gave him a quick nod, thanked Jenny, and hopped into the coach's stairwell. The hydraulics hissed again and the door slid shut.

Since my seat was right behind the driver (Carl, I learned), I could see the fourteen or so passengers reflected in the oversize rearview mirror mounted over Carl's seat. But I didn't see any obvious demons. For that matter, I didn't see any subtle ones. No leers. No slanty-eyed glances. No evil cackles.

In fact, the passengers all looked pretty harmless. The men had tended to sit on the left of the bus, and the women on the right. Most were with a companion, looking at a catalog or doing needlepoint or arguing over some indiscretion. A few were sitting by themselves, focusing on crossword puzzles or dozing.

None looked intent upon foisting a reign of evil onto the world.

And that, in a nutshell, is the problem when demons walk the earth. They blend in too damn well.

Most of the time, demons are simply out there in the ether, existing, but not interacting with us. Not that I'm all that keen on the idea of wading through a sea of demons every time I walk to my car, but it's better than meeting one in a dark alley. So long as a demon is incorporeal, he can't do much except watch us and long to be us. Demons have a real thing about wanting to be human.

Some demons want it so badly, in fact, that they go the possession route, stepping in to seize the body while the person's still alive, and trapping the victim's soul in some deep, dark crevice. Possession, however, isn't too subtle. For the most part, the Hollywood makeup department got it right with Linda Blair. In other words, those demons aren't going to be infiltrating the local PTA. At least, not without being noticed.

Fortunately (for all of us) possession is pretty rare. Unfortunately, the more common demon manifestation is less obvious. You know all those medical miracles that you hear about? Someone dying on the operating table and then— amazingly!—they're brought back to life? Someone walking away from a twelve-car pileup despite a massive blow to the head? Someone trapped underwater for close to ten minutes, but managing to survive?

I'll bet you think those folks are the lucky ones. Well, think again. Ninety-nine percent of the time we're not talking miraculous survival, we're talking determined demon.

Of course, not every body is a compatible host for a demon. Only the most powerful demons can infiltrate the body of the faithful, for example. Those souls *fight,* keeping the demons away until the gap closes.

And for the most part, demons avoid the elderly, preferring to infect the young, strong, and healthy (well, except for being dead). But I'd recently learned the hard way that in a pinch, demons will go for whatever's available.

Bottom line: Most demons look pretty much like everybody else.

Fortunately, though, corporeal demons do have a few idiosyncrasies that are useful for identification purposes. Holy ground, for example, stops a demon cold. Your average, everyday demon simply can't walk on sanctified ground. Or, it can, but it hurts like hell (literally). But since the odds of convincing Carl to make a quick detour so that I could parade the passengers through the cathedral were slim to none, I wisely crossed that option off my list.

The breath test is a personal favorite of mine. Demon-breath absolutely reeks. Sulfur mixed with decaying flesh and who knows what else tossed into the mix. Don't ask me why; I just know it's a universal demon characteristic.

The problem with using the breath test to locate demons is severalfold. For one, demons are wise to the whole stinky-breath thing. Altoids, Certs, Listerine—these trappings of modern-day hygiene have made it that much harder for Demon Hunters the world over. (Not that I'm complaining about hygiene, mind you. I'm just stating a fact.)

And even if a little stinkiness does make it past the breath mint, there's still the question of how to get in a demon's face without arousing his suspicions. Plus, there's always the possibility of running across a living, breathing human with breath that absolutely reeks. A social faux pas, maybe, but hardly the basis for justifiable homicide.

No, the breath test just isn't reliable enough. For locating a *possible* demon, yes. For definitively identifying a demon? No.

That leaves holy water. Which suits me just fine.

As definitive tests go, holy water is about as foolproof as they come. Convenient, too, since I'm rarely without a vial or two anymore.

Now all I needed to do was subtly figure out which passenger was Dermott Sinclair.

We'd reached the Coast Highway, and that meant we were about ten minutes from the high school. So I squeezed past Marissa into the aisle.

"People, people!" I called, then paused as all eyes looked up at me. "I just need to run you through a quick roll call before we get to the school." Marissa tapped one of her long, manicured fingers on my arm. I ignored her. "So if you'd just raise your hand when I call your name—"

"Kate."

"—and that way I can check you off the list."

"Kate!"

"Yes?"

"Kelly and I did that before we left Coastal Mists."

"Of course you did, Marissa," I said, in the same tone I use when I'm trying to calm Timmy. I saw her grit her teeth and knew she recognized the voice.

"Then there's really no need to repeat the process, is there?" She looked to Nurse Kelly for confirmation. Kelly, one of the most nonconfrontational women I've ever met, looked at her lap.

"I'm here as a chaperone," I said, grabbing the opportunity. "And that means I need to be familiar with all our charges. In case we need to locate someone at the school or if some sort of emergency comes up."

Marissa looked like she was going to respond to that, but I turned to smile at the passengers. "I know a lot of you already, of course, but not everyone. So if you'll just bear with me." I ran my finger down the clipboard to the first name on the list and started in with "Tamara Able." Ms. Able, a blue-haired and pink-cheeked bird of a woman raised her hand with a perky, "Right here, dear." I made a little check mark, just for show.

Between napping passengers and defective hearing aids, it took five full minutes to get to the "S" names. "Arthur Simms?" A man snorted, then his hand shot into the air. "Right here, girlie. Or are you blind?"

"Right," I said. "Got you." I cleared my throat. "Dermott Sinclair?" No response. My heart slowed in my chest. Had I been wrong? Had he left the nursing home by some other means? Or worse, was he still there, with Laura and my little boy?

I cleared my throat and tried again, willing myself not to be alarmed. Not yet. "Dermott Sinclair?"

Still no response, and that little bubble of panic was just about to lodge in my throat when I saw a pudgy, bald man—earlier, he'd answered to Edmund Morrison—shift in his seat. Beside him, a rail-thin wraith of a man sat staring out the window. Morrison's elbow connected with his companion's rib cage, and the wraith turned sharply, his eyes flashing hot with irritation.

I didn't even need to hear the rest. The wraith was Dermott Sinclair. And he was a demon. I'd bet good money on that. Even more, I'd bet my life. In fact, I was just about to do that.

Discretion might be the better part of valor, but it's also a pain in the rear. There I was in a motor coach full of elderly residents, a PTA vixen, the driver, and one potential demon. I needed to keep everyone safe, maintain my secret identity, and confirm Sinclair's demonic status. You'll forgive me if I was feeling a little stressed.

I was also feeling a little impotent. I'd wanted to get the task out of the way before reaching the school, but short of knocking Carl upside the head and hijacking the bus, I wasn't sure how to accomplish that. I had the holy water, sure. But if I used it, Sinclair would lash out—either in rage or in pain. Carl might lose control of the bus and send it tumbling over a cliff toward the rocky Pacific shore. I'd end up dead. Worse, I'd be late for Family Day.

Frankly, neither possibility worked for me.

Which meant I needed to wait until the bus stopped. And, ideally, I needed to get Sinclair alone. The question, of course, was how.

Three minutes later, we were pulling into the big parking lot by the football field, and I still didn't have a foolproof plan, but I did have Hershey's Kisses and a Ziploc bag full of baby wipes. Not typical tools of the demon-hunting trade, but I'm the woman who once helped her daughter make a diorama of the Vatican out of eggshells and soda crackers. I'd make do.

As Carl maneuvered the bus toward the back of the school, I rummaged in my purse, found the bag, and opened it. Then I opened the vial of holy water and dumped it in with the wipes. I could practically see the ad campaign: *Blessed be your baby's bottom . . . Now with Aloe!*

I shook myself and pressed on.

With the bag still hidden in my purse, I stood up, making a show of keeping my balance as I moved down the aisle toward Sinclair. "Okay, people," I said as I moved. "After the bus stops, we're going to get off, form two lines in the parking lot, and then go into the school together."

I leaned my hip against the seat in front of Sinclair and casually pulled out a Hershey's Kiss. "Would you like one?"

Sinclair grunted something that I took as a no. His seatmate, Morrison, looked tempted, then mumbled something about his blood sugar.

As I unwrapped the Kiss, Carl turned the coach into the lot, shifting the behemoth to the right. I accidentally-on-purpose fell over, then used Sinclair to catch my balance. And—oh, dear!—somehow managed to smear chocolate all over his sleeve and arm in the process.

Immediately, I started spouting apologies. Sinclair stayed stiff and silent. Possibly a tired old man. Possibly a pissed-off demon. I kept an eye on his face as I dabbed his sleeve with a Kleenex, searching his eyes for clues as to what he was thinking. More particularly, searching for some clue that he knew who I was. I hoped he didn't; I couldn't use the holy water until the others were off the bus (what with the whole howling in agony thing). And if he knew my secret, he'd hardly agree to lag behind so that I could help him clean up the chocolate mess.

The thing is, my identity as San Diablo's resident Demon

Hunter was no longer a secret, at least not among the demon population. After what happened this past summer, they knew me. Or, at least, some did. There are a lot of demonic beings floating around out there, and I had to assume their grapevine was at least as developed as my neighborhood gossip network.

But was Sinclair in that loop? I had no idea. His blank eyes revealed nothing, and neither did his breath, which was tinged with the sharp scent of cinnamon, courtesy of the packet of Trident I saw on Morrison's tray table. Which meant I had to proceed cautiously . . . and pray for luck.

Morrison shoved his tray back to the full upright and locked position, then squeezed into the aisle. Other folks started shuffling to stand up and gather purses and canes and the like.

Sinclair started to stand, but I kept him down with a firm hand on his arm. "Just hang on a bit. I should be able to get this cleaned up in a flash." I wasn't sure I liked the look he gave me in response, but he stayed. One point for Kate.

"Marissa," I called, as the passengers filed toward the front. "I'm trying to clean up Mr. Sinclair's shirt. Why don't you and Kelly take the others in and we'll be right behind you?"

"Honestly, Kate. If you weren't going to shoulder your burden, then why did you agree to help chaperone?"

Fortunately, she didn't seem to really want an answer. Instead she kicked into gear and started ordering the passengers to "Hurry, hurry, in one line, please!"

I rummaged in my purse for a wipe, then kept my hand clenched tight around it. "Carl," I said, tossing the name over my shoulder. "Maybe you could give them a hand out there."

To my complete amazement, he agreed and started gathering his things. Then again, maybe I shouldn't be amazed.

Marissa had spent a good portion of the drive describing the homemade cream puffs she'd dropped off at the school that morning. And, unless it was the sun reflecting off the ocean, I'm certain I'd seen Carl drooling.

"Okay, Mr. Sinclair," I said, keeping my voice especially cheery since Carl was still gathering his things at the front of the bus. "Let's see if we can't clean you up, then catch up to the others."

My cell phone blared, and I jumped. I think Sinclair did, too. I considered ignoring it, but since Carl was still on the bus, I decided to answer. Besides, unless my kids are safely in my line of sight, it's damn near impossible for me to ignore a ringing phone.

The caller ID read *Allie,* and my mommy-paranoia spiked. I flipped open the phone, fear for my kid almost blinding me to the potential demon at my side. "Are you okay? What's wrong? Where are you?" Our rule on Allie's cell phone use is stringent. Emergencies only. No exceptions.

"I won!" Allie's excited voice filtered through the tiny speaker. "They're going to announce it during the program. And I get a plaque and a check and everything."

I started breathing again, trying hard to downshift from terror to something a little more constructive. "You're okay?" I asked. "You're not bleeding? No broken bones? No emergency surgeries or strange men trying to lure you into cars?"

"Mo-*om!* I'm fine. Aren't you listening? *I won.*"

"The essay contest?" From the front of the bus, Carl was eyeing me curiously. I waved, signaling that all was well in my world, which I hoped wasn't a lie.

"Yes!" She'd spent a week of late nights at the kitchen table with my laptop, typing and editing a five-page essay on family and Christmas for a contest sponsored by the local paper. I'd proofed the final pages for her, and even managed to cry only a little bit.

"Oh, sweetheart," I said, downshifting even more from concerned irritation to maternal pride. "That's wonderful!"

"They want me to read it during the program. You're on your way, right? You won't be late?"

"Of course not. I'm practically there. Five minutes. Maybe ten."

Beside me, Sinclair started to push up again. I aimed a bright smile at him, and pulled out the baby wipe. Then, as Allie continued to rave, I used a tiny corner to attack the chocolate on his sleeve. I wasn't touching skin, and I hoped that if he was a demon, he'd be lured into a false sense of security. Mostly, though, I was stalling. If he was a demon, I anticipated some pretty loud histrionics once the holy water contacted his flesh. Best for all concerned if the cell-phone connection was broken when Sinclair released that first yowl.

All in all a calm, rational, analytical approach.

Unfortunately, it didn't work.

"—and they're actually gonna *publish* it," Allie was saying.

I tried to squeeze in a "good-bye" and a "tell me all about it in a few minutes," but I never got the chance. Sinclair leaped out of the plush seat, slamming into me with all the vim and vigor of a person possessed. I saw it coming, but not in time. I shifted to the right, but he caught me in the chest and sent me tumbling back over the armrest of the seat across the aisle. I cried out and the phone flew from my hand. I heard my daughter's terrified, *"Mom!"* then silence as the phone went dead.

Sinclair tried to sprint past, but I wasn't about to let that happen. I kicked out, managing to trip the undead bastard and land him with a *splat* on the rubber runner.

I was right behind him, leaping from my precarious position on the armrest to an equally precarious position on his back. Demon or not, this son of a bitch had just scared my kid, and for that, he really had to pay.

I still had the baby wipe in one hand, and now I slapped it down on his bald spot. I heard (and smelled) a satisfying sizzle, and Sinclair lurched in pain, his depths-of-Hell yowl filling the bus and threatening to burst my eardrums.

A riled demon is a strong demon, and he was on his feet in no time, with me still clinging to him like a leech. My arms were clasped tight around his neck, the still-wet baby wipe now pressed against the soft skin of his neck. The stench of burning demon flesh almost made me gag, but I kept my legs squeezed viselike around his waist.

I'd spent the last three months working my tail off to sharpen my atrophied skills in karate, tae kwon do, and a half dozen other martial arts styles. But I wasn't using any of those skills at the moment. Instead, I more closely resembled my son trying to avoid bedtime.

Since he'd been sitting at the back of the bus, we were probably only three yards away from the rear seat and the door to the coach's restroom. With me still stuck fast, he bounded in that direction, then whipped sideways, slamming my spine up against the angled protrusion where the wall of the bathroom extended slightly.

"Die, Hunter," he hissed as fiery pain shot through my entire body. He slammed again, then again, and again, adding a comment to me with each and every impact.

"You cannot win." *Crash!*

"Our forces grow." *Smash!*

"The wheels are already in motion." *Crunch!*

Not exactly the clearest of messages, but I wasn't too worried about interpretation. For that matter, the way my head was spinning, I wasn't too worried about anything. Except putting the damn demon out of my misery. And getting to Allie's ceremony on time.

Keeping my left arm tight around his neck, I reached back with my right hand and fumbled for the barrette that held my hair up and away from my face. As gross as it sounds, optical penetration is the best method of killing a corporeal demon. And the little metal strip on those cheap drugstore barrettes does the trick every time.

As soon as I let go with one hand, though, Sinclair dove forward with me still attached to his back like Velcro. He landed on his (and my) shoulders, then executed a sloppy but effective somersault that was so unexpected and painful that it completely shook me off him. My butt hit the floor, and I let out a little *oomph* as the wind was knocked out of me.

I tensed, ready to lash out, but instead of taking the offensive and rushing me, Sinclair barreled down the aisle toward the front of the bus. Barely seconds passed before I sprang back up, but that was all he needed.

Sinclair yanked the lever and the door hissed open. Then he turned, grinned in my direction, and started running toward the school.

Three

I was only seconds behind him, but demons move fast, and by the time I hit the asphalt, he was gone, lost in a sea of parents and grandparents, all rushing through the parking lot toward the gymnasium entrance. I rushed right along with them, searching every face as I ran, but not seeing Sinclair anywhere.

Damn!

I raced toward the school, part of me hoping Sinclair really had gone inside and part of me hoping he'd veered off toward some other destination. I wanted to nail the bastard, yes, but I also wanted him away from my daughter.

I burst through a cluster of elderly people, slowing only slightly when I realized that the cluster was made up of *my* elderly people. I didn't plan on stopping, but then I heard the tidbits of gossip—"What kind of vitamins did the doc put *him* on?"—and realized they'd seen Sinclair, and had probably noticed which direction he'd run.

I skidded to a stop. "Sinclair? Where'd he go?"

Mr. Morrison pointed toward a nearby door. "Right through —"

"Kate!" Marissa materialized beside me, her hand closing like a vice on my elbow. "Where have you been? It's like herding cats. Kelly and I need a hand here."

"I can't right now." I bounced a little, my gaze not on Marissa but on that one metal door. "I need—"

"To do your job?" She pointed to the group. "If you could just get everyone into two lines, then we can—"

I shifted from one foot to the other. "Right. Sure. I'll be right back. First I just need to—"

"*Kate!* What is your problem?"

"Looks like she's gotta pee," Mrs. Able said.

"Yes!" I jumped all over that excuse. I also ripped my arm out of Marissa's grasp and raced toward the school, her frustrated howl echoing behind me. Eventually, I'd have to deal with her wrath. Frankly, I'd just as soon face a demon.

I reached the door and jerked it open, then found myself on both familiar and unfamiliar ground. I never went to an actual high school, but in the few months since Allie had enrolled as a freshman, I'd pulled enough PTA duty to more than make up for those lost years of my youth.

The school had been built more or less in the shape of a Christmas tree, with the triangle-shaped top marking the academic sections, and the brown "trunk" hall playing host to the cafeteria, band hall and the like. The gymnasium made up the tree stand. In other words, a big rectangle at the bottom.

I was currently in the orange wing, which ran the length of one side of the Christmas tree triangle. I didn't see any sign of the demon, but I also didn't see anyone else. That was a good thing. With any luck, the students were already in the gym waiting for the Family Day festivities to start.

The demon had come in at the end of the hall, which

meant that he could have turned slightly to the right, tugged open the double doors, and entered the common area between the orange and blue halls. Or he could have veered right and had a straight path down the orange hallway.

Since barreling straight and fast seemed more in line with what a riled demon would do (Demonic Psychology 101), I raced that way, too. I reached the end of the hall, ripped open the door to the common area, and burst inside.

No Sinclair. *Damn!*

I hurried on through the room, oversized maps of the United States nothing more than blue-green blurs in my peripheral vision. Moments later, I plowed through the doors—then stopped dead. My daughter was standing right in front of me. Behind her, at the far end of the hall, I saw Sinclair retreating farther into the school.

"Allie," I squeaked, stupidly.

"Mom!" She threw her arms around me, squeezed, then apparently remembered that she was a teenager and stepped away, awkwardly jamming her hands into the pockets of her jeans. "God, Mom! I was ferociously worried. Are you okay?"

"I—" I clamped my mouth shut, forcing my eyes back to Allie and away from the demon, now disappearing in the distance. "I—Sure. Yes. I'm fine. Why? Don't I look fine?"

"Well, duh! We were talking and then you screamed, and—"

"Oh!" In all the ruckus, I'd completely forgotten. I threw my arms around her and squeezed hard. "I'm so proud of you! My daughter the published writer. It's fabulous." I took a step away. "But I really need to go—"

"Mo-om! You *screamed.*"

I stopped, resigned to finishing this conversation. "Right. I tripped." That sounded good, so I went with it. "I came on the Coastal Mists bus, and I was talking to you and I just tripped. I went sprawling, and the cell phone smashed all to bits." I actually had no idea where the phone was, but smashed was probably a good bet.

"Tripped?" she repeated, sounding more than a little dubious.

"Honest to God," I said, lying like a fiend.

"Jeez, Mom! You really scared us!"

"Oh, sweetie," I said, giving her a quick hug as guilt washed over me. "I'm fine. I'm so sorry I scared you, but— *us?*"

And that's when I noticed the man. Rumpled and professorial, he was hanging back a few feet, giving Allie and me space for our joyous reunion. Now, seeing that the conversation had begun to include him, he came over, clutching a cane and nursing a slight limp.

He looked to be about forty, with mahogany-colored hair that was starting to gray around the temples. His silver-gray eyes were mostly hidden behind wire-framed glasses. He was watching me with an odd familiarity, and I frowned, wondering if we'd met. Something about him was familiar to me, too, and I felt myself starting to fidget under his steady gaze.

"David Long," he said, holding out his hand for me to shake.

"I went and found him the second the line went dead!" Allie squealed.

Mr. Long's smile was indulgent. "I told her you probably weren't in mortal danger."

"Um, right. Thanks."

"Mr. Long teaches chemistry," Allie said. "I'm taking his freshman intro class next semester."

"On purpose?" I was having a hard time wrapping my fuzzy brain around the concept of "Allie" and "science" in any sort of close proximity at all.

"Um, yeah."

"Chemistry?" I repeated. "With the test tubes and the Bunsen burners and the fizzle and the smoke?"

"Mo-*ther*," she said, her tone suggesting she'd stepped in something gross. "It's not like I'm stupid or anything."

"Of course you're not," I said automatically. "You can handle any class you want."

"Right." She nodded, perfectly pleased with herself, then looked up at David Long and smiled.

I fought back the urge to whap myself on the forehead as comprehension dawned. My boy-crazy daughter had a schoolgirl crush. There was no other reasonable explanation.

I let that settle into my brain, trying to decide if I had a problem with my daughter having a crush on the chemistry instructor. I decided that so long as said crush got her signed up to take science classes, then I didn't. After all, I could trust Mr. Long to be purely professional. Anything inappropriate, and I'd practice a few of my more lethal moves on him in a dark alley.

The thought both cheered me and reminded me that I already had a man on my dark-alley dance card.

"C'mon," Allie said, tugging on my hand, her earlier worry all but forgotten. "I helped set up during study hall, and if we hurry, we can still get some of the little chocolate cakes before the ceremony starts."

I wanted nothing more than to eat cakes with my daughter, but demons take precedence over chocolate (hard to believe, but true). And today, demons even took precedence over my family. A little fact that almost ripped my heart in two, especially with Allie tugging on my hand, so eager for me to be with her despite the onset of puberty and raging hormones.

But what choice did I have? There was a demon loose in the high school. And to save my kid, I first had to hurt my kid.

Gently, I tugged my hand free. "You go on ahead. I'll be right behind you."

"But, Mom!"

"Honestly, Allie, I need to—" What? What could I possibly say that wouldn't increase the hurt I saw in her eyes?

And then Mr. Long stepped in, laying a firm hand on Allie's shoulder as he came to my rescue. "Your mom may have a few things she needs to take care of before she heads to the gym."

He turned to face me, his expression bland but his eyes piercing. "You're on the PTA, right? I bet you got stuck with a dozen last-minute projects."

"I did," I said, baffled but relieved. "I totally did." That, of course, was a lie. In what I'd considered a truly brilliant maneuver, I'd managed to sidestep all non-cupcake related duties. I'd felt a little guilty for not volunteering, but got over it fast. After all, eradicating the San Diablo demon population had to count for something, right?

I turned to Allie. "Why don't you head on down, and I'll meet you there."

"You'll be there before it starts?"

"Of course!" I said. And I intended to do everything in my power to make sure I wasn't lying.

"Come on," Mr. Long said to Allie. "I'll go with you." He looked at me. "One of my duties today. Herding the students to the gym."

"Herding," Allie repeated, rolling her eyes. "Like we're all cows or something." But she went with him without any more protest, and David Long and I shared a look that said simply, *Teenagers.*

As soon as they disappeared around the corner, I raced off in the same direction as Sinclair, turning corners and following the rainbow of colored hallways.

About two minutes later, I found myself at an intersection and realized I had no clue where the demon might be. I mentally flipped a coin, picked a direction, and hoped I'd find a demon.

And that's when I saw the door.

Cracked open slightly, the plain white door was the kind with a metal vent in the bottom panel. A place to allow nasty fumes from cleaning products to escape. I checked the little plaque by the door and, sure enough, this was the janitor's closet.

Logically, I knew that the janitor might have simply failed to pull the door completely closed. But logic wasn't entirely running the show here, and my instincts told me that it wasn't the janitor in there—it was Dermott Sinclair.

I hesitated, my hand pressed lightly against the frame. If I was wrong, I'd be wasting valuable time. The thing is, I didn't think I was wrong. And I was used to going on my instincts. I'd been doing it for the last fourteen years raising my kids and, so far, those instincts had worked out just fine.

So I went in. The door didn't open onto a supply room like I'd expected. Instead, it opened directly onto a set of stairs leading down to a basement. The stairs were lined on either side with shelves, and those shelves held a variety of janitorial products: Windex, bleach, a box of rags.

The stairs curved sharply, and right before the curve I saw a tool chest. Carefully, so as to not make anything scrape or rattle, I plucked out a screwdriver. Barrettes are fine in a pinch, but I wanted something with heft.

A few more steps, and now the stairs were below the level of the shelving, open to the basement, the only barrier a series of thin, metal posts supporting a battered railing. Two bare lightbulbs provided dim illumination, revealing a utility sink tucked into one corner, and there, on the far side of the room, Dermott Sinclair.

I held my breath and kept my body perfectly still. He hadn't seen me, too busy concentrating on the task at hand. Since his back was to me, I couldn't see exactly what he was doing, but I could hear the soft scrape of stone sliding against mortar. The muscles in his back tightened, and his arms moved in a rhythmic, alternating motion as he tugged on a cinder block lodged in the wall.

Why, I wondered, was he doing that?

I reached out, intending to grab hold of the handrail as I crept farther down the stairs. The top bar of the railing, however, had come loose from the vertical supports, and my touch knocked it off kilter, freeing the vertical metal posts. Talk about a building code violation. I mean, something like that could easily put out an eye.

A harsh metal noise accompanied the shifting of the rail, and Sinclair whipped around, his nostrils flaring. The cinder block was tight in his hands, and now he heaved it at me. I dove forward, the block clearing my head as my hands smashed against the cement floor. My purse spilled all over the floor, and the screwdriver went flying. I winced, but rolled over onto my back, my hand brushing something long and smooth. I grabbed it—whatever it was—then thrust my legs up and out in a practiced move that would make Cutter, my *sensei,* proud.

My shoes connected firmly with Sinclair's gut. He let out a howl as he stumbled backwards, then he plopped onto the ground. There's a certain satisfaction in seeing a demon fall on his rump, and I was riding that high for all it was worth.

I sprang to my feet, my fingers tight around what I now saw was a Christmas ornament. Specifically, a glass icicle, probably shoved into my purse by my little boy. The end had snapped off, leaving a sharp edge of glass. Exactly the kind of thing I didn't want Timmy to play with—for exactly the reason I was now glad to have it. These things are dangerous.

Sinclair was up now, too, and from the calculating look in his eye, I could tell he was itching for a fight. So was I. Threaten my kids, come on to my turf, and it's not just about duty. It becomes—like they say in the movies—personal.

He was watching me, wary, his hands in a classic fighting stance. His feet were in constant motion, a boxer waiting for the perfect blow. I didn't intend to let him have it.

"Why are you here?" I asked, my feet also moving. We probably looked like we were engaged in some strange dance competition. In a way, I guess maybe we were.

"That is no concern of yours, Hunter."

"Actually, figuring out why you're here is at the top of my job description."

His lip curled into a snarl. "Perhaps you should find a new job," he suggested. "Because you've failed here. The plan is already underway."

My stomach twisted a bit at that. *What* plan? But I didn't have time to wonder because he was lunging at me.

I lunged right back, leading with the icicle. He whipped his arm up, the glass first meeting resistance and then sinking deep into the yielding flesh. The wound was deep, but not nearly enough to stop a demon. And as I cursed in frustration, he kicked out, connecting solidly with my right knee.

I wish I could say I was ready for it, but I wasn't. A kick in the knee is brutal, and I went down, scrambling to keep some balance . . . or at least to keep my hand tight on the icicle.

I didn't manage either, though, and now Sinclair had the weapon—he tugged it out of his flesh and aimed it at me with a toothy grin. There was only a little blood—he was dead flesh, after all—and somehow the lack of blood made the entire situation that much more sinister.

I didn't have time to think about that, though, because

he was on me, my own arm up to deflect his blows as he tried to slam the icicle through my heart.

Old men may not be strong, but the same can't be said about demons and, from my awkward position on my back, Sinclair definitely had the advantage. We were by the staircase, and I grabbed the bottom step with one hand, trying to use the five inches of height to lever myself up while I fended him off with the other hand.

No use. Sinclair was on top of me; so close that the putrid scent of his demon breath came through even past the spicy cinnamon gum.

And that's when I saw it. *The screwdriver.* It had rolled under the yellow janitor's bucket, its orange-and-black handle barely peeking out.

With one hand, I shoved against Sinclair's chest, keeping him away, trying to prevent him from landing a fatal blow. With the other, I reached out, stretching until my fingers brushed the hard plastic handle. But I still wasn't close enough to grab it, and Sinclair was fighting hard.

Damn!

He rallied, this time coming in hard toward my face. I made one last thrust for the screwdriver. No use. Sinclair was on me, and at the last second, I whipped my outstretched arm forward, connecting hard with his throat.

He gagged, and dropped the icicle, but then he used his now-free hand to grab my wrist. I reacted without thinking and kneed him in the groin, screaming out in pain as I did so because my knee still hurt like hell from where he'd smashed it.

There wasn't a lot of force behind my blow—and demons are mostly immune to being kicked in the balls—but he stumbled backwards anyway, his grip on my wrists loosening just slightly.

That was all I needed. I stretched, pushing myself along

the floor until my fingers snagged the screwdriver. I tried to get up, but he'd recovered himself by then and lashed out, knocking my legs out from under me and destroying my precarious balance.

He leaped on me, his hand closing around the hand with the screwdriver. He slammed me backwards, banging my already battered hand, and then pried my fingers open.

I watched myself, like watching someone in a dream, as he hit a pressure point at the base of my thumb. My fingers slackened, and the screwdriver tumbled from my hand.

He caught it midair, then raised it, lunging for me even as he cried out, telling me in no uncertain terms that it was time to "Die, Hunter, die."

Images of my kids flooded my brain, and I screamed in defiance as I parried to the left. I managed to avoid the brunt of his blow, but the motion shifted both of us off balance. We crashed to the floor, and I rolled to the right, barely escaping his thrust of the screwdriver.

The icicle was right there, the end now even more jagged and sharp from having smashed on the cement floor. Good.

I grabbed it up and rocketed to my feet, ignoring the searing pain that shot through my injured knee. Sinclair was up, too, and we lunged at each other, me leading with a piddly little Christmas ornament, and the demon leading with a lethal-looking screwdriver.

Not the best of odds, but I didn't care. I didn't intend to lose. I just wasn't exactly sure how I was going to manage to win.

I was breathing hard now, instinct guiding my movements even as my head tried to come up with a good plan. Or, for that matter, *any* plan. We circled each other until the stairs—and the rickety railing—was right behind him.

And that's when I got the idea . . .

I leaped forward with the icicle, shifting at the last second to avoid his face, and instead slamming the glass deep into his thigh.

He'd braced for my attack, of course, but he hadn't expected the blow to his leg, and he reacted instinctively, turning away to protect his wound. I anticipated the move and scrambled the opposite direction, ending up behind him. Then I threw myself on his back, clutched his throat, and held on for dear life as he tumbled forward.

And then—using every ounce of willpower in my body—I aimed. And I prayed.

I heard a sharp crack, then felt a jolt as the metal post slammed home, sliding easily through the demon's bulbous gray eye. His low moan faded quickly, and I saw the familiar shimmer in the air as the demon departed the old man's body to return to the ether.

I sagged to the floor, my body limp with relief.

That emotion was short-lived, however. I'd gotten rid of one problem (the demon), but now I had a whole new one (his plan). He'd been down in the basement for a reason. I needed to figure out what it was.

The stone he'd tossed at me had been large, and it had left an equally large hole in the wall. A dark hole, actually, and I moved toward it with trepidation. I bent down and squinted into it, but I couldn't see a thing.

Since I'm not crazy about spiders and other basement-dwelling critters, I wasn't too keen on sticking my hand in the gap and feeling around, but I did it anyway. (This job is not for the squeamish.) Fortunately, I encountered nothing slithery nor slimy. In fact, I encountered nothing at all.

Well, damn. I'd been so sure that Sinclair knew what he was doing. Had someone beaten him to the punch? Or had Sinclair himself already squirreled the thing away? Maybe hidden it on his person?

I made a face as I considered that possibility, my fingers

still probing the dark. I'd changed a lot of nasty Pull-Ups in my day, but the idea of patting down a dead demon still had me cringing.

I'd about convinced myself that I really did have to frisk Sinclair when my fingers found a crevice in the stone. A place in the very back where the mortar no longer felt rough. Instead, it felt smooth and cool, with only the slightest hint of texture.

I felt around some more, my heart beating faster. I ran my finger down the length of the crevice until I encountered mortar again. That's when it hit me. *A book.* I was feeling the spine of a book lodged between two stones.

I settled my shoulder against the cool stone wall, hooked my fingertips around the edge of the volume, and pulled. It shifted, but only slightly, and I felt a momentary burst of irritation. If the book had been placed years ago and literally mortared in with the stone, then I'd need something a lot stronger than my fingernails, even with the Sally Hansen acrylic topcoat.

I took a breath and tugged again, hoping it had merely been placed in the wall for safekeeping, and not made a permanent part of the architecture.

This time, I got lucky. True, I ruined the polish on three nails and broke the nail on my forefinger off at the quick, but the book was in my hand, and I was victorious. Unmanicured, but victorious.

I pulled it out into the light and studied it, searching the outside for clues as to its purpose. None were apparent. The book was large—about the same size as Timmy's lap books but thicker than his battered copy of *How Do Dinosaurs Say Good Night?* About an inch thick, actually. And unlike Timmy's reptile-covered storybooks, this one was bound in dark red leather, cracked and scarred with age.

The spine may once have reflected a title, but now all that remained of the gilt lettering was tiny flecks of gold.

At one point, the book must have been extraordinary. But now the thing was battered and shabby, the embossing worn down so that there were no identifying marks at all, no title, no telltale demonic symbols. Just a hint of a raised design that may or may not have been a triangle.

Well, hell.

As a rule, I don't go around opening books that the demon population is scrambling for. You just never know what you might find.

But in this case, I wanted to know. No, it was more than that. I *needed* to know. Sinclair had said that I was too late. That the wheels were already in motion. He'd raced to the school—a place I'd always believed was safe. Willful blindness on my part, maybe, but it made the mornings easier when I sent my daughter out into what I knew, better than any mom, was a dangerous world.

The demons had a plan, and this book was part of it. I needed to know how. I needed to make sure nothing was going to happen now. That hordes of demons weren't about to descend on the school.

In other words, I needed to know that my kid was safe.

And so, with a holy water–drenched baby wipe held tight as a defense against any evil that might spew forth, I plunked the book on a worktable and then slowly lifted the cover.

The spine creaked in protest, but no evil emerged, and the flames of Hell didn't leap forth to engulf me. Thus encouraged, I opened the cover a bit more, then bent low and peered into the dark space between cover and flyleaf. I saw nothing, and so I continued until the cover was flipped entirely open.

Nothing.

And I mean that literally.

Not demons. Not incantations. Not even a copyright page with the Library of Congress information.

Just blank paper, brittle and slightly stained.

Frowning, I carefully flipped through the rest of the volume. Nothing.

Every page was completely blank. The book told me nothing. Absolutely nothing.

I turned to look at the grotesque form of Sinclair, the vertical beam protruding from the back of his skull.

"What's going on, Sinclair?" I asked.

The demon, however, stayed stubbornly silent.

Four

Disposing of a dead demon is a lot harder than it sounds, and if Marissa found me keeping company with a dead body, you can be damn sure Coastal Mists wouldn't be inviting me to the annual Volunteer Appreciation Dinner.

In the past, I simply would have called the kill in, and *Forza* would send a dispatch team to do the dirty work. But in the last decade or so, *Forza* has suffered staffing problems, and that simply wasn't an option. (I'd been a little surprised when I'd learned of the dwindling ranks within *Forza*, actually. But after I thought about it, I began to understand. It's a hard life. And what sounds like fun on a Nintendo Game-Cube loses a lot of its appeal in the harsh light of reality.)

I could try to hide the body myself—getting my new *alimentatore* to give me a hand with the heavy lifting—but that plan involved schlepping the body out of the high school, and that was too risky for my taste. I've wanted a lot of things in my life, but a future in prison was not one of them.

No, my best bet was to simply clean up any evidence of the fight, wipe off my fingerprints, and leave. The body was just a body now, so whoever discovered it would most likely believe that Sinclair had fallen victim to an unfortunate accident. I just needed to head up to the gym, find my kids, do my Mommy-At-Family-Day routine, and try my damnedest not to look distracted.

When it was time to head back to Coastal Mists, I'd feign concern and start a search. I could come back then and discover the tragedy. I probably still wouldn't win volunteer of the year (I mean, I *had* been in charge of the man), but I doubted anyone would suspect I'd killed him. I was on the PTA, after all.

On that note, I got busy cleaning up, wiping off finger-prints and picking up the junk that had scattered from my purse. I took the screwdriver, too, for good measure.

My forensic concerns allayed as much as possible, I gathered my things. The book was too tall to fit neatly in my purse, so I took off my cardigan and tossed it between the shoulder straps so it lay over the top of my bag, hiding the section of leather than peeked out from the Dooney & Bourke knockoff.

Then I hurried up the stairs, pausing at the door to wipe the dust off my clothes as I considered the situation. Since the assembly was already underway, I assumed the halls would be clear. With any luck, I could find the gym, find Allie, then slide into my seat with the efficient expression of a PTA committee member who's just finished doing her civic—academic?—duty.

Because I was having one of those days, the luck I'd wished for didn't materialize. David Long, however, did. I ran smack into him not two seconds after I'd turned from the purple hall to the brown.

"Oh!" I said, and he looked just as startled—and guilty—as I felt. Although, to be honest, I'm probably projecting the guilt part. Or maybe not. This was the students' big day, after all. Awards. Pomp. Circumstance. Shouldn't he be in the gym by now? I knew I should.

"Got a hall pass, Mister?" I asked, flashing what I hoped was a disarming—and charming—grin. I learned years ago that an offensive approach is almost always better than struggling to play defense.

He patted himself down, then shrugged. "Guess I left it in homeroom."

I made a *tsk-tsk* sound. "I see detention in your future."

"I teach chemistry," he said, deadpan. "I spend my days staring at dozens of blank faces who think a valence bond is an old Sean Connery movie. Isn't that punishment enough?"

I pretended to consider. "I see your point. I'll let you off the hook. This time," I added, in my most stern voice.

He nodded, just as seriously. "Yes, ma'am."

"What were you doing out here, anyway?" I asked.

"Still rounding up students," he said. "A lot of the kids will skip assembly. Hide out in the common areas. It's my job to wrangle them back." He leaned casually against the wall, his cane propped beside him, then hooked his thumbs in the front pockets of his slacks in a move so suddenly familiar it made my heart stutter in my chest.

Eric.

Mentally, I shook myself, willing myself not to slide into my memories. Lots of men are easy to talk to and have familiar mannerisms. Yes, David Long reminded me of Eric. But no, I couldn't afford to be rattled. Not today. Not with a stolen book in my purse, a dead demon in the basement, and a hellacious plot brewing.

I took a breath and forced myself to concentrate.

"Actually," he said, "I could ask you the same thing."

"Excuse me?"

"What you're doing here," he clarified, at the same time standing up straight and breaking the spell. "Aren't you supposed to be in the gym?"

"Right," I said. "Um . . . I got turned around. All these damned colored hallways."

"It's a challenge all right." He moved closer, and I saw his gaze dip down. My hand went automatically to my purse, pulling it closer to my side. My cardigan had shifted, and one corner of the book was peeking out. Not a lot, but enough to make clear to anyone who might be looking that I was schlepping a musty (and potentially demonic) book around. Damn.

When I looked back up, I found David Long searching my face.

"So," I said brightly. "I should probably get going." I took a tentative step, hoping he'd take the hint.

"Are you sure you're okay?"

I cocked my head. "Excuse me?"

"You're limping."

Damn. "New shoes."

He glanced down at the extremely comfortable, extremely broken-in loafers I'd matched with my linen slacks and sweater set. Not couture shoes by any means, but they were more practical than pumps for clamoring up ladders at nursing homes. And for fighting the odd demon.

"Uh-huh," he said.

"So," I repeated. "Which way do we go?"

For the briefest of instants, I thought he was going to say something else. Maybe criticize my choice of footwear. But he just lifted a finger and pointed. "Straight down. The gym's the dead end."

I winced, not too crazy about the way he said that. But I

took a step in that direction, then paused as I realized he was going the other way. Back the way I'd come. "Uh, Mr. Long?"

"David."

"Right. David. Aren't you coming, too?"

He shook his head just slightly. "I remembered something I need to check on." He gave me a friendly wave, then started walking. "I'll see you after the assembly."

Oh. Well. Damn.

I watched him go, unable to shake the feeling that he was heading straight for the janitor's basement. For a moment, I considered following him, but what would I say if he saw me again? That I'd developed a mad crush and couldn't bear parting ways? That I wanted to discuss Allie's future curriculum with him? That I desperately wanted to know what a valence bond was?

Somehow I didn't think any of those approaches would fly.

I reminded myself that I didn't know for certain that he was heading to the basement. It was, after all, in a completely different colored hall. And even if he was, so what? I certainly wasn't going to admit to any knowledge of the body beside the stairs.

Still, something about David Long made me itchy, and I wanted to keep him in my sights. I took a step in that direction, figuring I'd make up an excuse if he saw me, then was caught up short by the warm grate of a familiar voice: "Good God, Kate. Our girl's going crazy wondering if you're gonna make it on time."

I turned to see Eddie shuffling toward me, decked out in plaid golfing pants and an orange T-shirt that instructed passersby to *Kiss a Prince—The World Needs More Frogs.* I couldn't help but smile, especially at the "our girl" reference. As far as Allie's concerned, Eddie's her paternal great-grandfather, but the truth is a lot more complex. As far as I know, Eddie's no relation to Allie at all. Of course, both Eric and I were orphans, so in my more melancholy moments, I like to pretend that fate really did bring back my family.

Still, blood or not, Eddie really has become family. He's one of the few people who knows my secret, and he only knows it because he brought down more than a few demons in his day, too.

Eddie's wily, bad-tempered, can cuss a blue streak, and I love him like a father. And I'm pretty sure he loves me like a daughter. I know he considers Allie his own. Timmy, he isn't certain about yet. But once my boy moves from Pull-Ups to underwear, I have a feeling their relationship will shift, too.

In the meantime, I don't mind that Eddie's affection runs more toward my daughter. Tim has Stuart's parents to dote on him. To be fair, they dote on Allie, too, but she was old enough when I married Stuart to understand that Grandma and Grandpa Connor weren't really hers.

Eddie though . . . well, he belongs to our girl, and she cherishes that. As for me, I protect it.

Which explained why Eddie was still living in our guest bedroom even though he and Stuart hadn't exactly become bosom buddies, and even though he'd been promising for months to find a nearby apartment. It was a concession on Stuart's part that I appreciated and about which I felt no guilt. I'd made a lot of adjustments to accommodate his run for office. I figured the least he could do was open up the house to a long-lost relative, albeit a fabricated one.

"Come on, girl," he said, giving me a tap on the shoulder. "Time to get a move on."

"I haven't missed—?"

He shook his head. "Not yet. But you need to light a fire. As soon as that principal quits blathering on about all this hoo-ha, they're going to announce the awards. You won't hear the end of it if you miss it."

"Not going to happen," I said, any lingering thoughts of following David Long vanishing in a puff of maternal pride.

Still, I took a quick peek backwards as we hustled down the hall in the direction of the gym. All quiet. Not a hint of the man.

I told myself that it was pointless to worry. After all, if hell broke loose, I'd surely notice.

Principal George was still speaking when we arrived, which had the unexpected benefit of giving me an excuse to completely ignore Marissa, who was gesturing like crazy for me to join her and her Coastal Mist charges. I pretended confusion, pointed to Allie, and then started to climb my way over students and parents. Laura was already there, and Timmy clamored from her lap to mine.

As Principal George continued on through the hoo-ha, I kept checking the door, expecting David to enter. When he didn't, I started conjuring up scenarios where he'd found the body, called the police, and dozens of siren-spewing cop cars were now descending on the school, ready to cart me away in cuffs and an orange prison jumper.

Laura passed me my keys. "You're limping."

"So I've been told."

"Everything okay?"

"For now," I said. "I'll fill you in later."

She nodded, and I shoved thoughts of prison and demon carcasses out of my head, then took another look around the gym, this time searching for Stuart. Nothing. I mouthed his name to Laura, but she just shrugged.

Laura's husband, I noticed, was also absent. That, however, was to be expected. Paul is the CEO of a thriving fast-food enterprise, and spends a lot of time lately working out of his Los Angeles office. Considering Laura had recently begun to suspect that Paul's having an affair, I think she questions how much work goes on in Los Angeles. But she hasn't confronted the lying, cheating bastard yet.

Stuart, at least, was not a cheating bastard. Which meant he had no excuse for not attending Family Day. Which meant that I was pissed off. Particularly since he'd gone to such great lengths to assure me that he'd be there.

I didn't have long to revel in my righteous indignation, however, because Mrs. George had moved on to the various awards and other achievements that the school had racked up so far during the school year. "And the semester's not even finished!" she enthused as we all dutifully applauded.

There were a few athletic awards, some academic accomplishments, and then she introduced Stella Atkins, the Life & Arts editor of the San Diablo *Herald.* And then Stella introduced my daughter.

I squeezed Allie's hand, then choked back tears as she picked her way down the bleachers to Stella's side. She clutched the plaque, and I saw her eyes scan the crowd, focusing particularly on both sets of doors. I knew what she was thinking—her essay had been on Christmas and family. The loss of one dad and the joy of finding another. Not a replacement, but an addition. And a grandfather, too, to smooth out the rough edges.

I was there. Eddie was there. But Stuart was nowhere to be found.

I tapped Laura, then mouthed the word *phone.* She passed me her cell phone and I dialed Stuart's number, praying he was just outside the gymnasium doors.

Voice mail.

I snapped the phone shut, anger and disappointment settling over me like a thick blanket.

I sincerely hoped my husband wasn't expecting a hot dinner tonight. Because the only thing he'd be getting from me was ice cold.

I might have been seething, but Allie held it together despite the ache I knew she had to feel in her heart. She gave a wonderfully smooth acceptance speech in a voice that didn't even shake once, and in that moment, I think I was more proud of her than I'd ever been.

I'd expected the little pang in my heart back when she took her first steps. When she toddled off to kindergarten. When she learned to ride a bike. Those are the moments they tell you about in all those *What to Expect* books.

But these moments—the ones that sneak up on you, where your kid really rises to the occasion and you can't help but think that you did good and your baby's going to be all right—well, those are the moments that really get me in the gut.

As angry as I was that Stuart wasn't there, I also felt a little bit numb. Because it wasn't really Stuart that I wanted beside me that day. It was Eric. And as I listened to my daughter read her wonderful essay to the crowd, I had to fight the tears that threatened to overflow and spill down my cheeks.

Grief is a funny thing. Had I lost Eric back when we were both hunting, I think it might have been easier to handle. Death was part of the scenery back then. It was normal, expected. But Eric and I had hung up our demon-hunting hats. We'd retired from the *Forza Scura* and moved first to Los Angeles and then to San Diablo, one of the most demon-free towns in the country. Or, at least, it had been back then. We'd had our baby girl, and we'd ensconced ourselves in the trappings of suburbia.

We'd been happy. We had our normal life, our normal family, our normal town. Our problems centered around bills and car repairs and leaky plumbing. The most demonic creature we encountered was the principal at Allie's kindergarten. No longer were our evenings spent performing weapons checks, researching Grimoires, or brushing up on combat medicine. Instead, after we put Allie to bed, we'd snuggle on the couch and watch all the movies we'd missed during our oh-so unusual childhoods.

There'd been a time when I could have staunched a stab wound with my fingers or cauterized an artery by flash-burning gunpowder. But once Eric and I settled down, those skills deteriorated, and I'd been thankful. We spent ten wonderful years smoothing our rough edges and learning to be—and to feel—normal. We were happy and secure in the little fairy-tale world we'd built. But it had to be a fairy tale, because we knew the truth. There are giants and witches in the forest, and if you aren't careful, they'll slap you into an oven faster than you can say "boo."

And here's another truth: Demons aren't the only bad things that roam in the dark. There are bad people, too. One of them killed my husband. Took his cash and left Eric to die on a cold and foggy San Francisco street.

There's a cruel irony in Eric's story. My husband—the man who'd destroyed so many preternatural creatures, the man whose reflexes had once been a thing of wonder—taken out by a mere mortal and a 9-mm pistol.

There's probably a lesson there, too, but it wasn't one I wanted to think about. At the time, I'd only wanted Eric back. And my disbelief that he could have perished under such mundane circumstances had made my grief long-lived. It was still there, in fact. Hiding under the surface of my shiny new life. A life I loved so fiercely that my memories of Eric, and the pangs of grief that came with those memories, were always lined with guilt.

When I was young and brave and stupid, I never feared death. Now I dreaded it as only a mother can. I don't want to leave my kids. Not now. Hell, not ever, though I'm prag-matic enough to know that someday the time will come.

But I think the hardest part of Eric's death is the pity I feel for him. He'd been given a gift in Allie, and someone had ripped that away from him. He'd missed birthdays and kisses and cheerleader tryouts. He'd missed glaring at boys and setting curfews. He'd missed today, watching our beautiful daughter accept an award and read an essay to a roomful of people, without showing even the slightest hint of fear.

I didn't want to pity the man I'd loved, the man who'd been my partner. But I did. And my deep, horrible, dirty little secret? I was glad that if one of us had to die, that it had been him and not me.

By the time Allie finished, I was a teary-eyed mess.

"Mommy sad?" Timmy asked, rubbing his sticky palms on my cheeks.

I hugged him close and kissed the top of his head. "Mommy's proud," I said.

Beside me, Laura reached out to squeeze my hand. Across the hall, I could see her daughter, Mindy, grinning like a fiend from the riser on which she stood, surrounded by the rest of the choir.

The Duponts live immediately behind our house, and the girls have been best friends since the first day they laid eyes on each other. Laura and I quickly followed suit, and the Dupont and Connor females make good use of the back fence gates that allow us easy access to each other's homes.

Over the years, the only hint of jealousy that had ever reared its head between the girls appeared after the faculty committee anointed Allie, but not Mindy, with one of the three coveted freshman spots on the cheerleading squad. Thankfully, the tension eased after about a week. That's when the girls realized that Mindy has a voice that could give Celine Dion a run for her money, whereas my daughter sounds remarkably like Kermit the Frog. The universe shifted back, and the jealousy flitted off to annoy some other less-well-adjusted children.

Needless to say, Laura and I were greatly relieved. We could still be best friends even if our girls weren't. But it was a heck of a lot easier this way.

Around us, parents, kids, and teachers were shifting to stations that had been set up around the perimeter of the gym. Drama club, math club, surf club, cheerleading. And, of course, the snack table. I wondered idly what kind of cupcakes Laura had bought, but it didn't really matter. At the moment, all I cared about was my brilliant and accomplished daughter.

As the choir started up with a medley of Christmas songs, Allie bounded across the auditorium, all composure now abandoned. "A check!" she yelped, as Eddie caught her in a hug. "Mom, Eddie, look! I got a check for five hundred dollars!"

Eddie took it from her, then held it at arms length, squinting at it through his thick glasses. "Whoa-ho there, hotshot. Look at you. You're rich!" He ruffled her hair, and she didn't even duck away like she usually does when I show too much affection around her peers.

Eddie leaned in closer, his eyes on me as he spoke sotto voce to Allie. "Run," he said. "Run now. And if anyone mentions educational savings accounts, you shoot first and ask questions later."

I tried to look stern as Allie giggled and linked her arm through Eddie's. Beside me, Laura stifled a smile as she looked from one to the other. "Good luck," she finally said, giving me a quick pat on the shoulder. Then took off across the gym toward the choir risers, leaving me to deal with my insane family alone.

I sighed, and hoisted Timmy up onto my hip.

"So?" Allie said, bouncing from one foot to the other. "Can I buy an iPod? Please, please, *pleeeeeze?*"

"I don't know," I said, a little distracted because I saw Marissa stalking across the room toward us.

"Oh, come on, Mom! Eddie's right. It's my money. And I promise I won't use it during class."

That caught my attention. "I really hope you're kidding. Because if that's even an option at this school, we're going to have to seriously consider the value of a private education."

I was being serious, but that was lost on Allie. "Oh, Mom!" Then she looked at me with puppy dog eyes until I gave in.

I sighed. "It *is* your money—"

"Yes!" She shot her fist up in celebration. "You're the bomb, Mom!"

"I know," I said, amused. Timmy squirmed, demanding to be put down. I did, and then Allie grabbed his hands and did a little dance with her brother.

All in all, a nice little family moment. Except for the fact that we were missing part of the family.

A skinny girl with a long ponytail walked by with a tray of cookies and a determined expression on her face. Timmy immediately stopped dancing and looked at her longingly.

"Cookies!" Timmy said. "Want a cookie!"

Since the girl hadn't heard him, I reached for his hand, figuring that was as good an exit line as any, but Eddie got there first. "Come on, youngster," he said. "I'm gunning for one of them chocolate chunk monstrosities."

"Monsters?" Timmy said, looking more excited than scared. "I wanna see the monsters!"

I frowned and met Eddie's eyes, certain that he could read my mind. Because the last thing in the world I wanted was for my little boy to meet up with the wrong kind of monster.

"I've got him," Eddie said. "We'll find you in a few."

"*Mom?* Hell-ooo?" Allie waved a hand in front of me. "Where's Stuart? He *swore* he'd be here."

"Um," I said, cursing since I really should have been prepared. I mean, I'd definitely seen that one coming.

Fortunately, I was saved from responding by my arch-enemy. Marissa sidled up, her brow furrowed, her mouth a thin red line. "Dammit, Kate. Since you insisted on chaperoning, I'd appreciate a little help over there."

"Sure, Marissa. No problem. I'm just talking to my award-winning daughter."

"Hi," she said, barely acknowledging Allie. "You want to get over there and help me?"

I pulled myself up on my toes and looked over her shoulder. Four of our charges were still sitting on the bleachers, staying out of trouble as far as I could tell. The others were scattered around the gym, students at their sides and smiles on their faces. "I think most everyone is taken care of," I said. "Until it's time to go back, shouldn't we let them hang with their families?"

"Taken care of?" She crossed her arms in front of her chest. "I don't think Dermott Sinclair is taken care of."

Actually, he was, but I wasn't about to say as much. Instead, I tried to look appropriately baffled. "Sinclair? I thought he was with you."

"What are you talking about? I left him with you on the bus."

"Right. But then he hurried out. To find you guys, he said. I assumed he'd catch up to you in the gym." I kept my eyes on hers, daring her to call me a liar.

"Well, he didn't," she said sharply. "I'm so glad you signed on to chaperone today, Kate. You've been such a big help."

I forced a bright smile. "But it looks like you did just fine on your own. Everyone's here and happy."

"Except Sinclair."

"Yeah," I agreed. "That *is* odd." I scooted toward Allie and hooked an arm around her shoulder. "We're going to go make the circuit, okay? And we'll keep an eye out for Sinclair. He's got to be here somewhere. I mean, where else could he be?"

A loaded question, but not one I wanted answered.

Marissa fidgeted, but she didn't press the point. I took the opportunity to flee. Demons, I can handle. An irritated soccer mom? No thank you very much.

Allie was watching me curiously as we walked away, and I tried to run the conversation back through in my head, wondering if I'd said anything suspicious. Thankfully, though, demons weren't on my daughter's mind. Instead, she turned back to another uncomfortable subject: Stuart.

"So where is he?" she asked.

"On his way," I said. "Probably already here. He was in his car the last I talked to him," I finally said, desperately resorting to the kind of lies that would attract lightning from the Heavens.

"Oh. I was hoping he'd . . ." She trailed off with a shrug and a smile. "It's okay. He'll be just as impressed with the check. But there's no way I'm donating it to his campaign." The last was said with an impish grin, but I know my kid well, and her light tone was laced with hurt. Can't say I blame her. I'd skipped right over hurt and moved directly to enraged. Do not pass go. Do not collect two hundred dollars.

"He hasn't been here too many times," she said, rummaging in her purse and pulling out her cell phone. "What if he's wandering the blue halls? Should I give him a call?"

I hesitated, certain that the only wandering Stuart was doing was the kind that sent him meandering down the primrose path toward the promise of campaign dollars. Not entirely sure what to say to Allie, I chose the ever popular, "Um," response.

She started to dial.

"Allie!" I said, snatching the phone out of her hand.

"What?"

"You're only supposed to use your phone for emergencies," I said. "Stuart and I were perfectly clear about that."

She blinked at me, her expression befuddled. "Well, yeah, but you're here."

"Right. But Stuart's not. So when he sees that you're calling, he's going to think it's an emergency and worry." I put my hand on my hip for effect. "I know I did when you called earlier."

She actually looked contrite. "Right. So, um, I guess I won't call Stuart."

I nodded, hoping I didn't look too relieved. Then I slipped her phone into my purse. Just to be safe.

"*You* call him."

I blinked. "What?"

"Come on, Mom! It's not like he'll worry when he sees *your* caller ID, right? And I really want to tell him about the check. And you know Stuart. He's never going to call us and admit he's lost."

I frowned. The trouble was, I did know Stuart. And I knew the odds were good he was nowhere near this building.

But since I couldn't think of a graceful way to refuse to call my husband, I reached into my purse. I made sure to keep the book hidden, all the while praying that Stuart would draw on his fast-developing political skills to ensure Allie's feelings didn't get hurt.

It wasn't until I'd pawed through all the detritus in my bag, though, that I remembered. "I can't call Stuart," I said, hoping I didn't sound as gleeful as I felt. "I dropped the phone, remember?"

"Oh." She made a face. "Right." I could practically see the wheels turning in her head. "He might be trying to phone you. I should probably call and let him know you're okay."

I wanted to argue, but what would I say? We'd reached the point where it would be ridiculous for me to protest anymore. And, frankly, I was so irritated with Stuart for not having shown up, that I figured it was only fair that he get put on the spot. Passive-aggressive? Perhaps. Or maybe I was just tired.

At any rate, it didn't matter. Because just as I was about to hand Allie her phone, Mindy raced over.

"Did you hear! Did you hear! They found a dead guy in the basement. Isn't that just the grossest thing ever?"

"No shit?" That from Allie, who immediately shot me a mortified look. "Sorry. I mean, no kidding?"

"Honest! Mom and I were talking with Principal George when the EMS guy came in and pulled her away. I heard everything." She leaned in closer and added, conspiratorially, "They said his face was bashed in."

"Ew!" Allie squealed, as I tried to look both disgusted and concerned.

Laura, who'd been following Mindy at something less than a sprint, sidled up beside me. "A little drama in these hallowed halls," she said. "You've heard?"

There wasn't anything unusual about her tone or her words. Even so, I knew what she was asking: *Was this your handiwork?*

"Yeah," I said. "I've heard." And I really needed to know what was going on in that hallway. Did they believe it was an accident, or were they going to be looking for me?

"Come on," Mindy said, gesturing for Allie to follow.

"Hold on a second, girls," I said. "I don't think that's such a good idea."

"No way, Mrs. Connor! This is a totally good idea. I'm on the newspaper staff, remember? And they never give the freshmen anything to write except profiles of the teachers. This is like a total break for me."

"Forget it, Woodward," Laura said.

Mindy blinked. "Woodward?"

Laura just shook her head. "You're not prowling the halls to go see a dead body."

"But, Mom!"

"No," Laura said. "Now go. Shoo. Both of you." She pointed to the far side of the gym. Our girls hesitated, then shared one of those looks that all mothers of teenage girls are familiar with. The one that says, *My mom is a freak.*

"Whatever," my daughter said. Then off they went, their heads bent close as they ran down a list of their mothers' imperfections.

I turned to Laura, unable to stop my grin.

"What?"

"If I tell you *I'm* going, are you going to call me Bernstein?"

"Very funny. And you can thank me later for getting those two out of our hair." She cocked a head toward the door. "Let's go."

I hesitated only long enough to make sure the girls weren't watching and to scan the gym for Timmy. I found him and Eddie in a corner that the PTA had set up as toddler central. He (Timmy, not Eddie) was neck deep in a kiddie pool filled with plastic balls, the grin on his face so wide I could see it from yards away.

I waved, managed to catch Eddie's attention, and gestured for him to come over. He did, first making sure that one of the ladies standing nearby would keep an eye on my boy.

Laura and I met him halfway and gave him a brief rundown. "We're going to go see what's up," I said, ending the story in the vaguest way possible.

"You gals go on ahead," he said. "I'll watch the youngster."

"You're sure?" I asked.

He met my eyes. "Not my business anymore, is it?"

I nodded. Because the truth was, as much as I appreciated having Eddie around, I was the Demon Hunter in these parts. And at times, that responsibility weighed heavily.

As Laura and I hurried out, I heard a few of the PTA ladies calling to me. I pretended a sudden case of deafness and kept on going. Demons first. Refreshment Committee later.

We racewalked back through the halls until we saw the uniformed officers standing near the door. Yellow crime-scene tape had been spread across the hall, essentially barring anyone from passing. A stretcher—empty—took up a large chunk of space near the door. The stretcher didn't bother me. The cops, however, did.

I noticed David Long standing off to one side in a cluster of other teachers, and waved. "What happened?" I asked, since that seemed like a normal, I'm-not-involved kind of thing to say.

David stepped away from the other teachers, one of whom I recognized but couldn't place. From my new perspective, I also noticed the janitor, decked out in green coveralls and a sour expression. I couldn't blame him. I'd had a demon die in my kitchen a few months ago (or, more accurately, I'd *killed* a demon in my kitchen a few months ago), and it's put a pallor on cooking ever since.

"Damn kids," the janitor muttered, his voice so low I was reading his lips more than hearing his voice. "Always causing trouble."

The gripe seemed out of place, so I tossed another query into the mix. "Do they think kids did this?"

David looked surprised by the question. "I don't think so. Heart attack's what I've been hearing, not that they're giving us any solid information yet."

I pondered that. Considering Sinclair had a spike through his eye, "heart attack" seemed a tad unreasonable. Then again, the man *had* suffered a fatal heart attack. At least, he had originally. There were probably still signs. And if the EMTs assumed that he had an attack, and then fell on the spike . . .

Dicey, but I could hope. For that matter, I was willing to hope for anything so long as it meant that the cops would close the case and not go looking for a culprit. Namely, me.

I took a deep breath and kept my purse pressed against my side, my hand clenched tight on the hidden book. From the looks of things, I was in the clear with the cops. But ultimate evil? *That* I still had to deal with.

Five

"**Arthur Simms,**" Eddie said in a low voice. "Know that one from my stint at Coastal Mists. *He* could be a demon. Wouldn't surprise me none at all."

We were standing behind the choir risers, talking in low voices. "Simms isn't a demon," I said, glancing around to make sure we weren't being overheard. Not that I knew Arthur Simms well enough to be certain, but I did know Eddie. And I know when he's spouting off.

Eddie shrugged. "You're probably right. But if a High Demon's got his sights on that nursing home, you and I both know Sinclair's not the last of it."

"But the last of what?" I asked, frustrated.

"Don't know. But at least we know they're planning something," Eddie said. "That's more than you knew this morning."

He was right. I'd been in the right place at the right time, and had found myself face-to-face with a demon.

Killing Sinclair had undoubtedly slowed the plan down, whatever the plan might be. That, at least, was a victory. A minor one, but a victory nonetheless.

"Could be Goramesh again," Eddie said, referring to the High Demon I'd battled just a few months ago.

"Yeah. Or it could be someone totally new." I drew in a breath and let it out noisily. "Looks like I'll be spending more time at Coastal Mists over the next few days. Just to scope out the situation. You up for joining me?"

He met my eyes, his flat but firm. "If I never set foot in that place again, it'll be too damn soon. Not even if it meant holding off the goddamn apocalypse. You get me, girl?"

"I get you." I did, too. Eddie had been held and interrogated in Coastal Mists for months by a High Demon's minions. Under those circumstances, I could hardly blame him for avoiding the place.

"Now, if you want to fix me up with Stella Lopez," he said, giving the woman a little wave, and then letting loose with a wolf whistle that had the whole room turning to look at us.

"Eddie!"

"What? She's a babe."

I shook my head. "Never mind. We'll talk about this later."

I started to walk away, but he reached out and grabbed my arm. "Where's the book?"

"In the minivan," I said. After the cops had shooed us away from the crime scene, Laura and I had made a detour for the ladies' room, where I'd passed the book off to her. "I couldn't keep carting it around."

Laura was back in the gym now; she'd come in a few minutes before, flashed me a thumbs-up sign, and then made a beeline toward Mindy and the snack table. I was heading that way myself. I'd eaten the remains of Timmy's

Eggo for breakfast, along with three cups of coffee. Had I known what a workout I'd be getting, I would have loaded up on protein. As it was, I felt lucky not to be passing out from hunger.

Since I was near starving to death, naturally it took fifteen minutes to cross the short distance to the snacks. Everyone, it seemed, wanted to talk to me. A few other freshman moms. Sylvia Foster and Gretchen Kimble who share car-pool duty with me. Even Vice Principal Maynard, who wanted to "personally congratulate me on having such a talented daughter."

Everyone, that is, except Stuart, who still hadn't arrived on the scene. Yes, I know he's running for office. And yes, I know he's got to juggle dozens of obligations. But so what? I've been busting tail trying to raise two kids, keep the house in (somewhat) decent order, and volunteer for a ton of community projects. But I still manage to find time to hunt demons and generally make San Diablo safe for democracy (okay, maybe not that, but at least I'm making it safe to walk around after dark).

And yes, I realize Stuart doesn't know about the demon-hunting thing. But, dammit, he promised.

I pulled Allie's cell phone out and dialed Stuart. Voice mail. I scowled and resisted the urge to hurl the phone across the room.

"Problem?"

That from David Long, who was standing in front of me holding a plate with two slices of cheese, a few strawberries, and—thank you, God—two Krispy Kreme doughnuts.

"If that plate's for me, then all my problems have just vanished in a puff."

"Guess that makes me a hero."

I took a bite of the doughnut. "Definitely. If it were up to me, I'd erect a statue in your honor."

"Don't let me stop you." He turned and lifted his chin. "I think this is my best side, don't you?"

"I just don't know how to answer that," I said, fighting a grin.

"Hard to choose, isn't it?" He turned again. "This side's good, too."

"Mmm," I said. "I think I'll just stay quiet."

"Mrs. Connor, you wound me."

"Call me Kate," I said, my fingers closing around a strawberry. "Anyone who brings me food is automatically entitled to first-name status."

"All right, Katie."

The strawberry paused midway to my mouth. "It's just Kate," I said, probably a little too sharply.

"Sorry," he said. But he didn't seem sorry at all.

The thing is, only the people closest to me ever call me Katie, and then only rarely. Father Corletti in Rome. Stuart and Eddie.

Eric, though . . .

To Eric, I'd always been Katie. And there was just something about the way David said my name that made me want to cry.

I focused on breathing normally, trying hard to look casual. But I lost the battle when he pulled a mint from his pocket, unwrapped the plastic, and popped it into his mouth.

I took an unconscious step backwards. Surely David Long wasn't . . .

No. Lots of people suck on mints. That's why every restaurant on the planet has a tub of the things sitting next to the exit. Because the damn things are popular.

Still, I couldn't stop that little niggle of doubt. Not only was paranoia an occupational hazard, but this man spent every weekday in close proximity to my daughter.

Which reminded me of a question I had for Mr. Long. "Allie's not already taking chemistry classes, is she?"

He chuckled. "No, and I wouldn't be surprised if the bloom wears off before she has to pick her courses for next semester."

"Oh. Well, don't take this the wrong way, but why does she know you? I mean, do you make a habit of meeting all the freshmen? Has Allie developed a sudden affinity for hanging around the science hall?"

"She's developed an affinity, all right. But it's for surfers. Not science."

"Excuse me?"

"I'm the faculty adviser for the surf club."

"Allie *surfs?*" This was news to me.

"Not exactly," he said. "But she seems to enjoy the activities."

"Ah. What activities are we talking about, exactly?"

"That would be the watching boys in bathing suits activity."

That, I thought, sounded much more like the daughter I knew. Still, I was mildly irritated that Allie hadn't mentioned the club to me. I'd thought I knew all about her after-school activities. Surfing, however, had never come up.

"I'm teasing," David said. "Well, mostly, anyway. All the cheerleaders are involved at this stage."

"I'm probably going to regret asking, but what stage exactly are you talking about?"

"The exhibition," he said. "Allie hasn't mentioned it?"

"Oh!" I said, feigning total comprehension. "I don't know where my mind was. Of course she's mentioned the exhibition." Had she mentioned an exhibition? I frowned. True, I'd been a little distracted since I'd been drawn back into the *Forza,* but surely I would have remembered her mentioning an exhibition. Wouldn't I?

David continued on, oblivious to my fit of maternal insecurity. "The last few meetings, we've been planning the charity exhibition."

"Oh." I frowned, considering that. I was all for charity, but how much money could a bunch of teenagers surfing off Coronado Beach really raise? I mean, you could see the same thing pretty much every day—sunrise to sunset—during the summer.

But when I mentioned that tiny little problem to David, he only smiled. "No worries. We've lined up a special celebrity guest. Cool."

"Um, well, yeah, I guess it is."

"No, that's his name. Our celebrity. Cooley Claymore. They call him Cool. Unfortunately, that means I have to call him Cool, too."

"Right," I said, my estimation of David Long rising a notch. I'd keep an eye on the man, yes, but there was no denying the fact that I liked him. Even if the breath mints (among other things) meant that I didn't completely trust him.

"So do you surf?"

He shook his head. "Fortunately for me, the faculty liaison performs a purely bureaucratic role. In fact, Cool volunteered to step in and be a temporary coach. So he's training his team."

"And Allie? Is she supposed to surf?" The idea of my daughter breaking her neck just so she could be closer to cute guys didn't appeal to me at all.

"Not at the exhibition," he said. "In the spring, we'll have classes. Beginner level, I promise you. By the time summer rolls around, she should have the basics down."

"Hmm." I turned, my eyes searching the gym. I found Allie holding Timmy's hand, Mindy at her side, as they talked to a cluster of boys. She was laughing, her face lit up, and the boys were soaking it in, as if my daughter was a sunbeam. I stifled a sigh. Sometimes, I really miss not having had a normal childhood. How wonderful to have been worrying about boys and grades instead of demons and hellhounds. To have kept my backpack stocked with makeup and nail polish instead of holy water and crucifixes.

I may not have had that childhood, but at least my kids did. That's what Eric and I had wanted, after all. And, honestly, it was one of the reasons I'd let myself get drawn back into *Forza Scura*. I know the bad stuff that's out there. And I want to keep it the hell away from my kids.

"Kate?" I looked up sharply to find David watching me. "You okay?"

"Yeah. Sorry. Just thinking about how fast they grow up." I cocked my head, looking at him. "Do you have kids?"

"About a hundred and twenty," he said, sweeping an arm to encompass the gym.

"Any of your own?"

His hesitation was so short I could have imagined it. "No. None of my own."

An awkward silence hung between us. I cleared my throat. "So about the boys in bathing suits. Is he one of them?" I was looking at my daughter again, and the cluster of boys. In particular, I was focusing on a dark-haired boy in a denim jacket who was standing just a little too close to my girl.

"That's Troy Myerson," David said. "All the girls have a bit of a crush on him."

"Allie, too?" I'd heard *nothing* of this.

"Oh yeah," he said, his soft laughing suggesting that I was the only one in the entire gymnasium who *didn't* know that my daughter had a crush on the darkly handsome Mr. Myerson. I mean, talk about driving a stake through a mother's heart.

Fortunately, I didn't have long to be melancholy, because

Sarah Talbot, the head of the Refreshment Committee, scurried up. "Oh, Kate, good. We're getting ready to wrap up. Do you think you could help pack up some of the leftovers?"

David raised a hand in a silent good-bye, then left, leaving me to PTA hell. A hell that got just a tad hotter when Marissa stepped up and joined the conversation. "Kate's not available right now," she told Sarah. "She's chaperoning the Coastal Mists residents with me. We have to start rounding everyone up."

"Oh," Sarah said. She nodded toward the bleachers where several residents were clustered with Nurse Kelly. "It looks like they're mostly all there."

"Still," Marissa said, firmly taking my arm. "It's our responsibility."

Sarah shot me a sympathetic look, then aimed a glare at Marissa that would freeze nitrogen. Normally, I'd be right there siding with Sarah. In this case, though, Marissa was right. I hadn't exactly won the volunteer chaperone of the year award today.

"Now, don't you worry," Marissa said, patting my arm as Sarah stalked off to find another volunteer. "I'm sure none of the residents think you're responsible for Mr. Sinclair's death. But if any of them seem uncomfortable around you, you just come find me." When it comes to passive-aggressive, Marissa's got the technique nailed.

Since I was feeling a slight bit of guilt for having abandoned her to the task, I did as she asked without complaining. Basically, that involved circling through the gym, finding the residents, and herding them back toward the double doors. There, Marissa met us with a clipboard. She pursed her lips, then made six little ticky-marks. One for each of the residents I'd gathered.

"So that's everyone?" I asked.

"Apparently, yes."

"Great." I checked over my shoulder and found Laura. "Let me just make sure that Laura can take my kids home, and I'll go with you on the bus."

She sighed, then dropped the arm holding the clipboard. "You know what, Kate? Don't even worry about it. Kelly and I can handle it. Goodness knows we handled it earlier today." There it was again, that passive-aggressive thing.

"You're sure?" I asked. She probably expected me to step in and volunteer, letting her off the hook entirely. I, however, was rarely cowed by passive-aggressive behavior. And I was anxious to get home and find a safer hiding place for the book than my minivan.

Another sigh. This one deeper and more anguished. Honestly, the woman could emote. "Yes, I'm sure. I suppose it's for the best, anyway. I'd hate for any more passengers to die on the way back to the home."

Ouch. That one almost did it. I almost insisted on helping her out, but visions of a demonic book sucking my kids, Laura, Eddie, and the Odyssey into some horror movie hell kept me on track. "Nice," I said. "Very nice."

She tucked the clipboard under her arm and started to step away. Then she stopped. "Don't think you're off the hook. As far as I'm concerned, you've been completely useless."

"I already told you I'm sorry," I said, my patience wearing thin.

"Sorry doesn't do a damn thing. You owe me, Kate. And one day, I'm going to call in that marker."

"So are you going to give me the full scoop?" Laura leaned against my kitchen counter, a mug of freshly brewed Starbucks Sumatra in her hand. "I looked at that book, and there's nothing in it. So what's going on?"

I held up my hand for quiet, then peeked out of the

kitchen and into the living room. Eddie'd fallen asleep in the recliner, and the kids were spread out, the girls upstairs in Allie's room, and Timmy sitting too close to the television, his eyes glued to images of cheerleader Kim Possible jumping and flipping as she battled the evil Shego and her green-fire shooting hands.

For a half second, I considered telling Timmy to move away from the television. Or, worse, switching it over to something educational. I ignored that foolish urge. I needed to talk to Laura, and I was too tired for a full-fledged battle with an irate toddler. If the Disney Channel could buy me a few moments of peace, then I was happy to bow to the all-powerful Mouse.

"Well?" Laura asked, as soon as I went back to chopping onions.

I gave her a quick rundown, starting with what I'd learned at Coastal Mists and ending with Sinclair's rude encounter with a vertical beam.

"Ouch," she said, making a face.

"No sympathy for the demons, please."

"Sorry. So where's the book now?"

I eyed a nearby cabinet meaningfully. As soon as we'd returned home, Allie and Mindy had escaped to the upstairs. While Laura got Timmy settled, I'd returned to the garage and retrieved the book from the van, then hidden it where I knew neither Allie nor Stuart would run across it. In the kitchen. Among the pots and pans. I keep spare cash back there, too. So far, no one in my family has noticed.

"Good plan," Laura said. "Unless Stuart decides to whip up a casserole."

We both had a good chuckle at that, and then Laura turned serious. "So why do you think Sinclair needed that book?"

"I don't know." I added the onions to some ground beef

and tomato sauce I already had in a bowl. Meat loaf is one of the few dishes I can make without strictly following a recipe card and still have it come out edible. Not great, mind you. But edible. "Honestly, I'm not even sure he was getting it out."

"What do you mean?"

"Just that I don't really know what he was doing. Maybe he was putting the book *in,* not taking it out."

Laura cocked her head, studying me. "Yeah, but you would have noticed if he had the book on the bus, right? I mean, it's not exactly a paperback."

"Maybe," I said slowly, trying to articulate the thoughts even as they filled my head. "But what if someone was working with Sinclair. What if someone passed him the book?" An image of David Long popped into my head. I tried to blink it away, but couldn't quite manage. I liked the guy— I really did. And I didn't want to believe that he was involved with demons. Or, worse, that he *was* a demon.

I knew better than to trust him simply because I liked him, though. I'd been burned by that before. I didn't intend to be burned again.

"Taking it or hiding it, we still don't know why," Laura said. "I mean, it's just a blank book."

"It's got to be a lot more than that," I said. "I doubt Sinclair just wanted to journal about his deepest, darkest feelings."

"True," Laura said. "But what?"

"I'm still working on that one."

"Have you called Father Ben?"

"I left him a message." Once the book was safely tucked away, I'd gone upstairs to change into sweatpants and a T-shirt. I'd taken the opportunity to call my new *alimentatore* from the privacy of my bedroom.

Technically, Father Ben was a probationary *alimentatore.*

He'd learned about *Forza* for the first time a few months ago when Father Corletti had flown over from Rome to take charge of a powerful relic that the High Demon Goramesh had been after. Since I'd been in need of a new *alimentatore,* and since there were no fully trained mentors in *Forza* who could step into the job, Father Corletti had taken Father Ben into his confidence and invited him to train as my *alimentatore.*

Even though a fully trained *alimentatore* has years of experience, a wide knowledge base of all things demonic, and training in weapons and martial arts, I'd been perfectly okay with Father Corletti's suggestion. Father Ben might be inexperienced, but he was smart and eager, and I figured that had to count for something.

I'd left him a cryptic message about the book and the events with Sinclair, then promised to try him in the morning if I didn't hear from him first.

"What about the Italian guy?" Laura asked. "Did you call him?"

"Father Corletti?" I shook my head. "I tried. Couldn't reach him, either. He's doing missionary work in Africa or something. I left a message, but who knows when I'll hear back." Father Corletti headed up the *Forza Scura.* More than that, he'd been like a parent to me. I hoped he would call back soon. I wanted the reassurance of hearing his voice.

I finished shaping the meat, shoved the pan into the oven, and rinsed off my hands. "You and Mindy staying for dinner?" These days, Mindy and Laura ate with us about twice a week. We hadn't formally discussed it, but somehow it just seemed easier. Her house was too empty with Paul in L.A. so much. And mine was too empty with Stuart working late so many nights. Plus, the girls did their homework together. It just made sense.

The question was barely out of my mouth when I heard the familiar creak of our garage door. She caught my eye. "Thanks for the invitation, but I think we'll go order a pizza and have a girl's night."

"Good idea," I said. My heart was pounding in my chest, and while Laura left to gather up Mindy, I splashed cold water on my face, trying to will myself to be calm. And, more important, trying to rein in my temper.

I stood, rooted to the spot, as time seemed to slow. Since Stuart had yet to fix our ancient garage-door opener, it took almost two full minutes to groan its way to the top, and those minutes seemed to drag on forever.

Finally, I heard the car door slam. The noise kicked me into gear, and I started shredding lettuce into a large, wooden bowl.

The doorknob rattled and then there he was. I heard him rather than saw him. I couldn't look at him, afraid that if I did, I'd just yell. And did I really want a knock-down, drag-out before dinner? Ugly, brutal battles were better saved for after the kids were in bed.

"You're pissed," he said.

"Gee," I said to the lettuce. "What was your first clue?"

"That lettuce looks like confetti."

I checked the bowl, grimacing. He was right. I'd ripped the leaves into such tiny pieces they were good for nothing more than feeding Gidget, the hamster at Timmy's day care.

I shoved the bowl away and turned to face the inevitable. He was still in the doorway, a dozen roses in his hand.

"You are about a million miles past crazy if you think those roses are going make it up to me."

"Not for you, sweetheart," he said, coming up and kissing me on the forehead. "They're for Allie."

"Oh." Well, damn. My righteous indignation vanished

in a puff. I'd get it back, I was certain, but right then, I felt a quick tug of affection for the man who'd at least come prepared to offer a much-needed apology.

I gestured toward the upstairs. "Go supplicate yourself."

I held back, following him only after I heard Allie's squeal of delight. By dinnertime, all was forgiven. On the surface, anyway. From my perspective, this wasn't over. And if I know my daughter—and I'm pretty sure I do, Troy Myerson notwithstanding—the dozen roses only soothed the hurt; they didn't heal it.

Stuart wasn't off the hook. Not yet.

He knew it, too. He didn't say one more word about being late, but he did play Hi Ho! Cherry-O with Timmy (which consisted of Timmy tossing the tiny cherries around the living room and Stuart crawling on his hands and knees to retrieve them), then gave the munchkin his bath without me having to ask. And then—as if the bath thing wasn't miracle enough—he put Timmy in his pajamas, fixed a sippy cup of warm milk, and read three of this month's favorite books—*Good Night, Gorilla, Knuffle Bunny,* and the ever-popular *How Do Dinosaurs Say Good Night?*

He even brought the kiddo to me for a good-night kiss, then carried Timmy and Boo Bear upstairs to his room. Honestly, with this much help being offered, I almost wished that Stuart screwed up royally on a more regular basis.

As he finished up the domestic chores, I sat on the couch, pretending to flip through the latest issue of *Real Simple,* but really thinking about the mysterious book. I tried to shoot Eddie a meaningful glance—so we could sneak out to the back porch for a surreptitious conversation—but he'd dozed off again, leaving me all alone to fret.

Stuart came back into the living room holding two wineglasses. "I'm sorry," he said, handing me a glass and then sliding onto the couch beside me.

"Are you going to tell me where you've been, or am I supposed to guess?"

"Three guesses," he said. "But I bet you only need one."

"I don't even need that," I said, sinking back into the couch pillows. I took a long sip of Chenin Blanc and closed my eyes. "Was it worth it?"

"Missing out on seeing Allie? No. But there was some definite ka-ching involved."

"Good answer," I said, my eyes still closed.

"I really am sorry."

"I know you are," I said. I opened my eyes. "But sorry's not going to get today back."

"I know." His gaze drifted toward the stairs. "Think she's up for a few rounds of Monkeyball?" he asked, gesturing toward our GameCube.

I made a face. "It's late."

"It's Friday."

I pretended to consider. "One game," I said, because I knew Allie would love it. "And then tomorrow, *you* take her to the mall."

A horrified expression crossed his face. "Not clothes shopping? She's already got enough in her closet to clothe a small nation."

"Not clothes," I agreed, even though that really would be a suitable punishment. "I need you to pick up some Christmas presents," I said. "I have a list." That much was true, even if I did neglect to mention that I wanted him and Allie gone so that I could go visit Father Ben at the cathedral without anyone asking questions about what I was up to.

"Presents. Check."

"And she wants to buy an iPod."

"An iPod?" he repeated, his expression mildly disapproving. "She'll be hooked up to headphones twenty-four hours a day."

I raised an eyebrow. "If you've got a problem with the iPod, you should have raised it at the assembly."

"Right," he said. "Mall. iPod. No problem."

I grinned. "I love you. You're not off the hook yet, but I love you."

"I love you, too, babe. Don't ever forget that."

He pulled me close, and I heard the rustle of denim against upholstery across the room, accompanied by a low snort.

"Ain't that just heartwarmin'?" Eddie mumbled from the recliner, his eyes never even opening.

Stuart and I exchanged an amused glance. And then, because I couldn't help myself, and because I really did love him, I leaned over and kissed my husband. Hard.

He stood up and held out his hand. I hesitated only a second, and then took it, letting him tug me to me feet and lead me up the stairs.

Six

"Momma momma momma? You awake, Momma?"

I rolled over and pulled the pillow over my head.

Another poke on my side. "Mommy? Wake up, Mommy?"

"Mmphlf," I mumbled, trying to make sense of the world.

"MOMMY!"

I yelped and sat bolt upright, then looked down to see my little boy's innocent face grinning up at me. We'd moved him from a crib to a toddler bed five weeks ago, and Timmy was delighting in his newfound freedom.

"You awake, Mommy?"

"Am now, kiddo."

I reached over to poke Stuart—I wasn't going to be the only one suffering at seven A.M. on a Saturday—only to discover that he wasn't there. I scowled at his side of the bed, trying to process that information.

"Mommy! Come on, Mommy!"

"Timmy!" Stuart's voice echoed up the stairs. "Let your mother sleep."

"It's okay," I shouted back. "I'm already up."

A pause, then, "In that case, where do you keep that electric skillet? The one you use to make pancakes?"

"In the cabinet to the right of the dishwasher, all the way in the back," I called back. I yawned, vaguely thinking that an intercom system would be a good thing. "Why?"

"Can't a man make pancakes for his family?" Stuart asked, poking his head in through the door.

"I don't know? Can he?"

"I guess we'll find out." He gestured for Timmy. "Come on, sport. Come give your old man a hand."

As Timmy scampered merrily after his dad, I ran my fingers through my hair and scrubbed my face with my hands, trying to wake up. Something was off, and it was more than just the oddity of Stuart cooking.

I started to slide out of bed, thinking about the level of destruction that was about to descend on my kitchen. Pancake batter on the ceiling. Spilled milk. Sticky egg residue all over the countertops. And every single pot and pan dragged out of the cabinets as he looked for the skillet and a mixing bowl.

A mess. An explosion. A complete and total—

Disaster!

The book! I'd shoved the book right behind the electric skillet!

Suddenly, I was wide awake and racing down the hall, then down the stairs. I skidded to a stop in the kitchen, and smiled at my husband. "Hey. I thought you might need some help."

"I can handle it," he said. "I'm an extremely competent member of the male species."

"Right," I said. "Sure." I eyed the cabinet, which was still closed. "But can you get the skillet out without completely destroying my organizational system?"

He stared at me. "Organizational system?" he repeated. "*You* have an organizational system?"

"Yes, me, thank you very much." I tapped my foot and hoped I looked sufficiently indignant. I pointed toward the garage. "Now go get some bacon from the freezer, would you? Nobody wants pancakes without bacon."

He did, but not until he'd shot me one more incredulous look. As soon as he was of sight, I crouched down and tugged out the skillet. The book was still there, and I shifted a couple of frying pans to make sure it was well covered.

And, yes, I was probably being paranoid. After all, it's not like the book actually said anything. But it would raise questions I'd rather not answer. Which meant I either acted like a spazz and retrieved the skillet for Stuart, or I shooed him out of the kitchen and did the cooking myself.

Since Stuart offered to cook with about the same frequency as Haley's Comet, I wasn't about to choose door number two.

While Stuart did the testosterone-in-an-apron routine, I got Timmy settled in the living room. We'd recently invested in TiVo—an invention worthy of the Nobel Prize, if you ask me—which meant that *The Wiggles* and *The Backyardigans* were always available.

While Stuart poured batter onto the grill, I sat at the table nursing a cup of coffee and starting to come alive. He shot me a smug grin. "So, am I still in the doghouse?"

"You're almost out," I said. "Especially if they taste as good as they smell."

"I'm making banana pancakes for you," he said, then started peeling a banana as if to emphasize the point.

"You are looking for redemption, aren't you?"

"What can I say? I know when to pay penance."

I nodded thoughtfully. "Okay. Take Timmy with you to the mall and then you'll definitely be back in my good graces."

From the look on his face, I could tell he preferred the doghouse.

"Stuart . . ."

"I know, sweetheart, but you know how busy I am right now. I need to go into the office for a few hours this afternoon, and if I take Tim, it's going to add at least two hours to my day." He flipped four pancakes with an ease that I never seemed to manage. The big showoff.

"Besides," he added, "I won't be spending as much quality time with Allie. And isn't that the whole point?"

I tell you, the man's not a lawyer for nothing.

"Will it screw up your morning that much if I leave Timmy at home with you?"

I frowned, because what could I say? Yes, it would, because I need to head over to the cathedral to see about a new demon infestation in San Diablo? Not too likely. So instead, I just said, "Sure. Of course you can leave him with me. No problem."

"Great." He checked the clock. "The mall opens at ten. Considering how long it takes her to get dressed, we better make sure she's awake."

"I'll go roust her," I said. "The promise of bacon should do the trick." Allie had recently announced her intention to eat only fat-free foods and organic produce. I, however, had yet to see that plan implemented. And I seriously doubted she'd be starting this morning.

I'd just crossed the threshold into the living room when Stuart called me back. "I never did tell you why I was so late yesterday, did I?"

I shook my head, trying not to tense up. I'd forgiven him,

yes. But that didn't mean I wasn't still angry. "No," I said, "you never did."

"Tabitha Danvers came in to see me," he said in the same voice a little kid might use when he sees the pile of presents under the Christmas tree.

"Danvers," I said, trying to place the name. "Of the museum Danvers?" The Danvers Museum was to San Diablo what the Getty Museum was to Los Angeles. An amazing collection financed by a family so wealthy they could afford to open a museum here, a convention center there.

"Exactly," he said. "And, Kate, she's thinking about contributing to my campaign!"

"That's wonderful!" I meant it, too. If Tabitha Danvers had taken an interest in Stuart's campaign, then his scrounging-for-money days could be over.

He kissed my head. "There are just a few little things," he said, mumbling into my hair.

I tilted my head up and met his eyes. He held up a hand, warding off my protests in advance. "You don't have to throw a party," he said. "At least not for Tabitha's sake."

I nodded, mildly soothed. Given the choice between throwing a cocktail party and wading barefoot through a room filled with spiders, I think I'd take the spiders. And I *really* don't like bugs. "But?" I asked, because I could hear the "but" hanging in the air between us.

"But I do need you to come to a party tomorrow. A museum benefit. Tabitha thinks I should mingle, meet other potential donors. That kind of thing."

"On a Sunday?"

He shrugged. "Apparently, it's been set up for a while now. They're taking advantage of the museum being closed for a change of exhibits. At any rate, I just do what they tell me." He squeezed my hand. "Come on, sweetheart. It should be fun."

"Sure," I said. "No problem."

"You'll have to mingle, too," Stuart said, apparently wanting to make sure I understood what I was in for.

"I know, sweetie. I may not be the best at this political wife thing, but I do understand it."

"You *are* the best," he said, in a way that made me go a little weak in the knees. Then he kissed me. I moaned and leaned closer, my body reacting in all sorts of decadent ways.

"I'd better go wake up Allie," I said, finally pulling away. "Unless you want to get a really late start."

"**And you aren't sure** if he was removing the book or hiding it?" Father Ben asked. We were in his office—Father Ben, Timmy, and me—gathered around the battered oak desk that dominated the small room. The book dominated the desktop, dark red and ominous.

Timmy was on the floor, drawing pictures on old parish bulletins with a black Sharpie. I tried to pay attention, but I kept glancing down at Tim, afraid he'd end up coloring the carpet, and I'd feel obligated to have a genuine antique Oriental rug professionally cleaned.

"Kate?" Father Ben prodded.

"What? Oh." I rewound the conversation in my head. "I'm pretty sure he was taking it out, but I can't be positive." I lunged forward. "Timmy, *no.* On the paper, big guy." I sat back, and risked looking away from Tim just long enough to meet the padre's eyes. "Either way, the book was important to him."

" 'The wheels are in motion,' " Father said, repeating the demon's words that I'd relayed to him.

"Any idea what he was talking about?" I asked.

Father Ben nodded slowly, then sank back into his chair,

motioning for me to sit as well. I did, but reluctantly. I had a feeling this wasn't going to be good.

"We can't be certain, of course. Not without more research. But based upon the messages you left for Father Corletti and me, and your description of the book, we were able to do a bit of preliminary research."

"And?"

"And we believe the book may be the *Malevolenaumachia Demonica.*"

"Oh," I said, hoping I sounded duly impressed. "Wow. That's . . . I mean, *wow.*" In truth, I was impressed. Not by the whatever he'd said, since I had no clue what he was talking about. But by the fact that anyone could take my vague description and then announce that the book was something both evil-sounding and hard to pronounce. That was worthy of some serious props, as my daughter would say.

"Do you know what the *MD* is?" Ben asked.

"A doctor?" I asked, stupidly.

"The *Malevolenaumachia Demonica,*" he said, slowly and patiently.

"Ah, um, well, sure. I mean, mostly." I cleared my throat. "Actually, no. I don't have a clue. What is it?"

"You are familiar with a Grimoire?"

"Sure," I said. "It's like a manual for black magic."

"Well, if this book is the *Malevolenaumachia Demonica,* it's a hundred times worse than any potential Grimoire."

"Oh. Great."

He got up and came around his desk, leaning up against it as he faced me. "Have you ever seen *Raiders of the Lost Ark?*"

"Um, sure. It's one of my favorite movies. We even own the DVD." I bit back the urge to ask him what that had to do with anything. Unless my *alimentatore* was losing it, he'd get to the point eventually.

"Remember the scene with the French guy? What he says about the Ark?"

"A transmitter for talking to God," I said. I was getting a sick feeling in my stomach. "Are you saying—"

"Yeah," he said. "That's what I'm saying."

"The book is for talking to God? Or the book is for—"

"Talking to imprisoned demons."

"Oh. Well, isn't that just nifty?" I took a deep breath and considered what he was saying. "How?"

"The demons' words print upon the page."

"But then we're okay," I said. "The book's completely blank."

"Except that once the communication is read, it fades."

I shook my head, trying to get a handle on what he was saying. "So the demon says something, and it prints out across the page? Like, Hey there, Reader. Go stand in a pentagram?"

"That is the essence of it, yes."

"And then when someone reads that message, the page goes blank again?"

"Correct."

"Oh." I wasn't liking this. Understatement of the year, I know, but I really wasn't liking this.

"And can the reader talk to the demons?" I asked. "Like if they write in the book, would the demon read it and then erase the page?"

Father Ben shook his head. "That I don't know."

I nodded slowly, taking it all in. "And the demons that are doing the talking. You said they're imprisoned, right? I thought the demons were in Hell. Or all around us in the ether." As far as I've always understood it, a demon's power comes from Hell, and he'll go there to rejuvenate or vacation or whatever demons do in their leisure time.

But hanging out in Hell doesn't really have much demonic *oomph*. They want to be out here in the real world, fighting to become human. And, barring that, whispering to humans, their oily entreaties urging people to take the baser path even while our guardian angels try to lift us up.

Accounts by many of the saints report being able to see demons in the air all around. That's one serious black mark against being a saint, at least in my mind.

"Many theologians believe that demons are free to leave Hell and walk the earth," Father Ben said. "Certainly those of us affiliated with *Forza* know that to be true."

"Did you know it? Last year, I mean. Before you learned about me. And about *Forza*."

"I believed it," he said. "I didn't know it. I'd never seen evidence of a demon. I still haven't seen the horrors that you have, Kate, and I certainly haven't put myself on the front line the way you have. But still, I believed."

He reached out and squeezed my hand. And even though we're probably very nearly the same age, I felt warm and comforted. And at the same time, horribly sad. I'd never asked to see the things I've seen. My beliefs weren't grounded in faith. Not really. Instead, they were grounded in reality. And I had to wonder if that made me somehow lesser in the eyes of God. Would I, I wondered, be so devout if I'd never actually seen the devil amongst us?

Father Ben started pacing his office, warming to his subject. "Some believe that certain demons have even entered Heaven and been granted an audience with God."

"God has more patience than I do," I said. "I would have kicked their sorry butts right out of the pearly gates."

Ben smiled. "Yes, well, that is one of His traits. At any rate, Second Peter 2:4 tells of some angels who sinned so grievously that they were cast not just into Hell, but into a prison called Tartarus."

"I've heard of it," I said. "It's like the worst of Hell?"

"Exactly. Some believe that those demons mated with human women and created half-breeds. Nephalim, they're called. And for that horrific sin against nature, they were cast down. The ancient world considered Tartarus the worst pit of gloom and darkness. And those fallen angels are bound there in chains, without recourse or appeal to God."

"Wow."

"Exactly."

"An eternity in chains in Hell," I said thoughtfully. "Somehow that makes my filthy bathrooms not seem like that much of a burden."

"Eternity was the plan," Father Ben said. "But some demons have managed to escape over the millennia. Goramesh," he added, meeting my eyes. "He is believed to have once been bound in Tartarus."

"Oh." I shivered. I'd done battle with the High Demon Goramesh. And I sincerely doubted he had a warm, fuzzy place in his heart for me. Someday, I'd see him again. That much I was sure of. I was also sure that when that day came, my odds of walking away from the battle weren't good.

I straightened my shoulders and pushed thoughts of the High Demon out of my head. "What does all this have to do with the book?"

"Well, the lore is that although some demons have escaped, two are still imprisoned in Tartarus. The vilest. The most unrepentant."

I sat there a moment, letting Father Ben's words sink in. "Worse than a High Demon," I said.

He nodded solemnly. "Like nothing we've ever seen before."

"But they're imprisoned, right? I mean, that's the whole point. Gloomiest corner of Hell. Bound in chains. Right?"

"Right. Except . . ."

"Except some *have* escaped," I finished. "And you think these two want out, too."

"Wouldn't you?"

"Mmmm." He had a point. "And the book? The transmitter?"

"The title," he said. "*Malevolenaumachia Demonica.* Do you know what that means?"

"I'm a little rusty on the Latin, Padre."

"Demon's Malicious Struggle." He lifted a shoulder, his head tilting slightly to the side. "Well, that's a loose translation."

"Loose or not, it doesn't sound good."

"The point is, that lore suggests that the book is a transmitter. Not for talking to God, but for talking to the demons imprisoned in Tartarus."

"Dear God," I said, then crossed myself. "So how does it work?"

"That, I don't know."

I stood up and starting pacing the small office. "None of this makes sense. If it's a transmitter, what are they saying? And who are they saying it to? Sinclair? Other demons?"

He shook his head. "That, I can't tell you."

"And why? What are they trying to do? What's the plan?"

"All good questions," Father Ben said. "And I don't have a single good answer. All we know is that there *is* a plan. And I think it's a good guess that Tartarus demons want to escape from Hell. And perhaps they were using the book to give someone directions on how to make that happen."

"Dear Lord."

"That is, of course, all speculation," Father Ben said. "We can't even be certain the book is the *Malevolenaumachia Demonica.*"

"Great. I feel so much better."

"We also know that you've disrupted that plan. Or at least stalled it."

"Because we've got the book now."

"And it's secure."

"Where is it?" I asked.

"The altar," he said.

"Not the vault?"

"We have archivists cataloging the relics in the vault. They are in and out every day, and if they were to find the book . . ." He trailed off, shaking his head. "No, I don't believe there's a safer place in the world than the altar for something like this book. Except, perhaps, deep within the Vatican."

I nodded. Infused as it was with the bones of saints, the altar of St. Mary's Cathedral was impenetrable by a demon. The book, at least, was safe.

That didn't solve all our problems. But it was a start.

Timmy and I left the cathedral well before noon. We hit the T-Mobile store first, and I got a replacement for my missing phone, including the same phone number and a built-in camera. I snapped a few pictures of Timmy just to get the hang of it, e-mailed them to Stuart, then immediately wondered how I'd lived without the thing.

I needed to hit the grocery store, but first I wanted to fill Eddie in. I swung by the house and gave him the rundown. He didn't know anything more about the book than I did, but he agreed that the whole Tartarus demons run amok thing sounded pretty bad.

"You're going to help, right?"

He snorted. "Eh, why not? Chasing demons always brightens my mood. And killin' demons puts me in an even better one."

I ended up dropping him at the library, before heading on to the neighborhood Ralphs. He promised to call my shiny new phone when he was ready for a ride home, "Assuming I don't catch a ride with that hot librarian."

I wished him luck and set out to do some shopping.

For the first two years of Timmy's life, I'd been content to shop with my toddler in tow. Once I discovered the joys of day care, however, my tolerance for the extended process of shopping with a child decreased dramatically.

About the time Timmy grabbed his third can of some meat product off the shelf, held it up, and said, "This too Mommy? We need this?" I decided I'd had enough. If the folks on *Survivor* could live on bugs and berries, then surely we could survive on milk, pasta, and whatever happened to be hidden in the back of the freezer.

When we got home the garage was empty, which didn't really surprise me. Getting Allie out of the mall in under eight hours is an amazing accomplishment. Stuart had been borderline delusional to suggest anything less than five. Not that I'd been inclined to correct his disinformation at the time. . . .

I parked Timmy in front of the television, popped in the *Frosty the Snowman* video, then started to unload the groceries. The house seemed eerily quiet, and I fought a sense of unease, telling myself that just because I'd spent a good portion of yesterday fighting a demon didn't mean that they'd infested my house.

My earnest speech, however, did nothing for my mood, and I moved slowly from the living room into the breakfast area. The pitcher of orange juice I hadn't cleared was still there, but had it been moved just a little to the left? I frowned, not sure, as my gaze swept the room. Nothing else seemed out of place, and I told myself I was being ridiculous.

Naturally, I didn't really believe myself.

"Allie?" I called, loud enough to be heard in every corner of our house.

Silence.

Okay, that was good. The house was empty. Nothing was really out of place. And I just needed to get a grip.

I stood there for a minute, contemplating the get-a-grip plan. I decided that while that might be the rational thing to do, where my kid's safety was an issue, I was more than happy to be paranoid and reactive. And that meant getting Timmy over to Laura's while I searched the house. Just to be sure.

"Timmy?" I called, implementing step one of the paranoid-and-reactive plan. "Come here, kiddo."

He looked up, his features contorted with irritation. "Frosty, Mommy."

"I know, sweetie. But I need you to come here."

Nothing.

"Timmy," I said. "Come here this instant."

Again, nothing.

"Young man, don't make me count to three."

"I'm watching Frosty, Momma!" His little hands were fists at his sides, and I could see a full-blown tantrum coming on. Give in or hold fast? The age-old question of parenting.

I gave in, resorting to the only surefire method of ensuring toddler cooperation: bribery. "How about ice cream?"

He cocked his head to the side, looking just a little bit more toward me than the television. "Ice cream?"

"Absolutely. Come with me over to Aunt Laura's, and you can have ice cream. *And* you can watch Frosty over there."

He looked at me, his face scrunched up in concentration. "Chocolate ice cream?"

"Sure," I said, hoping Laura's freezer was well stocked. For that matter, I hoped Laura was home.

" 'Kay, Mommy." He tugged me toward the back door. "We go Aunt Laura's!"

And so we did. I popped out the video and turned off the television, then let Timmy drag me out the door. I double-checked the alarm system, then shut the door tight and locked it.

Timmy raced across the grass, with me following at a much more reasonable pace so that I could pull out my cell phone and give Laura fair warning. She answered on the first ring, and assured me that she was more than happy to watch the kiddo. It would, she said, save her from a fun-filled morning rearranging her Tupperware.

"Always happy to be of service," I said, as soon as we arrived at her back door.

"I hope you mean that," she said. "I swear I'm going crazy obsessing about my jerk of a husband. If I don't have something to keep me occupied, I'm going to start stalking the man."

"I can help you there, too," I said, as we got Timmy settled. "I'll bring you up to speed when I come back. But basically, I was hoping you could help me search the Internet." I'm not a complete idiot when it comes to computers, but I did think that Google was a children's video program until about six months ago. Laura's computer skills, however, had been honed and sharpened by years of online shopping. Give her a mouse and a cable modem, and she can find (and buy) pretty much anything. Isn't technology amazing?

She narrowed her eyes at me. "So why the last-minute babysitting? Everything okay over there?"

"I hope so," I said.

"Uh-huh. Can I help?"

I pointed to Tim. "Trust me," I said. "You already are."

Once Timmy was happily settled in front of the television with a bowl of ice cream in his chubby little hands, I sprinted back across our connecting yards to my house. Once again, I told myself I was being ridiculous. And once again,

I convinced myself that I wasn't. Demon-hunting's all about instincts. And, for whatever reason, I had a bad feeling.

Back in the house, I paused just inside the back door. "Allie? Stuart? Anybody home?"

No answer.

I checked the kitchen and the garage, just to make sure. No sign of Stuart.

Jimmy Neutron's theme song drifted into the kitchen, and I sang along with it, only a little mortified to realize I knew all the words. I froze suddenly. *I'd turned off the television!*

With my heart pounding in my chest, I made a beeline for the utility drawer. I pushed down on the little latch, then pulled the drawer open slowly, trying to avoid the telltale squeak.

Once it was open enough, I took out an ice pick and tested its weight in my hand. I'd invested in about six of the things last month, never expecting Stuart to notice. Of course that meant he did. I said they'd been on sale and that had satisfied him. After all, what woman can pass up a bargain?

Because of the configuration of our house, you can only see part of the living room from the kitchen area, and I entered carefully, watching my blind side until I'd swept the entire area with my gaze.

Nothing.

Or rather, nothing except the television that I was positive I'd clicked off. But maybe I hadn't hit the button hard enough, or aimed the remote the wrong way. After all, why would a demon want to watch *The Adventures of Jimmy Neutron?*

I wished I could believe I'd simply left the television on, but I couldn't quite manage it. Especially not once I noticed other things out of place. Knickknacks shifted on the hall table. The entertainment center door open just slightly.

Someone looking for something? The book, maybe?

I bit my lower lip and continued moving silently through the house. I'd known that returning to *Forza* would be dangerous. But for that danger to invade my home . . .

I shivered, guilt overwhelming me. If anything happened to the kids. To Stuart.

No.

I wasn't even sure there *was* a danger here. And as for Sinclair and his mysterious book, I didn't know what that was about, but I was determined to end it. And soon. No matter what, my first priority was keeping my family safe. And if that meant killing a few demons along the way, then so much the better.

A metallic screech rang out, echoing through the silent house like a shot and making me jump. *Upstairs.* Someone— or something—was upstairs.

I kept a firm grip on the ice pick as I eased up the stairs, careful to avoid the creaky third step. With any luck, my uninvited guest didn't realize I'd come home. Surprise, I hoped, would work in my favor.

I checked the master bedroom first, but found nothing there except a few dust bunnies huddling in terror under the bed. I assured them they weren't my priority for the day and moved on to Timmy's room.

The place was a disaster. Clothes and toys strewn everywhere. Broken crayons. Ripped bits of paper. Bedding on the floor.

In other words, it looked exactly like it always did.

I frowned, made a mental note to play off of Stuart's guilt and assign him room-cleaning duty. I paused midway to the door, a low, rhythmic *thump, thud* attracting my attention.

I turned in a slow circle, trying to find the source of the sound, but it was gone. And then, just when I was about to give up, I heard it again. A low reverb noise, and it was coming from the interior wall—the one Timmy shared with Allie.

In an instant I was back in the hall, my shoulders pressed flat against the wall outside of Allie's room. The door was cracked slightly open, and I could see that the light was off. From my limited perspective, I could also make out a variety of T-shirts littering the floor. Again, that wasn't exactly earth-shattering news.

That steady thumping, though . . .

I could hear it more clearly now, and I had no idea what it was. Someone opening and closing drawers, maybe?

Didn't much matter, because whoever they were, I was going to nail them. I drew in a breath, counted to three, and then burst through the door, the ice pick high and ready.

Allie's shrill scream just about shattered my eardrums.

Immediately, I dropped my arm, my heart pounding wildly.

"Shit, Mom!" she shrieked, and for once I didn't correct her language.

"Sorry! Sorry!" I eased the ice pick into my back pocket, but I knew it was too late.

She'd been laying on her back, her feet flat against the wall, tapping in time to some music I couldn't hear. Now she whipped her legs around until she was sitting upright, glaring hard at me with her hand at her throat.

"Sorry! I heard a noise upstairs and I didn't realize anyone was home."

"Jesus, Mom." She jerked the earpieces out and then exhaled loudly and dramatically. "You scared me to death. Haven't you been listening to all those lectures you and Stuart gave me? If you think someone's in the house you leave. You call nine-one-one. You don't creep upstairs with a freaking ice pick and terrorize your daughter! I mean, come on!"

"Right. You're right." What else could I say?

I took a couple of deep breaths, waiting until my heart slowed. "So, where's Stuart."

"Office," she said. "He left about three seconds after we got back." She gestured at the tiny gizmo she'd been tethered to only seconds before. "He didn't even want to see how it works!"

"Unbelievable," I said. "I'm going to go get Timmy from Laura's house. You want to stay here or come with me?"

She pointed toward her computer. "Busy, Mom."

"Right. No problem." Silly me. There was an entire Internet worth of songs out there, just waiting to be downloaded. Apparently my daughter wanted to get a headstart. At this rate, if we saw her again before college, it would be a miracle.

I bustled back down the stairs, giddy with relief. I collapsed on the couch and sat happily. Or, at least, I sat happily until my mind started whirling again. Then I sat in a sludge of random thoughts. The mess in Timmy's room, the mysterious book, my unfinished Christmas shopping, and the vast emptiness that was our refrigerator. The first, I'd assign to Stuart. The last, I could handle by ordering pizza. The Christmas shopping and decorating could wait until school let out. The book, though. That one still had me baffled.

Since Timmy would be perfectly happy at Laura's unless the cable went out, I decided to leave him there for a bit while I called Father Ben to see if he'd learned anything new. (Granted, I hadn't left him that long ago, but I was a teensy bit anxious. So sue me.)

I'd just picked up the phone when I noticed that the pantry door was slightly ajar. I shot a frustrated glance toward the upstairs. Our cat, Kabit, must be part raccoon, because he can chew through any and all bags of kitty food. Which means that unless we want Purina Cat Chow scattered on the floor like confetti, we have to keep the pantry door closed at all times. I remember. Stuart remembers. Even Eddie remembers.

My daughter, however, is physically incapable of latching a simple wooden door.

Frustrated, I moved to the pantry. Kabit was probably in there, gorging his little kitty face.

I tugged open the door to check, and—*"Aaaaaaayyyyy aaaaaaaa!!!"*

Something hard and fast hit me in a full-body blow, slamming me backwards against the granite countertops.

I grunted and tried to regain my footing, but the demon was on me, her eyes flashing and her red hair sticking out wild in a hundred directions. She looked deranged and vile and more than happy to kill me on the spot.

She thrust her arm forward, going for my neck, and I reacted immediately, my right arm whipping up to block hers, and my left hand smashing out to land a hard punch to her gut.

She stumbled backwards, then lunged for me again. This time, though, I was prepared and easily sideswiped her, adding my own shove to send her entire midsection slamming against the counter. She exhaled with an *ooph,* then whipped around to face me, a cookie sheet from my dish drainer tight in her hands.

She smacked me over the head, and I went sprawling, the wind knocked completely out of me.

As I gasped, she leaped, sending us both crashing down onto the floor. Despite the searing pain in my chest, I sprang to my feet, sending silent kudos to Cutter for sharpening my once-atrophied reflexes.

I kicked up and out as the woman tried to stand, catching her just below the chin and sending her head snapping back. A pretty nifty move, and one that would have laid a human flat. Instead, I was the one who ended up splayed out on the floor. In a movement that can only be described as preternaturally fast, the bitch reached up, grabbed my ankle as I was pulling in from the kick, and gave it a good, hard tug.

I went tumbling, crashing to the floor with a yelp that surely rattled the rafters and alerted my daughter. I didn't have time to worry about that, though, because the demon was on me, leaping on my chest with all the enthusiasm of a toddler on a trampoline. Her knees pounded my ribs, and I struggled to breathe as her hands closed around my neck.

"The book," she hissed, rancid breath washing over me. "Master needs the book."

"Tough luck for Master," I managed, snapping my knee up and into her groin in the hope that I'd get her off of me. No such luck.

"Where?" she said. "Tell. Or die."

I wasn't crazy about either option, but I didn't have a lot of choices here. I wheezed, trying to draw in enough air to think clearly, then turned my head, staring hard at the warming drawer beneath the oven. I closed my eyes, then looked back up at her. "No," I said. *"No."*

And then—because some demons are smarter than they look—she turned toward the warming drawer, too. And as a slow smile crept over her face, she shifted her stance. Not much, but it was enough. More, I was ready.

She kept one hand tight around my neck, but to reach the drawer, she had to shift her weight off of me. When she did, I twisted, then managed to get my hand out from under her and around to my back pocket.

By the time she realized what I was doing, it was too late. I had the ice pick out and aimed. And in one snap movement, I drew on all my strength and slammed the thing home.

She yowled, then went suddenly silent. And as the demon slipped out of the body, I let my head fall back onto the tile floor as I coughed and gasped for air. I needed to get rid of the body before Allie came downstairs and found a dead woman on the kitchen floor.

First, though, I needed to breathe.

Seven

I laid there a moment longer, sucking in glorious oxygen, and then I forced myself to my feet. The house was silent. "Stupid bitch," I whispered, leaning over the body. "You don't put paper in a warming drawer." I may not be much of a cook, but even I know that.

I scowled at her again, just because she was making my life miserable. Or, more specifically, her master was making my life miserable. And who was that? One of the Tartarus demons? Had they been talking to their minions through the book, and now the minions were desperate since I'd shut down their handy little intercom system?

Or was the master someone else entirely? A High Demon, not bound by the chains of Hell? Maybe a demon who wanted the Tartarus demons free. After all, those Tartarus dudes sounded pretty powerful. And they'd probably be pretty grateful to be set free. If you're a High Demon looking to build an army, a demon who'd served time in Tartarus would be a fine addition to the team.

I pondered the questions a bit longer, frustrated because I had no answers to throw into the mix. Worse, I had a body to deal with, and I stared down at her, trying to decide what to do. (Honestly, I understand that *Forza*'s not the organization it used to be, but a little more focus on assisting the Hunters with the disposal of demonic carcasses would be very much appreciated.)

I decided on the garage. For one thing, I could drag the body there without going through the living room (and possibly running into Allie, who I couldn't believe had been deaf to the scuffle). For another, Stuart had shoved several paint tarps in the corner of the garage, supposedly for when he repainted the master bathroom. Since I figured that my husband wouldn't be seeing the inside of a Home Depot until well after the election, I could get away with hiding the body under the tarps. At least until I could come up with a better plan.

I'd just hooked my hands under the dead demon's armpits when Allie's cry of "Mom!" rang out through the house.

"Hang on!" I dropped the body, letting the head land on my foot so as to not make too much noise, then hustled into the living room. No Allie. "What do you need?" I shouted up the stairs.

Her head appeared around the corner, her forehead creased. "What was that noise?"

"Noise?" I repeated, utterly unimpressed with my daughter's reaction time.

"Yeah. I heard something. A minute or so ago." She started down the stairs. "You didn't hear it?"

"Oh!" I held a hand out, motioning for her to stop. "Right. That. No big deal. I just dropped a cookie sheet. Makes an awful clatter on the tile floor."

"You're making cookies? Mom! You know I'm not eating anything with trans fat!"

"I was just moving some things around," I lied. "And you ate pancakes this morning, smothered in butter and syrup."

"Extenuating circumstances."

"Mmmm."

She held on to the banister and half hung there, swinging a little. "So, like, you don't need help then, right?"

"Nope," I said, cheerily. "Totally under control."

"So I can go back up?"

"Far be it for me to keep a girl from her iPod."

She rolled her eyes, then pounded back up the stairs.

I gave her enough time to get settled, then moved back into the kitchen. The demon was still there, staring blindly at me with the one intact eye. I looked away. I've done this countless times—and I get a nice little buzz of satisfaction every time a demon bites the dust—but there's still a definite ick factor involved.

Once again, I got a grip on the demon, and once again, I was interrupted. This time by the shrill ring of the telephone. I left the demon where I'd dragged her—halfway into the garage, the door banging up against her shoulders—and ran to snatch up the handset. "Hello?"

"It's me," Laura said. "I was starting to get worried."

"Everything's fine now," I said. Then I looked at the body. "Although, there is one little thing you could help me with . . ."

"You're sure about this?" I asked, as we bent down to grab the tarp-wrapped body, me at the head and Laura hoisting the feet.

"Oh yeah," Laura said. "I'm positive."

She and Tim had come over about fifteen minutes ago. After we'd settled the munchkin in the living room with a box of Legos and a *Dora the Explorer* video, I'd dragged Laura into the garage, where I'd left the demon in a heap in front of our stand-alone freezer.

"I need to get her to the cathedral," I'd said, pointing to the body. Father Ben might be new, but he'd already proved his worth by coming up with a workable demon disposal plan. And now the crypts beneath the cathedral were being put to good use hiding demon carcasses.

The trouble with that system was that the families of the truly dead person (the one who'd had the body the demon had invaded) were left believing their loved one had up and disappeared. Unfortunately, we didn't have much choice. We could dump the body somewhere, true. But there wasn't any way to repair the damage from a spike to the eye. And cops tend to get all antsy about things like that. They'd investigate. And if their questions led back to me—well, what could I do then? I really didn't want Christmas with my kids spent in the visiting room at San Quentin. And I didn't want Mindy visiting Laura there, either.

Which was why I reiterated my original proposition. "We can put her in the Odyssey."

But Laura shook her head. "No. Without a trunk, it's too obvious."

"She's wrapped up," I said, but Laura just looked at me. I shrugged. She was right. A body wrapped in a tarp pretty much resembles a body wrapped in a tarp.

"We'll shove her in Paul's trunk, and we can drive over to the cathedral after dark."

"What if Paul wants his car?"

She made a face. "He won't. He took his new Thunderbird to San Diego. He's got some sort of conference for all his franchisees. He won't be home until late tomorrow."

"It's still a risk," I said. "We've wrapped her up tight, but there's no way we can be sure there won't be trace evidence in the trunk." Did I sound like a *CSI* buff or what? The

truth is, once I realized that I was going to be responsible for demon disposal for the greater San Diablo metropolitan area, I'd started doing a little research on crimes and forensics and all that.

"Honestly, Kate," Laura said. "Just pick her up already. If Paul ends up nailed for murder, at least I'll know where he's sleeping at night."

She had a point. And since one of my strongest rules is to never argue with a pissed-off wife, I grabbed the demon's head. Laura hoisted the feet, and we shuffle-walked the body the short distance to the Lexus's trunk. Laura had pulled in backwards and popped it open, so all we had to do was squeeze between the front of the Odyssey and the stack of Christmas boxes Stuart had retrieved from the attic last week, but which I had yet to unpack.

"On three," I said, as soon as we were in position. "One . . . two . . . three!" We swung our demon inside, where she landed with a thump.

At the same time, the door between the kitchen and the garage opened. "Mom?"

Yikes!

As Laura screamed, I slammed the trunk shut, then whipped around to face my daughter.

"Jeez, Mom! You guys scared me to death!"

"Scared you! What are you doing sneaking up on people like that?" I pointed to Laura. "You just took ten years off her life!"

Allie looked at me like I'd gone insane, not an unreasonable expression under the circumstances. "I wasn't sneaking. I was looking for you." She squinted at Laura's car, her brow furrowing. "What are you guys doing, anyway?"

She took a step forward, and I moved quickly in to intercept. "Nothing."

"Nothing?" She raised an eyebrow, a challenge in her

voice. "Doesn't look like nothing to me. And what's Mrs. Dupont's car doing in our garage anyway." She took another step, craning her neck as if she were trying to see into Laura's trunk. I turned back around quickly, just in case. Yup, closed tight.

"You're as bad as when you were six," I said. "Remember when you found the Barbie playhouse?"

She glanced again at Laura's car, comprehension playing across her face. "You went Christmas shopping!"

"Inside," I said, making shooing noises. "And stay in there, or I'll take everything back to the store."

"Yes, ma'am," she said, and I laughed. Allie only remembered to say "ma'am" when she wanted something. She opened the door to the kitchen and then paused, turning back to face me. "I completely forgot why I came looking for you in the first place. Someone left you a present, too."

"What?"

"A package," she said. "I found it on the front porch when Stuart dropped me off. I forgot to tell you earlier. You didn't see it? I left it on the breakfast bar for you."

Laura and I followed her back inside. Sure enough, among all the detritus, there was a small package, wrapped in brown paper, about the size of a juice box.

"Gee," I said, glancing at the schoolbooks, CDs, Post-it notes, action figures, and Play-Doh sculptures scattered about. "I wonder why I didn't see it."

"Dunno," Allie said, apparently not recognizing my sarcasm. "It's been here all along." She peered over my shoulder at it. "Who's it from?"

"No return address," I said. I hefted it in my hand, the weight minimal. "For that matter, there's no address at all. Just my name."

"So someone dropped it off themselves," Laura said. "They didn't mail it."

"Maybe you have a secret admirer," Allie said. "Stuart's going to freak."

"I don't have a secret admirer." Did I?

"Maybe it's Stuart, then," Allie said. "Maybe he's making up for yesterday."

"Then the present would be for you," I said.

She shrugged. "I'm okay. We talked. You know. It was good."

I studied her. Not the most rousing endorsement of my husband's parenting skills, but I was pleased nonetheless. Stuart had screwed up, but at least he hadn't scarred my daughter for life.

"It's probably from Marissa," Laura said. "It's about the size of a cell phone. I bet she's just returning the one you lost."

That actually made a lot of sense. "Not really worth the trouble," I said.

"Open it, Mom. It might be something else."

I hesitated, running my fingertip over the brown paper packaging. It probably was my cell phone; what else would it be? But why wrap it? Why not leave it in the mailbox or simply in a small shopping bag?

If it wasn't my phone, did I really want to open the package in front of Allie? No, I thought, I didn't. The way my week was going, I wasn't sure I wanted to open it at all.

I turned to Laura, hoping to buy some time. Or distract Allie. Or something.

"I should go," she said. "Um, you want to come with me, Kate? I'm going to, um, go hide that big present."

Subtle, my best friend isn't. But at least I knew what she meant. She was going to take the Lexus—and the demon—back to her house.

"I'm going to do some more shopping, too," she said. "I could use the company. The mall's a madhouse this time of year."

Allie cocked her head. "You guys are still up to something. What? Are you planning something for me and Mindy?"

"Keep asking questions, and you're going to find nothing but coal in your stocking, young lady." I turned to Laura. "Sure. I'd love to come with you." To Allie, I said, "Watch Timmy, okay? We'll only be gone a few hours."

Not that I intended the kids to stay alone in the house. Before Laura and I got out of the neighborhood, I was going to grab Eddie from the library and bring him back home.

Probably an unnecessary caution, but a demon had just attacked me in my kitchen, and I wasn't going to leave the kids alone. Eddie might be old, but he could still roll with the best of them. And I knew he'd do whatever it took to protect my kids.

I also knew he'd keep the doors locked, the alarm system armed, and he wouldn't open the door to strangers. That's the nice part about being old and curmudgeonly; you can piss off neighborhood callers and no one takes it personally.

Allie, however, was having none of it. "No way! That's so totally not fair!"

"Alison Elizabeth Crowe, you know part of your allowance is compensation for watching your brother."

"No, no, no. *That's* fine. I'll even play Candy Land with him. But you can't go yet." She made frantic gestures toward the package. "Open it!"

"Allie," I said sharply. "Just drop it."

"Jeez, Mom, what's the big deal?"

I frowned, wondering if I were pushing too hard, bringing into sharp relief all my secrets for my daughter to see.

"*Mo-om.* Come on! It's probably a Christmas present someone dropped off." She bounced a little. "Just open the thing!"

I glanced at Laura, who shrugged.

I drew in a breath, wishing I had X-ray vision, psychic powers, something. I didn't anticipate something dangerous—the danger, after all, had just attacked me in the kitchen. But danger takes forms other than the physical, and I could think of at least a dozen things that would have my daughter asking the kinds of questions I didn't want to answer. Questions I wasn't ready to answer.

Then again, maybe now was the time. I'd been younger than Allie when I'd started training, about her age when I'd killed my first demon. My heritage was her heritage, and someday I really was going to tell her. I just hadn't planned on today.

I considered the box. I could stall, or I could open it and field whatever questions Allie asked.

Was I prepared for that? Prepared for my daughter to learn about my past? To ask questions about my present? To worry and fret and—God forbid—get involved?

No, I wasn't. But I hadn't been prepared for the sex talk, either, and I'd made it through that one relatively unscathed.

I'd make it through this, too.

I reached for the box, dragged my nail under the tape, and started peeling it back slowly.

"Could you move *any* slower?" my daughter asked, in a tone that suggested her mother was a complete loser. "It's brown paper. Just rip it off!"

"Hey, you open your mysterious packages your way, and I'll open mine my way."

She made a face and bounced some more.

Honestly, her eagerness was catching. I ripped the rest of the paper off and revealed a plain white gift box.

I drew a breath, hesitating.

"Open it already!"

I did, yanking off the top before I could talk myself out of it. We both stared down. "A key?" Allie said, the confusion in her voice reflecting my own.

She reached down and snatched it up. A simple silver key. "Well, shit." A look of horror, then, "Sorry, Mom."

I didn't bother to reprimand her. I was too busy looking at the key. I took it from her, then squinted at it. A number—287—was stamped in the metal, but other than that, there were no identifying markings.

"I think it's a safe-deposit box key," Laura said.

"No kidding?" Allie leaned forward to get a better look. "So it's like spy stuff. Someone's sending you secret clues, and you have to put them all together." She nodded, pleased with that scenario. "Pretty cool, Mom."

"Hmm," I said.

"So let's go," she said.

"To the mall?"

"Duh. To the bank." She reached over and took the key. "I mean, this is *so* Sydney Bristow."

"I'm not sure—"

But Allie cut me off. "Come on, Mom! Aren't you curious?"

Desperately curious, actually, but I wasn't about to admit that to Allie. Actually, now that I had some time to think about it, I realized I should simply have told her the key was mine. That I'd dropped it, and Marissa had returned it.

A nice little lie, but it had come to me way too late.

I snatched the key back. "It's a key, Allie. Nothing more. There was probably supposed to be a note. It's probably not even a safe-deposit key. It's probably for a locker. Some storage locker filled with fake flowers that Marissa wants me to sort in penance for falling down on chaperone duty yesterday."

"So call her," Allie said. "And if it's not, we'll go check at the bank." She snatched up the phone and held it out.

But before I had the chance to take the phone from her, it rang. "Probably instructions from your handler," she said, then answered with a quick, "Spies 'R' Us."

I looked at Laura and rolled my eyes. "No more *24* for her, and I'm going to hide all the *Alias* DVDs."

As she listened, Allie's cheeks flushed bright pink. I shot Laura a knowing look. *A boy,* I mouthed. Sure enough, the next thing out of Allie's mouth was, "No, no. It's me. Hi, Troy. No, of course you're not interrupting anything. I can totally talk now."

With the phone pressed tight to her ear, she skulked away, heading upstairs where she would, undoubtedly, lie on the bed with her feet on the wall, and spend the next three hours on the phone. Not with Troy, of course. But with the post-call analysis with twenty-eight of her closest friends to get their take on every little nuance of Troy's words, tone, and attitude.

In other words, where the key was concerned, I was off the hook.

Laura cocked her head toward the garage and whispered, "Do you really want to go with me to, um, move the package?"

I shook my head. "We'll do it tonight, like we planned. But I do want to go check this out." I held up the key. "Want to go with me?"

Laura hesitated, then shook her head. "I'm up to my eyeballs in laundry over there," she said. "And Mindy's probably home from choir practice by now. Besides, I think I'd be a nervous wreck if I couldn't check on the car every six or seven minutes."

I nodded, understanding exactly what she meant. "I don't want to leave the kids alone, though. Can you take my car and go get Eddie?"

"Sure," she said. And while Laura left to retrieve Eddie,

I moved through the ground floor of the house checking the locks and sticking my head into every room, every closet, and under every bed. (Well, except Allie's, but only because I couldn't think of a reason for snooping.) All secure.

I found Timmy in the living room, about eight inches away from the television, completely naked.

I sighed, dragged him backwards so that I could at least later tell the Mayo Clinic surgeon that I tried to protect his eyes, and then shoved his legs into his Pull-Ups. "Why'd you take off your Pull-Ups?" I asked.

He peeled his eyes away from the television just long enough to answer me. "Gotta dance, Momma."

Right. I mean, how can you argue with that?

"Stay here," I said. "Any closer, and Dora goes bye-bye. You understand?"

A somber nod.

"And keep your pants on."

"Not pants. Pull-Ups."

That's my kid, literal as they come.

"Mommy's going upstairs. I'll be right back. You be good." But I'd lost him. He was back with the map and the girl and the talking monkey. Not a bad place to be, I thought, all things considered.

"Feet off the wall," I said automatically, as I knocked and then opened the door to Allie's room.

"Hang on," she said into the phone, then rolled over to face me.

"I'm going out as soon as Laura gets back with Eddie," I said, hoping the telephone call had distracted her from her desire to go with me. "Help him keep an eye on your brother, okay?"

"Sure thing, Mom. No problem. Want me to do a couple of loads of laundry, too?"

Because I am not a naïve woman, my senses immediately

kicked into overdrive. "Sure," I said. "And maybe you could clean the bathrooms, too? I think the cure to Ebola is growing in your bathtub."

"No problem," she said happily.

Yup, something was definitely up. "Give," I said. "What do you want?"

"Nothing!" she said, her expression managing to reflect utter shock that I would paint her with any ulterior motive.

"Okay then," I said, turning to leave.

"Um, Mom?"

I turned back. "Hmm?"

"I was wondering if, well, if I could go to the beach this afternoon."

"The beach?" Clearly there was a catch. We live in a coastal town. Usually requests to go to the beach aren't accompanied by offers to do the laundry and scour the toilets.

"Yeah. Okay?"

"With who?"

"Mindy will be there."

"So you and Mindy are going together?"

"Um, not exactly."

I moved and sat on the edge of the bed. I glanced at the phone. "Mindy?" She nodded, and I picked up the receiver. "She'll call you right back," I said, then hung up.

"Now," I said, focusing on my kid. "Spill."

"It's just that Troy Myerson asked me to come, and, well, it's *Troy Myerson.* And I really like him, Mom."

"So I gathered," I said, thinking of David, who'd been clued in to that little fact long before me. (I mean, I'm just the Mom.)

"Can I go?"

"On a date?" I shook my head. "You know we've talked about this. I don't care what everyone else is doing, you aren't dating until you're sixteen."

"I know! But this isn't a date." She pointed to the phone. "Mindy even agrees."

"Oh, well, if *Mindy* says so . . ."

She made a face. "It's like a party. And he called because he wants me to come. But it's not like I'm his date or anything. It's the whole surf club. They're doing a barbeque. And Mindy's going to be there, too, and a lot of the cheerleaders, and just because Troy's going to *coincidentally* be there, too, doesn't make it a date." She paused for breath.

"Coincidentally?"

"Okay, maybe not so much of a coincidence, but please? Can I go? Honestly, Mom, if I can't go I might as well just curl up and die now because my life will be so totally over." She flopped back on the bed, my little drama queen.

"Chaperones?"

She sat back up, smelling victory. "Sure. Totally. Mr. Long will be there. It's the surf club barbeque. They're doing a cookout, and then the surf team's practicing for the exhibition at sunset."

"The exhibition?"

"Uh, yeah? I've only mentioned it nine thousand times."

"Right." I stifled a frown. Okay, so maybe she had told me. Has my attention span really been that deficient since I rejoined *Forza*? "The exhibition. Of course."

"You could even come for the practice part," she said, apparently unaware of my descent into guilt. "I'd totally be okay with that."

I lifted an eyebrow. "Really?"

"Sure. I mean, don't come too early. But the guys are really good on the waves. It'd be fun. And you could even see Troy."

I noticed that she hadn't said I could meet him. Apparently at this juncture I was only allowed to watch from afar.

"Stuart can come, too," she added, then frowned. "I mean, if he's not working and all."

I made a show of moving slowly through her room. I opened the closet, ran a finger along the top of her bookshelf, then peeked under the bed. No demons. This was a good thing.

"Come on, Mom. Pleeeeeze?"

"Do I have to drive you?"

She shook her head. "Bethany's picking us up. Me and Mindy and JoAnn, too."

I considered that. JoAnn was Marissa's oldest girl, but I tried not to hold that against her. Bethany was the head cheerleader and student-body president. She was a senior and seemed reasonably responsible. What's more, I knew her mom. I also knew that her parents had bought her a Volvo. Lots of airbags. Lots of safety features. I usually didn't protest too much when Bethany was driving.

"All right," I finally said. "You clean the bathrooms, do your laundry, vacuum under your bed, *and* change the cat box, and we have a deal."

She squealed and threw her hands around my neck. "You're the best, Mom!"

I hugged her back. The sentiment may have been entirely induced by the fact that she'd just gotten her way, but I still really loved to hear it.

Eight

"Find anything?" I asked, as Eddie plowed through the front door. I waved at Laura, who was idling in the driveway. She waved back, then pulled out as I followed Eddie inside.

"Not a damn thing," he said.

"Well I found a demon in the kitchen," I whispered, cocking my head so that he followed me in there. I brought him up to speed quickly—about the demon and the mysterious key—then asked if he had any theories about either.

"Not a one," he said. He looked at me, his face tight with concentration. I held my breath, wondering if he'd had an epiphany; if he'd remembered something from his past that would shed some light on this whole freaky situation.

"Got any of those mini-corndogs left?" he finally asked. "The ones you fed to the boy the other day? I'm so hungry I could eat the rear end of a rhinoceros."

I sighed, then turned toward the kitchen. "Watch Timmy," I said. "I'll go heat some up for you." Clearly the only flashes of brilliance I could rely on here were my own. Unfortunately, I wasn't flashing, either.

While the corndogs were heating, I made an errand list. The bank was first—I wanted to check out that key, and now that Allie was distracted, I had the perfect opportunity.

After that, my list delved away from intrigue and into the mundane. Since my trip to the grocery store had been cut short, I still needed to make another run. A quick glance into the refrigerator and pantry revealed that we still needed all manner of dairy products (we were nearly out of milk and the cheddar cheese was starting to sprout fuzz) along with the basic life staples supplied by Chef Boyardee and Kellogg's.

The pile of laundry in the utility room was threatening to reach the ceiling, but I'd pawned part of that disaster off on my daughter. And while the house needed a thorough cleaning, I decided that my investigations into the demonic were much more important. (I love it when my justifications for avoiding housework are actually legitimate.)

I tapped the pen against the pad, trying to think what else I needed to do while I was out. Timmy needed new clothes since he'd outgrown everything he owned. For that matter, I realized that I did, too. Need new clothes, that is. The museum party required a nice dress. Without drool stains or smears of ketchup that had only partly come out in the wash. Unfortunately, much of my wardrobe had that particular element of toddler chic.

I might have something in my closet that would work, but I didn't bother looking. I was in the mood to splurge. Since my husband works for the county—and since I have two kids who need new outfits about every seven seconds—our discretionary clothes budget tends to be allocated first toward the kids, then to Stuart (who legitimately needs suits, ties, and shirts with clean collars). Anything leftover trickles down to me. Usually the trickle barely pays for a T-shirt at Kohls.

Today, though, money wasn't a problem. I'd been back on *Forza*'s official payroll for almost three months now, and my monthly stipend was deposited directly into a brokerage account held for me in trust and in secret. We're not talking a lot of money—I could probably make more selling Pampered Chef products—but I didn't return to *Forza* to get rich.

Although I intended that the money go to the kids someday, at the moment, I figured a few hundred for a decent dress and shoes wouldn't detrimentally impact their futures. And it would totally boost my self-esteem. It's one thing to wear Kmart couture to a cocktail party being held in my living room. It's an entirely different matter to forego Donna Karan for the latest Jaclyn Smith duds while mingling with the rich on their own turf.

(And if you're worried that Stuart would be suspicious, the answer is no. The man is entirely clueless as to the cost of women's clothing. I could tell him that a pair of Jimmy Choo sandals costs $49.99, and he'd not only believe me, he'd be shocked by the expense. *Men*.)

I glanced at the clock. One-fifteen. Our bank closes at three on Saturday, so I assumed most of the others in town did, too. If I hurried, I thought I would be able to check a few places before they locked up for the weekend. (I hoped the key would open a safe-deposit box at my own bank, but I couldn't imagine being so lucky.) After that, I was heading to Nordstrom.

I shoved my to-do list into my purse, tucked the key into my wallet, grabbed my car keys, then headed into the living room to say good-bye to my brood.

I found Eddie asleep in the recliner, the *Herald*'s real-estate section open on his lap, and a stubby pencil loose in his hand. The television was still blaring, but Timmy wasn't anywhere to be found.

"Tim!"

Beside me, Eddie snorted and shifted, but he didn't wake up. From upstairs, I heard Allie call down, "Did you say something?"

"I'm looking for Timmy," I said.

"Not here."

"Where's here?"

"Duh. I'm in the bathroom. Scrubbing the stupid toilet, remember?" She didn't sound happy about it, but at least she was doing it. "Hold on, I'll check his room."

I could hear her steps in the hallway as she moved in that direction. Meanwhile, I checked the den and Stuart's study. Nothing. I also checked all the doors. Everything was locked up tight. So where was my kid?

Honestly, I wasn't *too* worried. It's a big house, and we'd taken down the baby gate a few weeks ago, so Tim had the run of the place. Still, the whole demon-on-the-prowl thing made me a little nervous. I wanted to know where my boy was, and I wanted to know now.

"Timmy!" I yelled, this time making Eddie jump.

"What? Who? What!"

"I'm looking for Tim," I said.

"Right there in front of the—oh." He dropped his out-stretched finger. "That little one's a pistol."

"Mmm." I tried again. "Timmy! You answer me right now, or no television for the rest of the day!"

That worked. Which probably says something about bad habits and my parenting skills, but I wasn't inclined to think about that.

"But I *want* TV!" The little voice came from upstairs, followed by the patter of footsteps and then a much more concerned yelp of "Mommy! I WANT TV!"

"He's here," Allie shouted unnecessarily. I heard her make shooshing noises, and then, "Oh, man. You're in for it, squirt."

Since I didn't like the sound of that, I took the stairs two at a time and met them in the hallway, just outside of the master bedroom. Sure enough, Mom was not a happy camper. There my little boy stood—his mouth completely rimmed in bright red lipstick and his eyes so encircled by purple eyeshadow that he looked like a raccoon on an acid trip.

"*Timmy,*" I wailed. I checked my watch. I *really* didn't need this.

"Pretty!" he said.

"I thought Eddie was watching him," Allie said. "It's not my fault! I was cleaning." She held up her Playtex encased hand as if to demonstrate the point.

I just sighed. "Come on," I said, holding out a hand to Timmy.

"*The Wiggles?*" he asked.

"Don't push your luck, sport. We need to get you cleaned up, and then we have to go run some errands."

Honestly, I'd rather shove bamboo under my fingernails than take Timmy clothes shopping with me, but I didn't see any other choice. Allie was going to be gone before I could get back, Laura was tethered to her garage until we passed the demon off to Father Ben, and Eddie was no longer on my list of approved babysitters.

I told myself it would be okay. I'd pretty much saved the world just a few months ago. Surely I could manage to buy one little dress despite having a two-year-old attached to my hip.

Couldn't I?

I didn't let myself think too much about that, though, since I was a little bit afraid of the answer. Instead, I focused on wiping the makeup off Timmy's face and hoped the smell of cold cream wouldn't warp his masculine sensibilities.

"Funny!" he said, looking at his Ponds-slathered mug in the mirror.

"Hysterical," I acknowledged as I quickly wiped the bulk of the makeup away. I gave him a washcloth and let him help ("help" being a relative term). In the end, I had a sweet-smelling little boy with very smooth skin, and a slight hint of blue around the eyes. His lips looked like they might have been sunburned (when Maybelline says long-lasting, they mean it), and I feared he might randomly strike a Cover Girl pose.

Still, it was good enough, especially since we didn't have time for a full-blown bath. I hoisted him up on my hip and hurried down the stairs, calling out to Allie that we were leaving and that she should lock up behind her.

She grunted in reply, and I figured that was about the best I could do. At least I was getting clean toilets out of the deal.

Five minutes later we'd said good-bye to Eddie, Timmy was strapped into his car seat, and I was back in the living room desperately trying to find Boo Bear. I managed to locate him under the sofa, then returned to the van in triumph.

Timmy, who'd been whimpering softly, immediately changed his attitude, looking at me with complete adoration. God, but I love that kid.

"We ready?" I asked, buckling myself in.

"Ready!" he howled, shoving a little fist in the air. "To infinity, and beyond!" he added, which made our errands sound a whole lot more exciting than I anticipated. Frankly, I wasn't sure that was a good thing.

Stuart and I have a joint checking and savings account at First Mutual on California Avenue. We also have a safe-deposit box there for the kids' birth certificates, the house deed, life insurance policies. The usual. And since I'm the one who usually goes to the box, I also knew that our shiny gold key didn't look a thing like the silver one that had mysteriously appeared on my doorstep.

Even so, I decided to try there first. The tellers know me and, for all I knew, maybe gold keys signified the better boxes. Or maybe the bank had access to some sort of booklet that identifies safe-deposit box keys. I wasn't completely optimistic about this plan, but I figured it was worth ten minutes.

Eleven minutes later, I wasn't so sure. My favorite teller, Nancy, had no clue, and even the manager on duty couldn't help. "I could make some calls," she offered.

I shook my head. "Thanks, but I don't want to be any trouble." Mostly, I just didn't want to draw too much attention to myself. Not that I was doing anything illegal, untoward, or even strange. But there was still something very cloak and dagger about the whole situation.

Nancy handed Timmy a watermelon-flavored Dum-Dum, and we went back the way we came, my little boy happily sucking on the lollipop. I was trying to remember what other banks were in the area when I heard a familiar voice call my name.

I turned around, searching the lobby, and finally saw Cutter rising from a couch near a sign that read *Loans*. Cutter—actually Sean Tyler—is my *sensei*. That is, he's my martial-arts instructor, training partner, and friend. He doesn't know my secrets, but he's astute enough to know I have them.

He's also training Allie, Mindy, and Laura, all of whom I want in fighting shape. To my infinite pride, Allie's definitely at the front of that pack. Even more, she's kept up with the training despite the addition of cheerleading and a bunch of other extracurriculars to her schedule.

I like to think it's because she's good and wants to stay fit. More realistically, I think it's because Cutter is a particularly fine-looking male specimen. And my daughter is fourteen and boy crazy.

I am nothing if not a realist.

As soon as he saw Cutter, Timmy jerked free of my hand and trotted over, holding out his candy for Cutter to inspect.

"Looks good," Cutter said.

"You can have some," said my son, displaying just how much he liked my martial-arts instructor. For Timmy, the sharing of candy marks the absolute highest level of affection.

"Thanks, kiddo, but I'll pass."

Timmy looked confused—how could anyone say no to a Dum-Dum?—then popped the thing back into his mouth, apparently realizing that since the invitation was turned down, there was more candy left for him. He sucked hard, his slurping noises underscoring my conversation.

"What are you doing here on a Saturday?" I asked. "Don't you have a class to teach?"

"Lunch break. My landlord wants to sell, so I either have to buy the dojo or find a new location." He waved, indicating the loan department. "So here I am, wasting another lunch hour filling out small-business loan applications."

I made sympathetic—and sincere—noises. If Cutter moved I was going to be severely inconvenienced. His studio was located in a strip mall right at the entrance to our subdivision, less than five minutes away from my house. Even better, there was a 7-Eleven right next door, which meant that I could bone up on kip ups and jump kicks, pick up milk and bread, and be back home in less than the time it took for Allie to get dressed for school in the morning.

"Anyway," he said, "it's a pain in the butt—sorry, *rear*," he said, looking at Timmy, who happily yelled out "Baby butt!" just to embarrass me.

Cutter mouthed an apology, then took Timmy's hand. On the sidewalk, Timmy kept up with the "Baby Butt" song, but eventually lost interest, and started pulling leaves off a decorative shrub instead.

"I hope you get your loan," I said.

"I will. I just have to find the right bank." He looked at me sideways. "Sort of like you."

I reached out and grabbed the back of Timmy's shirt before he could launch himself off the sidewalk. "Not following you," I said to Cutter.

He took Tim from me and hoisted him up to his shoulders. Timmy yelped and squealed and pulled at Cutter's hair. No pain registered on Cutter's face, proving once again that the military training he listed on his bio was absolutely true.

"I overheard you in there," he said, taking off his sunglasses and tucking them into a pocket before Timmy destroyed them. "What's the deal? You're trying to find a bank to match your safe-deposit box key?"

"Something like that," I admitted.

"Because people are always trying to match up mysterious keys," he said.

"Cutter . . ."

He held his hands out, surrender-style. "Can't blame a guy for trying."

"Actually, I can," I said, but with a grin. The truth is I trust Cutter. Not enough to tell him about my secret identity, of course, but I do trust the man. For one thing, he's known from the first day I showed up in his dojo—and pretty much beat the pants off of him—that I wasn't what I seemed. He'd questioned, but he'd never pushed. And, honestly, that had meant as much to me as the training he'd given me over the past few months.

He flashed a trademark Cutter grin, then leaned in close to my ear. "One day, Kate Connor," he whispered, his voice flowing over me like warm honey. "One day you're going to tell me your secrets."

"You're probably right," I said, lowering my voice to match his. "But today's not the day."

I stepped back, and looked at him. Our eyes locked, and for just a second, I thought that he was going to push the point. Then he blinked. The moment faded, and I let out a sigh of relief. I'd meant what I said. Someday, yes. But not now.

"So I'll see you at practice?" he asked.

"I think so. But a few things have come up lately, and my schedule is crazy." That, at least, was the absolute truth.

"Fair enough, but are you still interested in finding another sparring partner?" A few weeks ago, we'd talked about finding me someone else to spar with. Someone whose moves I hadn't started to anticipate.

"Of course I am. Why?"

"I may have someone. New guy. Seems pretty competent. I'll give him the once-over, and if he passes muster, I'll give you a call."

"All right." I held my arms up, signaling for him to pass me my kid. "We need to get going. I'm late for my secret mission."

"You're a riot, Kate. You know that, right?" He swung Timmy to the ground, then held out his hand. "Let me just see the damn thing."

"Damn's a bad word," said Timmy helpfully, as I reached my free hand into my back pocket and pulled the key out. I passed it to him, and he studied it, then passed it back.

"What do I get if I can tell you what bank it's from?"

"*Can* you tell me what bank it's from?"

"Maybe."

"You'd get my deep admiration and devotion."

"I already have that."

"Oh, right," I said. "Okay, how about a blind date with a

single PTA mom?" I could think of three or four who'd leapfrog over each other for the chance to go out with Cutter.

He considered for a moment, then shook his head, his eyes hard on me. "No."

"Fresh out of ideas, Sean," I said, using his given name just to tick him off. I hoisted Tim up onto my hip. "Either help me or don't, but I've got to go. The banks close at three on Saturday, and I've barely started."

"Try County Mutual," he said. "And they're open until four."

"And you know this because . . . ?"

"Because that's where I bank."

I studied him, hating the suspicions that filled my head. Was this a convenient coincidence, or was Cutter my secret deliveryman?

As hard as I looked, though, I couldn't find anything suspicious on his face. For that matter, maybe the key led to something completely innocuous. That, however, I really didn't believe.

Timmy squirmed on my hip, drawing my attention away from Cutter. I slid him down to the ground, then held tight to his hand as he tugged hard, trying to get away and making me list to the left as I finished up with Cutter.

"The bank's at Pacific and Amber Glen, right?"

He nodded. "Right. There's a McDonald's across the street."

At that, Timmy stopped pulling, every other thought in his head pushed out by one compelling demand: "Happy Meal!" he wailed. "Want a Happy Meal!"

Cutter chuckled. "Sorry."

"You owe me big time," I said. To Timmy, I promised a Happy Meal if he stopped trying to pull me down the sidewalk, *and* if he behaved at the next bank, *and* if he agreed to eat applesauce with his Happy Meal instead of French fries.

Since Happy Meals are really all about the toys, he smiled and saluted. "Aye-aye, Mommy!"

Cutter raised a brow.

"SpongeBob," I said, by way of explanation. I may not be able to tell you the top-ten prime-time television shows or the number-one box-office hit, but Nickelodeon I've got down.

Once Timmy and I reached County Mutual, my little boy amused himself by running the length of the lobby, touching the wall, and then running back again. I probably should have told him to stop—another Happy Meal threat would probably have done the trick—but I was in a mood, too. Running hard and fast sounded like a damn good idea, actually. And if I couldn't burn off my excess energy and thoughts that way, at least my little boy could.

We were there about five minutes before the bank officer who handled the safe-deposit boxes called me to her desk.

I took a minute to get Timmy settled with one of the little tubs of Play-Doh I keep in my purse, then handed over the key. "I need to get into this box."

I'd decided to be vague on the whole question of whose box it was. Not hard, since I was clueless on the point. I was hoping that she'd look the information up on her computer and then she'd tell me.

I know enough about how banks work to be dangerous, but in the movies, you can never access a box with just the key. Your name has to be on the account, too. So I doubted I'd be getting any final answers today. But with any luck, I'd have the name of the box owner. And that, I figured, was a baby step in the right direction.

The bank officer—Ms. Sellers, according to her name tag—tap-tapped at her keyboard. "Here it is," she said. She looked at me. "You must be Katherine Crowe?"

The room shifted, and I held on tight to my chair just so

I wouldn't slide off. I forced myself to nod. More, I forced myself not to cry.

Apparently I wasn't doing a good job of looking normal, because her brow creased and she leaned toward me. "Ms. Crowe? Are you feeling okay?"

"I'm sorry." I wiped my eyes. "Yes, yes, I'm fine. And yes, I'm Katherine Crowe. Or, I was. My husband passed away five years ago. I'm remarried. It's Katherine Connor now."

"I'm sorry for your loss," she said.

"Thank you," I said, automatically, but still unsteadily.

I'm not sure what I'd expected here, but certainly not my name in that computer. I also wasn't entirely sure how to handle the situation.

I took a deep breath, then leaped into the deep end. "Um, obviously it's been a long time," I said. "I don't remember getting this box."

Her brows lifted. "Oh? Then why are you here?"

A good question. "I found the key," I said. "In my jewelry box," I added, because I'd learned that the more specific a lie the more convincing the lie. "So when did we, um, rent the box?" The "we" was a guess.

She looked at me, and I saw compassion, but something else, too. "I'm sorry," she said. "But I think I should probably see some identification."

"Right. Sure. No problem." I took out my driver's license and handed it to her.

"Do you have anything that shows you as Katherine Crowe?"

I did, actually. My old license. I don't really know why I keep it, but I do, tucked into the back of my wallet under the pictures of my kids. You're supposed to turn the old one in when you get a new license, but I claimed that I'd lost the thing. No one even asked twice.

Now, I pulled it out and handed it to the woman. She

took it, compared the number to the number on her computer screen, and nodded.

"We don't have any record that Mr. Crowe passed away. You should bring in the paperwork and we'll get the box and account transferred to your name alone. We've already got your signature card on file, so the process will be relatively simple."

"Wait. There's an account, too?"

"Yes, we provide safe-deposit boxes only to account holders."

"I see." I frowned again. "How much money is in the account?"

She tapped at the keyboard. "Eight-hundred thirty-seven dollars and twenty-three cents."

"Oh." This was getting weirder and weirder. That the account existed at all had surprised me. After all, Eric and I had done all our banking together, and we'd never used this bank.

Except they had my signature on file.

That was strange, but explainable. Eric had probably brought a card home for me to sign. Since I let him handle all the paperwork, I wouldn't have paid that much attention.

So Eric opened an account, then put money into it. Call me crazy, but it seems to me that any man who has a bank account he keeps secret from his wife, isn't going to add his wife to the account in the first place. And he'd stuff it full of money. I'm not scoffing at eight hundred dollars, but it's hardly enough to run off to Rio.

Except Eric would never have run off to Rio. Not without me, anyway.

So what the hell had he been up to?

I needed to get into the box, but I still had questions, and I wanted to ask them right now, when Ms. Sellers was talkative and at least a little sympathetic to my plight.

"So when did we open the account?" I asked.

She checked, then rattled off a date. My stomach clenched. Just one month before Eric had died.

"Ms. Connor?" She frowned at me. "Are you okay? Does that help?"

I held up a hand and forced a smile. "I'm fine. Really." I cleared my throat. "What about activity? Anything happening on that account?"

She checked. "No. Nothing. It looks like the only funds that have ever been withdrawn, in fact, have been the safe-deposit box rental fees."

"I see," I said, although of course I didn't. Not completely. Not yet.

I stood, motioning for Timmy to do the same. "I appreciate all your help," I said, taking my little boy's hand. "Maybe I could take a look at the box now?"

"Of course," she said, then led the way into the vault. We each inserted our keys, then she opened the door. I pulled out the small box, surprised to find it weighed next to nothing. Ms. Sellers showed me to a tiny room where I could examine the contents of my box in private. I pictured folks richer than me in the surrounding rooms pulling out piles of gemstones and running their fingers through them like confetti.

As soon as she'd left, I pulled the door closed, locking Timmy and I in the claustrophobic little room. "Okay, kiddo," I said to Tim. "This is it."

"Present?"

"I don't know, big guy. But I'm thinking no."

I took a deep breath, then lifted the lid, not at all sure what I'd see.

Nothing. I saw absolutely nothing.

I frowned. That couldn't be right.

I held the box on end and shook it. Sure enough, a folded piece of paper fell out. I stared at it, somehow knowing that it was from Eric. I wanted to touch it, to smell it, to hold it to my heart. The one thing I didn't want to do was read it. It was bad news. Somehow, I just knew that whatever was on that paper was bad news.

I considered pocketing it for later, but abandoned the idea. I couldn't walk out of this room without knowing what that note said. Doing that would be like walking away from Eric.

The paper had a ragged edge, as if it had been ripped from a notebook, then folded over on itself four times. I unfolded it slowly, hesitating only briefly over the final fold. Then I opened the paper, smoothed it on the table, and read these words:

My darling Katie,

I'm writing this because I'm afraid that I've gone too far. If you're reading this, it's because my fears are correct. I'm sorry. So sorry. And I love you. You and Allie are my whole world. My everything. And I wouldn't trade our years together for anything. Please, don't ever forget that. And please, don't ever doubt it.

But there were things I had to do, and for that, I hope you can forgive me. I want you to know what happened, Katie. I need you to finish what I started. I hate asking you to do that and I regret opening the door in the first place. But some doors, once opened, can never be closed again. We tried, though, didn't we? And I wish I could say that we succeeded. But we didn't. There's a crack, and everything we thought we'd left behind is rushing through it.

I know you don't understand. Not really. And I wish I could say it plainly, but that's impossible, too. I can't be certain that it will be you who finds this. So I can't risk telling you the full story. But if you look to the best of us, you'll see that you already have all the pieces you need.

At least to get started.

But darling Katie, be careful. Watch your back. I didn't pay
enough attention. Please, sweetheart, don't make my mistake.
Eternally yours,
Eric

I read the note twice, only stopping because I couldn't
make the words out through my tears. I blinked, and the
tears streamed down my face, falling in fat drops from my
cheeks to the paper. I wiped one away, then pulled the paper
to my heart, hugging it close.

"Momma?" Timmy was by my side, stroking my arm. I
managed a watery smile, then hoisted him up onto my lap,
hugging him tight, too. He looked at me with big, serious
eyes, then somberly kissed my cheek. "Kiss and make better," he said. "Momma better now?"

I nodded and forced the words to leave my throat. "Absolutely. Thanks, big guy."

But it wasn't true. Not at all. Because as cryptic as this
note was, it made one thing crystal clear: Eric hadn't been
the victim of a random mugging all those years ago.

Someone had intentionally murdered my husband.

Nine

I think Timmy could sense my mood, because he not only be-haved beautifully all the way home, but he kept blowing kisses from the backseat to the front. Do I have a great kid, or what?

I needed those kisses, too. Because the truth was, I was smothering under a blanket of guilt. *Murder.* The San Fran-cisco police had never even suggested premeditated murder. The theory had always been a mugging gone bad. Murder, yes. But not planned. My husband had simply been in the wrong place at the wrong time. We'd been ten years out of the demon business. Our lives were boring. Wonderful, but boring. Murder wasn't even on my radar.

Now, though, that little bubble had burst, and I was kicking myself for not having been suspicious. For having blithely gone along with what the police had told me. Why didn't I see? Why didn't I know?

Because there'd been nothing suspicious about his death. Nothing, that is, except the fact that he'd died at all. And the fact that a mugger had actually been able to take down my husband. We might not have been actively training every day, but Eric hadn't been a slacker. He'd never let his body go soft.

I thought about that, my stomach tightening more and more as the reality of the situation settled in my bones. My husband had been murdered. And I, the woman who knew and loved him best, hadn't even suspected.

I tightened my grip on the steering wheel, thinking about the odd timing of the note's appearance. Could it be fake? A trap?

Part of me wanted to believe that, but I knew it wasn't true. Too many phrases in the note sounded like him. And even after all these years I recognized the handwriting. No, the note was from Eric.

How the key had landed on my doorstep, though. Well, that was still a mystery.

I glanced toward the passenger seat and my purse. The note was inside. For five years, I'd let Eric down, and I couldn't help but believe that the key was some sort of silent accusation. A shout out to me that I'd failed.

Not anymore. Somehow, I was going to find out what had happened. I was going to interpret his cryptic message and I was going to find the truth.

I only hoped that after five years of doing nothing, the trail hadn't gone completely cold.

I steered the car home on autopilot, ignoring the list of errands I'd planned to do while I was out and about. While the garage door creaked open, I tried to think what Eric could have meant. *The best of us?* What was that? I really didn't have a clue. And, unfortunately, that was where I needed to start. That was me, a demon-hunting Nancy Drew.

The first thing my sleuthing discovered was a note on the table. Short and to the point, Stuart had said that he'd come home for a bit, but he had to get back to work. He was going to miss both dinner and Allie's beach party. And he was sorry.

I closed my eyes, expecting a rush of irritation. Lately I was seeing evidence of my husband (damp shower stalls, laundry on the floor, rumpled sheets) more than the man himself. For weeks now, that little fact had been driving me crazy, a flash point for frequent fights when we did cross paths.

But the annoyance didn't surface. This time, I only felt relief. My senses and memories were full of Eric. I wanted to wallow. And unless I wanted more fights added to our regularly scheduled program, I knew that wallowing about the dead first husband in front of the second was a really bad idea.

Not that I had time to wallow. For better or for worse, life with kids prevents deep descents into morbidity. I needed to get Timmy settled, check on Eddie, hide a body, and then get myself to the beach.

Not that I *had* to go to the beach, but I had a feeling that the number of times Allie was going to invite me to accompany her when she was on a date (or, rather, a pseudo-date) were exactly one. In other words, this wasn't an opportunity I was going to let slide by.

I found Eddie where I'd left him, sound asleep in the armchair, the television blaring. I clicked it off, then opened the cabinet and pulled out Timmy's tiny toy piano. He honed in on it immediately, and I figured I'd just bought myself a solid—if noisy—ten minutes.

Normally, I'd ask Laura to babysit, but even though Mindy wasn't in the surf club, she'd decided to go to the cookout. And she'd also granted Laura permission to come to the beach party ("so long as you promise not to do *any-thing* that would embarrass me"), and that meant we needed to move our date with the demon earlier in the afternoon. As in, right now. Either that or leave a body in the trunk while we frolicked at the beach. And I didn't think Laura was up for that. The risk, or the frolicking.

After this morning's experiment in cosmetology, there was no way I was leaving Tim with Eddie. Not unless I wanted to find the house in shambles, my son swinging from the curtains, and every bit of makeup I owned converted to war paint.

I grabbed the cordless phone and started dialing the other women in the neighborhood. Ten minutes and three conversations about the dead guy in the school basement later, I found one who could watch my son.

"You're sure?"

"No problem," Sylvia Foster said. "This is Carl's week-end to have Susan," she said, "so I'm all alone in the house anyway. Frankly, you're probably doing me a favor."

Sylvia and Susan live at the other end of our block across from the community pool. Susan usually goes into school early for band practice, but when she doesn't, she's part of our car pool. When the girls were in seventh grade, Sylvia and Carl had divorced. I don't see Susan often, but even I could see the change in her disposition. Lately, she'd gotten some of her spunk back, but it was two years coming.

I thought of Allie and those years after Eric had died. And then I thought of Stuart and how frustrated I was by his recent absences. I made a mental note to sit him down and talk about this. There are a lot of things in this world worth fighting for. More, even, than keeping demons out of the neighborhood. My family was tops on that list.

"I really appreciate it," I said to Sylvia, then made plans

to drop Timmy off on my way out of the house. "And if there's anything I can do to return the favor . . ."

She jumped all over that one. "Actually, I'm having a Pampered Chef party a week from today. Maybe you could come?"

"Sure," I said, thinking about the heart attack Stuart was going to have when I told him I'd just ordered another half dozen kitchen items, none of which would actually improve my cooking skills.

Sylvia promised to be available, and I rushed upstairs to change. Timmy was still banging away, and Eddie was still sound asleep. That's about as calm as my house ever gets, and I was actually a little depressed to be leaving. Then I remembered: Allie, beach, bathing suits, boys. Oh, yeah. I was so outta here.

Since the bathing suit part of the occasion was for the kids only, I chose a pair of white drawstring pants that I'd bought at Old Navy during one of Allie's back-to-school shopping sprees. I topped that with a purple T-shirt, then finished the outfit off with plain, white sneakers.

I pulled my hair back into a ponytail, grabbed my purse, then checked myself in the mirror. Not bad, really. Definitely nothing about my appearance that would make my child spend the evening avoiding me.

Years ago, I dressed for practicality. Military gear designed to hold weapons and facilitate movement. Now, I dressed for my family. Practical clothes that made errand-running easier, decent outfits appropriate for Stuart's political functions, and, now, a mom-ish outfit, carefully chosen so that my daughter could acknowledge me publicly without melting into the sand in embarrassment.

One day, I thought, it might be fun to simply dress for me.

The only thing wrong with the image in the mirror was

the clunky brown purse. Way too much for an evening at the beach. I found a small cloth bag I'd picked up at a street fair one year, and was just starting to switch the contents of the purses over when I heard the doorbell ring.

"DEMONS!" Eddie cried, his voice reverberating through the house. "The beasties are everywhere! EVERYWHERE!"

I grabbed my half-filled purse and raced down the stairs. Eddie's been through a lot over the years. So much, in fact, that it's a wonder he's kept his grip on sanity. That grip, however, is significantly more tenuous when he's asleep.

For the most part, I write his dreams off as merely that— the nightmares of an old man. That seems to satisfy Allie, who's so enamored of having a grandfather in her life, that he could probably brandish a battle-ax and she wouldn't care. I'd thought Stuart would be more concerned about Eddie's outbursts. I was wrong. Stuart's managed to tune Eddie out so well that I don't think he even hears them.

The neighbors, however, were not prepped to my pseudo-grandfather-in-law's foibles, and I raced down the stairs, desperate to get to the front door before Eddie did. Or before whoever was out there heard Eddie's cries through the door and ran screaming down the block.

"Stop!" I cried, sliding into the front entrance hall with about as much grace as a Little Leaguer sliding home. Eddie was standing there, eyes wild, a lethal-looking stiletto clutched in his hand.

"At the door, girlie," he said. "The demons are coming through the damn door!"

"Eddie, no." I closed my hand over his, taking the knife. "You were having a dream and the doorbell woke you up." I looked in his eyes. "It's okay. It's safe. It's *fine*."

In the living room, Timmy started wailing. Honestly, I couldn't blame him. At the moment, I'd like to wail a little, too.

"Momma, Momma, Momma," he cried. "Where you at, Momma?"

"In here, sweetie," I said. "It's fine. Mommy'll be right there." To Eddie, I said, "You okay?"

He cast a suspicious look toward the door, but nodded.

I hesitated, wanting to be sure, but the bell rang again, this time accompanied by Sylvia's voice. "Kate? Are you okay in there?"

I lunged for the dead bolt, squeezing in between Eddie and the door. I flung it open, hoping my smile looked genuine. "Sylvia! Hi!" I shoved the knife behind my back and leaned against the wall. "I, um, thought I was bringing Timmy to your house."

On cue, Timmy called for me again.

"Coming!" I shouted back.

"They can just smell when you're leaving, can't they?" Sylvia said, stepping around me and into the hall. "I had to run to the Seven-Eleven, so I thought I'd swing by and see if you'd rather I picked him up." She held out her hand to Eddie. "Hi. I'm Sylvia."

"Mmph." He took her hand, then tugged, pulling Sylvia right to him before either she—or I—could do anything about it. He took a long sniff of her breath, then nodded at me. "She's okay," he said.

Try as I might, I couldn't convince the floor to open up and swallow me.

Eddie turned back to the living room. Sylvia gaped at me. "I promise he's harmless," I said. "He just wakes up a little disoriented."

She stared.

"Why don't I bring Laura with me to the Pampered Chef party?" I asked, in a not-too-subtle attempt to distract her. Everyone in our neighborhood knows that Laura is physically incapable of not buying cooking supplies. We go out of our way to avoid Williams-Sonoma, just to ensure that she and Paul are able to pay their mortgage.

"Oh, yes," she squealed. "You have to bring Laura."

Behind me, the front door swung open, and Laura stepped inside. "Bring me where?" she asked.

"Pampered Chef," I said. "Next weekend. Can you make it?"

"Are you kidding?" she answered, as if I'd asked her if she'd like twenty million in cash. "Just tell me when and where."

Because Sylvia's no fool, she jumped all over that, and while she and Laura discussed the joys of kitchen gizmos, I gathered Timmy's things and gave Eddie a hug, reminding him to lock up and set the alarm if he went for an evening walk.

Laura drove, and we dropped Timmy at Sylvia's on our way out since I wasn't crazy about him driving in someone else's car, even someone I trusted as a babysitter. I ran down all of Timmy's idiosyncrasies, suggested a few bedtime books, then made sure she had the phone numbers for Stuart and the hospital. I gave her mine and Laura's, too, of course. But cell service is spotty at the beach, so Stuart was on point tonight.

"Ready?" Laura asked, turning the key in her ignition.

I checked my purse, found my keys, wallet, and sunglasses, and nodded. "Let's go."

About the time we reached Rialto Boulevard, the main street into our subdivision, Laura turned to me. "Are we going to be okay? Not waiting until dark to take the demon out of the trunk, I mean."

I shrugged. I'd been considering that very question. "I think it'll be okay. The Saturday mass doesn't start for another hour."

She made a face. "That's still cutting it close," she said.

"I know. But Father Ben said we should come around to the service entrance. He said no one's ever back there on the weekends."

"I hope he's right," Laura said. "I need tailored clothes. I'd look horrible in prison chic."

"We could wait," I said. "But then we'll miss the surf thing."

She sighed. "If we miss it, they'll never invite us back."

"I know."

She took a deep breath, then grabbed the steering wheel with both hands. "All right. Let's get this over with." She shot me a quick glance. "Honestly, Kate. Sometimes I think life's more exciting now that I know your secret. And sometimes I wish I'd just stayed home that night."

I'd told Laura because I'd had no choice. She'd followed me one night, then witnessed a rather graphic demonic death. I had to either tell her or let her think she was losing her mind. "If it's any consolation, I'm glad you know. I'd hate to have to go through this all by myself."

"I'm glad I know, too. But on days like today . . ."

"Yeah," I said. "I know."

We drove in silence for a few minutes. Then Laura turned to me. "Actually, maybe we *should* wait until dark. If we're not at the cookout, we can't embarrass the girls."

"Good point," I agreed, happy that my universe was shifting back to normal. I'd never intended for Laura to be involved, but now that she was, I realized how much I needed her. Both for helping me schlep bodies and for moral support. "You got the embarrassment lecture, too?" I asked.

"Lecture, memo, reminder phone call." Her eyebrows rose behind her sunglasses. "It would be irritating if it weren't so damned amusing."

"List of do's and don'ts?" I asked.

She patted her purse. "Right here."

I tapped my temple. "Left mine on the dresser."

"I'm particularly fond of item eight—no adjusting Mindy's hair in public. With extra demerits if there's a boy within five hundred feet."

"No participating in karaoke," I added. "As if that were really a worry in the first place."

"I like karaoke," Laura said.

"No embarrassing *me*," I retorted, deadpan.

"You know," she said, thoughtfully. "There wasn't anything on my list about naked hula dancing."

"Mine either," I said. "Obviously a blatant oversight."

"Or flirting with the teachers," she said.

I thought of David Long and had to silently acknowledge that that one might do well to be on the list. "Are we allowed to acknowledge blood relation with them?" I asked. "I mean, I think it's important to understand the rules here."

The conversation pretty much disintegrated from there, as we came up with more and more outrageous ways to embarrass our daughters. Everything from asking each boy if he thought our daughters were pretty to snorting Diet Coke up our noses.

By the time we pulled in behind the cathedral, the imaginary Kate and Laura were surfing with the boys, decked out in bras and panties because we didn't have our bathing suits, while singing karaoke and inviting the whole crowd back to our neighborhood for a block party.

St. Mary's Cathedral dominates the highest point in San Diablo, a focal point for the entire town. It's a splendid piece of architecture, and dramatic, too, in the way it perches on top of the cliffs, the ocean beating a rhythm below.

And it's not just dramatic visually. There's also high drama in the way the cathedral fights evil, by nothing other than its mere presence. The cathedral, in fact, was one of the reasons Eric and I moved to San Diablo. Built centuries ago, the structure is home to some of the holiest of relics. Even the mortar is holy, having been infused with the bones of saints.

There were only four cars in the parking lot, and I recognized two—Father Ben's and Delores Sykes's, the volunteer coordinator. "Pull around behind," I said, pointing to the thin driveway that exited on the far side of the lot, then curved around the rectory, the Bishop's Hall and the other buildings until it dead-ended near the back of the cathedral itself.

While Laura parked the car, I called Father Ben, and he met us outside. "We should be able to do this unnoticed," he said. His face was pinched, and he looked tired. "Where's the body?"

"What's wrong, Padre? Have you learned anything more about the book? About any of it for that matter?"

He shook his head. "No, I'm afraid not. Just a moment of pity for this woman who won't get a decent burial. And her family, who will never be able to say good-bye."

"Yeah," I said. I hated that, too, but none of us could see a way around it. Father Ben had even talked with Father Corletti at the Vatican. But the head of the *Forza Scura* had no better suggestion. "At least she'll be buried with the bones of saints surrounding her."

"Yes," he agreed. "That does give me some peace."

He looked from me to Laura. "We should begin."

Because of the way my week had been going, I expected the worst. But God must have decided I'd had enough drama in my life (or that I wouldn't look good in prison chic, either) because we managed to get the body out of the trunk and into the cathedral without incident.

After that it really was easy. We readjusted our grip on the body, then followed Father Ben down the dark hallway that led from the back door to the sacristy. We didn't make it that far, though, turning off at a thick metal door that Ben opened with an ancient-looking key.

I'd been down there once before, but Laura hadn't, and Ben cautioned her to watch her step. The stairs were narrow, and carved out of the rock, and we followed their curve until we hit the bottom and found ourselves in a cavelike room with raw stone walls.

While Laura and I kept a hold on the body, Father Ben took a flashlight from its hook on the wall, then shined it to the right, illuminating yet another door. "That's the crypt," I explained to Laura. "The cathedral's priests are entombed there."

"Right," she said, looking just a little green.

Father Ben held the door open, and we entered the damp space. "We're under the altar now," he said. A massive crypt loomed before us, ornate stone tablets appearing as decorations, but serving the more practical purpose of sealing the individual tombs.

A metal pry bar was propped against a far wall, and he took it now, placing it carefully between the stone and the surrounding crypt. He shoved, but nothing happened. Laura and I set the body down, and I joined him, all of us tugging on the count of three. The stone shifted, came loose, and we carefully tugged it out of the space, then set it gently on the ground.

"Oh, wow," Laura said softly.

She was looking into the tomb at the decaying robes of a priest, only the edges of his vestment and the bottom of his feet visible from this angle.

"That's Father Michael," Ben said. "He served the church in the late 1800s."

I closed my eyes and crossed myself, saying a quick thank you to Father Michael for helping us out here.

"You don't think he'll mind?" Laura asked. "I mean, buried with a demon . . . ?"

I shrugged, and let the padre field that question.

He stayed silent for a moment, then spoke softly. "When Father Corletti came from Rome and told me what happened last summer—when he told me what you were doing, Kate— I almost couldn't believe it. Seminary didn't prepare me for that. Nothing I'd seen or heard or read prepared me for it."

"I know," Laura agreed shakily. "But it's real. I couldn't believe it, but I also couldn't deny it."

"And it's vile," Father Ben said. "And as soon as Father Corletti asked me to help—to train to be an *alimentatore*— I knew that I had to say yes. Because the way I see it, nothing I can do in this life is more important than being a part of God's army against evil. I try to do that in my homilies, to prepare my congregation to fight Satan's influence. But to actually stand here and see the tangible results of that fight . . ."

"It's okay," I said, taking his hand. "We understand."

"I know you do. But my point is that these priests would have made the same decision. So to answer your question: No, I don't think they would mind. I think they would welcome the chance to help in any way they can."

"Right," said Laura, looking dubiously at the crypt. "Too bad for them that means having some body a demon hijacked shoved in their resting place."

Father Ben cracked a smile. "Well, we can't all be out there kicking a little demon butt. We do what we can."

"Father!" I said, feigning shock.

"Get on with it, you two," he said, gesturing at the open crypt. "It's going to be a tight fit."

He was right, but Laura and I managed, gritting our teeth against the squishing sound as we shoved the body inside the tight space. Father Ben may revere what I do, but there are times when the details of the job really gross me out.

Once the demon was safely ensconced with Father Michael, we replaced the end stone, sliding it back into the space until it was almost impossible to tell that it had ever been removed.

We followed Father Ben back up the stairs. The cathedral was still silent, and I wondered if the saints in the cathedral's mortar were watching out for us. Just in case, I said a silent thank-you. I needed all the help I could get.

We said our good-byes, then got back in Laura's car. She'd maneuvered us all the way down to the Pacific Coast Highway before I realized she hadn't spoken one word.

"You okay?"

One shoulder lifted in a dubious gesture. "Just coming to grips, you know?"

I did know. And because I did, I reached for her free hand. "We did good," I said.

"Gold stars on my permanent record?"

"A whole box of them," I promised. "Although . . ."

She shifted in her seat long enough to eye me suspiciously. "Although?"

"Demerits can be fun, too," I said as she turned into the beachfront parking lot. "Embarrassing our girls should be worth five or six at least, don't you think?"

"More if we do the underwear surfing." She was grinning now. For that matter, so was I.

As Laura maneuvered the rows looking for an empty space, I pulled the collar of my T-shirt out and took a mournful look inside. "I don't think I can go there," I said. "My bra's just too boring."

"Mine's not," Laura said, her tone mischievous. "Damn, this lot is full."

"Try the hotel," I said. "Valet park if you have to."

The Coronado Crest Hotel is a one of those charming mission-style hotels that sprang up back in the Hollywood heyday, when stars would escape Los Angeles for romantic trysts to the north. It had oversized rooms with fireplaces and balconies, excellent service, and a world-class restaurant with both indoor and outdoor dining. The patio looked out over the beach, and you could sit and drink wine and listen to the sound of the surf.

Eric and I had stayed our first week in San Diablo at the Crest, our days spent searching for a house and our nights spent listening to the ocean. I loved that hotel, but I hadn't walked through its doors since Eric died.

Laura found a space in the self-parking area, and pulled in. We wove our way through the mishmash of cars until we hit the boardwalk that runs from the hotel to the north, staying parallel with the Coast Highway and the high-priced artsy area that makes up the old-town heart of San Diablo. To the west of the boardwalk is nothing but sand and ocean, and that's where we'd find our daughters.

We started out on the boardwalk, the beach to our left, and the hotel to our right. "You realize that I haven't forgotten your comment," I said.

"Comment?" she asked, her voice a little too innocent.

I reached a finger inside the collar of my shirt and tugged out a hint of bra strap. "Your comment," I repeated. "Tell."

She grinned deviously, looked around as if to confirm we had no audience, then unbuttoned the top two buttons on her blouse. She pulled it open quick and flashed me, showing off a satin and lace red push-up bra.

"Whoo-woo," I said. "I guess you really did come prepared for underwear surfing."

"No one's seeing me in these things except Paul."

I cocked my head, finally getting with the program. "You're pulling out the big guns?"

She gazed at her 34B chest. "I'm not sure how big they are, but I'm not too proud to use them," she said. "I spent Thursday afternoon at the mall buying out Victoria's Secret."

I took advantage of a bench to sit down. "What did Paul say?"

Her eyes darkened. "He hasn't been home since Thursday morning." She made quote marks in the air with her fingers. "Working."

"He might really be working," I said, mostly because I wanted it to be true. "You don't know that he's—"

"It's okay. You don't have to make me feel better. I mean, it makes some sense. We've been married for almost twenty years. And even if he's not—" She cleared her throat. "Even if he's totally faithful, that doesn't mean our marriage can't use a little oomph, right? I mean, everyone gets complacent over time, don't they?"

"Of course," I said, giving her the answer I knew she wanted. But I wondered if it was true. Were Stuart and I getting complacent? Was that why it was so easy for him to spend all those late nights away working on his campaign? Because I'd just become part of the scenery? His wife, his house, his kids, his car.

The thought both worried and angered me. Even after ten years, Eric had never once gotten complacent. The comparison was unfair, and I knew it. They were different men, and I loved them both. But Eric had one thing that Stuart never had. Eric understood with microscopic precision just how fragile life is. How every day is a gift. He never took me for granted because he couldn't. People had been ripped away from us our whole lives. And as far as Eric and I had been concerned, just surviving until dawn was a miracle to be cherished.

I frowned, my thoughts turning back to Eric's mugging. Was that why I hadn't been more suspicious? Had I been complacent? Had I spent our entire marriage knowing the Sword of Damocles was hanging over us? And when it finally fell, although it was a tragedy, it wasn't really a surprise?

I shook my head, not liking the direction of my thoughts. It had looked like a mugging. I'd believed it had been a mugging. There'd been nothing in our lives back then—nothing—to suggest that Eric had been intentionally murdered. Maybe I had failed him by not investigating, but he'd failed me, too, by not telling me what was going on.

And, honestly, that hurt as much as Stuart's long hours away from home.

"Earth to Kate."

"Sorry," I said.

"I've lost you, haven't I? You've left my love life for the equally fascinating topic of demons."

"I should be thinking about that," I said. "Especially since we're still clueless about that damn book. But no. I'm thinking about something else." And then, because Laura needed a distraction as much as I needed a friend, I told her about the note. And the implications.

"And you still don't know who left the package on your door?"

"Not a clue," I said. That had been bugging me a lot, actually. Eric was dead. The safe-deposit box had been in both our names. No one in San Diablo had known our secret. So who could he possibly have entrusted the key to? And why wait all this time to give it to me?

"Something weird's going on," Laura said, which pretty much summed up the obvious. "You need to be careful, Kate. This whole thing feels off. And don't you think it's more than a little freaky that it shows up at the same time as all this stuff starts up about the book?"

"I know," I said. "But I have to at least look into it. If he was murdered . . . If his murderer is still out there . . ."

"It's been five years. Any leads are probably cold by now."

"I have to try," I said.

"I know. Just don't let it distract you."

I dragged my toe through the sand in front of the bench. "What do you mean?"

"Just what I said. Don't let it distract you. Don't go running around searching for clues about Eric and forget about that book. Eric's dead, Kate, and nothing's going to bring him back. But our kids are alive, and that book was hidden at their school. If there's something going on—"

"I know," I said. "I'm going to figure it out. And I promise you, nothing's going to happen to our kids." A fool's promise, maybe, but it was one I absolutely intended to keep.

She sniffed, then blinked, then nodded. "Sorry. I know you wouldn't ever—I mean, I know you're watching all our backs. I didn't mean to suggest that you—"

"It's okay. And if you ever think I need a reality check, you just feel free to smack me around, okay?"

"No problem."

We started trudging down the boardwalk again, passing beside the patio of the restaurant. Couples were up there, poised to watch the sunset. I looked out toward the sea and the sun that was starting to dip low in the sky, then I shifted back to look at the hotel, remembering the nights that I'd sat there, too, holding hands with Eric and waiting for that green flash when the sun hit the horizon.

"Have you ever—" I began, wondering if Laura had done the same with Paul. Her expression stopped me, though. She was staring at the patio, her mouth wide open, and her hand up, just a little, as if she wanted to point to something but couldn't quite manage.

"Laura?" Alarmed, I took her arm and gave her a little shake. "Laura, what is it?"

"Paul," she whispered. And then her hand did manage to

point. A couple, off to one side and near the back, mostly hidden in the shadows. My heart stuttered in my chest, and even as I told myself that she had to be wrong, I knew that she wasn't. Paul was there, with a woman. And this wasn't a business dinner.

"It might not be him," I said, lamely. "It's really hard to see from here."

"It's him." Her voice was flat, resigned.

"Maybe it's innocent."

She looked at me. Just looked.

"Or maybe it's not. What do you want to do? I could slam an ice pick through his eye. Or we could try a calmer approach and just go talk to him."

"Tempting," she said. "The ice pick, I mean. Not the talking."

She drew in a breath, then another. Then she closed her eyes and as she did that I counted to ten. Sure enough, right when I'd finished counting, she opened her eyes, squared her shoulders, and pointed toward the beach. "I'm not going to waste any of this evening on Paul Dupont," she said. "I'm going to go see my daughter. I'll ask him about it when he gets home. Maybe he does have an explanation for having dinner with a woman at San Diablo's most romantic hotel when he told me he was out of town. I mean, I have to give him the benefit of the doubt, right?"

I doubted, all right. But in true best friend fashion, I just nodded. "Right. Absolutely right."

"Okay then." She started walking again. "We better hurry. I don't want to miss out on the hot dogs."

We walked the rest of the way in silence, Laura taking tense, careful steps, and me keeping an eye on her. She was doing okay, though, and by the time we reached the north end of the beach and the boardwalk fizzled out into sand over by where the cliffs started, we could hear music and see the smoke rising from a campfire just past the tide pools. Kids were scattered about in the inlet marked by the cliffs, some dancing, some running in the surf, some riding the waves.

"Smells good," Laura said, her voice high pitched and overly chipper. "I'm starved."

"Me, too."

A few more minutes of walking in silence, then, "So what do you think they want it for?"

I didn't even pretend to misunderstand. We were talking about the book now, both out of necessity, and to get our minds off Paul. "I wish I knew," I said. "Maybe the local demons want to start scrapbooking."

" 'The wheels are in motion,' " Laura whispered, pulling her sweater tighter around her shoulders.

"So I've been told," I said. "We just have to figure out how to derail the damn thing."

"You know I love you, so don't take this the wrong way, but sometimes I really miss the days when our most serious decisions turned on whether we should join World Gym or Curves, and the darkest secret I knew was that Jennifer Tate was taking her daughter's Ritalin."

I shot a sideways glance at Laura. "She was?"

Her cheeks immediately bloomed pink. "You didn't know?"

"No, I didn't know. Why didn't you tell me?"

She lifted a shoulder. "It was a secret. I'm good at keeping secrets. You know that."

That I did. But still. "Her kid's *Ritalin*?"

"Shhh!" Laura hissed, turning in a circle and scanning the area for prying ears. "Just drop it and tell me what I need to do about *your* secret."

We didn't have any more time to discuss it, though, because we'd climbed over the battered rock marking the tide pools, and David Long was waving at us from just a few yards away. He reached into an ice chest, grabbed two bottles that looked suspiciously like wine coolers, and started heading our way.

He didn't have his cane, but he moved gracefully, albeit with a slight limp. By the time we met him somewhere in the middle, I was seething. This was a school-sponsored event! The faculty adviser was supposed to set a good example, not press alcohol onto every adult who wandered in. Was he letting the seniors have beer? The freshmen?

I was just about to give him a piece of my mind, when he pressed a bottle into my hand. "Here you go, Mrs. Connor." I read the label and immediately deflated. Sparkling water.

I twisted the cap off the water and took a long swallow, feeling a little like an idiot. "Thanks," I said. "And call me Kate."

Allie brought Troy over about ten minutes later, and after much blushing and shuffling of feet, I got to say a few words to the boy. When she smiled and gave me a quick hug, I figured I'd passed. Dress, conversation, attitude. All appropriately appropriate for a mom attending a school function.

And, I have to admit, Troy acted appropriately, too. He introduced me to the other members of the surf team who'd come to the cookout, explaining that only about half had been able to make it since the pre-practice cookout was a last-minute thing. "I'm glad you could come, Mrs. Connor," he said, then beamed at my daughter, who blushed down to her toes.

Although I watched like a hawk, I didn't catch one ill-mannered move toward Allie. He brought her sodas and food, made her laugh, and went out of his way to clear a place on one of the oversized beach blankets for her to sit. All in all, I had to approve.

I wasn't going to lift my no-dating rule, but maybe—just maybe—we could invite this kid over to watch a movie. With the lights on. And me and Stuart (and Eddie and Timmy) in the room, too.

By the time the sun was hovering just above the horizon, Laura and I were sitting with a few other parents, all of whom were also watching their kids. I watched as David circulated among the kids, pulling the surfers aside, and sending them off to gather at the water's edge.

When he got to Allie and Troy, I saw Troy squeeze Allie's hand before leaving. Then David said a few words to Allie, and a broad smile split her face. I had no idea what he'd said, but I had to admit that he was good with her. From what I'd seen, he was good with all the kids.

In fact, I couldn't think of one thing that was wrong with David Long. So why did that little warning light go off in my head every time I was around him?

I leaned toward Laura. "Him," I said, nodding toward David.

"Are we playing Twenty Questions?" she asked. "What about him?"

"You can start your research with David Long."

She shifted on the blanket so she was facing me, then glanced around to make sure no one else was listening. No one was. The other parents were gathering up their things, anticipating moving closer to the water to watch the surf team do their thing.

"You really think he's up to something?" Laura said. "He seems so nice."

"That's what I don't like," I said. I'd met David the same day all of this had started. He was either a demon, a mysterious key-leaver, or in the wrong place at the wrong time. I wanted to know which one.

"Honestly, Kate, you didn't used to be this paranoid."

I just stared at her.

"Right. Okay. Paranoia is good. I can see that. So what do you want to know about him?"

"Whatever you can dig up. How long has he been teaching? How long at Coronado. Where's he from? Is he married? You know. The usual."

"I'll see what I can do," she said. She hauled herself up to her feet. "Meanwhile, I'm going to go watch the guys surf."

We moved closer, and from our new vantage point, I could see the surfers standing with their boards, all lined up for a picture. The guy in the middle—tall and blond and definitely not high-school age—seemed familiar to me, but I couldn't place him.

"That's Cool," Laura said, when I asked if she knew. "You know, the surfer."

"As a matter of fact, I didn't know. And I'm amazed that you do. Do you know all the local basketball players, too?"

She made a face. "He's been in the news, Kate. If you wrangled the remote away from Stuart and Eddie, maybe you'd see something more than political coverage or old Match Game reruns."

"My repertoire's broader than that," I said. "I'm thoroughly versed in each and every episode of *The Backyardigans*. And I always know who the *Sesame Street* celebrity guest's going to be."

"Yeah? Well, Cool is the celebrity guest here. It says so on the sign by the hot-dog stand."

I cocked my head, looking at him more closely. If he was that much of a local celebrity, I probably had seen him on the news or in a local commercial. I certainly couldn't imagine where else I'd have seen a six-foot-something, tanned and oiled surfer dude. I mean, I haven't watched an episode of *Baywatch* in years.

Laura lifted her bottle of sparkling water. "I'm switching to the hard stuff," she said. "Diet Coke. Want one?"

I shook my head, realizing that I'd already finished off four bottles of water and was beginning to feel it. I hauled myself to my feet. "Be right back," I said. I looked around, orienting myself, then pointed back toward the hotel. "The only bathroom's that way, right?"

Laura nodded. "We passed one just after we got off the boardwalk. It's pushed up against the base of the cliffs and there's a little concrete path leading up to it. You can't miss it."

I set off that direction, still thinking about Cool. Yes, there were demons afoot. And yes, something was definitely brewing. But that didn't mean I had to be suspicious about the surfer simply because he looked familiar. The low-budget commercials the local merchants aired on television were usually pretty bad, but they hardly crossed the line to demonic.

The public restroom was deserted and remarkably clean. I attributed that to the fact that it was December. Although you can go to the beach year-round in San Diablo, only the hardiest of souls actually brave the water during the winter months, and the tourists are conspicuously absent. The Pacific's cold enough during the summer; drop the ambient temperature a few degrees and you have a situation more suitable for polar bears than people.

Not that the water temperature was slowing down the surfers. As I came out of the restroom, I could hear the laughter and applause from the students as they cheered the surfers on. From this vantage point, my view of the kids on the beach was blocked by an outcropping of rock. But I had a clear view of the ocean, and I could make out six surfers, bouncing on the waves, waving at the crowd, and generally having a good time.

As I hurried down the path, I passed a sanitation worker coming up, one of those broom/dustpan combinations in his hand. His familiar green coveralls caught my eye. For that matter, they probably saved my life.

Because if I hadn't been eyeing him, I might not have seen the way he slowed. The way his hand tightened on the broom handle as he dropped the dustpan aside.

And I definitely would have missed the way he lashed out with the stick in a deadly maneuver aimed straight for my throat.

Ten

I thrust my right arm up in a lightning-fast move designed to protect. At the same time, my left arm whipped across my body in a defensive motion. I snatched the handle, my fingers closing tight.

My attacker howled in frustration, his volume only increasing when I yanked the broom out of his grasp. I jammed it down hard on the concrete, using the heel of my foot to snap off the whisk part.

All that took less than a second, and I spun the staff, then jammed it out, catching him in the gut with the end of the stick. His breath escaped with a *whoof,* and he tumbled backwards, clutching at his middle.

I recognized him right away—the green overalls, the fleshy face. And, of course, the "Coronado High School, Ernesto Ruiz" monogram on the pocket was a dead giveaway (no pun intended).

I'd been attacked by the high school janitor.

Since I doubted he'd jump me simply because I'd messed

up his supply room, I was pretty certain that the janitor was a demon. "Why are you here?" I demanded, my voice low and deadly. "And who is your master?"

He tightened his hands around the staff, trying to release the pressure on his belly. "Fool," he rasped. "You cannot win. Give us what we seek and we'll let you live."

"The book? I burned it."

"You lie!" he hissed.

"You can look for it in Hell," I said, lifting the staff just long enough to slam it down once again, this time through his eye.

I didn't make it, though. I'd underestimated his strength, and as I released my hold, he reached out, managing to grab the long-handled dustpan. He swung it up and out, the metal scoop part slicing across my belly and ripping my shirt. I cried out against the sharp pain, withdrawing reflexively for the briefest of instants.

But that was enough. He was up and on his feet, snarling as he slammed the dustpan down hard on the pavement in a move that mirrored my own. The scoop part came off, leaving him with a stick the approximate length and weight of mine.

He held tight, lunging toward me and waving the stick in choppy but lethal motions. I hadn't fought with staffs in over twenty years, and as I lunged and parried, I made a mental note to suggest a curriculum change to Cutter. I definitely needed a refresher course.

Not that my lack of training mattered much. Formal skills weren't really on the agenda at the moment. This was street fighting. Down and dirty and no holds barred. Training would help and hone, but tonight it was my mood that would get me through.

Because, frankly, I was pissed.

Attack me in my house? Leave inexplicable demonic

books lying around? Make me late for the only date my daughter will *ever* invite me on?

Oh yeah. I was ready to kick some demon butt, and this demon would do just fine.

We went at it like wild things, lost in a flurry of lunges and thrusts. My moves were primarily defensive, as I tried to stay alive while looking for an opening during which I could slam my staff through his eye.

My purse had tumbled free earlier, and now I saw it on the ground. I started to lunge that way, then remembered. I'd been interrupted switching purses. My holy water, knife, and other handy tidbits were still in my bag at home. *Damn.*

He rushed me, the end of his staff aimed for my face. It was a ridiculous move, and easily blocked by an upward thrust of my own staff. As I did that, though, I took a step backwards . . . and found myself sprawled on the ground, my foot in a tangle of metal and chain.

Frisbee golf! I'd tripped over a half-buried Frisbee golf goal.

As I tugged my foot free, the demon leaped on me, his knees tight around either side of my waist as he held me down with a hand to my throat.

My hands were pinned under me, and I struggled to move, but could manage little more than a squirm. His foul breath washed over me, and I sent up a silent prayer. This couldn't be the end. Not now. Not when I had two kids to raise. Two kids to protect from the demons out there in the world.

His hand tightened around my throat, and I struggled uselessly, the world starting to turn gray.

"Where?" he whispered again, his voice as rough as gravel. He got right in my face, and I almost gagged from the stench. "Where is it?"

I opened my mouth and pretended to try to speak. His eyes narrowed, but he didn't loosen his grip. I wiggled my hand some more, twisting my body as I did in a mock struggle that I hoped camouflaged what I was really doing: digging deeper into the sand, trying to free just that one limb.

"Where?" he demanded again.

I forced out a sound. Just a gurgle really, then coughed. I tried again. Another sound. And this time, thank God, it actually worked. The demon loosened his grip on my neck. Not much, but enough. "The book," I croaked. "Just go . . . go . . ."

"Yes?"

"Just go to Hell!"

His eyes went wide, as much from my words as from my now-free hand that I'd shot up and out, catching him in the throat just about where he'd caught me. He reacted instinctively, pulling away and that gave me the opening I needed.

I thrust up with my knee and the heel of my hand, managing to knock him off me. Then I rocked back and up in a kip-up maneuver that got me to my feet.

Now I had the advantage, and intended to use it. "Are you trying to free the Tartarus demons? Why do you need the book? For instructions? A ritual? *What?"* I snapped out the questions as I circled him, waiting for the right moment to attack.

"You'll learn soon enough, Hunter," he said. He lunged for me, and I moved to defend. But instead of attacking, he reached down, scooped up a handful of sand, and before he was even fully upright again, he tossed it right into my face.

I howled in pain as the sand dug into my eyes. Only a split second passed before I remembered to react, but it was already too late. I braced for his attack, and then . . . *nothing.* I squinted through the pain, my eyes streaming tears. He was gone. Instead of attacking, he'd run, and I could see him sprinting down the beach away from me. And, more important, away from the students.

I considered going after him, but ruled it out. I'd need to find and eradicate him, no question about that. But I'd rather not do it now if I didn't have to. For one thing, I didn't have any decent weapons. For another, I'd have to hide the body.

I could drag him into the surf or dig a hole in the sand, but both of those things would take time, and weren't very effective anyway. And if any of the students walked up while I was in the process of burying their janitor, what would I say? That he wasn't keeping the cafeteria sanitary? Somehow, I didn't think that would fly.

No, I knew about the janitor now. Best to let him go and follow up on that kill later.

I thought back to the time I'd seen him at school, standing in the background as the police had hauled Sinclair's body away. Had he been a demon then? I didn't think so. For one, it would have made a lot more sense to have a janitor-demon search for (or hide?) the book. Why send Sinclair when he might be detected by yours truly?

Also, he hadn't seemed particularly demonic when I'd seen him. Of course, appearances can be deceiving, but he'd been mumbling to himself, grumping about the damn kids. Not the usual litany for a demon, but probably a common complaint for a high school janitor.

The demon was still on my mind when I returned to the party. Laura gave me a curious look, her eyes going wide when she saw the rip in my shirt.

"What—?"

But I waved her questions away, zipping my jacket to hide the damage to my shirt.

I'd tell Laura, of course. But later.

I'd had my fill of drama for the night. And although I'd keep an eye out for demons and other nasties, I figured I was entitled to spend the rest of the evening off the clock, pretending I was a normal mom with a normal life in a normal town.

That illusion lasted for exactly two hours and thirty-six minutes. After that, Allie, Laura, Mindy, and I returned home to find my door wide open, and three police cars parked in front, their blue, white, and red lights illuminating the neighborhood like some perverted carnival.

Timmy!

Fear pounded through me as I shoved the car door open and scrambled out before Laura even had time to slow down. I sprinted toward the door, screaming for my little boy, a thousand hellish images dancing in my head.

A uniformed officer stood in the doorway, his hand outstretched as if to stop me. I smacked his arm away and barreled through the door, practically tripping over Sylvia.

"He's fine," she said, putting both hands on my shoulders and looking hard into my eyes. "We're all fine. No one's hurt. The place was robbed. It's a total mess, but no one's hurt."

"Where is he?" I demanded, not willing to believe anything until I saw my baby.

But Sylvia didn't even have to answer, because my little pajama-footed boy came racing into the entrance hall, a pair of handcuffs dangling in his hand. "Momma, Momma! I'm a defective!"

I scooped him up and hugged him close, my eyes shut tight against the horror. Allie and the Duponts pounded into the house as well, and I felt Allie's arms go around us both, her quiet sobs just about enough to break my heart.

"It's okay," I said. "He's fine. It's okay." I kept repeating that, figuring that if I kept it up, maybe I'd start to believe it.

After holding my kids for an eternity, I passed Timmy off to Allie. He really did seem fine. She still looked about as shook up as I felt. And no wonder. She and her brother had been in one hell of a scrape (literally) at the tail end of the summer.

Timmy's nightmares had faded, but I knew the memories still preyed on Allie. I also knew that there wasn't anything I could do except let her know that I love her. We've all got demons to face. And we each have to do it in our own way.

In my case, of course, a lot of those demons are real. And back in September, I'd spent days weighing my decision to go back on active duty. In the end, I'd decided that San Diablo needed a Hunter. Needed someone trained to stand up against evil. Someone to fight on the side of good.

Now, though, I couldn't help but wonder: Had I done the right thing? And if I'd made a mistake, was it too late to fix it?

I didn't know, and it wasn't a question I could answer right then, not with my daughter looking with horror around our ransacked home, and my little boy running around waving the handcuffs and chasing after the young blond officer who'd willingly cast himself in the role of "bad guy."

"What happened?" Laura asked. She'd moved beside me, and now she took my hand, squeezing my fingers in a silent show of support.

A shadow crossed Sylvia's face, as she told us about how she'd heard a commotion and stepped outside her house, then saw the lights and police cars at our end of the block. She'd been concerned, but not overly so. But then she tried to call our house and got no answer.

She thought that perhaps something had happened to Eddie—that maybe an ambulance had arrived—and she felt like she had to go see. So she and Timmy had walked down the street and learned that the house had been ransacked.

Eddie had gone out for a walk, and in the time it took him to make the four block circle, someone had gone in and trashed the place.

Eddie had called the cops the second he'd arrived back home, but, of course, there was nothing they could do.

"Where's Eddie?" I asked. "He must feel terrible."

"He's in the kitchen," Sylvia said. "He was, I don't know, a little freaked out. Kept going on about demons. But he's okay," she added, hurriedly. "The cops said that they see weird reactions to robberies all the time. So it's not like he's, you know, psychotic or anything."

"Good to know," I said. I shot Laura a pleading look.

"I'll go check on him," she said, then hurried toward the kitchen before I could even say thanks.

"I need to call Stuart," I said, to nobody in particular.

"I called him," Sylvia said. "I left him a voice mail. And the police called, too." She shook her head. "He's probably really busy with the campaign, huh?"

I counted to ten. Now really wasn't the time to tell my neighbor how I was feeling about that damn campaign.

I drew a breath. "So what happened next?"

"They've just been looking the place over. The weird thing is that the burglars didn't take your electronic equipment or anything. I think they wonder if maybe the whole thing was political. Someone who doesn't want Stuart running for office."

I considered the idea and told Sylvia that it had some merit. That was a lie, of course. Because I knew what the burglars had been looking for.

But the book wasn't there. I'd taken it to the cathedral for safekeeping.

That plan, at least, had worked.

The larger plan—the one where I keep my family safe

and warm and well away from my demon-hunting life? That plan, I'm afraid, wasn't working out nearly as well.

"You gonna tell me why you keep me around? Not exactly earning my keep." Eddie clasped a mug of hot tea with both hands, and he looked at me over the top of his glasses, his eyebrows twitching like bushy gray caterpillars.

I put my hand over his. "Because we love you."

The cops and Sylvia had finally left, and I'd sent Mindy and Laura home, too. Laura had wanted us to come stay at her house, but that felt too much like giving in. Plus, I didn't expect any more drama tonight. The search had been thorough, and they hadn't found the book. The bad guys wouldn't return. Not tonight, anyway. Especially not with the cops making frequent passes in front of our house.

Eddie closed his eyes and his shoulders started to shake. "I'm getting old. I'm already damn near useless. And then I go and forget to set that damned alarm."

"A mistake, Eddie. It could have happened to anyone."

"It shouldn't have happened to me." He drew his hand back, taking the teacup with him, and took a long swallow. "Dammit," he said again, "it shouldn't have happened to me."

And then he hauled back and let go, sending the teacup flying until it shattered on the far wall of the kitchen. Tea splattered against the white paint, then dripped in lazy streams down the wall as Kabit yowled and raced like a shot for the living room.

"Well," I said after a moment. "At least you didn't do that *after* I'd cleaned up."

The slightest hint of a grin touched his mouth. "The way you keep house, you really think anyone's going to know the difference?"

and most of the living room. *That* was a mess that couldn't be hidden. Nor could it be blamed on my housekeeping skills, however inadequate they might be.

"Holy crap," he said. "What happened?"

"If you'd check your cell phone once every few hours," I said icily, "maybe you'd have a clue."

"The batteries died," he said. "And I can't find the damn car charger. The last time I took Timmy to the—"

I held up a hand. "Oh, no. You are not blaming your lack of communication on your son. So don't even go there."

"Kate . . ."

"We were *robbed,* Stuart! And you're telling me some bullshit story about your phone charger!"

All the color had drained from his face. "Where are the kids?"

I clenched my fists, wanting to hold on to my anger. And, yes, wanting to punish him. Petty, small, and mean, but, dammit, that's the way I felt. And as soon as I realized it, the bubble burst. My breath hitched and—despite all my training, all my anger, and all that stupid self-control I'd drawn so deeply on over the last few months—I started to cry.

"Jesus, Kate," Stuart said, grabbing my shoulders. "The kids? *Where are the kids?*"

"They're fine," I managed between snuffles. I buried my face in his chest and let him hold me tight, raw emotion flooding my body as the adrenaline drained out of me. "They're upstairs. They're fine."

"I'm sorry," he murmured. "I was trying to get a handle on that subdivision mess I've been dealing with at the office. I knew you were at the beach with Allie, so I wasn't worried about getting home early, and it didn't even occur to me to call from the office. And then when I was in the car, I realized I couldn't call at all." He stroked my hair. "If only I'd known."

"Watch it, old man," I said, but I think he could tell I was glad to have the old Eddie back.

Footsteps clattered on the floor, and Allie skidded around the corner, Timmy tight in her arms. "What was that?" she asked, breathlessly.

"Big noise!" Timmy shrieked. "Big, big noise!"

"Eddie dropped his mug," I said.

Allie looked at me, looked at Eddie, then looked at the wall. "Right," she said. "Can I break something, too?"

"What the hell." I slid my own mug—now empty—toward her. "Have at it."

She did, sending it flying with a speed that probably would have gotten her picked for the girl's softball team. The mug shattered, and she high-fived Eddie. She met my eyes, hers shining. "I think I feel better."

"Good," I said.

"Me, too, Momma! Me, too!"

Eddie chuckled, and I did some quick mental gymnastics, wondering if I let Timmy smash one mug, if all of our dishes were going to end up in shatters.

In the end, I decided I didn't much care. "You, too, sport," I said. I got up and found two ugly-as-sin mugs in the cabinet. "I'll even join you."

I handed him a mug, then counted to three, and we both let it rip. Mine smashed to bits on the tile just shy of the wall, the sharp *smash-crack!* of the shattering ceramic surprisingly cathartic.

Timmy's mug traveled about six inches, then landed at his feet, the handle breaking off and a fissure snaking down from rim to base. Not nearly as satisfying as my million-piece smash, but even so, he was now jumping up and down yelling, "Again! Again!"

"I think once is enough," I said. And then, before he

could think about that and decide to wail, I added, "Why don't you and Allie pick up the fuzzies in the living room."

"Right," Allie said, not even blinking that I'd just enlisted her to clean up upholstery innards. "We'll do that, and then I'll give him his bath." She cocked her head. "Where's he sleeping tonight?"

"We're all sleeping in my room," I said. "We'll pile some blankets on the mattress. Won't even notice the rips."

"All of us?" Allie repeated, one eyebrow cocked.

"Not me," Eddie said. He hooked a thumb my direction. "That one snores."

"Thank you very much," I said, as Allie laughed. "And you have my permission to sleep wherever you want."

"My room'll do me just fine, thank you."

"Get Eddie some blankets to put over the rips in the mattress," I said to Allie. "Then work on the living room."

"I'll get my own damn blankets," he said. "*That* much I think I can handle."

"Eddie . . ." I reached for his hand, but he was already up and waving me off.

"I'm fine. And I'm going to bed."

I watched him go, my heart aching a little, but I had no idea how to make him feel better.

Allie pulled out a chair and sat at the table, Timmy balanced on her lap. "So your bed's gonna be kinda crowded, huh?"

"Cozy," I said.

"Stuart's the one who snores," she said.

"That's true," I agreed.

"And we haven't seen much of him tonight."

"No," I agreed. "We haven't." I glanced again at the phone that still hadn't rung, despite me having left two messages for Stuart already. I'd say I was irritated, but that would qualify as the world's biggest understatement.

"So, um, is he sharing the bed, too?"

I met my daughter's eyes. My very perceptive, growing-up-too-quickly daughter. "No," I said. "He's not."

With perfect timing, the sharp creak of the garage door echoed through the kitchen.

"Speak of the devil," Allie said.

"Not the devil," I corrected. "But he will have hell to pay."

I stood up. "Why don't you forget about the fuzzies and take Timmy upstairs now? Get into bed. Watch a Timmy-approved movie if you want. I'll be up in a little bit."

"Okay," she said, gathering up her brother. "Stuart's in for it, isn't he?"

"Oh yeah," I said. "It's going to be ugly."

When Stuart finally walked into the kitchen, I was standing there waiting for him, my arms crossed over my chest, and my fury rising like mercury. He looked at me, then held out a single red carnation.

"All the florists were closed," he said. "They had a bucket at Seven-Eleven."

"You brought me a flower," I said, my voice sharp enough to slice bread.

"If I got you chocolate, you'd just complain about your waist."

The man does know me.

"And isn't it the thought that counts?"

I leaned against the counter and shook my head. "Not today."

His brow furrowed as he looked from me to the rest of the room. The kitchen was still a mess, but not that much worse than my usual post-dinner–disaster area. When he reached the table, though, he had a clear view of the smashed cups

"It's okay," I said. "It's okay." It wasn't, though, not re-ally. Both of our jobs were seeping over into our home life, into our marriage. And, honestly, I wasn't sure our marriage could take it.

"Kate?" He tilted my chin up and brushed a kiss across my lips. "What is it?"

"Nothing," I said, automatically. Then, "No, wait. That's not true. I feel like you've got a mistress or something. Only I'm the one who has to sneak in time with you."

He stroked my hair. "It's hard now," he said. "I know that, and I love you for putting up with it."

"I know," I murmured. "And I love you, too." I took a deep breath, and then another. Then I pulled myself up on my tiptoes and brushed a kiss across his cheek as the cat emerged from hiding to rub figure eights around my legs. "But tonight, my darling, you get to sleep on the couch."

I traipsed upstairs to join the kids, wondering vaguely if I was being hypocritical. I mean, at least I knew what Stuart was up to on those long nights away from home. Stuart, however, had no idea what I was up to.

And the truth was, I never intended to tell him.

Eleven

I am not unfamiliar with the concept of guilt. Last summer, for example, I erroneously thought that Stuart had thrown in with a particularly nasty demon bent on taking over San Diablo and, eventually, the world. An honest mistake that any wife could have made, but I still feel guilty about it. And Stuart had been reaping the benefits for months—not that he ever knew the reason for my sudden shift into über-wife mode.

The point of which is to say that I recognize guilt-motivated behavior when I see it. I'd seen it just yesterday, as a matter of fact, and now it was déjà vu all over again, this time with chocolate chip pancakes, orange juice and coffee delivered on a tray to the master bedroom's sitting area.

"Rise and shine, family," Stuart said, opening the curtains.

"Wow," I said, blinking against the sun. "Pancakes, huh?"

"Practice makes perfect. Besides, the skillet was still on the counter." He tugged on the blanket. Allie groaned and yanked it back over her head. "Come on, you guys. We have just enough time before mass to eat and get dressed."

I propped myself up on an elbow, watching him. I go to mass at least weekly, and I take the kids every Sunday. But Stuart's another matter. He goes, but reluctantly. And I think the number of times that Stuart's actually initiated a church outing adds up to exactly zero.

Oh yeah. I was definitely witnessing guilt on overdrive.

I, however, am not picky, and so I rolled out of bed, rousted the kids and started getting ready.

My pleasure at Stuart's sudden shift to both the spiritual and the familiar took a southerly turn as we were finishing breakfast.

"I thought we could swing by a couple of furniture stores on the way home," I said. "The mattresses are trash. And now's as good a time as any to get a new sofa." We'd been holding off until Timmy passed the age of leaky diapers and spilled sippy cups. But our sofa had a decidedly sour smell that even the Pottery Barn slipcover I'd splurged on couldn't hide.

Stuart, however, didn't look nearly as enthusiastic.

"What?" I demanded, as I wiped maple syrup off Timmy's hands (and his face, and his legs, and the tops of his ears).

"Nothing," Stuart said. But he was now clearing the dishes and I smelled additional guilt.

"Uh-huh," I said.

"I just thought we could take two cars."

"Two," I repeated. "And we'd want to do that why?"

"Kate . . ."

I lifted my hands in surrender. "Fine. You have to work. I get it."

He came up behind me and slid his arms around my waist. "The museum benefit's tonight. I just need to make a few calls about that, and catch up on some other things, I'll be home by seven. I promise."

"So we can turn around and go to the benefit." I fought the urge not to cringe. I still needed to buy a dress for that thing.

"Sweetheart—"

"I know, I know. That's fine."

He looked at me dubiously. "You're sure?"

"Absolutely." I wasn't thrilled, but I had work of my own to do. "Just don't be surprised if you come home to find I've bought a new couch."

"Would probably serve me right."

"Probably would," I agreed.

Twenty minutes later, we were dressed and climbing into the cars. Allie and I went in the Odyssey and Stuart and Timmy in the Infinity. I'd have both kids after mass, but for at least a portion of the morning, I could listen to the news rather than Radio Disney.

I'd hoped to catch up with Father Ben after mass, but to my surprise, he wasn't there. The bishop presided over the service, which he often did on Sundays, but usually Father Ben participated in the mass. Today, though, Father Ben was no where to be seen.

Mass ended about noon, and after we all filed out and said a few words to the bishop, Stuart kissed me and the kids good-bye, then left with a promise to be home by seven. Today, of course, I didn't care if he was late. I'd much rather stay home in my jeans and eat peanut butter sandwiches than mingle at a benefit, especially when I'd be as much on display as my husband.

This time, however, I was certain my husband would be on time.

Once Stuart was gone, I left Timmy on the playground with Allie while I went and found Delores. "Father Ben?" she asked, in answer to my question. "He went down to Los

Angeles last night. Said he wanted to do some research in the archives."

"Did he say what he was working on?"

"Not a word."

"Right. Thanks."

I stifled the urge to call Father Ben's cell phone, and instead went to find my kids. He'd let me know when he had something concrete, and in the meantime, I had my hands full getting my house back in order.

Not too surprisingly, Allie didn't object to my plan to spend a few hours at the mall. And once I offered to throw in a new outfit from the Gap, she even agreed to take charge of her brother and do some of our holiday shopping while I did some shopping of my own.

I hit Pottery Barn first, but couldn't justify spending that much on a sofa, no matter how comfortable it might be. Especially since I knew I'd have to spend the next two years hiding it under slipcovers if I wanted it to stay even remotely clean. I tried to find a store priced for the middle-income-with-toddler set, but soon learned that all the major furniture stores were located outside the mall in their own freestanding buildings.

Nice for them, bad for me. Because now I was trapped in a mall with a teenager who'd just begun to shop. And even though I'd only agreed to buy one outfit, I knew my daughter well enough to know that choosing said outfit could take upward of four hours.

That's when I remembered that I needed an outfit, too. I'm not sure how I'd forgotten, actually. Wishful thinking, I suppose. If I had nothing decent, maybe Stuart wouldn't take me.

I scowled, annoyed by my train of thought. This election was important to Stuart. Which meant it was important to me, too. And yes, I was irritated (which is the politically correct way of saying that I was completely pissed off) by his more and more frequent absences from hearth and home. But that was between him and me. The election was between us and the voters. Because, whether I liked it or not, I was a political wife now. And I wasn't about to let my spite ruin his chances of getting elected.

In other words, my mission was to buy a dress. A this-candidate-has-a-great-wife-let's-vote-for-him kind of dress. With matching shoes. And, just because I wouldn't mind having my husband home on time for a change, I figured I'd take a page from Laura's book and swing by Victoria's Secret as well.

The perfect dress came in every size but mine, but the almost-perfect dress fit beautifully. A twist on the little black dress, this number sported a tight waist accentuated by a red belt, a fitted bodice, and a skirt that swished when I walked and flared when I turned. I'm by no means a clotheshorse, but put a couple of these in my closet, and I might be willing to convert.

Of course I bought the thing. I even bought a pair of matching black pumps. I considered buying a new wrap, but decided I'd done enough damage to our credit card. And, yes, I was injuring *our* credit card. My original plan to spend my *Forza* money on a dress dissolved in a puff of smoke about the time that Stuart announced he was a no-go for Allie's beach party. And when he wasn't there after the robbery? Well, that's when the shoes were added to the tally. Highly unreasonable, but it felt really, really good.

So good, in fact, that a full two hours passed before I caught up with Allie and the munchkin.

Even buying for herself and Timmy, Allie's splurge totaled significantly less than mine. We stopped at the cookie stand, then parked ourselves on a bench as she gave me the rundown of her purchases (with the notable exception of the Christmas goodies). Although she went through each item in intricate detail, it all boiled down to clothes and toys. The toys being the far more interesting, where I was concerned.

"You bought him an arsenal?" I asked looking up from the shopping bag into which I'd been peering.

"I thought it would be fun," she said. "Water pistols for Timmy and Stuart. And the super-squirter things for you and me."

I pulled out one of the pistols and tested the action. Not bad for a cheap, cartoon-licensed plastic toy. And I had no doubt that these purchases would provide the family at least an hour of entertainment. After that, I imagined they'd get lost somewhere in the backyard, then broken by the lawn-mower come summer. I'd been through this before.

But I didn't complain. An hour is an hour, and the idea did sound like fun.

As soon as Timmy finished his cookie, we toted our shopping bags to the car, Allie pushing the stroller and complaining about how difficult it was to shop with Timmy underfoot. I kept silent. Somehow, I thought that was best.

We hit the furniture stores next, and while Allie tried hard to keep Timmy from bouncing on every single cushion, I hijacked a salesman and seriously upped his overall sales average. By the time we were back out the door and into the van, starvation was looming. We pulled into the first McDonald's we saw. Not exactly thrilling for either Allie or me, but it made the munchkin (who'd been slowly descending into crankiness) happy. Considering how loud the boy can wail, I'm all about staving off crankiness.

The line for the drive-through was insane, so I pulled into a slot, foisted my purse on my daughter, and told her to get me a Big Mac, Timmy a cheeseburger Happy Meal, and her whatever she wanted. She left, seeming perfectly happy about that plan.

When she came back, though, I couldn't help notice that she seemed significantly less happy. Downright moody, actually. Since frequent mood shifts are par for the course when one lives with a teenager (my moods and hers), I didn't think too much about it. I did ask, though. But she cut me off neatly with a surly, "I'm fine. I'm just tired. It's no big deal." Then she stuck her feet on the dash, sank low in her seat, and closed her eyes.

Great. Fight crankiness on one end and get hit with it on the other.

The rest of the afternoon was spent much more pleasantly. Allie wasn't exactly a ray of sunshine, but she wasn't moping around, either, and I attributed her earlier morbidity to falling blood sugar.

Even more significantly, the day passed blissfully demon free. Allie and I made a dent cleaning the disaster that was the house while Timmy proceeded to add to the mess in his room. Eddie made a show of helping, but I had to give him such specific directions that I didn't object when he announced that he was heading for the library, which opens at two on Sundays. (I'm pretty sure his ignorance of basic vacuum-cleaner operation was a ruse, but I decided not to call him on it.)

About four, Laura and Mindy came over and we all went for ice cream. Or, rather, Laura and I ate ice cream. I'm not entirely sure Timmy ingested any, but if anyone ever determines a connection between an ice-cream facial and perfect skin, then I can safely say that my boy is going to have the world's best complexion. The girls both ordered teeny-tiny scoops of sorbet, then proceeded to take teeny-tiny bites, ultimately throwing most of their scoops in the trash when we finally left.

"Why not just drink water?" I asked.

My daughter and Mindy shared a pitying look. "Cuz then we wouldn't get the taste, Mom. I mean, it's not like we're into deprivation or anything,"

Like Allie would say, *Whatever.*

I dropped everyone off at Laura's house before heading home. I hadn't discussed the evening's arrangements with Allie, but she didn't raise a protest. After last night's robbery, I didn't expect that she would.

Eddie was a different story, as he had earlier insisted on staying home, and promised to "kick the sorry ass of any demon-loving freak who's unlucky enough to try to break in." Since that sounded just fine to me, I didn't argue with him.

Neither Eddie nor Stuart were home yet, so I had the whole house to myself as I showered, and went to work on my makeup. My hair tends to hang limp around my face. That's one of the reasons I pull it back in a ponytail so often. At least then it's hanging limp, but out of my face.

I can, however, force it into submission when I really need to, and I had a feeling that a Tabitha Danvers gala fell into that category.

So I spent the next twenty minutes putting all manner of goop in my hair, then blow-drying it. An altogether humbling experience, I might add. I'm the woman who once cleaned out a nest of vampires while wielding a wooden sword in one hand and a crucifix in the other. But none of that matters in the hair-care arena. Because I am apparently genetically unable to wield both a blow-dryer and a round brush.

Despite my ineptitude, my hair did manage to dry. And it even had some body, which basically means that it wasn't hanging as limp as it normally does. I resisted the urge to pull it back into a familiar ponytail and instead heated up my curling iron. I might not have a clue what the demons in this town were up to, but by God I was going to beat my hair into submission.

Thirty minutes and half a bottle of hair spray later, I looked pretty damn good, if I do say so myself. My face was surrounded by a sea of curls, my eyes looked even wider with the three layers of mascara I'd applied, and my lips were red and full. I expected the makeup to slough off within half an hour and my hair to fall by the time we reached the museum, but at least my husband could see the results of my efforts.

I pulled on the dress, then checked the time. A quarter to seven. In another lifetime, I would have expected Stuart to get home early. No more. Which meant I had fifteen minutes to kill, and I needed to do it in a way that wouldn't crinkle my dress, make my nose sweat, or rumple my hair.

I clicked on the television and channel surfed, but despite the fact that we have more than three hundred channels, I found absolutely nothing interesting. I gave up and turned the thing off. Then I grabbed my purse and pulled out the note from Eric.

I read through it once, then again, my heart aching as I did. Both for Eric and the life we'd lost, and for Stuart and the life we had.

I closed my eyes, the note pressed against my chest as I thought about Stuart. As much as I hated to admit it, for all the time that I've been married to Stuart, I've compared my marriages. Not overtly. Not really even consciously. But how can you help it? I certainly couldn't. And one simple fact always stood out: Eric had known my secrets. He'd known my past. Hell, he'd lived it with me.

Stuart didn't know that part of me, and that made me a little sad. Because in my first marriage there hadn't been secrets. And I think I'd put my first marriage up on a little pedestal. A representation of some marital perfection that Stuart and I could never reach.

Horribly unfair to Stuart. I know that. But feelings and fairness don't always go hand in hand.

Now, though, I had to wonder if maybe that pedestal was crumbling. Because the world I'd imagined with Eric was an illusion. I'd believed we'd had no secrets. But that wasn't true. The safe-deposit box had shown me that.

It all boiled down to one inescapable conclusion: My husband had been murdered for a secret.

A flicker of rage burned through me, and I couldn't help but wonder: If he'd told me the truth—if he'd asked me for help—would Eric still be alive today?

And if so, what would my life be like now?

"You look absolutely stunning," Stuart said, as he held out his arm for me.

We were on the sidewalk in front of the museum, standing just in front of the stairs leading up to the grand entrance. Behind us, the valet put the car in gear and drove away. I hooked my arm through Stuart's and smiled. "You've already said that."

In fact, he'd already said it three times. First when he'd come home, again after he'd changed clothes, and once again before he'd opened the car door for me.

In all fairness, I'd said it right back to him. Stuart's not too shabby on any given day, but he's positively dashing in a charcoal-gray tailored suit, his shoulders squared, and his eyes bright with anticipation.

In fact, he looked so delicious, that I decided to repeat myself, just for the record. "*You* look amazing," I said.

"And I look even better on your arm."

"Well, sure," I said. "That goes without saying."

We both laughed, and I felt warm and light, the memories of when we'd first started dating washing over me. I'd barely been free of the funk I'd slid into after Eric's death, and the thing I remember most about those first weeks was the way Stuart had made me laugh. And the way he could always surprise me. A drive down PCH and dinner at Spago in L.A., when I'd only expected a quick burger. A night curled up on the couch with *Monty Python and the Holy Grail,* complete with Chinese food and wine spritzers. A weekend trip to Catalina Island after Allie had mentioned that she'd never been and really wanted to go.

And, of course, the thing that really got me: He'd asked my adolescent daughter for permission to marry me.

"You okay?"

Stuart was studying my face, and I realized that my eyes were brimming with tears.

"Oh no!" I yelped. "Handkerchief! This mascara isn't waterproof!"

"Did I miss a crisis?" he asked, as I dabbed at my eyes, kicking myself for not going with my Maybelline standby.

"I'm fine," I finally said, after I'd checked my reflection in my compact. "I was just thinking about the day you asked me to marry you."

"Ah," he said. "Well, now the tears make perfect sense."

I lifted myself up on my toes and kissed him, hard. "I love you," I said. "Now let's go in there and rake up some serious campaign donations, okay?"

I started to pull open the door, but he stayed my hand. "Thank you," he said simply.

I turned, looking at him quizzically. "For what?"

"For this. For everything. I know you never signed on to be a politician's wife." His mouth quirked, revealing a reluctant dimple. "And I love you for putting up with it."

"I married the man, Stuart. Not the job. And I love you no matter what."

I only hoped that if he ever discovered my secret life that he'd feel the same way about me.

I'll say one thing for Tabitha Danvers—that woman knows how to throw a party. Even I, who tend to avoid these kinds of functions as much as possible, had a reasonably good time. Which is to say that I drank the free wine, made small talk when necessary, then wandered through the museum to look at the various things on display.

Truly, the best part of these parties is escaping the crowd.

The museum was technically closed until January so that the staff could do inventory and set up new exhibits. But Tabitha had opened the place up for us, making clear that we could wander throughout the museum, and even get a sneak peek at some of the coming exhibits.

I greedily took her at her word, wanting to escape the crowd. Most of the guests, though, stayed in the atrium, where they could be close to both my husband and the bar.

I actually know the Danvers Museum pretty well. When I was pregnant with Timmy, I did the obligatory please-kick-me-into-labor-NOW walk around these halls for the entire last week of my pregnancy. (It didn't work. The little bugger was six days late, entirely blowing that old wives' tale about second children arriving early.)

After that, I burned off my baby weight by walking these halls with Timmy strapped papooselike to my chest in the BabyBjörn carrier I'd splurged on in a postpartum-induced shopping frenzy. (I also walked at the mall, but those walks always seemed to cost money. With a new baby and a government-salary husband, I figured the least I could do to stabilize the family budget was avoid any enclosed place with a Pottery Barn, a Gap, and a Brentano's.)

Considering I'd spent so much time here when he was young, it really was no wonder that Timmy still enjoys the museum. He walks by himself now, and we explore the natural history section, looking at the exhibits of fossils excavated from the area or the whale skeleton suspended from the ceiling. We'd been here just a week ago, actually, right before they closed for the exhibit change.

I moved through that room now, my heels clicking on the tile floor, the giant whale looming above me. The next room housed traveling exhibits, and I was curious as to what they were installing. I paused at the threshold, nodding politely at the guard standing just outside the door.

And then, because I'd been attacked only yesterday by a demon in uniform, I gave him a second look. His stance hadn't changed, and he was hardly paying any attention to me at all. I relaxed, but only a little.

You just can't be too sure about demons.

The room itself was odd, housing only a glass display case, the contents of which I couldn't see from the doorway. Black velvet draped the walls and ceilings, and the only illumination was provided by a black light.

I stepped up to the case, and saw that it was dominated by a large stone tablet covered in geometric shapes that seemed to glow under the purple light. Triangles on triangles. Squares on squares. Squares bisected into triangles.

I took a pamphlet from beside the main display case, and quickly scanned it. All the artifacts, it said, were Macedonian relics, discovered last year as part of an archeological dig funded by the British Museum. According to the text, the relics dated back thousand of years before the birth of Christ.

I don't know a lot about history, but I thought that

sounded pretty fascinating. More so since experts were unsure as to the function of the tablets or the meaning of the symbols.

I sat down on a bench and slid off my new shoes, wiggling my toes in ecstasy. I was out of practice in heels, and my feet ached.

I was massaging the ball of my foot when I realized someone was in the doorway. I looked up, embarrassed, to see the tall, sun-baked blond hunk—*Cool.*

I had one of those V-8 moments when I finally realized why he looked so familiar—I'd seen him here at the museum. Not the kind of place I would have expected to find a celebrity surfer, but people surprise you all the time.

I slipped my shoe back on and got up to go over and make polite conversation, but by the time I got to the doorway, he was gone.

I shrugged and moved on to the next room, where at least the light was normal and the objects recognizable. Bowls and spoons. For those, I didn't even need a pamphlet.

Since I hadn't checked on the kids, I pulled out my cell phone and called Laura. They were fine, she reported, and Timmy was already asleep. Did I want to just retrieve both kids in the morning? I thought about it, and decided I did. Once Timmy's awake, he's impossible to get back to sleep. Better to not disturb him once he was down for the night.

I continued through the exhibit, half paying attention, but mostly letting my mind wander. To demons, to Stuart, to Eric, to my kids. Stuart found me there, coming in and sliding his arms around my waist. "Hey," he said. "You ready to go?"

I checked my watch. Still early. "Are *you* ready to go?"

He kissed the top of my head. "I've mingled. I've schmoozed. I've played the politician. And now," he added, turning me in his arms and pulling me close, "I think it's time for me to play the husband."

"In that case," I said, baffled but pleased. "I think I can probably tear myself away."

The next morning I retrieved Timmy from Laura's at the crack of dawn, hurried him off to day care, then hurried back, eager to dive into the mystery of the book and the demons. I'd called Gretchen yesterday, explaining I anticipated a late night, and begging her to cover my car pool. So it was more than a little ironic that I was now camped out at Laura's coffee table half an hour before I'd normally be dressed.

"Eager much?" she asked, yawning and pulling her robe tighter around her.

"Just ready to kick a little butt." It's amazing what a romantic night in a child-free house can do for your world view.

"You and your daughter. What's with the attitude this morning?"

I frowned, thoughts of demon butts shoved aside by concern for my kid. "What are you talking about?"

"Don't know," she said as I followed her into the kitchen. "That's the point. Last night she hardly said two words to me. And when I mentioned it to Mindy this morning, she said that Allie didn't say anything to her, either."

"Well, damn," I said. "She was quiet yesterday after the mall, but I thought it was the hunger." Now I didn't know what to think. Not talking to me or Laura fell within the normal parameters for the fourteen-to-sixteen age group (at least, according to every parenting book I've ever read). But not talking to Mindy? That was a mystery.

"Maybe they like the same guy?" I suggested.

"Maybe," Laura said dubiously. "But I thought you should know."

"Thanks." Not that I had any flash of insight as to what I should do with this newfound knowledge. That's the problem with parenting. Every time you get one problem—like potty training—taken care of, a new one pops up.

And even though the infant issues like croup and baby-proofing and the first day of kindergarten had scared me to death, it was the older-kid issues that were really frightening. Boys and drugs and fast cars and sex. And because my life wasn't already complicated enough, I had demons to throw into the mix.

Honestly, some days it doesn't pay to get out of bed early.

"I'm sure it's nothing," Laura said. "Anyway, it's not why I called."

I drained my coffee, then stared at her. "Called me? When did you call me?"

"Last night. You didn't get my message?"

Heat settled in my cheeks, and I cleared my throat. "Ah, um, no. We didn't exactly check the machine last night. After the fund-raiser, I mean."

"Oh, really?" Her eyebrow cocked with interest.

I leaned forward, then lowered my voice, as if the neighbors might otherwise hear my confession. "I followed your lead," I said. "Victoria's Secret."

"And I gather it worked?"

"Oh yeah," I said, unable to stop the ridiculous grin. "It worked like a charm. Although considering Stuart's mood, I think Sears lingerie would have been just as effective."

I cleared my throat, my grin fading as I remembered why she'd mentioned the sexy undies plan in the first place. "Have you talked to Paul?" I asked.

"Yeah," she said, almost too casually. "He actually called yesterday morning. And without me even bringing it up, he told me how he had to drive all the way back up here to wine and dine some key client who couldn't make it down to the conference."

"So he was home last night?"

"Um, that would be a negative. He *also* said that he'd planned to come home, but that he'd gotten an emergency call and so he'd had to turn right around and go to L.A." She shrugged. "Sounds plausible, don't you think?"

I decided to sidestep that question. "Do you believe him?"

She closed her eyes and took a long sip of coffee. "Let's just say I'm giving him the benefit of the doubt. For now."

I reached across the table and clasped her hand. "I hope it works out okay."

"It will." She gave me a watery smile. "However it ends up working out, I'm going to be just fine."

She got up quickly and moved to the sink, then stared out the window. After a second, she ran some water, shut it off, then turned back around to face me. "Anyway, none of that has anything to do with why I called you."

"Right," I said. "I'm sorry I didn't check the messages."

"Doesn't matter. But you need to see this." Her voice had turned serious.

"All right," I said, a little alarmed. "Tell me."

She got up and moved toward her phone, then started digging through a pile of papers. "I found it on the Internet last night, and printed it for you. I didn't want to risk not being able to find the site again."

"What?" I said.

"Hang on. I'll get it." She tossed a few manila folders aside, papers scattering along the countertop. "Wait. Here it is."

She plucked one free, then slapped it onto the table in front of me. "I'm sorry, Kate," she said, before I even finished reading it.

I skimmed the article, feeling sicker as I absorbed each

word. The article was dated several months ago. And it described a nasty car accident. The kind where the police expect no survivors.

But in this case, the driver had survived. A teacher at Coronado High School who'd suffered a busted kneecap and a broken tibia. And, miraculously, no other injuries at all.

The teacher's name, was David Long.

Twelve

I lunged for Laura's phone and started dialing, waiting impatiently through the rings until, finally, Allie's voice came over the handset, telling me she couldn't get to the phone right now, but to leave a message.

I redialed. Once again, I got dumped into voice mail.

I slammed Laura's phone down. "Damn it, I'm just going to head to the school."

"I'm coming with you."

"You're not dressed."

"Two minutes," she said, tearing toward her bedroom.

True to her word, about three minutes later we were in her car, heading for the school.

"It's going to be fine," Laura said. "Neither of the girls have any classes with him, right? And Allie's been around him for days and days and nothing's happened. There's no reason anything bad would happen today. Right?" she asked, stopping at an intersection and turning to look at me. "Right?"

"Mysterious keys. Geriatric demons. Demonic janitors. And one completely tossed house. All over the course of a weekend. I don't know. Somehow I don't think we can blame Mercury for being in retrograde."

"Yeah, well, when you put it that way." She gunned the car across the street.

I was clutching the armrest for dear life when my cell phone rang. I snatched it up, answering without checking the caller ID.

"Mom?" she asked, not even waiting for me to say hello. "What's wrong? Is it Timmy?"

"No, no," I said in a rush, my eyes catching Laura's and nodding at her a silent *Allie?* "We're all fine. How are you?"

A long silence, then, "Um, I know you've been acting kinda freaky and all, but I'm supposed to be in English class right now, and I had to beg for a bathroom pass because my stupid phone rang twice, and it kept making my purse vibrate. So, like, aren't you only supposed to call me if it's an emergency?"

"It is," I assured her. "It was urgent that I get in touch with you."

"Right. So . . . ?"

"So?"

"Mom! Why'd you need to get in touch with me?"

To make sure you hadn't been attacked by a demon. But I could hardly say that. "I, um, just needed to check some stuff. You have a second?"

"Mom! I'm standing in the hall missing English. What's going on?"

"Any classes with David Long today?"

A long pause, then, "I don't have *any* classes with Mr. Long. Why?"

"What about surf club? Is it meeting after school?"

"Mo-*ther!*"

"Just answer the question, Allie."

"No. Surf club is not meeting today. Satisfied?" I could picture her standing in the hall, the phone tucked against her ear, her foot tapping.

"So you won't be seeing Mr. Long today?"

"No. God, Mom. I've told you like twelve times. I don't even think he's in school today. Bethany heard he had a substitute. Why? Do you need me to find him or something for you?"

"No. No, no. I just . . . heard some things about unorthodox teaching methods. I want to look into it."

Silence.

"Allie?"

"You're losing it, Mom."

"Maybe," I agreed, signaling for Laura to turn the car around and head back home. "You're home late tonight, right? Cheerleader practice?"

Another pause, then, "Yeah, but I'm skipping it."

That got my attention. "Skipping? Why? Is something wrong?" She hadn't missed a practice since she made the squad. And for the last month—at least until she'd discovered the amazing Troy Myerson—she'd been living and breathing cheerleading.

"I gotta go." And then she clicked off. No "I love you." No "good-bye." Just *click.*

I thought about what Laura had said, and a finger of worry snaked up my spine. Something was up with my daughter. And I didn't have a clue what it was.

Since Monday is my normal Coastal Mists volunteer day, and since I wanted to sneak a peek at Sinclair's things anyway, I went straight to the nursing home from Laura's.

I found Jenny in Delia's room, taking a beating from the older woman at checkers.

"Isn't it awful?" Jenny said. "Poor Mr. Sinclair. I mean, to wake up from a coma, then to turn right around and have a heart attack."

Delia shook her head. "Wasn't right in the head, that one. I talked to him once after he woke up, and all I can say is he just wasn't right in the head."

"How so?" I asked, wondering if Sinclair had blurted the demons' plan out to Delia. "Did he say anything in particular?"

Delia looked up at me, blinked. "Who, dear?"

"Never mind."

I made small talk for a few more minutes, before easing the conversation back around to Sinclair. "I thought I'd sort through his things," I told Jenny. "You know, get everything in order for his family. Is everything still in his room?"

"I think so," she said, as if my request wasn't in any way bizarre. She frowned at the checkerboard, lost in concentration. I took a step backwards toward the door. She looked up. "Except, I think it's already been sorted through."

"Oh." I stopped. I was afraid of that. "So it's in a box in the administrative offices?" I *could* break in there and take a peek. But I didn't really want to.

"Oh, I don't think so. I just meant that his nephew already went through it all. He's *so* dreamy!"

"His nephew?" I asked, wishing it was easier to carry on a linear conversation with Jenny.

"Oh, yeah. And he actually *talked* to me."

"Jenny, what are *you* talking about?"

She blew out a frustrated breath. "He's a celebrity, Mrs. Connor! I didn't even know Mr. Sinclair had any relatives, but then his nephew shows up and he's, like, a total hunk!"

"Got his picture in the newspaper and everything," Delia confirmed. "One hot number, that guy."

"Hot number?" I asked, but Delia was already rummaging on the table for yesterday's paper. She flipped through, found the Life & Arts section, and handed it to me. And right there, on the first page, was a picture of Cool at Saturday's cookout, front and center with the surfers lined up behind him.

Sinclair was Cool's uncle? Maybe. But if not, then what reason did Cool have to snoop through a dead demon's belongings?

Needless to say, my interest was piqued.

I figured I'd gotten as much information as possible from Jenny and Delia, so I left them to their game and went down to Sinclair's old room. As I'd expected, it had been picked clean. I searched diligently, though, just in case. The only contraband I found was a Snickers tucked between the mattress and the box spring. Fattening, maybe, but hardly demonic.

I shut Sinclair's door, perched on the edge of his now-stripped bed, and called Laura's cell phone. No answer. I tapped my fingers on my knee, waiting for her voice mail to pick up, and then when it did, I had to fight back the urge to blurt everything out. I was pretty sure Laura was the only one who ever checked her cell phone messages. But I wasn't positive.

So in what was probably more cloak-and-dagger than necessary, I left her a cryptic message about how I'd learned some interesting stuff about the local celebrity we'd been talking about, and maybe she could see what she could find out about him online.

Seemed pretty clear to me. Hopefully, it would to Laura, too.

I'd just clicked off when my phone rang again. I checked

the display, saw that it was Cutter, and smiled as I answered. "Hey there. What's up?"

"My banking advice work out?"

"Sure did. You're brilliant."

"Win me any brownie points?"

"Five, actually. Ten more and I'll have to officially label you a good guy."

"How many points until you tell me all your secrets?"

"Careful there, Cutter," I said, my voice stern despite my smile. "Keep pushing and you'll start earning demerits, too."

"Damn. And I was so close."

I laughed. "What's up?"

"You're coming in today, right?"

"Sure." I worked out with Cutter most every Monday. We'd developed a nice little routine, and I was honing my atrophied skills. "Why?"

"That new student I mentioned, the one who needs a sparring partner? I told him to come by around four. That okay with you?"

"Too late now if it's not," I said. Cutter had invited the guy to arrive right when my private session was scheduled to begin.

"He's good, Kate. And he'll make you better."

"He's *that* good?"

"No. Not yet. But he's surprising. And he's not me. You're getting lazy."

"The hell I am."

He laughed. "Yeah? Prove it to me this afternoon."

"You're an ass, Cutter."

"I know. But I'm an ass who puts up with you."

So true. I told him I'd be there, then clicked off, looking forward to sparring with this mystery man. A little fresh meat would do me good.

When I'd first started working out again, I'd been surprised how quickly I'd slid back into familiar routines. But there's a satisfaction that comes with knowing you can kick the shit out of someone and, truth be told, I'd missed that.

I'd found replacements, sure. I mean, there's also an intense satisfaction in helping your kid learn to count, in making sure your family has clean clothes (most of the time) and decent meals (if not gourmet). And although I disdain all things housekeeping, there's even a perverse satisfaction that comes from getting the layer of soap scum off the inside of the glass shower doors. (Lemon oil. Works like a charm. Trust me on that one.)

But none of that matches the thrum of satisfaction that races through you when you execute a perfectly timed kick and nail your opponent cold.

I spent the next few hours doing my typical volunteer routine at Coastal Mists. I asked the residents about Sinclair, but no one had much to say other than the usual ghoulish commentary on how horrible his death was, and how unfortunate to have a heart attack and end up with a spike through your eye.

That got me thinking all over again about everything that had happened, and how much I didn't know. By the time I arrived at Cutter's place, I was ready to let off some steam.

"I hope this guy is good," I said, "because I'm in the mood to kick a little butt."

"I'm good," came a familiar voice. I looked up, startled, and sure enough, David Long stepped out from behind the curtain that separated the workout floor from the changing rooms. "Or at least I used to be." He held up his cane. "But I may not be a match for you."

My breath caught in my throat, and I realized I was standing there like a statue, just staring at him.

"Kate?" Cutter frowned at me. "What?"

"Nothing," I said. Except that I wanted to rip David's demonic little throat out right then and there. What kind of a game was he playing? Getting close to my daughter— getting close to me—and then setting himself up to spar?

Damn demons are getting ballsier every day.

"It doesn't look like nothing from here," David said. He took a step toward me. I took a step back. "Are you feeling okay?"

"I feel just fine. How about you? Leg doing okay after the accident?"

"What accident?" Cutter asked, looking between us.

"Mr. Long was in a car accident. Busted his knee. Broke his tibia."

"That was a while ago," David said. "I'm doing just fine now. A slight limp, and I keep the cane handy in case the leg gets tired."

"I didn't realize you two knew each other."

"Oh, yeah," I said. "David and I are old friends. Aren't we?"

"Yeah," he said, his eyes never leaving mine. "We are."

I shivered, goose bumps rising on my arms as I fought the urge to run. I don't know where and I don't know why, but something about his words. Something about his voice . . .

I shook myself, forcing the moment to pass. "I don't think this is such a good idea," I said to Cutter. "I don't like to fight men with canes."

David spun the cane like a staff, then slammed it down on the mat not two centimeters from my foot. "Why not? Figure you'll be at a disadvantage?"

"Give it a rest, you two," Cutter said. His voice was firm, but he shot me one more questioning look. I kept my face stoic and looked pointedly away. "Kate, David is going to spar with the cane."

"I figure so long as I'm stuck with the thing, I may as well make the most of it and turn it into a weapon."

"Your call, Kate. But I think it'll do you good."

"Fine," I said. I'd wanted to practice with staffs anyway, right?

I moved to the middle of the mat. "Bring it on."

David looked me up and down. "You're not going to change?"

"I'll ditch my purse," I said. "But I can fight in jeans. And I don't think anyone who attacks me on a dark street is going to let me run home and change into my Gi."

A shadow crossed his face, and he nodded. "True enough."

I gave him a quick nod, then went to drop my purse off. I watched their reflection in the wall of mirrors, and when David turned away to talk with Cutter, I slipped my bottle of holy water out and tucked it into my pocket. Then I pulled my hair back and clipped it up with my favorite barrette. The kind with the long, sharp metal back piece.

As soon I knew for certain that David was a demon, I was taking him out while his flesh still burned and sizzled. Cutter would see, of course, but there wasn't much I could do about that. David had gotten too close to my little girl for me to let him off the hook. He wasn't walking out of this building alive. And if that meant that today was the day that I finally revealed all to my *sensei,* then so be it.

And, honestly, part of me was looking forward to making that revelation.

I stood up, rolling my shoulders and neck, then crossed the mat to where David stood, his cane tucked under his arm.

"I promise to be gentle," he said, with the tiniest of grins.

"I don't," I countered.

And then, before Cutter even signaled for us to start, David lashed out, leading with the cane, and knocked my knees right out from under me. So much for gentle.

Cutter yelled a protest, but I rolled to my side and snapped to my feet, keeping my eyes on David while I gestured to

Cutter that it was okay. We sparred lightly for a while, simple jabs and thrusts designed to test each other's reflexes.

Despite myself, I felt a growing respect for the man, even if he was a demon. He knew what he was doing. His moves were practiced and clean, and his reflexes were every bit as good as I wanted mine to be. The limp didn't slow him down at all, and the cane that might otherwise be a liability had been turned to an asset.

If the man hadn't been a demon, I really might like him.

No, the trouble was I *did* like him. And I hated what I'd learned.

He sensed that my mind was wandering and kicked into high gear, using the cane to jab and thrust in a pattern that had my feet dancing defensively even as I looked for a way to take the offense.

I found it in the pattern of his thrusts and instead of leaping to the left to avoid a jab, I slid right and caught the cane against my arm, then drew my other hand over to close around the shaft. I whipped it up and out, effectively disarming him. And surprising him, too. That much I could tell from the expression on his face.

"Not bad," he said. "But now that the fun part's over, let's see about getting down to business."

I tensed, my body at the ready, and he held his hand out in a come-on gesture made famous by Laurence Fishburne in the *Matrix* movies. Then he tapped his nose and pointed a finger at me. I tensed. I'd seen only one person ever make that motion. Just one in all the years I'd been fighting.

Eric.

My breath hitched in my throat, I wavered, and David Long laid me flat. He'd been waiting for the weakness, had known it would come. And for that, right then, I hated him.

He was on me, holding me down, his hands on my wrists and his knee pressed against my waist. "Do you concede?"

The room turned red with my fury, and my fist tightened around the cane I still held in my hand. Concede? *Concede?* To some goddamn demon who'd stolen my husband's move? Used it against me to throw me off? Played me for a fool?

No, I didn't think I was conceding, and in an entirely illegal move, I slammed my head up, cracking my forehead against his. Pain shot through me, the red haze over the world shifting to a blurry gray that I had to fight against.

I was motivated, though, and as David reeled back in surprise, I fought through the pain and brought my knee up against my chest, then shot my heel out and into his pelvis.

Behind us, I could hear Cutter shouting my name. I was even vaguely aware that he was running toward me. I didn't care. As Cutter's fingers grazed my shoulders, I leaped forward, knocking David backwards until I was straddling him, the cane tight against his throat, restricting his airway. He struggled, his skin taking on a bluish pallor, as Cutter yelled and pulled, trying to get me to let go.

I did, but only with one hand. And with my free hand I reached into my back pocket for the bottle of holy water. I stuck it in my mouth and screwed the lid off with my teeth.

David watched me, his eyes wide and bloodshot.

"Goddamn it, Kate!" Cutter howled. He'd given up on trying to move me, and now he dove to the mat and wrestled the cane out of my hand.

I didn't even try to fight him, because I had the bottle open now. And I dumped the contents on David's face, then held his arms down, anticipating the fresh wave of strength that would come with the pain.

Nothing happened.

I waited, tense, my hands tight around his triceps.

Still nothing. Or, rather, nothing except David sputtering and coughing.

I couldn't quite believe it. And yet, oddly, it wasn't

clue who the Tartarus demons were talking to. Or, more important, why.

All in all, I didn't like the score, and I had a feeling time was running out.

I forgot all about that, though, when I saw Timmy. He looked up, beamed, then raced into my arms. I swung him around, generating peals of laughter from my little man.

"What did you do in school today?" I asked him as I strapped him into his car seat.

Silence.

I gave him Boo Bear and tried again. "Nothing, Momma," he said, then shoved his thumb into his mouth.

I shut his door and moved around to the driver's side. Once we were back on the road, I tried again. "Come on, sport. I know you must have done *something*. Tell me about your day."

In fact, I knew they'd played with shaving cream, because that's what the little note in his cubby had announced. Timmy, however, guarded that fact like it was a state secret.

"Can't tell you, Momma. I'm sucking my thumb."

"Right," I said. "That makes sense. Maybe you could take your thumb out long enough to clue in your mom?"

More silence, except for the mild slurping sounds associated with rampant suckage.

"Timmy? Come on. I really want to know."

I adjusted my rearview mirror so I could see him. The thumb came out of his mouth, and his eyes got wide.

"Momma," he said, his exasperated voice a little too familiar. "I *told* you. Is a secret!"

"Right. A secret." What the hell? I smiled to myself and decided not to press. After all, I knew all about secrets.

I was still grinning when I opened the door that leads from our garage into the kitchen. Timmy barreled inside, yelling about *Blue's Clues* at the top of his lungs. I followed

embarrassment but relief that washed thr
Long wasn't a demon. I could like him witho
an idiot. More important, I didn't have to kill

Cutter crouched beside us, the cane tight in
"Dammit, Kate," he whispered. "You have got t
chill out."

He stood up, then held out a hand for me. I
sheepishly, managing to fire off "sorry," toward David
rolled over onto his side and continued coughing as soc
I was off of him.

I waited for him to catch his breath, then offered my ow
hand. He looked at me dubiously, then took it, and I tugged
him to his feet.

"Um, sorry about that."

"I don't suppose you're going to explain?"

"That's just Kate's way of getting to know you," Cutter
said wryly. "Good luck getting her to say anything more."

I just smiled and tried to look mysterious. "Forgive me?"

"If I say yes, are you going to douse me again?"

"I think you've been doused enough." At least, I hoped
he had. I had to reluctantly admit that I'd been duped by
the holy water test before. Still, I wanted to believe the results. David Long just didn't seem demonic. Strange,
maybe. And even a bit mysterious. But demonic? I didn't
think so.

Especially considering how baffled he looked, I figured I
could cut David some slack. I'd trust him. For now. But I'd
also keep an eye on him.

I spent the drive from Cutter's place to Timmy's day care
thinking about demons and David and how I still had more
questions than answers. David might not be a demon, but
something was definitely up with that man. And I still had

him in, my smile fading as I saw my daughter sitting at the kitchen table, her eyes puffy, her cheeks flushed, and tearstains marring the thin layer of powder she'd dusted onto her cheeks.

"Allie? Sweetheart, what is it?"

I dropped my purse and went to her side, trying to put my arms around her. She twisted away, avoiding my touch. Since I can take a hint, I pulled out one of the other chairs and sat facing her, my heart pounding in my chest as I waited for my daughter to tell me what was wrong.

"Allie? Is this about a boy?" I didn't believe that it was, not really. But I hoped. Oh, how I hoped that it wasn't my secret that had brought tears to her eyes.

"A boy," she said, then shook her head. "No, I guess it's not really about a boy." She looked up at me, and from my new, closer vantage point, I could see just how bloodshot her eyes were.

"Sweetheart . . ."

She cut me off, waving a piece of paper. "It's from Daddy."

I froze, the blood in my veins turning to ice. "From Stuart?" I asked, pushing my words out as if through molasses.

But I knew the answer. Even before she spoke. The letter was from Eric. And somehow, someway, our daughter had found it.

Thirteen

"Are you going to tell me what's going on?" Allie said.

I shook my head slowly, too shell-shocked to say anything at all.

"Mom? I've got a right to know. If there's something weird going on about my dad, you have to tell me."

"That's a letter from Eric?" I asked, my eyes never leaving the paper."

She pressed her lips tight together, her eyes blinking fast. "Yeah."

I held out my hand, and she passed me the note. This is what I read:

My darling Katie,

If you're reading this, I presume you've also found the safe-deposit box. (If you haven't—if you simply stumbled across this letter—I need you to go to County Mutual. Tell them you've lost your key and give them your name. They should take care of you.) My other letter explains the why of it. Or, at least, it gives you a hint as to the why of it. And I don't want to say anymore here. I need you to find the retired teacher, our friend from our days in Los Angeles. Do you remember him? Find him, Kate. He will know where to send you next.

I love you and Allie more than anything. Keep that truth safe in your heart.

Eternally yours,
Eric

I finished reading the note and set it on the table, ignoring the tears that ran down my cheeks. "Where did you find this?"

Allie shook her head. "Nuh-uh. No way, nohow. Not until you tell me what's going on."

"Alison Elizabeth Crowe, don't you dare play games with me. I'm really not in the mood."

"Yeah? Well, I'm not in the mood, either," she shouted. She stood, snatched up the letter, then waved it in front of my face. "This is my father writing this! I have a right to know what's going on!"

I knew I should step in, remind her that I was the mother and she had no right talking to me like that. But part of me said that she *did* have a right. That this was about Eric. And that she deserved to know the truth. If not all, then some.

From the living room, Timmy started wailing.

"Coming!" Allie tossed the letter at me, then stalked out of the room. I just sat there, numb, taking deep breaths as I tried to regain my equilibrium.

Finally, I pushed back from the table, then went into the living room where Allie was rocking Timmy on her lap. She looked up at me, then immediately back down at the floor. "I scared him," she said. "I shouldn't have yelled."

"He'll be okay." I sat down on the couch and put my arm around them both. I don't know what I'd planned to say, but when I opened my mouth, it all seemed so simple. "I don't know why yet," I said. "But I think your father was murdered."

She stiffened in my arms, but stayed silent.

"I found a note the other day. That key? It led to a safe-deposit box. I didn't remember Eric and I getting it, but we must have, because my name was on the box, too. And all that was inside was a letter to me."

"Why didn't you tell the police?"

"And say what? The note was cryptic. A lot of nonsense, really." I didn't say that the police would probably be useless. Eric had been a Demon Hunter. Once upon a time, I'd believed his death was unrelated to his work. I didn't believe that anymore.

"The note didn't tell the whole story," I added. "And I didn't know where to go next."

"Yeah," she said. "I know."

I looked at her, comprehension dawning. "You've seen the first letter." It wasn't a question. I was absolutely positive I knew what the answer would be.

She nodded guiltily. Timmy took that opportunity to squirm free. Allie scooted to the far side of the couch, then hugged a pillow close to her chest, looking at me over her intertwined arms. "When I got into your purse at McDonald's," she said. "I didn't mean to snoop, honest I didn't. But I could see some of it, and I recognized Daddy's handwriting, and I—"

She squeezed her mouth shut, blinking furiously.

"It's okay, sweetie. I understand." I don't believe in all that subconscious psychobabble BS, but I *had* left the note in my purse. And I had let my daughter rummage her little heart out. If anyone was taking the blame here, it was me. Not Allie.

"But how'd you find that note?" I asked, pointing toward the kitchen, where I'd left the new note on the table.

"Daddy told you where it was," she said, in the same tone she might use to tell someone they were an idiot.

"Apparently Daddy told *you* where it was. I had no clue."

"'The best of us'," she said. "That's what Daddy used to call me, remember?"

I did remember, and as soon as she said it, the answer was obvious. "Your baby box." I'm not much of a scrapbooker, but I do keep trinkets in an old hatbox. Baptismal souvenirs (the church program, the baptismal candle), birth stuff like the now-dried pink mum the hospital had hung on the door of my private room. Her first pacifier. The hospital baby blanket I'd smuggled out in her carrier. Stuff.

And not stuff I ever go back to look at, either. It's just there, in the closet, ready to be pulled out and examined when the time was right. Like when Allie has a baby of her own.

"It was wrapped around the candle," she said. "And the candle and the note were both in the candle box."

"I'm impressed," I said.

"So when are we going to Los Angeles?"

"Excuse me?"

"The teacher guy," she said, tapping the letter. "You're going to go talk to him, right?"

"Yes," I said. "*I* am." I hadn't seen Father Oliver for years, but I was certain that's who Eric meant.

"I'm coming with you," she said.

"Allie, in case you've forgotten, you've got this thing called school tomorrow."

"I'm totally ahead in all my classes."

I didn't even bother to hide my disbelief. "*All* your classes?"

She sucked in her cheeks, then blew out some air. "Well,

not life sciences, but, I mean, like why do I care about photosynthesis anyway?"

Since I wasn't entirely sure what photosynthesis was, much less why she should care, I decided to avoid the question entirely. "You can't skip school on a whim, Allie. And you can't not study something just because it doesn't involve boys or cheerleading."

"I like algebra," she said.

I gaped at her. "Are you sure you're my daughter? Because I'm thinking you're a pod person."

She made a face. "Don't even try to change the subject. I'm coming with you tomorrow, and that's all there is to it."

She crossed her arms over her chest and leaned back in her chair, looking so much like me at that moment, that it was eerie.

"I really don't think it's such a good idea." What if Father Oliver blurted something out about our demon-hunting days?

Her body seemed to sag, and I was certain I'd won the battle. "It's just . . . It's just that I'm starting to forget him."

My heart started to break around the edges. "Daddy?"

She nodded, then wiped the back of her hand under her nose. She looked small and young and lost, and I couldn't bear the thought that she'd ever, *ever,* forget her father.

"I don't want to, but I was only nine, you know? And I look at pictures and it all comes back, but I'm really afraid, Mom. What if I look at a picture someday and that's all it is?"

"Oh, baby." I was crying now, too, and I opened my arms wide, hugging her close. Timmy lost interest in his television show and came over to join us, crawling up on the couch between us and snuggling.

I still wanted to say no. So help me, I wanted to scream no at the top of my lungs. But in my heart, I knew she had to come with me. If Allie found out the truth tomorrow, I'd deal with it then.

After all, I thought, isn't that what this whole parenting thing is all about?

Because Allie was anxious, she woke me up at the crack of dawn—even before Stuart had rolled out of bed.

He sat up, blinking in the dark. "Wha—?"

I kissed his forehead. "Go back to sleep," I whispered. "You still have twelve minutes before your alarm goes off."

By the time I was showered and changed, Allie was waiting at the kitchen table, Timmy's lunch already packed, and the boy himself eating dry Honey Nut Cheerios and drinking milk out of a sippy cup. "Can we go?"

I melted into one of the chairs. "Administer at least one dose of coffee intravenously. Then we'll talk."

"Mo-om."

"Tim's day care doesn't even open for another fifteen minutes. I have time for one cup."

"Fine. But I'm putting it in Stuart's commuter cup. If you're not done with it in five minutes, you can take it with us."

Exactly five minutes later, we were in the van, the Starbucks cup tucked into the console beside me. We got to KidSpace with three minutes to spare, and ended up waiting in the parking lot for Nadine to unlock the doors.

"Why can't you do this on a school day?" I asked, as soon as we were underway. "Do you have any idea what a hassle it is getting you up in the morning?"

She just rolled her eyes, then kicked her feet up onto the dashboard. "Can we drive through McDonald's for a sausage biscuit?"

"What about your no-fat, wholly organic, must-be-a-paragon-of-food virtue diet?"

"Road trip, Mom. I can bend the rules for a road trip."

"Right." And since a sausage biscuit sounded pretty tasty right then, I pulled into the first McDonald's I saw. Why not? With this latest insurgence of demon activity, I was burning an insane number of calories. And besides, we had a long drive ahead of us. More than an hour without traffic, but since Los Angeles's morning rush hour covers a four-hour window, I expected that we'd be moving at the speed of lethargic snails once we hit the outskirts.

Since I didn't want to spend the entire day in the van, we avoided the Coast Highway, picking instead the significantly less scenic 101. Allie, naturally, dozed off about ten minutes after she finished her biscuit, leaving me to my mishmash of thoughts and questions. All familiar territory. What were the demons up to? Which demon was their master? What secrets would Father Oliver reveal to me? And the biggest question of all: Why had Eric kept secrets from me?

Around and around the questions spun until I was so sick of my own thoughts that I clicked on the radio. A CD was in, so the first thing I heard was "Hot Potato." I actually listened through the entire song and the beginning of "Shaky Shaky" before I remembered that when Timmy wasn't in the van, I wasn't required to listen to his *Wiggles* CDs. I switched over to the radio and tuned to an oldies channel, letting Wham!'s "Wake Me Up Before You Go-Go" fill the car.

The song did the trick, too. Beside me, Allie stirred, then reached for her Diet Coke and downed about half of it in one swallow. "This music is lame," she said offhandedly. Then she flipped down her visor, checked her reflection in the mirror, and touched up her lips.

"You're gorgeous," I said, ignoring the music critique.

"I'd be better with eyeshadow," she said, hopefully.

"Nice try," I said. "You don't need to wear eyeshadow to school. It's not a fashion event."

"I'm not at school right now," she pointed out, quite reasonably I thought. Really, the girl should join the debate team.

"School hours," I said. "No eyeshadow during school hours."

"How about on dates?"

"Sure," I said. "As soon as Stuart and I say you can go on dates, you can wear eyeshadow."

"Sixteen, right?"

I checked my rearview mirror, changed lanes, then nodded. "Right"

"So, if it's a double date, I should be able to go when I'm fifteen. I mean, that makes sense, right?"

"I can't even begin to describe how much that does *not* make sense."

"Mom! Of course it does. You're just not paying attention."

"Allie. Sixteen. That's the rule."

She flopped back in her seat. "Whatever."

"And take your feet off the dash."

She dropped them to the floorboards with a huff that represented the start of a snit that lasted another fifteen miles. Then she yawned, stretched, and twisted around to face me. "So how about you talk to Stuart? If he thinks I can double-date, will you at least think about it?"

"Allie . . ."

"Come on. Please? I'm responsible. Aren't I?"

I stifled the urge to close my eyes since we were currently doing eighty, but I did let my shoulders slump. "Yes, you're responsible. I'm very proud of my responsible, manipulative daughter."

"So you'll talk with Stuart?"

"Yes, I'll talk it over with Stuart."

She settled back in the seat, a grin slathered across her face. After a bit, the wattage decreased a bit. "You *can* talk to him, right? I mean, he's not around a whole lot these days."

"Of course I can talk to him. What do you think? We leave each other Post-it notes in the bathroom?"

"I dunno. Mindy says her mom and dad hardly talk at all anymore. She thinks they're going to get a divorce."

I turned sharply. "She does?"

"Yeah." A pause, then, "Are you and Stuart okay?"

"Oh, baby. Yeah. Stuart and I are great. He's working his tail off, and, yes, I get annoyed when he's not home as much, but there's nothing wrong with our marriage."

"You're sure?"

I reached over and squeezed her knee. "Positive." I wasn't positive, though. Not really. Things had changed in the last few months, shifting slightly off their axis. I didn't see a divorce on the horizon, but I also wasn't taking our marriage for granted anymore. Probably a good thing when you thought about it, but it still made me a little sad.

"How about Daddy?"

"What about him?"

"I dunno. I guess, I mean, well, you always tell me how much you loved him."

"I did love him. I do still." I glanced sideways at her, trying to think like a fourteen-year-old and figure out where she was going with this.

"Well, yeah, but he kept all this stuff secret. Doesn't that make you mad?"

"No, of course not." I spoke automatically, coddling my kid with lies. The truth was harder, because I did hurt. The glass through which I'd looked back at my first marriage was losing its rosy tint. But this was my daughter, not my best friend, and there are some things you don't share with your kid.

Her eyebrows lifted a good two inches. "You're really not mad?" she asked, in the same voice she'd use if I told her I'd taken a job as a professional chef. "Daddy has some secret so huge that he's leaving clues all over the state, and you're not even a teensy bit annoyed?"

Smart girl, my daughter.

"Your daddy loved secrets," I said, thinking of the way he and I had gotten unofficially married well before our official ceremony. And no one but the two of us had known. "You two even shared a few secrets from me, right?"

Her cheeks colored. "Well, yeah. Sure. But that's not the same. Those aren't as much like a secret because two people know. It's like a thing you share. But the key and the notes and all that. I dunno. It's just different."

Yeah. Definitely a smart girl.

"It really doesn't make you mad?" she asked, pressing her point.

"I'm surprised," I said. "And I hate the idea that there may have been something I could have helped him with before he died. But this doesn't change anything about the way I feel about your dad. I loved him and he loved me. But everyone has secrets, Allie. Everyone."

I knew that better than anyone. I'd just never expected Eric to keep his secrets from me.

"I guess." She twirled a strand of hair around her finger, apparently in deep thought about my brilliant words of wisdom. (I was actually pretty proud of myself. As parenting moments went, I thought I was handling myself pretty well.) "Sort of like you and Stuart, right?"

"How so?"

"Well, I mean, does he know about the note from Daddy?"

I tightened my grip on the steering wheel. "No," I said, trying for casual. "He doesn't."

"Right," she said. "Secrets." She started picking at her nail polish, peeling it off in strips. "So how old were you and Daddy when you met?"

I almost commented on the change of subject, but since I was more than happy to shift conversational gears, I didn't. "Thirteen."

"Did you know right away? That he was the one, I mean?"

"Well, he was a much more sophisticated fourteen, and so I figured there was no way he'd be interested in a kid like me."

"But he was."

"Not at first, actually." I smiled, remembering how Eric had protested when he'd been assigned to work with me on my very crappy knife-throwing skills.

"But he came around, right. I mean, by the time *you* were fourteen, you knew you wanted to be with him always, right?"

"Yeah," I said. "He came around."

She shrugged, and when her cheeks flushed pink, I understood.

"Your father and I were unique. Our whole situation, in Rome, in the orphanage. We bonded more than we might have, you know?" I stopped there, because Allie really didn't know any more details. "We were lucky to have found each other so early, but we missed out on a lot, too. Most people, they go out. They date. They have fun and see a lot of different men before they finally meet the guy who sweeps them off their feet. It doesn't have to be the guy you fall for when you're fourteen."

She slunk down in her seat and looked out the window. "God, Mom. I know. I'm just, you know, making conversation."

I let that one sit for a while as we maneuvered down the 101 Freeway, through Reseda, Encino, Sherman Oaks. I concentrated on the signs until I found the exit for Pasadena. Once I'd merged onto the 134 and picked a lane, I relaxed a little.

"So tell me about him," I said.

"Who?" Allie asked, looking a bit like a bunny confronted by the big, bad wolf.

"Santa Claus," I said. "Who do you think?"

"Oh, Troy?" she said, just a little too casually. "We're just friends."

"Uh-huh."

"I mean, I like him and all. And, well, I think he likes me. But . . ."

"But your pain-in-the-butt mom won't let you date?"

"I didn't say that."

"No, and I love you for it." I considered only for a moment before diving in. "How about you invite him over for dinner Friday. Give Stuart and me the chance to meet him."

"Really? And you won't, like, embarrass me? I mean, you're not going to pull out the baby pictures or anything, are you?"

"Pictures? No way. I figure the videotapes are much more effective."

"Ha-ha. My mom is such a comedian."

"I'm not saying you can do a car date—or even a double date—but once we meet him, you can probably go out as a group."

"I do that already."

"A group *date*. And when do you go out?"

She lifted a shoulder. "I dunno. Surf club, I guess. He's always at the meetings, and I go watch him practice all the time."

"All the time?" I repeated.

"Well, it's not like it's just me. I mean, the other guys on the team are there, too. And sometimes Mindy comes. And JoAnn and Bethany almost always come, too."

"Wonderful," I said. "A whole gaggle of teenagers in bathing suits on the beach without adult supervision."

"Honestly, Mom. It's not like we're living in the olden days."

"I know. I'm just so pathetically old fashioned."

She rolled her eyes. "Anyway, we do have a chaperone. Cool's been to almost every practice."

That caught my attention. "He has?"

"Sure. I mean, he's already brilliant on a board, but he's got to practice. And he's like the coach. He's shown the guys all sorts of cool tricks. Troy's tons better now."

"Mmm." The idea of my daughter in such close proximity to Cool gave me the willies, and it wasn't just his bizarre name that had me worried. Anyone who hung out at Coastal Mists—who'd searched the room of a resident-turned-demon—was suspicious in my book. I had nothing more concrete to base my fears on. Not yet, anyway. But where my kids are concerned, a single bad vibe was one too many.

I drummed my fingers on the steering wheel, trying to decide what to do. I wanted to forbid her to go anywhere near Cool, but if I did that, I'd have to fabricate a reason. And nothing rational sprang to mind.

"Is Cool the only adult at these things?"

"Mr. Long's always there, too."

"Right," I said, immediately relieved. "He's the faculty adviser, isn't he? So of course he'd be there. Okay. That's good."

Allie was turned in her seat, looking at me as if I'd lost my mind.

"What?"

"We're not babies, Mom. And we're not rolling around in the sand making out like porn stars, either."

"Thanks," I said. "I feel a lot better now."

"I just mean that you raised me right, okay? So chill out."

I couldn't help my grin. "Right. Chilling."

"Jeez," she muttered, but loud enough for me to hear.

She was right, too. I'd done a good job with this kid. My only regret, in fact, was that I hadn't started teaching her how to kick a little butt from the time she was age three. But still, better late than never. And at least David Long was around to keep an eye on things.

Considering that only a day before I'd thought him a prime candidate for demonic infestation, my sudden relief that he was there to watch over my kid seemed a little abrupt. But the reaction was honest. For better or for worse, and despite all my lingering questions, at the end of the day, I did trust David Long. And until I could figure out a way to keep Allie away from Cool, I thanked God that David was there to be a buffer between them.

"Here!" Allie yelled. "Turn here!"

She waved the map in one hand and gestured wildly with the other.

I slammed on the brakes, but missed the turn. "Okay, okay. No problem." I did an illegal U-turn, braced myself for the sound of police sirens, heard none, and then gunned it onto the street.

We were in Pasadena now, following the directions to St. Ignatius Catholic Church that Allie had downloaded from MapQuest. Father Oliver had been the pastor there until his retirement. After that, he'd continued working in secret as an *alimentatore.* He'd never been my mentor, nor Eric's, but we'd both known and respected him.

After Eric and I had retired from *Forza,* we'd moved from our base in Italy to Los Angeles. Father Oliver had been our only connection to our old life, and even though we'd left *Forza* willingly and with no plans to look back, sometimes we wanted to be around people who understood. Who shared our knowledge of the bad things in the world. Not because they'd seen a movie or read a book, but because they'd lived it, too.

Father Oliver filled that role. And although we'd never joined his parish, we'd used to meet him for hot dogs at Tail O' the Pup in West Hollywood. We'd sit and watch the traffic go by and talk about completely mundane things. Never about demons. Never about hunting. But somehow, just the act of being normal around someone who *knew* made the whole world seem safer, too.

We'd lost touch with Father Oliver after we'd moved to San Diablo. Or, at least, I had. I'd always assumed that Eric had, too. That he'd lost himself in suburbia with me, relishing our new life in our safe new town.

Now, though, I had to wonder. Had Eric kept in touch with Father Oliver all those years? And if he had, then why?

Allie gestured frantically toward a nearly hidden driveway, and I turned in. The church loomed in front of us, a mission-style structure that had been built into the hills hundreds of years ago. The parking lot was mostly empty, which wasn't unusual for a weekday. I drove the length of the driveway, squinting at the signs as I tried to find the residence hall.

Like so many parishes, St. Ignatius provided housing for retired priests. I didn't see a sign, though, and I stifled a frown. I'd been so certain he lived on site. If he had an apartment somewhere with an unlisted phone number, I was going to have a difficult time tracking him down.

Inside the office, a twentysomething brunette greeted us with a perky smile.

"Hi," I said. "I'm an old friend of Father Oliver, and since I happen to be in town, I thought I'd drop in and visit. But I can't seem to find the residence halls."

"Oh, wow. Like, the residence halls are just back there." She pointed vaguely out the window. I started to thank her, but she wasn't finished. "The thing is, though . . . I mean, Father Oliver passed away last year."

"Oh, *man.*" That from Allie, though I totally agreed with the sentiment.

"I'm sorry to hear that. Was he ill?" Father Oliver wasn't young, but he'd been in good health the last time I'd seen him.

"Cancer," the girl said. "We all really liked him. I miss him a lot. He used to eat with me on my lunch break sometimes."

"He didn't happen to leave anything, did he?" It was a longshot, but I had to ask. Father Oliver was my last link to Eric. If he was truly a dead end, then I really had failed my husband.

"Like what?" she asked.

"I'm not sure. Letters, maybe? Or specific bequests, like in a will."

"I think he left everything to the church."

"His stuff, sure. But maybe he left notes for his friends. It sounds like he knew he was dying, and I just—" My throat hitched, suddenly clogged with unexpected tears.

"We're wondering if he left my mom a note," Allie said. "Or maybe one for my dad?"

"I don't think so," the girl said. She shot me a worried glance, as if she was afraid I was going to melt into a pile of blubber right then. "But let me ask Father Carey. What are your names?"

"Crowe," Allie said, seeming decades older than fourteen. "Katherine or Eric Crowe."

The girl got up, then slipped silently through a door at the back of the room.

"You okay, Mom?"

I sniffed, loud and wet. "Fine." I drew in a shaky breath. "When exactly did you grow up?"

"If I'm so grown up, why can't I go out on dates?"

"And smart, too," I said. "I've got one heck of a clever, grown-up child."

"No fair going with the flattery thing," she said.

"No fair being so smart."

"I'm not going to win this one, am I?"

"Give it a couple of years. I'll give in eventually."

"Thanks," she said. "Thanks a lot."

I was spared having to come up with a snappy retort by the receptionist's return, this time on the heels of a silver-haired priest with stooped posture and a friendly smile.

"Good morning," he said. "I'm Father Carey. You must be Katherine Crowe?"

I nodded. "Connor now," I said.

"Yes, of course. I heard about your husband's death. My deepest condolences."

"Thank you," I said automatically, even as the import of his words struck me. "You heard about Eric's death? From Father Oliver?" I supposed that made sense. After all, I'd notified everyone I knew in *Forza*; a few had even made it to the funeral. But Father Carey wasn't a member of that group, and I was surprised Father Oliver would mention Eric's death to him.

But then Father Carey continued, surprising me even more. "I'd so enjoyed chatting with him during his visits with Father Oliver. Your husband was a very charming man."

"Yes," I managed, hoping I didn't sound as startled as I felt. "He was the best."

Allie was looking between me and Father Carey, her face

pinched with thought. "So, um, did Father Oliver leave anything for my mom?"

"Gretchen mentioned that you were inquiring as to that. No, I'm afraid that Father Oliver left no specific bequests. I went through his belongings personally, and I can assure you that I saw no papers or correspondence that would seem to be of any interest to you."

"Oh," I said. "Well, um, thank you."

I started to turn away, then stopped. "One more thing. How often did Eric come see Father Oliver?"

Father Carey's gray eyes seemed to soften. I didn't want his pity. Didn't want anyone—least of all Allie—to know that Eric had kept these visits from me. But I had to know.

"I would say about once a month," he said. "At times more frequently. But often, significantly more time would pass."

"I see. And do you know what they discussed?"

"That would be confidential, between a penitent and his confessor, and I would feel bound not to share that with you even now that Eric has passed."

"But—"

He held up a hand. "It's a moot point, my child. I enjoyed Eric's company, but I had no conversations with him that I would consider substantial. And Father Oliver never revealed to me the nature of their visits."

I nodded, strangely satisfied. So it was over. I'd followed the only lead that Eric had left me, but I'd followed it years too late.

I'd failed. And my husband's murder would remain unavenged.

After hearing Father Carey's news, I didn't want to do anything except head home, sleep, and feel sorry for myself. Since I had Allie with me, that wasn't an option. And, honestly,

there's nothing more mood-altering than a shopping extrav-
aganza with a fourteen-year-old. If you're in a good mood, it
will surely make you surly and irritable. But if you start out
in that mood already, well, your spirits have nowhere to go
but up.

We bought decorations for the house, electronic gadgets from Brookstone and Sharper Image for Stuart, and a
house full of toys, videos, and books for Timmy. Eddie was
harder to shop for, but we ended up going with an engraved pocketknife that Allie described as totally bad ass.
I couldn't really argue. Allie admirably restrained herself
from begging for new things. She did, however, compile a
detailed list.

By the time we left the Beverly Center, my attitude had
been through a serious adjustment. (Our credit cards had
been put through the wringer, too, but I had thirty days before the bills came in, and I'd work up the courage to break
the bad fiscal news to Stuart sometime before then.)

During the ride back, Allie entertained me with stories
about Troy, cheerleading practice, and goofy things her
teachers did. "Mr. Creasley pats everyone on the head when
we're supposed to be reading," she said. "It's totally freaky."

"Creasley? Isn't he your English teacher? The bald one
with the sprayed-on comb-over?"

Allie giggled. "That's him. So, like, maybe the head pat
is Freudian?"

We analyzed that for a while, then Allie switched gears
and was off and running analyzing all her favorite television
shows. I listened, commented, argued, and generally had a
great time chatting with my kid. I was also grateful. Because the truth is, Allie rarely talks on trips. She's a car
sleeper. But this trip, I had no doubt she'd been trying to
distract me. Did I raise a great kid, or what?

As we pulled into our driveway, Allie swiveled in her

seat, staring at the assortment of bags. "Stuart's going to have a cow."

"It's Christmas," I said. "Ho, ho, ho."

"Maybe we should tell Stuart not to come into the garage because his present is out here. And then we can smuggle all these bags in when he's not looking."

"Brilliant," I said. And then my brainiac child and I headed into the house, to dupe my husband about both the reason for our trip to Los Angeles and the amount of money we spent.

As soon as we walked through the door, Allie made a beeline for the answering machine. I kept going, moving through the house to find Stuart. His car was in the garage, so I knew he had to be around somewhere. I found him, eventually, in Timmy's room.

"Hey," I whispered, coming up and putting an arm around him. In front of us, my little boy was sound asleep, Boo Bear clutched in his arms. "How'd you get him to sleep so early?" It wasn't even seven. Lately, it was like pulling teeth to get the kiddo down before nine.

"Sick," Stuart said. "Poor kid. The medicine knocked him right out."

"Sick?" I bent over and felt his forehead. Cool enough. "What happened? Why didn't you call?"

"I did," he said. He leaned over and tucked Timmy's blanket around his shoulders, then gestured for me to follow him into the hall. "I called your cell twice," he said after he'd pulled the door shut. "Apparently so did the day care. I picked him up about one."

Great gobs of guilt washed over me. "Oh, Stuart. Oh, my poor baby."

"Don't worry," Stuart said. "I'm fine."

I made a face. "Not you. What's wrong? Did you take him to the doctor?"

"Ear infection, and yes."

"I should have been here." I shifted my shoulders, adjusting the mommy guilt to a more comfortable carrying position.

"Why? I managed."

"Yes, but—"

I cut myself off. Stuart had managed. And considering his absences lately, he was due for a serious dose of daddy duty. Which did nothing to ease the mommy guilt, and I took a little comfort in the fact that it would be mommy on deck tomorrow. The day care's policy was strict—fever free for twenty-four hours before they could return. So school tomorrow was out for Timmy. I imagined he'd be able to return on Thursday. Timmy had yet to have an ear infection that didn't respond immediately to a nice big dose of nasty pink medicine.

I leaned past Stuart and pushed the door open one more time. I could hear him breathing—my two-year-old snores—but other than that, he was sleeping like an angel. I pulled the door closed, making sure it clicked quietly into place, then followed Stuart down the stairs to the living room.

We found Allie there, a phone pressed to her ear. She saw us come in and told whoever it was that she'd call them right back. Mindy, I presumed.

"Oh my God, Mom! Remember Mr. Creasley? The one I was just telling you about?"

"The English teacher? The head-patter?"

"Yes! He almost *died.* Can you believe it?"

"I—" I bit back my automatic response that yes, I could most definitely believe it. "What happened?"

"He went boating early this morning or something. I guess he goes out a lot before school to fish or whatever. Anyway, they found him around lunchtime half-drowned. Isn't that the freakiest thing?"

I agreed that it was incredibly freaky.

"I'm so glad he's okay. Troy thinks Creasley's a jerk, but I like him okay. I wish he'd stop with the head patting, but otherwise he's all right."

But I barely heard her. I was too busy wondering what the healthy Mr. Creasley would be up to this evening. And if there was any way I could intercept him. New demons are at their most vulnerable within the first twenty-four hours, but Hunters aren't usually in tune with the new demon roll call.

This was an opportunity I didn't want to pass up.

This was also incredibly inconvenient. On a normal night, Stuart would be plugging away at the office and I could finagle my schedule to give me some time to prowl the town. But now that I wanted to escape, Stuart got it into his head that tonight would be a good night to rekindle our marriage.

I gave him an A-plus for the thought, and a D-minus for the timing.

"So, um, where's Eddie?" We'd had dinner, Allie had retreated to her room, and now we were snuggled on the couch, both with glasses of red wine. Stuart's thoughts were obviously amorous. Mine were tuned to distraction.

"Left about thirty minutes after I got home with Timmy. Said sick kids aren't his thing, but I think it was mostly me."

I didn't bother to correct him. Eddie really didn't know what to make of Stuart. And vice versa. "Where'd he go? It's almost ten."

"The Paramount's showing Christmas classics all day every day until New Year's Day. He said he was going there."

Somehow I couldn't picture Eddie getting too worried about whether Mr. Potter was going to take over Bedford Falls. I hoped Father Ben had come back and the two of them were holed up somewhere, making tons of progress. My fingers itched to pick up the phone and call the cathedral, but I stifled the urge. Ben would call when he knew something. And Eddie would come home in his own sweet time.

I had a hard time worrying about that for too long because Stuart shifted on the couch and started to massage my shoulders. Yes, I'd been a little bit ticked at my husband for putting his campaign before his family, but we're talking a shoulder massage here. And he *had* earned major brownie points in the child-care department today. And, honestly, my shoulders ached and his touch felt good. Even better when his hands started roaming and his lips found my neck.

I needed to be out there hunting demons, I knew that. But under the circumstances, with my husband right there, silently insisting that I not go anywhere except upstairs with him . . . well, that kind of persuasion is hard to resist.

I woke up with a start, then rolled out from under Stuart's arm so I could check the clock. Just past two.

I turned carefully, then propped myself up on an elbow as I examined Stuart's face and listened to his breathing. Definitely asleep.

I waited a little longer, just to make absolutely sure. Then I slid slowly out of bed, careful not to bounce the mattress, shift the sheets too much, or do anything else that would clue my sleeping husband in to the change in status quo.

I paused, watching him in the dark, but his breathing stayed nice and even, his eyes shut tight. I checked the baby monitor, and it was on. I turned the volume all the way up, just to make sure Stuart could hear it. If Timmy woke up crying, Stuart would realize I was gone. But that was a contingency that I'd deal with if I had to.

In the meantime, I padded into the bathroom. I found a clean pair of sweatpants in the closet, and I tugged them on, then topped my fashion statement with a black T-shirt courtesy of my husband's clean laundry hamper. I tugged on socks, shoved my feet into running shoes, then pulled my hair back and away from my face. Ready.

I turned off the bathroom light, then opened the door and tiptoed through the bedroom, sparing one last glance for my husband. Still asleep. Good.

I opened our door just enough to squeeze through and then eased into the hall. And then, only when the door was closed tight behind me, did I breathe again.

One feature I love about our house is that there is a regular staircase leading up to a small attic, not one of those annoying pull-down ladders. In fact, the door and the attic itself resemble the room Greg and Marsha Brady fought for, as Allie has pointed out to me during her sporadic pitches to convert the space to her own private suite.

Not that our attic has the love beads and psychedelic colors. We haven't gone that far. But it does have a finished floor, insulation, a decent light, and lots of storage boxes filled with all the things I'm not willing to keep in our hot, bug-infested storage shed.

I closed the door behind me and crept up the stairs, stepping carefully since Stuart was directly below me. I navigated around all the boxes—until I reached the far side of the attic and the leather and wood trunk I'd hidden under a stack of musty sheets.

I pulled the linens off and gave the lock an automatic tug, finding it still tight. Good.

I'd hidden the key on a small nail on the backside of one of the rafters, and I dragged an old chair over, teetering on it until my fingers closed around the key. The lock was sticky, but it turned. The hinges creaked as I lifted the lid, and I cringed slightly, wishing I'd thought to bring some WD-40.

Inside, I saw the shallow tray exactly as I'd left it, filled with a mishmash of articles I'd ripped out from various women's magazines. Anyone who bothered to look closely would likely be suspicious—I'm hardly the soufflé type, and I can barely spell decoupage, much less know what it is—but for the most part, the pages served their camouflage purpose well.

I lifted the tray out to reveal the black velvet cloth covering my tools. I peeled it back and considered the weapons. I don't like to travel with much—I can hardly wander the San Diablo streets with a crossbow slung across my shoulder—and in the end I picked the lean, mean stiletto knife that Eric had given me for our third anniversary. Completely custom-made, the switchblade knife boasted a double-action release system. I preferred simply pushing the bolster to release the blade, but the knife also presented the option of opening manually.

I set it aside, then pulled out my battered leather jacket. I'd tried my hand at sewing only twice in my life. The second was when I valiantly attempted to make a baptismal dress for Allie (we ended up buying one). The first attempt, though, had actually been successful. I'd stitched a tight strip of elastic into the left sleeve of the jacket.

Now, I put the jacket on, picked up the knife, then slid the handle under the elastic. I shook my arm, making sure the knife was secure. Years ago, I'd been able to reach over and pull out the knife in seconds flat. I wasn't back up to my old speed, but I'd been practicing, and getting better with each try.

I already had holy water in my purse, but I'd stocked up over the last few months, collecting holy water in gallon jugs. Now, I filled a few vials and tucked them in my jacket pockets.

I sat back on my heels and wondered what else I should take. I didn't need the crucifix. While corporeal demons hated the things, crucifixes were a weapon only against vampires. Nothing else looked particularly useful for tonight. For a second, I fingered a sheathed Japanese sword, wishing I could take it. Eddie had a similar one, and I smiled at the memory of us comparing weapons, sharing a little bit of Demon Hunter bonding.

I put the sword back and repacked the chest. The larger weapons I'd already decided against, and none of the trophies from my past hunting days would be of any use.

Decided, I carefully shut and locked the trunk. Then I stood up, armed, dangerous, and as ready as I'd ever be.

Since demons rarely leave a calling card with directions to a lair, I really didn't know where to go patrolling. I ended up at the marina, since Allie had mentioned that Creasley had been "injured" in a boating accident. When nothing demonic jumped out at me there (literally and figuratively) I patrolled the beach for a while, particularly by the bathroom where the janitor had jumped me. Also nothing.

I was getting discouraged and considered calling it a night when I had one more idea. *Coastal Mists.* Creasley hadn't been a resident, but Sinclair certainly had been. Couple that with the knowledge that Cool had gone through Sinclair's stuff, this seemed like a good place to start. Besides, I didn't have a better plan.

Unfortunately, I also didn't have a *concrete* plan. More of a vague idea. And that involved walking the perimeter of Coastal Mists, peeking into windows, and generally scoping the place out. If that turned up no demons, I'd go in the front door and fake an overwhelming urge to chat with the insomniac residents.

I parked on the street, then walked up the road toward the Coastal Mists driveway. I stayed to the outside, veering around the perimeter and walking along the edge of the cliff until I was behind the nursing home. Then I crouched low and scurried toward the back of the home and the yard into which the residents weren't allowed to go because there was no barrier blocking access to the cliffs. It did, however, mean there was a hell of a view from the windows on this side of the home, and a ton of windows to take advantage of it.

No lights shone from any of those windows, though, and I didn't see any movement inside. Frustrated, I weighed my options: go inside the building, walk the grounds, or give up and go home. Since I'd already wasted more than an hour on this excursion—and since Timmy ensured a six-thirty A.M. wake-up call—I decided on home.

I was just starting to turn around when my head was jerked backwards by the force of someone using my ponytail to yank me to me feet.

I screamed in pain, then found myself flying through the air. I crash-landed in a graveled garden area, my face too close for comfort to a cactus, and the sharp blade of a knife pressed against my throat.

Fourteen

"Up, Hunter." The gravelly voice whispered in my ear, his putrid breath carried on the wind along with the scent of eucalyptus.

The flat edge of the knife pressed against the soft skin under my chin, the cool metal a counterpoint to the anger flaring through me. The knife blade barely grazed my throat as I rose, my attacker still unseen behind me.

Cool stood in front of me, the moon on his white-blond hair contrasting with the dark anger in his eyes. He took a step toward me, and I tensed, my mind whirring with possibilities. Considering the blade against my neck, none of them were particularly promising.

"Where?" he whispered, his face mere inches from mine.

"Right here," I said, hoping the fissures in my bravado weren't showing. "Right here, right now. Just call off your attack dogs and let's finish this thing."

His eyes narrowed, and then the bastard laughed. He

took a step backwards, and he actually laughed, his hands clapping in a mockery of applause.

"Glad I could bring some amusement to your otherwise dreary life."

"Oh, you do," he said. "This *will* end. But by my hand, not yours. And definitely not here."

"I don't suppose you'll tell me where?"

"I don't suppose you'll tell me where you've put the book?"

"Not a chance," I said, with more bravado than I felt.

He cocked his head slightly. "Refreshing," he said.

"What's that?"

"That old cliché of 'over my dead body.' I'm impressed you didn't use it."

My pulse pounded in my ears and I resisted the urge to turn my head and search for an escape. The blade was still there, sharp, and the slightest turn would fillet me.

"It would have been appropriate, though," he said, then took a step closer. "Now. *Where* is the book?"

My hands were clenched in fists, and I forced myself to relax. To think. To plan. "It's not here," I said slowly.

He didn't answer, just nodded to my captor, who shifted the knife until the point pressed against my throat. I felt a sharp prick, then the trickle of blood. "Kill me, and you'll never know," I said.

"Tell me."

I pressed my lips together, weighing just how foolhardy I was willing to be. On the one hand, I didn't think they'd kill me. Not until they were certain I wouldn't tell them what they wanted to know. On the other hand, I could easily see torture as being on Cool's list of acceptable methods of persuasion.

I also didn't know who was holding the knife, which meant I didn't know who—or what—I was up against.

"Tell me!" He howled the words, and as he did, his form shifted with the force of his rage, all the more powerful, I was sure, because he couldn't simply dispose of me.

The stench of sulphur and decay swirled around us, and Cool seemed to pulse, each beat of his heart destroying the image of what was human and pulling forth the snarling beast that was the demon within. His eyes flashed fire, and when he stared at me, it was like looking into eternal damnation.

I felt cold and my heart skittered in my chest, and I fought the urge to scream. I'd seen this before, more times than I'd like to remember, but you never get used to looking into Hell.

Even my attacker—a demon himself, if the state of his breath was any indication—was taken aback by the spectacle. The knife pressed against my flesh relaxed just slightly.

Since I didn't know if a better chance was coming, I decided to take the risk. I shot my fist straight up from waist level, connecting solidly with his wrist. *Yes!* His knife arm went wild and I spun, holding on to his arm as I did, and relishing the satisfying *snap* as the bone broke.

I lashed out with a solid kick at the same time, managing to send him sprawling. As he fell backwards, I wrested the knife from him, then pounced, aiming the point for his eye even as I recognized the man who had once been my daughter's English teacher.

I slammed the blade forward, but as it was mere millimeters from sliding home, something grabbed my legs and pulled me backwards. My aim faltered, and the point of the knife cut a shallow path down Creasley's cheek.

Whoever had yanked me back let go, presumably to get a better position for attack. I rolled over just as Ernesto Ruiz, the janitor, pounced. From my new vantage point, I could see Cool still behind us, still raging and still in a demonic state. That was one pissed-off puppy, but I didn't have time to worry about him, because a bigger problem was trying to get a choke hold on my neck.

We rolled, grappling across the ornamental lawn toward the cliffs. My adrenaline peaked, every sense on overdrive as I expected Creasley to jump into the fray. He didn't, though, and as I pondered that oddity, I managed to get on top of Ruiz even as his hands closed around my throat.

His hands were out, thumbs pressed against my throat as I gagged and choked and tried to suck in air. I'd either been wrong about that no-kill plan or Ruiz was pissed off enough to ignore it.

Either way, I was in trouble.

I still had one trick up my sleeve, though. And even as my brain screamed for oxygen, my right hand reached for the knife. My fingers closed over the hilt, and I pushed the bolster the instant the knife slid free, sliding the blade into place.

Ruiz's eyes widened in surprise—a pretty helpful instinctive response under the circumstances. With both his hands around my neck, he was screwed, and he knew it. That fact had about a millisecond to register on his brain. Then I slid the blade home. The hands around my throat relaxed as the demon inside Ruiz was sucked out with a shimmer and a hiss.

I rolled off, then sprang back up, my knife at the ready.

There was, however, no one to fight.

I frowned, not quite believing that, as I turned in a slow circle, scoping out every inch of the moonlight-lit yard.

Nobody.

How odd.

Actually, Cool's absence didn't surprise me. Kill a corporeal demon, and all that happens is that the demon is sucked out and returned to the ether. Once it finds another body, it can come back again.

But kill a demon in its demonic state and that's another story. That demon's history.

The problem is that demons don't reveal their natural state very often. That Cool did was testament to how angry he was at me—and to the importance of his plan. Whatever the plan might be.

Creasley's absence was more surprising. As a rule, demons aren't chicken. He wouldn't have run simply because I'd won round one. So where was he?

No answer sprang to mind. And since I didn't have time to worry about it, I pushed the question aside in favor of another one: What the hell was I going to do about this body?

I found the answer about twenty yards away. The cliffs. I rolled Ruiz that way, then paused to look down. Here, there was no beach to speak of, just the surf crashing over battered rock.

I took a deep breath, pressed my foot against Ruiz's backside, and shoved.

He tumbled down the cliff, finally landing with a *thud* on the rocks. I would have preferred delivering the body to the cathedral, but that was impossible. At least the rocks were out of the way, and the beachcombing crowd was significantly less in December. By the time the body was discovered, the wildlife should have erased any sign of the knife through Ruiz's eye.

Brutal, I thought, but satisfying.

The house was dark when I snuck back inside, and I paused in the kitchen, waiting, afraid the creak of the garage door might have awakened my family.

Silence.

I waited another minute, watching the second hand on our clock make its slow parade around the Roman numerals. Ten . . . eleven . . . and finally clicking back to twelve.

Still silent.

I exhaled in relief, then tiptoed toward the stairs. I made it up without hitting any squeaky floorboards, then padded down the hallway to the double doors to my bedroom. Still closed, which I figured was a good sign since it meant that Stuart probably hadn't awakened during the night and gone looking for me.

I carefully closed my hand around the doorknob and turned. As soon as the latch cleared the frame, I pushed the door open about eight inches and squeezed inside. Stuart was there in bed, his sleeping form illuminated by the soft streams of moonlight filtering in through our gossamer drapes.

I stood for a moment, making sure I hadn't disturbed him, then continued on to the bathroom. I shut the door, changed back into my pajamas in the dark, then crept back into the bedroom.

I sat carefully on the edge of the bed, then eased carefully under the covers. Finally in, I let my head sink into the pillow and closed my eyes.

Made it.

"Have a nice time?"

I jumped, coming bolt upright, and turned to look at Stuart, who had rolled over and was watching me with expressionless eyes.

"I . . . um . . ." How's that for a brilliant cover? Demon hunting I can handle. Blatant fabrication? There, my skills are sadly lacking.

Stuart reached for the bedside lamp and flicked it on. I squinted, trying to avoid both the light and my husband's stern gaze.

"Do you want to tell me where you've been?"

"Um, no?" That was the truth, after all. And wasn't I constantly admonishing Timmy not to tell fibs?

Stuart exhaled through his nose, his jaw tightening in what I knew was an effort to control his temper. I'd seen that expression before, but it had always been directed at the kids. Never at me.

"Kate—"

I held up a hand, cutting him off as I tried to take control of this little drama. "I'm tired. We can talk about this in the morning." By then I should be able to fabricate some plausible excuse for sneaking out after midnight.

"Kate." His voice was sharp, demanding.

"I mean it, Stuart. I'm tired." And the only excuse I had at the moment was a desperate urge to run to the grocery store. I could try to make it work. But somehow, I didn't think he'd believe me.

But he wasn't about to let the matter drop. "This isn't the first time you've gone out at night, Kate. I'm not an idiot, and I'm not blind. You owe me an explanation."

I fought the urge to shut my eyes in defeat. He was right. Over the last two months, I'd gone out on semi-regular nightly patrols, anytime the newspaper reported a deadly accident and, miraculously, a survivor. I'd make the rounds that night, hoping to encounter the newly minted demon. Sometimes I succeeded. Sometimes I failed. But always, I tried.

From Stuart's perspective, I imagined that my jaunts did seem a little suspicious. I just wasn't sure how to handle the situation.

He reached over and took my hand. "Is it that karate guy?"

I blinked, recoiling as if he'd slapped me. "Cutter?" Dear God the man was insane. Cutter's a great guy, and sure, there've been a few odd sparks between us, but I'd never—

I yanked my hand back, my temper flaring. "You son of a bitch! You honestly think I'm having an affair with Cutter?"

Most of the tension melted from his face. "Not anymore. But if it's not Cutter—"

"Whoa there," I said, interrupting. "I am not having an affair. Not with Cutter, not with anybody. I love you. Even if you have been driving me absolutely crazy lately, you're the only man on this earth that I love."

"Then why—"

"Because of you," I said, poking him in the chest. I wasn't being fair, and I knew it. But dammit, he'd pissed me off. And, yes, payback can be a bitch. "The only times you haven't been absent lately are when you're apologizing. So it's either leave the house to drive around and think, or have a knock-down, drag-out fight and terrify the kids. I decided to take the more civilized route."

I sat back against my pillow, my arms folded sulkily across my chest as I wondered if I'd be going to Hell for my lies. I made a mental note to go to confession this week, just in case a demon got the best of me.

Beside me, Stuart had completely deflated. "Oh, babe. I'm sorry." He rolled over and stared at the ceiling. "You're right. I've been so absorbed in all of this, that you and the kids have been getting the shaft. It's just that I never . . ." He trailed off.

"Never what?"

For a second, I didn't think he was going to answer, then he turned onto his side and faced me. "I just never expected that anyone would have the kind of faith in me that Clark does."

"Stuart!" I said, shocked.

"No, I'm serious. I know I'm a good lawyer. But to actually be a representative for the people. Honestly, it's more than I'd ever dreamed of. And now that it's a real possibility,

I want it." He rolled over again, facing up rather than me. "But I don't want it if it's going to ruin us. And it's only going to get worse before it gets better."

"I know," I said. Stuart would file formally in January. Then he'd bust tail until the primary in March. If he won that, it would be more months of campaigning until the election in November.

"Can we handle it? Because if we can't, I'll quit. I'll call Clark right now and tell him he's got to find someone else to support."

"You'd do that?"

He turned his head and smiled at me. "Of course I would."

I shivered, wondering if I could say the same. I hadn't asked to be pulled out of retirement. At the time, I'd fought it tooth and nail, desperate to protect the normal life I'd built.

But now that the dust had settled, I couldn't imagine walking away. Secret or not, what I did was important. Crucial even. More, I loved it.

It was, I realized, the same for Stuart. In a way, the county attorney fights demons, too. And Stuart wanted to be there on the front lines.

I loved him for offering to give it all up. I couldn't, however, let him do it.

"Just try to make it home for dinner once in a while," I said. "And give me at least twelve hours notice if I have to put on a dress and makeup. Sixteen if I have to clean the house for company."

"I can handle eight and ten," he said, the grin I loved so much flashing briefly.

"Ten and fourteen," I countered.

"Done." He held out his hand and we shook. Then he tugged me closer and wrapped me in his arms. "It's past five," he said. "I'll be getting up in just over an hour. Hardly seems worth going back to sleep."

"Mmm," I murmured, as he kissed my ear. "But it's so chilly. I hate to get out of bed before I absolutely have to."

"Don't worry," he said. "I can think of a way to keep us busy and warm until the alarm goes off."

He reached over and flipped off the light, and I lost myself in the dark heat of my husband's arms.

The sharp toot of a horn pierced the early morning chaos.

"Allie!" Timmy yelled at the top of his little lungs. "Car pool!"

"Coming, coming, coming!" My daughter pounded down the stairs, her ninety-eight pound body managing to create about the same reverb through the house as a herd of small elephants.

"Hold up," I said, rushing to meet her in the entrance hall.

"Mom! Late!"

"Just one second." I opened the door and waved to Sylvia, then held up one finger. She lifted her arm and made a show of tapping her watch. I nodded, then turned back to Allie. "So what's on your agenda today?"

She blinked, then yanked her earbuds out of her ears. "Huh?"

"Have you got any surf club things, I mean? Anything going on to prepare for the exhibition?"

"Well, yeah. I mean, it's on Saturday. I'm like ferociously busy this whole week."

"Right." Not the answer I wanted. "At the beach?"

She shot me a hooded look, then sagged against the wall, apparently overcome by the exhaustion of having to deal with a freak for a mother. "No, Mother. The planning meetings are held in the chem room with Mr. Long."

"Sure. Right." That was good. "But what about Cool? I suppose he's right there pitching in with the planning?"

Sylvia tooted the horn twice. I waved. She threw her hands in the air and gestured for Allie to get a move on.

"I gotta go." Allie took step, managing to scoot past me out the door. I watched as she raced down the sidewalk, then slid into the car next to Susan, Sylvia's daughter.

I told myself there'd be no reason for Cool to be there. After attacking me last night—and, worse, revealing himself as a demon—I figured he was probably going to avoid the school and Coastal Mists until whatever plan he'd set in motion was underway. In the meantime he'd spend his days and nights running around San Diablo wreaking all sorts of demonic nonsense. He had no reason to bother my daughter. No reason at all.

Except, of course, that she *was* my daughter.

No, no, no!

I raced back to the kitchen and snatched up the cordless phone. Then I dialed Allie's number and waited impatiently for her to answer.

"Mom?"

"Hey, hon."

"Um, don't take this the wrong way, but, like, what's up with you today?"

"I just never got an answer from you, that's all. Is Cool at all these planning meetings?"

"Why?"

"Allie," I said, using my I'm-the-Mother voice. "Just answer the question."

"Fine. No. He never comes to the school. Only the practices at the beach."

"Right. Good. Okay, then."

"Mom?"

"Yeah, hon?"

"You wanna tell me what's going on?"

I didn't, of course, but she needed to know something. Not only was she going to think her mother was insane if I stayed silent, but I wanted her to be on her guard.

"I've heard some things about Cool," I said. "I don't want you around him."

"What kind of things?"

"I'll tell you later," I said, hoping that by the time later rolled around, she'd have forgotten the question.

"Mom . . ."

"I'm serious, Allie. Now's not the time or the place."

"Fine. Whatever. But you're wrong about him. He's not just some brain-fried surfer dude. He's like totally smart." A pause, then, "Hang on." I heard the muffle of discussion as she kept her hand over the microphone, then, "Susan says he's not just smart, but he's totally into the community. And his girlfriend's even a museum docent. I saw her last week, and she's totally mousy."

"And this is relevant why?"

"Because if he's a sleaze, he'd have some bimbo bikini-babe girlfriend, right?"

The holes in her reasoning were large and looming, but now really wasn't the time. So I complimented her and Susan on their astounding feat of logic, asked them to humor me and avoid Cool, and made Allie promise to come straight home after her surf club meeting.

When I hung up, I felt only mildly better. At least David would be at the meeting. If nothing else, he'd keep Allie safe.

I reluctantly shoved thoughts of surfer-demons out of my head. I would have liked to have spent the day scouring the city in search of Cool, but that wasn't an option. I had a sick boy at home. Plus, I had furniture deliveries scheduled. The demons might not be taking a day off, but I had no choice.

"Mommy?" Timmy padded into the kitchen, Boo Bear under one arm. "Is it a school day?"

"No, kiddo. Today you're home with me." I bent down and felt his forehead. Cool, thank goodness. "School tomorrow, unless you get sick again."

He puffed out his little chest. "I'm not sick."

"Nope, you're totally healthy. Want to read some books?"

"Wockets!" he shouted. "Wockets and pockets!"

I readily agreed, more than happy to wile away some time with Dr. Suess.

I found the book, settled Tim on my lap, then started to read, laughing as he bounced and blurted out the nonsense (and real) words. After that book (twice) we moved on to *One Fish, Two Fish,* and then *The Cat in the Hat.* After that, I begged off, fearing if we read any more, I'd think in rhyme for the rest of the day.

"Let's check the TV," I said, clicking it on. *Dora the Explorer* burst onto the screen and my kid made happy noises.

"Sit with me, Momma!"

"Sure, kiddo." I snuggled up with him, and let myself get lost in the show, feeling the pain of Dora, Boots, Tiko, and the others as they tried to get to the City of Lost Toys to find their missing treasures. I was humming along, when Laura tapped at the back door. I extricated myself from Timmy and unlocked the door for her, careful to close it and reset the alarm.

Since Timmy was entranced, we retreated for the breakfast table. "I've got news," Laura said, as soon as we sat.

"So do I. Cool's a demon."

Her entire expression crumpled. "Well, damn! What's the point of being the research sidekick if I can't even tell you something you don't know."

"If it's any consolation, I never got the chance to check

him with holy water. But I watched him change into a Hell monster. Not a pretty sight." I explained about the newly minted Creasley-demon and how I'd gone looking for him. "I found him," I said. "Him and Cool."

"Wow," Laura said. She reached into her tote bag and pulled out some computer printouts. "Here," she said, pushing one toward me. It was a newspaper article dated from late November. The story reported a terrible wipeout by celebrity surfer Cooley Claymore, known to his fans as Cool. " 'A sigh of relief swept over the entire surfing community after an unconscious Cool was resuscitated by quick-acting lifeguards who performed CPR and mouth-to-mouth, despite the surfer having been unresponsive for over eight minutes.' "

"Well, now we know how long he's been a demon," I said. "We just don't know what he wants."

We spent the rest of the day tossing around useless theories and trying to track down Cool. Laura found an address on the Internet, but when we called the apartment complex, we were told he'd moved out.

Laura left when the furniture deliverymen came, promising to keep working. I didn't hold out much hope, though. The demon Cool wouldn't want to be found.

On a whim, I called the school and asked to speak to David Long. Miraculously, he called me back within the hour, explaining that I'd called right before his off period. "So what's up?"

"Cool," I said. "Do you have an address?"

"In the market for a celebrity boy toy?"

"Absolutely," I said.

"Hold on. Let me check my file." I heard him rifling through papers, and then his voice came back on the line. He read off an address, but I didn't copy it down. Laura and I had already called; I knew that Cool had moved on.

I confirmed with David that Cool was definitely not going to be anywhere near the planning session that afternoon. Then I signed off and drummed my fingers on the table until the furniture guys signaled to me. Then I spent the next hour showing them where the various pieces went, and telling them which of the destroyed items they could cart away.

I spent the rest of the afternoon moving furniture this way and that, pretending like I had even an inkling of talent in the interior-decorating department. Finally, I just shoved the couch back where the old couch had been and called it a day.

Allie came home, pronounced the new furniture "okay," then went upstairs to do homework. Timmy immediately got chocolate smears on the sofa. Eddie announced that the floral print was "too damn frou-frou." And Stuart wandered in so exhausted that he didn't even notice.

Nice to know my domestic efforts are appreciated.

As soon as I'd put Timmy into bed, I followed suit, anxious for this day to be over and tomorrow to arrive. At least then I could get back to demon hunting. My efforts there might not be acknowledged, but at least I knew they were appreciated.

Fifteen

I was so anxious to get back to work Thursday morning that only the tiniest bit of mommy guilt peeked out as I dropped Timmy at day care. And when Miss Sally told him that they were going to be finger painting that day, the guilt vanished in a puff, erased by the toothy grin that spread across the face of my soon to be purple, orange, and blue child. (No matter how hard the school insists that the kids wear smocks, my child always comes home in psychedelic colors. That, however, is a small price to pay for guilt reduction.)

Back home, I made a fresh pot of coffee and tried to decide where to start. As the coffee brewed, I skimmed the paper, my heart stopping when I saw the small article on the front of the Metro section.

Jason Palmer, a junior at Coronado High School, was found beaten to death in an alley near the community college. "Mr. Palmer held a 4.0 grade point average, was a member of the marching band, editor of the newspaper, and the treasurer of the surf club." The article ended with details regarding the funeral and memorial.

I'd just finished reading it, when the phone rang.

"Did you see that article about Jason?" Laura asked, as soon as I'd answered.

I told her I'd just finished reading it. "Allie's going to be devastated," I said. "I don't know the boy, but she must if he's in the surf club."

"Mindy, too," Laura said. "From the newspaper staff. Do you think . . ." She trailed off, but I knew where she was going.

"I can't be positive. But the way everything has been going lately . . ."

"Yeah," Laura said ominously. "And now everything seems to tie back to the high school. I swear I'm going to pull Mindy out. St. Mary's has a Catholic school, right? Better yet, a convent. Maybe Mindy would take to being a nun."

I laughed. "You're not even Catholic."

"A minor detail," she said.

She was joking, of course. At least about the nunnery. But I knew how she felt about the school. The same thoughts had crossed my mind, too. "At least today's Thursday," I said. "Today, tomorrow, and then they're off for two weeks. Surely we'll figure out what's going on—and stop it— before the new semester starts."

Actually, I thought I might just keep Allie home tomorrow, and then come up with some excuse to keep her away from the exhibition on Saturday. I didn't know what, but I had a feeling bribery and threats would have to be involved. I could do that. When it comes to saving my kids, I'm really not proud.

After that, it was total family time, and I intended to do my damnedest to keep my daughter locked in the house, the alarm system on, a crucifix around her neck, and Christ-mas carols playing in the background.

The phone beeped, signaling an incoming call, and so I signed off with Laura and clicked over.

"Katherine? Sei tu?"

My hand went to my throat, and I dropped back into my chair. Stupidly, my eyes filled with tears. "Father Corletti," I said. "It's so good to hear your voice."

"Father Ben has told me of your recent trials," he said. "You are well?"

"I'm fine. My family's fine. But I'm worried."

"Ah, *mia cara,* my heart and prayers are with you."

"Thank you," I said. "But we could use a few more Hunters here."

"You know that is one request I cannot grant. Our resources are too thin, and the need is great elsewhere in the world as well."

"I know," I said, feeling like a petulant child. "Our problem isn't even so much manpower," I admitted. "It's information. We haven't figured out what the Tartarus demons are up to. We're working blind, here."

"Si," he said. "But if we are correct and this book is the *Malevolenaumachia Demonica,* then these events could bring forth a reign of evil such as we have never seen."

I shivered. Father Corletti is not prone to exaggeration. If he says the book could spark a crisis like nothing ever seen on the earth, I certainly wasn't going to argue with him.

"Be strong in your faith, *mia cara.* You will find the answer soon. Of that, *I* have faith."

"Thank you, Father," I said, feeling like a little girl being praised by a parent.

I started to say good-bye, but stopped myself, remembering one other question I had for him. This one, about Eric.

I heard Father's soft chuckle, and realized that he knew exactly what I was thinking. "What do you wish to know, child?"

My breath hitched in my throat, because I realized what he was offering me. Father Corletti knew what Eric had been up to. The trail Eric had laid out for me might have gone cold, but I could still learn the truth. Or I could walk away from the mystery, bid good-bye to Eric, and concentrate on the family I had now.

I closed my eyes, trying to think rationally, to parse my decision through both logic and love. In the end, I made the only choice I could. I asked Father to tell me about Eric.

If he was disappointed in me, he didn't show it, and for that, I loved him all the more. Instead, he told me to sit down, that what he had to say might be hard to hear.

I sat, mindlessly ripping a paper napkin to shreds as Father Corletti told me things about my first husband that I'd never imagined.

"Eric visited Father Oliver because he was studying to be an *alimentatore*," Father said.

I tried not to be shocked, but the world was spinning under me. "When? When we were in San Diablo?"

"*Sì.*"

"But . . . but . . . why didn't he tell me?"

"That, my child, I do not know. I assume he had not completely made up his mind to return to *Forza,* and he did not want to unnecessarily worry you."

"That's nuts," I said. "There must have been some other reason."

"Child, I have no more information—or comfort—to give you. Other than to say that Eric Crowe loved you very much."

I snuffled a little, but nodded, even though Father couldn't see me. "I know that. I do. It's just, hard. All this coming at me at once."

"Katherine? Are you still there?"

"I'm here," I said, suddenly tentative.

"There is something on your mind, my child?"

I couldn't help my smile. Father knew me better t[...] most anyone. He'd been teacher, trainer, father, nurse[...] sat for hours at my bedside when I'd succumbed to pn[...]nia after battling a demon in the Paris catacombs [...] dead of winter. And on my sixteenth birthday, he'd [...] me the delicate silver crucifix that I still cherished.

I couldn't keep secrets from Father Corletti. And[...] estly, I wouldn't want to.

"I've been thinking about Eric," I said.

"Ah, my child. You and Eric shared a wonderful lov[...] you must let go. Keep him in your heart, always. But [...] the husband you have now."

"I know," I said. "I do. Or, that is, I try." I swallo[...] "The thing is, Father, I found a note."

I explained about finding the cryptic notes from Eri[...] words spilling out. My uncertainty as to how much t[...] Allie, and when. My hurt that Eric kept secrets from m[...] crets that seemed to grow with every bit of informat[...] discovered.

"But I've reached a dead end," I said. "Father O[...] passed away, and he left no information for me. What [...] Eric wanted me to find is gone. I feel like I've failed [...] Father. But at the same time, I'm so hurt—so angry—[...] he hid something this huge from me."

"I understand, child. It is never easy to learn that v[...] you believed is not entirely true. But even in a marri[...] there is still autonomy, no? You are one as a unit, while [...] maining unique in the eyes of the Lord."

"I . . . well, yes." Not that his words made me feel [...] better. I mean, Eric had still been keeping secrets.

"Perhaps you should speak to Father Donnelly."

"Why?" Father Donnelly was on the short list of priests poised to take the helm at *Forza* once Father Corletti retired.

"He supervised Father Oliver's work with Eric. Perhaps he will have more information for you."

"Okay."

"If you are certain you wish to pursue this, I will transfer you to Father Donnelly's extension."

"I'm sure."

"Very well. And Katherine, remember that God is with you always. And, my child, so am I."

I heard *click-clicking* on the line as Father Corletti put the call through. A ring, then another, and then a male voice. *"Sì?"*

"Padre Donnelly? Is he available?"

"Not at the moment," the voice replied in crisp English with only a hint of an accent. "May I take a message?"

I decided not to leave my name. Assuming Father Corletti didn't mention my call, I might be able to catch Father Donnelly before he'd had the chance to think about his responses. "Never mind," I said. "Thanks so much."

I'm not sure how long I sat there, my head in my hands. Then I heard the scuff of a chair across the tile and looked up to see Eddie peering hard at me.

"What's on your mind, girl?"

"What?"

"Either you're constipated, or you're thinking deep thoughts. Which is it?"

I frowned slightly at his choice of words, but I wasn't his mother, so I let it slide. "Deep thoughts," I said.

"Good. We're out of prune juice."

"Thanks for the update," I said.

"So what is it? The book? Your daughter's love life?

Damn demon-bugs that keep crawling over this godforsaken town?"

"Actually," I said, "I'm thinking about Eric."

His bushy eyebrows rose above his glasses frames. "My grandson, eh?" He pulled out a chair. "In that case, I'll have a seat and you can tell me all about it."

At the moment, Eddie was the closest thing I had to a father. And since I needed a shoulder to cry on, I took him up on his offer and basically spilled my guts.

Laura tapped on the back door just as I was finishing my story. I let her in, then brought her up to speed as we traipsed back to the table. Eddie was still there, his fingers tapping out a rhythm on the Formica.

"Father Donnelly," he said. "Interesting."

"Why?" I asked, my ears perking up at his tone.

"Just that he's as crooked as they come. If Eric was working with that one, then he musta been crooked, too."

I reeled backwards with as much force as if he'd slapped me, rage bubbling up. "What the hell are you talking about? This is Eric! You didn't know him. You can go around pretending you're part of this family, but you're not. You don't know us, and you sure as hell don't know Eric."

I pushed back from the table, my hand clapped over my mouth, ferocious anger warring with total mortification. I ran out of the room and up the stairs, then fell onto my bed, pulling a pillow tight against my chest.

I knew I was overreacting, I *knew* it. But I'd been hit too hard lately to even bother trying to rein my emotions in. *Damn Eddie!* What right did he have to trash Eric's good name? My husband wasn't corrupt. The idea was completely absurd.

I closed my eyes and buried my face in the pillow. As pissed as I was, I still hated myself for lashing out. I may have only known Eddie for a few months, but I did love him, and I knew he loved me. He was brash and obnoxious and often thoughtless, but he'd never hurt me on purpose.

On accident, though. Well, he'd definitely got me good, there.

I heard a soft tap on the door, then felt the mattress shift as someone sat down next to me. I opened my eyes to see Eddie peering at me. "Wanna take a punch at me? Just do it in my gut. Be a crime to ruin such a perfect nose."

I smiled despite myself. "No punches. I'm sorry I yelled at you."

He stroked my hair. "No, girl, I deserved it. Never liked Father Donnelly, and I opened my mouth without thinking. Maybe he ain't corrupt after all. Father Corletti likes the pansy-ass jerk, so maybe he's okay."

I propped myself up on my elbow, still listening.

"And even if the rat-bastard's as crooked as the day is long, well, that ain't no reason for me to go accusing Eric of throwing in with him. Eric might not've known. Or maybe he was trying to trap Donnelly."

Laura sat down on the other side of the bed. "Like a sheriff going in to clean up an outlaw town."

"That's it, girlie."

I almost managed a grin, liking the picture of Eric stepping up to battle corruption wherever he found it. I still didn't like him keeping the battle a secret from me, but if he had to have a secret, I wanted it to be a noble one.

Actually, the more I thought about it, the more plausible Eddie's revised-and-more-palatable theory sounded. After all, chasing after corruption can easily get a guy killed . . .

"Kate?" Laura pressed a hand to my shoulder. "You okay?"

I sat up, nodding and feeling a little foolish. "I'm fine. I'm sorry," I said to Eddie.

"No need," he said. "And that offer to punch me still stands."

I shot him a wry look. "I'll save it for when I really need it."

I splashed water on my face, and we all traipsed back downstairs. I'd just poured a fresh cup of coffee when the phone rang. I answered, surprised to find David Long on the other end of the line.

"I need to talk to you," he said. "Can you meet me?"

"What? Right now?"

"Yeah. Right now."

"I . . ." I made a shooshing gesture to Laura and Eddie, who were asking who it was in very non-whisperish stage whispers. "David, what's this about?"

"Have you read the paper this morning?"

I tensed, fearing I knew where this conversation was going. "Yeah."

"Then you saw the article about Jason Palmer."

"Yes, I did. I'm so sorry. He sounded like a good kid."

"He was a good kid." I heard David draw in a noisy breath. "It's all related," he finally said. "Jason. The dead guy in the janitor's basement. And more."

Uh-oh.

I stayed silent.

"Kate?"

"I'll meet you," I said. "At the cathedral." As much as I hated to admit it, I still wasn't certain about David Long. There were too many questions. He may have passed the holy water test, but he knew too much, and I wasn't going to be completely satisfied until he walked on holy ground. And even then, I wanted a damn good explanation.

"The cathedral," he repeated, speaking slowly.

"Is that okay?"

A pause, then, "Yeah. Sure. I can do that."

"Great. See you there."

I hung up the phone and looked from Laura to Eddie. "I guess now we'll see what David Long is made of."

Eddie and Father Ben were with me, the three of us sitting on a step just in front of the communion rail, when David stepped through the doors. He paused, then saw us and lifted his chin in silent acknowledgment.

"Come join us," I said, watching him carefully.

He hesitated, but he came, taking one step and then another down the aisle toward the altar. I searched his face for hints of pain. Nothing.

I still wasn't sure what David's story was, but at least I knew he wasn't a demon.

"I didn't realize we'd have company," he said, as soon as he'd reached the three of us.

I shrugged. "Father Ben and Eddie are interested in the kind of story you're here to tell. Besides, I'll tell them after the fact, anyway. They might as well hear it firsthand."

He considered that, then nodded, reaching out to hold the communion rail. "I don't suppose you're going to tell me what you three musketeers are up to?"

"You suppose right," I said. "You came here to tell me something. So tell."

"It's about the boy who died. Jason Palmer. He was badly mutilated. But he was wearing a surf club jacket and so the police brought me in, hoping I could identify the body."

"Could you?" Father Ben asked.

"Yes." He shivered, looking a little green. "Yes, I could recognize him."

"I'm so sorry," I said, reaching out to brush his sleeve.

"I saw something," he said, shaking himself and squaring his shoulders. "When they brought me in. The boy had a ring. He wore it on a chain around his neck."

"A ring?" Eddie asked. "What kind of ring."

"Thick, like a class ring, but with planetary symbols engraved all over it." He watched our faces, but none of us reacted. Maybe Ben and Eddie had a clue, but I didn't know why I should care about a planet ring.

"Asmodeus," he finally said, his voice flat. "We're dealing with Asmodeus."

"*We're* dealing with?" I repeated, even as Eddie blurted out, "Holy Mother of God," then crossed himself. "Sorry 'bout that, Father."

"The feeling is mutual," Father Ben said. And then, to David, "You're sure?"

"About Asmodeus? No. How could I be? But with the ring—with everything that's been happening—I'd say it's a damn good bet."

"Wait, wait, wait," I said, holding up a hand and turning to rail on David. "Who the hell are you and why do know about demons?"

"I'm on your side, Kate."

I shook my head, holding firm. "That's not good enough. Not good enough by a long shot."

"Kate." Father Ben's hand closed on my arm. "Look at where we are." He swept his arm out, indicating the length and breadth of the sanctuary. "There's work to be done here. For now, let's trust him."

I looked from the padre to Eddie, who nodded. I drew in a breath, fisted my hands, and gave in. They were right. "But we're going to talk," I said. "And it damn well better be good."

"We'll talk."

"Asmodeus," Father Ben said, getting us back on track.

"Hold on," I said. "I'm about five minutes behind you guys. Who's Asmodeus?"

"A demon," David said.

"Thank you," I retorted. "That much I figured out."

"A High Demon," Eddie said. "And one of the tricksters. He teaches his followers skills to entice, then bequeaths them with a special ring."

"With planets on it," I said. "But what's so special about the ring?"

"It bestows on his followers the power of invisibility."

"Wow," I said, looking to Father Ben for confirmation. "Really?"

"I've read a little bit about this demon," he said. "He is said to have possessed Jeanne des Anges, a nun at Loudun. That takes extreme power. He's not a demon you want to mess with."

"But he's here," I said. "Messing with us."

"It looks that way," David said.

"But if Jason had the demon's ring, then we must be getting close to an answer, right?" I asked. "I mean, he must have got it from someone. Or somewhere." I looked at the men. "Could it have come through the book? Do you know about the book?" I added, the question directed to David.

"I figured it out," he said, the answer making me frown. "But I don't know whether the book can produce a ring."

Honestly, the possibility seemed ridiculous. Although when you tossed an invisibility ring into the mix, maybe it wasn't so absurd.

"Don't think so," Father Ben said, apparently not thinking the idea was ridiculous at all. "From what I've read, the book can only conjure words. Although . . ."

"Although? Although doesn't sound good."

"Under certain circumstances, the book can conjure spirits," he said.

"Other demons?"

"I'm not certain," he admitted. "But the book definitely can't conjure objects."

"So someone had to give the ring to Jason," I said. "But who?"

As soon as I said the question, I knew the answer. "Cool," I said. "It has to be Cool."

David's forehead creased. "What makes you say that?"

I shot a questioning look at Father Ben, who nodded. I drew in a breath, hoping we weren't wrong about David. Then I filled him in, telling him what we'd learned about Cool, Coastal Mists, and Dermott Sinclair.

"So Cool's a demon," he said. "But is he the demon Asmodeus? And if he is, what does he want?"

"I've got a couple of ideas about that," Eddie said. "Our buddy Asmo used to be one of the order of seraphim, right?"

"Well, don't look at me," I said. "I just work here."

"Right," David said. He shifted his weight from one foot to the other. I looked at him, my eyes narrow. "My off period," he said. "If I'm not back in time, *I'll* be the one called to the principal's office." He nodded at Eddie. "But I've got some time. You were saying?"

"Seraphim's one of the highest orders of angels. So Asmo had the farthest to fall. And he's probably pretty ticked off about that, don't you know?"

"Revenge?" I asked.

"Bingo," Eddie said. "He frees those demons in Tartarus, and he's got some damn powerful allies. A nearly invincible army to wreak hell on Earth."

"Okay, but how?" I asked. We all looked at each other, clueless.

"Looks like it's back to research," Father Ben said.

I checked my watch. "If it's time for research, I think that's my cue to leave. Besides, I need to go rescue Laura from my son."

"I need to get back to school," David said.

Eddie said he'd stay and do some research with the padre,

and Father Ben promised to deliver him home sometime that evening.

David and I walked to the parking lot together, the silence between us an odd mixture of tension and familiarity. Or maybe it was the familiarity that was making me tense.

"Get in," I said. "We need to talk."

"I've got my car."

"Just get in."

I thought he was going to argue again, but then he nodded. He kept one hand pressed against his stomach as he climbed into the passenger seat, then leaned back and closed his eyes.

"You look a little green." He did, too. And his forehead had broken out in beads of sweat.

"I'm fighting a cold," he said.

I shot a frown his direction. I didn't like the unhealthy way he looked, but at the same time, I knew I was being foolish. The fact that he looked like shit *now*—away from the cathedral, in a car, on the asphalt—was purely coincidental. There was absolutely no way he could have stood in that cathedral and talked to us if he were a demon. My suspicions were not only absurd, they were petty. Like residual distrust from the way he'd waltzed in all knowledgeable about Asmodeus. As if I were jealous that David had stolen the limelight or something. Dumb, dumb, dumb.

Beside me, he closed his eyes and rubbed his temples.

"I think the cold is winning," I said.

He opened his eyes long enough to aim a weak smile at me. "And here I thought I had this fighting thing down."

I wasn't sure what to say to that, so I didn't say anything, just concentrated on driving. By the time we reached the bottom of the hill and turned onto the Coast Highway, David's eyes were open, he was sitting up straight, and his skin no longer looked green.

"Better?"

"Yeah. I don't know. Maybe something I ate. It comes and goes. Right now, I guess it's going."

"Good." I glanced at him. "What's your story, David Long?"

"Damn. I thought my invalid status would postpone the inevitable."

"Sorry. No such luck."

"What do you want to know?"

"Well, for starters, why do you know so much about demons? And why did you feel the urge to call and tell me about Jason's ring?"

"You seem like a woman with discriminating taste in jewelry?"

"Nice try, but no."

"Do I get points for creativity?"

"David . . ."

"It seemed like the thing to do. Find a ring that suggests demonic activity, who else would you call but a Demon Hunter?"

I tensed, my arms on the steering wheel going rigid. "I don't know what you're talking about."

"No? Well, I can fill you in. Katherine Connor, née Andrews, formerly Katherine Crowe. Level Four Demon Hunter with the *Forza Scura,* recently reactivated after fifteen years of retirement."

His words sent a cold chill through me, and I ripped the steering wheel to the right, slamming on the brakes as we hit the shoulder. At the same time, I reached into the map pocket with my left hand and pulled out the ice pick I'd stashed there. My right arm shot out in a bastardization of a protective motion, catching him across the throat as I twisted to face him, jamming the steel point against his carotid artery.

"Jesus, Kate!"

I kept my voice low, dangerous. "There are only a handful of people on this planet who know what you just said. You're not one of them."

"Kate, no. I'm on your side."

"How do you know all that?" I hissed. "And if I don't like the answer, I'm sliding this through your throat. And your eye, too, just to make sure."

"You think I'm a demon?" He made a little *hmmm* sound and nodded. "Yeah, well, I guess under the circumstances that makes sense."

I jabbed the pick, drawing a tiny drop of blood. *"Talk."*

"I know about you because I know Hunters."

"Are you in *Forza?*" I couldn't imagine that he was. After my pathetic plea for help, surely, Father Corletti would have told me if another Hunter was in town.

"I'm not," he said, after the briefest of hesitations. "I'm rogue. And I called you because when I saw the ring I realized this was too big for me to handle alone."

"*Forza* Hunters aren't in the habit of sharing information with rogues," I said. A lot of rogue hunters were dangerous, willing to sacrifice humans for the "greater good" of eradicating the demon parasites from the face of the earth. To my mind—and to *Forza*'s—that decision rests with God.

"I never intended to be a rogue," he said. "I swear. But there's a need. Dammit, Kate, you can't deny that there's a need."

I watched him, saying nothing as the van rocked in the wake of the outside traffic. He didn't blink, didn't sweat, didn't cower. Just looked straight ahead, and waited for me to decide.

I took the ice pick off his neck, but kept it poised and ready. I was starting to trust him again, but I wasn't there yet. "Who?" I said. "Tell me who these Hunters in *Forza* are that you know so well. The ones who told you all about me."

He closed his eyes, and I saw his chest rise and fall as he drew in a breath, then exhaled. He turned to face me, his gray eyes sharp. "Kate, do you really have to ask?"

A shiver ripped through me and the pick tumbled from my hand as I lifted it to my mouth. He bent forward and picked it up, holding the steel and passing it back to me. I ignored it.

"Eric?"

"He was . . . Let's just say that I knew him well."

"You left me the key."

He nodded. "Eric asked me to."

"But why now? After five years?"

"A lot of reasons," he said. "But it boils down to finding you. It just took me that long."

"Why?"

He sighed. "Some other time, Kate. If you don't trust me, then you can put that ice pick to good use. But I'm not living those years again right now. Not even for you."

I let that settle in, then decided I could live with it. Not that I had a choice. I wanted to hear about Eric. About how David knew him. About the conversations they'd had and the things David had seen. I wanted to draw every ounce of my husband from this man, then hold it tight in my heart.

So I had to trust him. I needed him.

I think he knew that.

Frustrated, I jerked the car back into drive, waited for an opening in traffic, and gunned it. We went the rest of the drive in silence, and I pulled into the parking lot at the school just as classes were changing. "Right on time," I said.

He opened his door and got out, but leaned back inside before shutting the door. "I'm going Cool hunting tonight," he said. "I'll be on the boardwalk, by the lifeguard stand between Main and Ocean at seven. Will I see you there?"

"I don't know," I said, even though I did. So far we'd had

no luck finding Cool. I doubted we'd get lucky enough to find him hanging around the surf, but I had to at least try.

I'd have to extricate myself from my family, of course. But I'd manage somehow.

"Kate?" David was watching me, his hand poised to slam the car door.

"I'll be there," I said. Somehow, I'd be there.

Sixteen

I leaned against the door of the pantry, wondering if my family would notice if I served Cat Chow for dinner. Probably. I debated ordering pizza, decided that would take too long, then put some water on to boil. Mac and cheese it was.

What the hell, right? Stuart would undoubtedly be late, Allie would pick at her food and then eat graham crackers in her room, and Timmy would be out of his mind with glee.

As if he could hear me thinking about him, Timmy scampered in from the living room, Boo Bear tight in his hands. "Cookie, Mommy? Want a cookie."

"No way, sport. It's almost dinnertime. We're having macaroni and cheese."

He stared at me. His lip quivered. I tensed, but it was too late. "NOOOO. Turkey and apples! Don't like stupid macaroni!"

I crossed my arms over my chest and stared him down.

"Timothy Connor, you love macaroni and cheese. And stupid's not a nice thing to say."

"*You're* stupid!" he yelled, just as Eddie wandered into the room.

"Okay, young man. Time-out." I took him by the arm, steeling myself against his ear-piercing howls of protest. I parked him in the corner, then shot a warning finger when he started to walk away. "Stay," I said in my most firm Mommy voice. He puffed out his lips in a pout, but he stayed.

In the kitchen, I pulled a package of sliced turkey from the fridge, along with a shiny red apple. As I washed the apple, then started to skin and dice it, I cradled the telephone handset against my ear and dialed Laura's number. "Any chance you can watch Timmy tonight?" I asked.

"Hot date?"

"Hot as Hell," I said, thoughts of demons mixing with thoughts of David.

"When do you need me?"

"About an hour? Should be easy enough. Allie's in her room doing homework, and Timmy just got a time-out, so he'll be happy to have someone around to coddle him."

As if on cue, Timmy called out for me. "Is time-out over?"

"It's over," I said. "Come on in here and eat your turkey and apple."

His voice filtered back at me through the wall. "Noooooo! Mac and cheese! Mac. And. CHEESE!"

I resisted the urge to succumb to a primal scream. "No problem, sweetie. Mac and cheese it is." To Laura, I said simply, "Help."

She laughed. "I'll be right over."

True to her word, she and Mindy appeared at my back door about ten minutes later, just as I was dishing mac and cheese into Timmy's bowl, the third course in his meat, fruit, pasta meal.

Mindy bounded up the stairs, and Laura followed me back into the kitchen. "I know where Stuart is," she said. "But where's Eddie?"

"Still with Ben, I think." I filled her in on everything we'd learned from David. "I hope they're making some progress, because I don't have a clue what Cool is planning."

The garage door creaked and I jumped a mile. "Stuart?" I shot a glance toward Laura. "He's never early!"

Still, unless someone else had commandeered our garage door opener, my husband was about to walk through that door. And I'd lay odds that he'd come home early as a concession to me. To eat dinner with me. To have a nice little family moment.

Unfortunately, I had a date to go demon hunting.

"Hey, there," he said, tossing his briefcase on the kitchen counter and giving me a kiss on the cheek. "And hey to you, too." He planted a kiss on Timmy's head.

"Mac and cheese!" Timmy said happily.

"So I see. Hey, Laura."

She waved a feeble hand.

"Got enough Kraft for me, too?"

"Just about," I said. "But . . ." I trailed off, looking at Laura helplessly.

"I've kind of commandeered Kate for the night," she said, jumping in like a true best friend. "I, um, I hope you don't mind. I need her to, you know, help me with some stuff." She gestured vaguely toward her house.

"I'm sorry, sweetie. I didn't realize you'd be home for dinner, so I told Laura I'd, you know, help her."

"Right," he said. "Sure." I could see the disappointment in his eyes, and for a moment, I let the guilt wash over me. I figured I deserved it.

* * *

I left Timmy with Stuart (who surprised me by not protesting too much) then headed over to Laura's to help with her fabricated project. I hadn't been able to sneak up to the attic, so my only weapon tonight was the holy water in my purse, my handy-dandy barrette, and a barbeque skewer I borrowed from Laura. That was okay. I'd make do.

Because I also didn't have a car, I borrowed Laura's Lexus to go meet David. All of which put me about ten minutes late arriving at the lifeguard stand. I waited, turning a slow circle as I scoped out the area for David . . . and for any potential demons.

Nothing.

I checked my watch. Fifteen past seven. And no sign of David. Damn.

I shifted my weight from one foot to the other, trying to decide what to do. Not that hard of a decision, though. I was there. David wasn't. Which meant I was going hunting on my own.

I walked down the boardwalk toward the Coronado Crest Hotel, keeping an eye out for any known demons.

I wasn't seeing anyone, though. No one except tight groups of Christmas shoppers ducking in and out of the little shops across the street, and a few couples walking hand in hand on the beach.

My eyes darted to the hotel patio as I passed, thinking about Paul and Laura and me and Stuart. I shook my head, shooing the thoughts away. I was a walking target out here; I needed to stay focused.

The boardwalk ended at the hotel parking lot, and I stood for a second, trying to decide what to do. I could cross down the beach to the surf and continue walking, or I could backtrack, checking out the passersby again, and see if David had shown up at the lifeguard stand yet.

I decided on the second option. As much as I wanted to find Cool and company, I really didn't have any reason to believe he was here tonight. And if I was going to wander the beach, aimlessly looking for a neon sign flashing "demon" then I wanted company.

I'd walked about twenty yards when I heard it—soft footfalls behind me, keeping in step with me, and pausing when I paused. I tensed and stopped. The footsteps stopped, too.

"You're late," I said, then spun around to find David grinning behind me.

"*You* were late," he said.

"No excuse to sneak up on me."

"You knew I was there," he said. "By definition, I wasn't sneaking."

"I'm sure there's a flaw in your logic," I said as he fell in step beside me. "But give me a little time to figure out what it is."

"I'll give you all the time you need," he said.

I glanced sideways at him, wondering at both his tone and his words. But his face was blank, his eyes focused on the area.

I took my cue from him, and we spent the next hour hunting demons . . . with absolutely no success. Frustrated, I stopped on the boardwalk and looked around, taking in the beach and the stores across the street. If we called it a night, I could squeeze in some Christmas shopping before the stores closed at ten. "Let's make one more pass through the area, and if nothing jumps out at us—"

"Literally."

"—then we'll wrap this up," I concluded, shooting him a "be serious" look.

We walked the length of the boardwalk again, then cut

down to the beach. We walked along the water, not talking, both of us listening and looking.

Beside us, the ocean churned about as noisily as the thoughts in my head. I hadn't patrolled with anyone since Eric had died. Even on the few occasions that I'd wanted help with the footwork, Eddie and I had covered different sections of the town. So now, to be walking alongside this man, well, the whole situation was surreal.

Bittersweet, too, especially since David had known Eric. Time and again, I tensed, turning just slightly, the words right there. But I couldn't make them come. I wanted so badly to ask him about Eric. To share stories. To have him tell me funny little things that would make my husband come alive to me again.

I couldn't do it, though. Now wasn't the time. And, honestly, I'm not sure it ever would be.

We walked along the water until we were even with the lifeguard stand again. Then we plodded through the sand back up toward the boardwalk.

"No one," he said. "I'm disappointed, but not too surprised."

"Me, too."

We stood at the corner, waiting for the light to change to cross PCH and get over to the shops on Main, lovely little art galleries, jewelry shops, ice cream parlors, and beach gear stores. In other words, a mishmash of goods geared mostly for the tourists, but still fun for locals.

The light changed and I started to cross, David at my side. "I want to pick up something for Allie and Laura," I said. "But I have an idea about Cool. You up for shopping?"

"Shopping?" He looked pained. "I suppose it won't kill me."

"Probably not," I agreed. We turned into the first store,

Escape, a tiny boutique with a range of everything—carved wooden boxes, silver and beaded jewelry, funky wall art, and trinkets made from seashells. I picked up a nautilus shell and held it out for David to see. "I think the ocean must have something to do with it," I said. "Whatever *it* is."

"I'm listening."

"Why else would Asmodeus pick a surfer body?"

"He may not have picked it," David said. "Demons tend to not be picky. They take whatever body comes available."

The man had a point, and I considered that, shifting my theory as I ran my hand over a display of ankle bracelets made from polished stone beads. "What do you think? For Allie?"

He took it from me and held it up. "Pretty. Does she like blue? She's always seemed more the pink type to me."

I laughed. "When she was little, she went through a phase where she wore only pink. Thankfully, we moved through that one without damage to life or limb."

"Probably best not to rouse the beast, then." He grabbed a bracelet off the rack and passed it to me. "How about this one?"

Muted oranges and browns, natural colors that would not only look great against Allie's tan, but also fit nicely in her organic, earth-friendly, eco-awareness phase.

"I'm impressed," I said. "A male of the species with a reasonable shopping suggestion."

"Don't tell anyone," he said. "They'll revoke my membership in the Manly Man Club."

"I'm amazed they let you join in the first place."

He put a hand over his heart. "Kate, you wound me."

"Wait a second," I said. "I think we're onto something."

"We?"

"All right. *I'm* onto something. What I said a minute ago about not letting you into the boy's club in the first place."

His mouth twitched. "You think Cool's a member?"

"What I think, Mr. Comedian, is that this surf exhibition is somehow key."

"Go on."

"When did you add Cool to the ticket?"

"About three weeks ago," David said.

"He wiped out about a month ago," I said. "So unless he needs the surfers or the beach or the ocean, why would a demon bother with a high school surf exhibition?"

"Jason brought Cool to the surf club," David said thoughtfully.

"What do you mean?"

"The exhibition was originally going to be just that. The kids showing off a few tricks. We'd sell some food, some raffle tickets. Still for charity, but we weren't planning on bringing in that much money."

"And then Jason shows up one day with the idea that Cool step in as a celebrity surfer? Someone who'd really sell tickets?"

"Exactly," David said.

"And now Jason's dead. It doesn't make sense."

"It does if Jason didn't realize what he'd gotten himself into—"

"And didn't want anything to do with it," I said, finishing his thought.

"Exactly."

"It's not just the ocean or the beach then. This whole thing must center around the exhibition."

"Saturday," he said. "Whatever Cool's plan is, it sounds like it's going to happen at noon on Saturday. That gives us just over thirty-six hours to save San Diablo. Maybe the world."

"Great," I said. "I was afraid we were going to be rushed."

*   *   *

"Mo-*om*! Have you gone mental?"

"For suggesting you stay home from school today? Why is that mental? I thought you'd be kissing my feet?" Allie and I were faced off, her at the top of the stairs, me at the bottom. She was dressed for school, fully decked out in cheerleader garb for the last-period assembly that would kickoff Christmas vacation.

"I've got responsibilities, Mom! I'm on the end of the first row in the second routine. If I'm not there, the whole thing's gonna crash and burn."

"Right. I'm sorry. You're right." I held up my hands in defeat. I may not have done the high school thing, but I was smart enough to know when I was beaten. And David would be there. At least I knew he'd keep an eye on her.

As soon as Allie was out the door, I packed Timmy into the van and took him to KidSpace. On the drive back, I tried to think what to do now. I had the entire day laid out in front of me. An entire day without husband or kids. A full, uninterrupted span of time I could devote to eradicating demons from the face of the earth.

Too bad I had no idea where to start.

I got back home and grabbed the 409, then started going over the kitchen countertops with a frenzy borne of nervous energy. It was the last day of school before vacation and the day before the exhibition. All points were converging on tomorrow, but I didn't have a clue what to do now.

If I didn't figure something out soon, my house would be spotless. Not a bad deal for my family, but for San Diablo as a whole, I predicted dire consequences.

Eddie padded into the kitchen, grunted at me, and made a beeline for the coffee.

"Learn anything yesterday?"

His eyes narrowed, but he didn't say anything, just moved to the kitchen table and took a sip. I scowled at him, then threw down my rag and grabbed the Swiffer WetJet from the pantry. While I attacked the floors, Eddie attacked his coffee.

I'd scrubbed the entire kitchen and moved on to the breakfast room when he finally grunted at me. "Not a damn thing. Thousands of books in the cathedral archive, and not one mention of the *Malevolenaumachia Demonica.*" He pointed a bony finger at me. "You want to fight demons, you need information. Damned organization is behind the times, that's what. Living in the damned fifteenth century."

"Behind the times? *Forza?*"

"Databases! PDF files! Scans and uploads! All that techno mumbo jumbo your daughter blathers on about all day. You wanna tell me why not one of *Forza*'s research books are on the Internet? Far as I know, your esteemed ancient organization doesn't even have a website."

I leaned against my Swiffer handle and stared at him. "You want computerized information? Has Hell frozen over? Are monkeys flying?"

"You laugh, but I'm right. You mark my words."

"Is this about Allie? Or that librarian you like?"

The tips of his ears turned pink. "You leave her out of it. That woman knows her stuff. She's not trapped in the past."

"Right," I said, turning away to hide my grin.

Eddie grumbled something I couldn't quite make out. When I'd managed to get my face well enough under control so that I could turn back, I found him scowling at me.

I held my hands up in supplication. "I'm not disagreeing with you. But you're the man who until a month ago thought the Internet was a high-speed freeway in Germany."

"I never thought any such thing."

"Uh-huh."

"Well, they call the damn thing a superhighway," he muttered.

"At any rate," I said, falling into the chair opposite him. "I take it you haven't found anything useful. In books or online?"

"You take it right," he said. He frowned at me. "The padre and I kept at it until about ten last night. When I got home, lover boy said you were out with Laura. Some crisis or other. She okay?"

The warmth in his voice made me smile. As with the rest of us, Eddie had adopted Mindy and Laura as if they were family. "She's fine," I said. "Well, she's not, actually. The whole thing with Paul is eating at her. But I wasn't with her last night."

Eddie's bushy brows waggled. "Oh, no? Where were you then?"

"Patrolling," I said. "With David," I added to the table-top, feeling unreasonably guilty.

"Oh, ho," he said. "And you didn't want Stu-boy to know."

"I didn't want Stuart to know about the *patrolling*," I said sharply. "David had nothing to do with it."

"Right," Eddie said. "Sure."

I got up and poured myself a cup of coffee. I needed to keep my hands busy so I wouldn't throttle the man. "Are you finished giving me grief?" I asked, my back to him. "Or should I wait a little longer to tell you what we learned?"

"Wait a little longer," he said. "I'm still amusing myself watching you squirm."

"Eddie!" I whipped around, glaring at him. "It's the surf exhibition! The exhibition that Allie's desperate to go to to-morrow! Now do you want to be serious? Or shall we just leave it to chance that our girl's going to be okay?"

His shoulders rose and fell, his eyes darkening. He took a

sip of coffee, then put the cup down hard on the table. Then he looked at me, every trace of humor gone. "Tell me everything," he said.

And I did.

Half an hour later, I'd run him through all that had happened. From learning that David was a rogue, to hunting with him last night, to finally reaching our theory that everything centered on the exhibition.

"It's a good theory," he said. "What are you going to do about it?"

"I don't know," I admitted. "Keep Allie away, that's for sure. And in the meantime, hopefully figure out what Cool is up to and stop it. But you and Ben haven't figured anything out yet, and we're running out of time."

"You're going to have to tie that girl down to make her stay home," Eddie said. "Either that, or tell her the truth."

My stomach twisted. "Yeah. I've thought about that." I wasn't big on the truth plan. Not yet. But I might not have a choice. If it came down to a choice between letting my daughter walk into danger or revealing my secrets to convince her to stay home . . . well, put that way, it was a no-brainer. Just not a no-brainer I particularly wanted to confront.

"And David's the one who told you about Jason, right?"

"You mean about Jason recruiting Cool for the exhibition? Yeah." I peered at him. "Why?"

"Just wondering if you should trust David. If you're being smart about this."

"What are you talking about?"

He shrugged. "You're the one who said he brings back memories of Eric. Maybe he's playing off that."

I swallowed, fighting the bile rising in the throat. But

Eddie was right. David had known Eric. And because of that, I wanted to be around him even as much as I wanted to run home and cry.

Still, I couldn't discount what Eddie was saying, even if I did think he was dead wrong. "I didn't trust him at first," I said. "Remember? I'm the one who tossed holy water on his face."

"And that convinced you?" Eddie's eyes burned into mine. Years ago, nothing would have convinced me more.

"Not just the holy water," I said. "The cathedral, too. We were inside, in the sanctuary, for almost an hour. He carried on a conversation. He spoke clearly. He was focused. He couldn't be a demon."

"He looked a little green around the gills to me."

"I've already thought of all this, Eddie. I even asked him. He told me he was fighting a cold."

"And you believe him."

"Yes! If he were a demon, we'd know. No demon could survive that long beside an altar, and especially not the St. Mary's altar."

"So maybe he's not a demon," Eddie said.

"Isn't that what I've been saying all along?"

"Maybe he's something else."

That threw me. "Something else? Like what?"

"Don't know. But if a demon can slide into a body, then why not a soul? I've heard rumors, you know. Whispers of *alimentatores* seduced by the possibility. Grabbing on to immortality by sliding their soul into a dying human."

"What exactly are you suggesting?" I asked, my voice little more than a whisper.

"I'm not suggesting anything. I'm just talking. But if someone were to dabble in the dark arts—and if that someone played dangerous games with their own soul—well, he'd be changed, right? Not a demon, but not human anymore, either. So is he good? Or is he bad?" Eddie peered at me, his eyes dark and narrow. "Has malevolence touched him like a disease?"

"You're saying that Eric might have . . ."

"Hid out in David's body?" His bony shoulders rose and fell. "Eh. It's possible."

"No," I whispered, shaking my head. "Eric would never—"

"Are you sure, Kate?" he asked gently. "Do you really know what Eric was or wasn't capable of?"

But I couldn't answer that. I'd lost all my words, and I could only sit there lost and hopeless, my head filled with memories of the man I'd thought I'd known and the letters that proved I hadn't.

Could David really be Eric? And if he was—if Eric had slid into David's body—then what did that mean? Was he still my Eric? Or was he something else entirely?

Seventeen

It was almost a relief when the phone rang. I'd sent Eddie off on the pretense that I wanted to be alone, and now I needed to either let it ring or answer it. Since I was craving distractions, I answered, actually praying for a telemarketer.

I wasn't prepared to hear David Long's voice on the other end of the receiver. "Can you come to the school?" he asked, his voice low. "Creasley's here. But he's on his way out. I was in the office and overheard some of the staff talking about him. I've got students for the next two periods, but if you come right now, you can follow him from the parking lot. Maybe he'll even lead you to Cool before you nail him."

"On my way," I said, relieved I wouldn't have to see David. And a little too excited about the possibility of sending a demon packing back to Hell. What can I say? I was a little stressed out, and I was definitely in the mood to kick some demon butt.

"Good. Meet me at Cutter's at five. You can fill me in on how you nailed the SOB. Then we can get in some sparring."

I paused, wanting to protest, but the words never came. And as I stayed silent, he begged off, saying he had students waiting. I found myself listening to the dial tone.

It took only a few seconds to pull myself out of my funk, though. I had a date with a demon, after all. I grabbed my keys and purse and then made a quick run through the house to check the locks. I pushed through the curtains that covered the back door, saw the face just inches from the glass, and screamed.

The sound had barely left my throat when my brain caught up with the situation. *Laura.* Her skin red and splotchy, tears cutting a path through her powder, and dark smears of mascara under her eyes.

I yanked the door open. "Laura! Dear God, what is it?"

"Paul," she wailed. "The bastard filed for divorce."

She fell against me, and I hugged her close, my own sobs joining with hers. I thought about Creasley, the demon who'd been on my afternoon agenda. Killing him was my responsibility; I was the Demon Hunter in these parts, after all.

Didn't matter. As far as I was concerned, my appointment with Creasley had just been bumped. He'd been pre-empted by a demon of the human variety. A lying, cheating, bastard of a husband.

For now, at least, Creasley lived. Because I had other responsibilities in San Diablo, too. And one of them was to be there when my best friend needed me.

I yanked open the glass doors to Cutter's dojo at ten minutes to five, and found myself staring at my daughter, her leg out thrust, as David Long went sprawling.

Her head snapped up at the sound of the bell over the door, and a wide grin spread across her face. In an instant, she went from Martial-Arts Queen to Homecoming Queen as she bounded across the mat toward me, squealing about how she'd totally nailed him.

"Did you see? Wasn't it ferociously cool? I've been working with Cutter for weeks and weeks, but I didn't think I had it down, but I did. I *so* busted him!"

I looked over to the busted "him," who'd rolled over and was now sitting up, watching my daughter with amusement and affection.

My stomach twisted a little and I couldn't help but wonder—was he watching *his* daughter, too?

Allie took my hands, still bouncing. "Tell her, Cutter! Tell her how fabulous I did."

"It's true," Cutter said from behind his desk. "The kid's doing great. She kicked David's sorry ass."

"Thanks a lot," David said, climbing to his feet.

I saw that his cane was a few yards away, and I wondered if he'd fought with it or set it aside while doing battle with Allie.

He snatched up the cane and looked at me. "You okay?"

"Fine," I said. "Just a little light-headed." I pulled Allie into a hug. "You are amazing."

"I know," she said, then bounced happily around the room until she reached Cutter. He pulled her aside and sat her on a bench. I watched as he analyzed each of her moves, his hands moving in elegant illustration.

This wasn't her usual class day, and I realized that she must have called Cutter and made a special appointment. I wondered how often she'd done that, and made a note to ask Cutter. If what little I'd seen was any indication, not only was she practicing frequently, but her practices were paying off. My little girl, it seemed, was learning to kick a little butt.

"I didn't realize she'd be here," David said. I'd moved to

his side, and he spoke softly, his words meant for me only. "Actually, I didn't realize Cutter would be here."

"How were you planning on getting in?"

"Key," he said. "I've been practicing here after hours. Cutter's a good guy. I trust him."

I cocked my head. "Exactly how much do you trust him?"

"Not that much," he said, understanding my meaning. "So what happened with Creasley?"

I glanced over, but Allie and Cutter were still deep in conversation. "I didn't go," I said. I gave him the short version of Laura's dilemma. "I needed to stay with her."

"You stayed with Laura instead of nailing a demon?"

"Yes," I said, my voice tight. "I just told you." I tensed, ready to lash out if he said anything critical. I almost hoped he did. However unreasonable, I wanted a fight with this man, whoever he was.

He didn't look critical, however. Instead, he looked amused, and his eyes were dancing as he jerked his head sideways, signaling for us to walk to the far side of the room.

I fell in step beside him, both grateful for the silence and strangely off-put. It hung between us, as thick as fog, and I fought the urge to blabber on about the latest PTA drama, just to break the silence.

We stood looking out the window at the people going into and out of the 7-Eleven and the traffic along Rialto. After a few more minutes of silence, David broke it for me. "You have a good heart, Katie-kins."

"What did you just call me?" I asked, my voice remarkably stable.

"I called you Kate. That's your name, right?"

"No," I said. "You called me Katie-kins."

Eric used to call me that. I hated it, but he'd say it anyway, just to get a rise. It had started when we'd first met, me thirteen and him a year older. He told me later that it had been love at first sight for him, too, but I never really believed him. How could I when he'd spent so much of his time tormenting me?

David glanced up and to the left as if trying to remember. "Yeah, I guess I did."

"Why?" I managed to force the question out even though my mouth and throat had gone completely dry.

"Why?" he repeated.

I wanted to confront him. To insist he tell me the truth. But maybe I didn't really want to know, because "Eric used to call me that," was the best I could manage.

"He did?" David said, his eyes strangely soft. "I don't know, Kate," he said. "It just sort of rolls off the tongue. Hell, maybe Eric told me he called you that. I just don't remember."

I blinked at him, then swallowed. "Right," I said. "That makes sense."

I clenched my fists, wondering what I'd expected. For him to reveal all? To say that, yes, he was Eric. That he was sorry for leaving me, that he was sorry for the secrets.

That he loved me.

And then . . .

I frowned, turning away from David as I studied the floor. And then what? Could the Eric I loved ever really come back to me? And even if he could, so what? Time changes everything. I had a new life now. A new family. Even if this man was Eric, did I really want to know?

I wasn't sure, but at the same time, I *had* to know. I wasn't sure if I was obsessing on the question because of hope or fear, but I couldn't get it out of my head. I also couldn't get it out of my mouth.

But while I might not be able to voice the question, there was one other way that I could be sure—a fight. And a real one this time, not the scrabbling to douse him with holy water we'd played at earlier.

I'd known Eric's rhythms. Known his style, his pattern. I hadn't been paying attention the first time I'd sparred with David. But I wouldn't make that mistake this time. And if Eric was buried somewhere deep in David, I'd know.

What I'd do with the answer, though . . .

That, I wasn't yet sure of.

"This is so cool. You guys are really going to fight?" Allie bounced in front of us, clearly thrilled at the prospect of seeing her mom and her teacher battle it out.

"Don't you have homework?"

"Not much."

"Allie, you should go home. You're already in hot water for not telling me you were coming here today." I shot a look at Cutter and put my hands on my hips for emphasis. "Considering how well you're doing, I'm thinking that my little girl's been keeping a few secrets about her practice schedule."

"You're the one who wanted me in shape!"

"And now I want you to go home."

"You want me to walk?" She said the words with the same outraged inflection as if I'd told her to perform a belly dance.

"Yes," I said. "I want you to—"

I cut myself off. Our house was about a mile away, and I really *didn't* want her walking by herself. "Never mind," I said. "I'll drive you." I shot a quick glance toward Cutter and David. "We'll do this some other time."

"Mom!" Allie howled, at the same time Cutter and David voiced equally powerful protests.

"It's not like the kid hasn't seen you fight, Kate," Cutter said.

I wanted to put up more of a protest, but I knew I was beat. Besides, I figured too much protest would only raise Allie's suspicions. She'd never seen her father fight; it wasn't as if anything David did could possibly trigger a memory with her. It was my reactions I was worried about. But no matter what I learned here, I could keep my emotions and my expressions under control. After all, it wasn't like I didn't have practice.

"Fine," I finally said with a toss of my hands. "You win." I turned to David. "Looks like it's you and me."

This time, David sparred without the cane. We started out easy, just testing each other's rhythms. A few jabs and parries as we scoped out reflexes and reactions, Cutter and Allie cheering us on from the sidelines.

He broke the pattern first, and we went at it with gusto until we were both out of breath, neither one at the advantage. He was good, and I had to admit we were pretty evenly matched.

He got the advantage first, catching me in the chest with a kick. I'd seen it coming at the last second, and I defended with a sidestep, then grabbed his leg and tried to knock him flat. He surprised me, though, nailing a damn tricky move by spinning around, and jerking his foot free. At the same time, his hands hit the mat, and he kicked back, catching me under the chin and knocking me down.

I sprang back up, my adrenaline now truly pumping. I'd seen that spin before, and not just in practices with Cutter. The move was difficult, and every fighter moves with certain nuances. And the man now circling me on the mat moved like my first husband.

My heart stuttered, and David picked up on my hesitation, moving in with a jab that I blocked automatically, then dropped and rolled to one side, wanting both distance and time to think. I was back on my feet before he could reach me, but in the split second I'd been down, I'd noticed the lights in the dojo. Never important before, they'd always blended into the background. Now, though . . .

Now the metal fixture fluorescent bars surrounded by the solid wire cage seemed to call to me. And as David rushed me, I did exactly the same, sprinting toward him, even while I blurted out the key words of "Hail Mary!"

He blinked, but stopped short, and I could swear I saw him nod. I kept on, expecting him to grab my waist and toss me into the air as Eric had so many times before.

It was our "Hail Mary" move, named after the football play, and something we'd concocted together. It only worked in certain fight situations, but we'd extricated ourselves from many a sticky situation by Eric tossing me up, giving me a new vantage point from above our foe.

This time, the move didn't work nearly as well. Instead, reality smashed up against my expectations. And by "smash," I mean literally.

I barreled straight into David, barely registering his startled expression as we tumbled to the ground. Allie and Cutter cried out and rushed toward us, and I lay there on the mat, staring up at the light fixture I'd been aiming for and wondering what had gone wrong.

Except I knew what had gone wrong: David wasn't Eric, and some little part of me had known that all along. More, I'd been foolish to even let the thought enter my head. Eric would never have used black magic to slide his soul into another body, and I couldn't quite believe that I'd let my imagination run off with Eddie's wild theory.

As I lay there—Cutter, Allie, and David staring at me with baffled expressions—the reality of the situation flooded through me. *This man wasn't Eric.*

I closed my eyes and breathed deep, barely hearing Allie's worried cries of "Mom? Mom!"

I shouldn't be sad. I didn't *want* to be sad. I was happily married. An undead husband would only wreak havoc on this life I'd put together and loved so much. So, no, I really, really, really didn't want to be sad.

Didn't matter, the tears threatened anyway. I managed to blink them back, but I could tell by the expressions on the faces around me, that I wasn't doing a good job of hiding my emotion.

David knelt beside me. "Kate? Are you okay? What happened?"

"I . . . I misjudged a move. I was trying something new. It didn't work."

"No kidding," Allie said. She was down beside me, too, now, her hand on my elbow. If she or the others thought my "Hail Mary" outburst was odd, no one mentioned it.

David studied me through narrowed eyes. "You don't look that great. Do you feel okay?"

"I'm . . ." I shook my head. "You know what? I don't. I'm feeling a little woozy." Right then, I wanted nothing more than to escape. And I wasn't above faking an illness to do it.

"Go home," he said. "Besides, don't you two have company tonight?"

"We do?"

"Troy, Mom!" Allie said. "Mr. Long's right. I've gotta go get ready." She stood up, tugging me along with her.

"Right," I added, with a queasy smile to Cutter and David. "And I've got a dinner to make."

I dropped Allie at home so that she could do the primping thing, then picked up Timmy at KidSpace. On the way home, I stopped in at Laura's to beg help. I told myself that I didn't want her at home by herself brooding about Paul, but the truth was I wanted her kitchen gadgets, her recipe books, and her kitchen equivalent of a green thumb.

She's not a neat or organized cook, but the end result always came out edible. And so long as I trailed along after her cleaning up the mess and putting the broken pieces back together, I was pretty sure we'd come up with something worthy of Troy Myerson by the time he arrived at eight.

"You're sure you don't mind?" I asked her. We were in her kitchen, putting a variety of Pampered Chef products into a box. Each and every one, Laura assured me, absolutely essential to bringing off a fabulous meal.

"I promise," Laura said. "In fact, I'm glad you asked. Otherwise I'd just be sitting around plotting ways to kill him." She shot me a piercing look. "I mean, I already know where to hide the body, right? I'm halfway there."

"We definitely need to get you in the kitchen," I said. "In fact, maybe you and Mindy should come for dinner, too. How's Mindy doing, by the way?" I asked gently.

"She doesn't know," Laura said. "Well, I think she suspects, but that's not the same. We're going to wait until January to tell her. I told Paul that I'd take him for every last cent if he spoiled Mindy's Christmas."

"Yeah?"

She smiled thinly. "Of course, I plan to take him for every last cent anyway. But he doesn't know that."

"I'll keep my fingers crossed. Maybe you and Mindy should plan on spending a lot of quality holiday time over here."

"Sounds good to me," she said. "Even tonight, for that matter. But is that kosher? Another teenage girl at the table when the boy du jour is present?"

"I'm not sure, actually. I'll have to check the manual."

I pulled a face. "Oh, wait. Teenagers don't come with a manual. Someone really ought to do something about that."

As Laura continued to pack enough cooking utensils to supply a five-star restaurant, I called the teenager in question, grateful to discover that in this particular case, etiquette gave a big thumbs-up to the presence of best friends.

I relayed the news to Laura, then peeked into the last box she'd packed. "We're just feeding a high school boy, you know. He's not the monarch of a small country."

"Allie's crushing on him," Laura said. "You don't want her blaming a crappy dinner if it all falls apart. Do you?"

Since she had a point, we loaded all the boxes (five!) then raided Laura's refrigerator and freezer. Between the two of us, she assured me that we had enough for a decent meal. Considering the Odyssey was packed to the gills, I believed her.

Once we'd brought the supplies back to my house and she'd put me to work dicing onions, the conversation shifted around to demons. Some women discuss soap operas with their friends. Laura and I dish about the undead.

I checked to make sure Allie was out of earshot, then brought Laura up to speed, ending with the theory David and I had concocted that somehow this all had to do with the exhibition.

"And he's a rogue hunter, huh?" She slammed the knife hard against the cutting board, neatly slicing a bell pepper in two. "I don't seem to have any luck with the buttoned-up corporate types. Maybe I should see if your academic demon-hunting friend is looking for a date. Because apparently I'm in the market again." Her voice had risen, along with the speed and fury of her knife blows.

I watched silently, waiting for her to calm down. When the pepper was nothing more than tiny bits of green goo, she looked up at me with a beatific smile. "Cooking's very cathartic, don't you think?"

"Absolutely," I said. I cleared my throat. "Actually, there's something about David I wanted to talk to you about."

"Oh really?" Her perfectly arched brow quirked upward. "Is this the part where you tell your best friend to back off, because you've got your sights on the guy? Poor Stuart. His wife, thinking about another man."

"Pretty much," I said.

That got her attention and she stopped chopping mushrooms long enough to turn to me. "Kate, what are you talking about?"

I closed my eyes and drew in a breath. "God, Laura, I'm such an idiot. I got myself all worked up, thinking that David was Eric. But—"

"Whoa!" She held up a hand. "David is *Eric?*"

"No, no. I just thought maybe he was. But I was wrong. I had to have been wrong."

A long moment passed while she stared at me, searching my face for signs of a recent mental breakdown. Since she started talking again, I'm assuming she didn't find any. "You're serious," she said. "You really thought that? But why? I mean . . . *how?* How could he possibly be?"

I ran down Eddie's theory, then concluded by telling her about the failed Hail Mary. "So I figure that means he's not Eric. And, honestly, I was being ridiculous to even consider it for a second. Eric would never have hijacked someone else's body."

"Are you sure?"

I opened my mouth to say that of course I was sure, but I couldn't quite get the words out.

"Maybe it is him. Maybe he doesn't remember all the little details like your fighting code words," Laura suggested. "Maybe it's some sort of weird amnesia where he thinks his past life was as a friend or something."

"Maybe," I said, trailing off. "I mean, I guess it could be

possible." But would Eric do that? Dabble with dark forces that way? A week ago I would have emphatically said no. Now, I wasn't as sure.

"Or maybe it's Eric and he remembers perfectly well," Laura continued.

I frowned. "Then why not just tell me? Why tease me by calling me Katie-kins?"

"Slip of the tongue?"

"I don't know," I said, not sure what I wanted to believe anymore. "Why even pretend to be David in the first place?"

"What would you do if he told you?"

"I don't know." That was a question I'd been asking myself all day, and I still didn't have an answer. "I just keep thinking about how Eric knew me so well, but with Stuart I have this secret life."

"You could tell him," Laura said.

"I can't," I said. "I don't want *Forza* to be part of my life with Stuart. That wasn't in the original package, you know? And I don't want him to wake up and find out he married some other woman. A woman who prowls the streets with holy water and a stiletto. The only time I want Stuart thinking about me and stilettos is if he takes me to a fancy restaurant."

"Kate . . ."

I held up a hand. "I'm not that woman with him, Laura. And I don't want him looking at me that way. Thinking about the things I've done, the things I've seen. Telling him might give him the truth, but it wouldn't really be honest. Because the woman I'd be describing isn't the woman he comes home to every night."

"Yes, Kate. It is."

I closed my eyes and let the truth of that settle over me. "Maybe, but I don't want it to be."

What that said about my marriage, I didn't know. But I

loved my husband and I didn't want to lose him. And the one thing I hadn't shared with Laura was that I didn't know how Stuart would react if I did tell him. Would it close the chasm between us? Or would it make it that much wider?

Because the truth was, I'd already lost one husband because of demon hunting. I don't think I could stand to lose another for the exact same reason.

"I didn't mean to start another big thing," Laura said. "This started with the whole David-Eric question, and that's gnarly enough."

"No kidding," I said.

"It could be true," Laura said. "David does seem to be around Allie a lot. And if Eric came back, he'd want to see her. Want to see what she's been up to and how she's grown up."

"And he'd keep the secret from me," I said, more to myself than to Laura. "After all, I'm remarried now."

Laura shot an ironic look my direction. "Yeah, you with two husbands, and I can't even manage to keep one."

"Oh, sweetie. I'm so so sorry."

Laura waved a hand. "Never mind. I didn't mean to start it all up again." The timer dinged, and Laura blew out a loud breath. "And we don't have time for it anyway."

Maybe I'm a bad friend, but I was relieved we had the interruption. I felt horrible for Laura, don't get me wrong, but my mind was too overwhelmed with husbands of my own, both past and present.

Not to mention the demons.

"You're sure I look okay? 'Cause I could wear the blue top." From her makeshift runway at the top of the stairs, Allie held it up for illustration purposes. "Oh, man," she whined, leaning against the railing in a fit of abject helplessness. "Mo-*ther,* can you please give me some help here?"

"The yellow," I said. "Definitely go with the yellow."

"You're sure?"

"Absolutely. I couldn't be more certain."

"Can I wear eyeshadow?" She clasped her hands in front of her, as if in prayer. "Please? I promise I won't ask again until I'm sixteen. No, eighteen. But please, please, pleeeeeeze can I wear it tonight."

"Eighteen?" I said. "You swear?"

"Cross my heart," she said, adding the appropriate motion for emphasis.

I didn't believe her, of course. For that matter, I figured the question would come up again in about a week, when she started going with her friends to the holiday parties. Then I'd get hit again after the new semester started. I'd held fast for an entire semester, despite horrific odds and a whining teenager. By spring break, odds were good that I'd have given in completely on the subject.

"Hang on," I said. "Let me check the stove and I'll meet you in my bathroom." I held up a warning finger. "Don't touch."

"Hello? I'm not Timmy!"

She had a point. But just in case, I intended to make sure that she didn't apply makeup with as heavy a hand as her brother.

All of Laura's concoctions looked to be cooking or boiling or simmering just fine, so I figured it was safe to leave the kitchen. Actually, considering my natural ineptitude in that department, I might be giving the meal a better chance by leaving it to cook in peace.

Laura had gone home to change after making sure everything was under control, and that I'd read and understood her scribbled instructions. She promised to be back—dressed and with Mindy—in time to do the last-minute tweaking. I glanced at the clock. Almost eight. The Duponts—and the guest of honor—should be arriving any minute.

I don't often wear makeup—most of the time, I really don't see the point—but my natural skills in that area are significantly more fine-tuned than my cooking skills. So I felt confident that we'd selected a perfectly appropriate, not overly dramatic, eyeliner and shadow.

With her hair curled and clipped up, my pearl earrings, and the soft-focus makeup job, I have to admit I got a little choked up. My little girl was growing up. (That fact was registering with me on a regular basis lately. I'd experienced pretty much the same moment two months ago when we'd gone to the mall for bras and discovered that Allie and I now wore the same size. This was a blow to my ego from which I'm still trying to recover.)

Since nothing can turn a dinner party south faster than unexpected toddler crankiness, I'd fed Timmy earlier. Now Allie and I got him to bed, then called Stuart up for the requisite bedtime kiss.

With that chore handled, and a few minutes left before Troy was due to arrive, Allie prowled the living room, picking lint off of cushions, organizing the magazines so that *Newsweek* and *Time* were top of the pile, artfully placed to conceal *Vogue, Redbook,* and *Entertainment Weekly.*

She scowled at Stuart, who had his feet on the coffee table, double-checked that I'd bought actual napkins (instead of our usual paper towel segments), tuned the television from yet another presentation of *Miracle on 34th Street* to CNN, and begged Eddie to keep any off-color jokes to himself.

I sat quietly—fearful that actually reading a magazine would incur my daughter's wrath—until Mindy and Laura arrived at the back door. If I'd thought their presence would lighten up the mood, I was sadly mistaken. Mindy was just as antsy as Allie, and they held whispered conversations, then moved around the room, straightening pillows and knickknacks, and, yes, dusting. I would have felt totally incompetent as a mom and housekeeper if I hadn't been so amused.

My amusement faded, though, about eight-fifteen. I'd been staring blankly at the television, absorbing not a word of the commentator's discussion of the latest fiscal crisis, when I realized that Allie was doing the same. Her foot was bouncing and she glanced toward the clock about every ten seconds, the time in between spent checking the digital time displayed on the cable box as well as her wristwatch.

No doubt about it. Troy was late.

Another five minutes passed without him. Then another. Then another.

"Maybe he's lost," Mindy suggested hopefully.

Allie jumped all over that idea, and the girls raced to the kitchen to call Troy's cell phone.

No answer.

When the mantel clock chimed the half hour, the consensus was in: My little girl had been stood up.

"Allie," I said, moving to the arm of the sofa and putting a hand on her shoulder.

She jerked away, then stood up, not quite meeting my eyes. "It's okay," she mumbled. "Something probably came up. Or he's late. Or something. Not like I care or anything." She pressed her mouth together in a thin line, then concentrated a little too long on the carpet. "I'm gonna go wait upstairs."

Mindy stood up, apparently understanding that she was welcome where parents weren't.

"Bastard," Stuart whispered as soon as the girls were out of earshot. "If I ever get my hands on that son of a bitch."

I nodded, feeling exactly the same. And when I met Laura's eyes, I'm certain she could read my expression. Right then I wished Troy Myerson were a demon. Because nothing would feel better than shoving a blade through his eye.

I gave myself about an hour to calm down, figuring Allie and Mindy needed the time, too. Then I couldn't stand it any longer. I pushed up off the couch, pointing upstairs in response to Stuart's questioning glance.

"Chocolate might help," he said.

"Good point." I gave him a kiss on the cheek, then turned and walked the opposite direction to the kitchen. When I came back through the living room to our staircase, I had a bag of Oreos, two glasses, and a gallon jug of milk.

"Ah. The heavy artillery."

"I have a feeling I'll need it."

I tapped on the door, then pushed it open. The girls were on the bed, long T-shirts tucked over their knees. Allie's eyes were red and swollen, and Mindy didn't look much better. She looked over at me helplessly, and I hooked my thumb toward the hallway. "Your mom could use some help with the dishes." A transparent ploy to get rid of her, but nobody minded.

"Sure thing, Mrs. Connor," she said, She leaned over and gave Allie a tight hug, then slipped beside me into the hall.

Allie rolled over, hugging her pillow. I sat on the bed beside her and stroked her back, the same way I used to when she was a little girl and would wake up with a nightmare.

"What's wrong with me?" she whispered, after an eternity had passed. "Why'd he stand me up?"

"It's not you, baby. There's nothing wrong with you. You're perfect. Isn't that what you're always telling me?"

She didn't roll over, but her shoulder twitched, and from my perspective, that felt a whole lot like a smile.

"Any guy who stands up my little girl obviously is a guy

lacking in taste and discernment," I said. "Basically an idiot. A big fat idiot, actually." No reaction. "Probably eats boogers, too."

At that, her shoulders really did start to shake.

"I mean, did you really want to go out with a booger-eating moron? He probably wouldn't have even liked what Laura made for dinner."

"That is *so* not funny, Mom," she said into her pillow. But the shake in her now-spasmodic shoulders told a different story.

She rolled over and faced me. "I'm not Timmy, remember? You can't get me with gross-out jokes."

"I can't?" I grinned at her as I stroked her hair. "Well, in that case, I stand corrected."

"He has been showing signs of being a moron lately," Allie said. "He was so nice at first. But lately . . ." She trailed off.

I rubbed lightly on her shoulder. "So what happened? Did Troy start liking some other girl?"

"I wish," she said. "No, it's not even like he ditched me for a person. It's that stupid surf club," she said. "I mean, no offense to Mr. Long and all."

"I'm sure he doesn't take it personally," I said, trying to keep my voice light despite the way my insides were twisting and my muscles were screaming for action. "So what happened?"

"I don't know. Once they started practicing for the exhibition, he just got tenser and tenser, and . . ." She shrugged. "And he didn't even seem all that upset when we heard the news about Jason, you know? I mean, I told myself it was because it was such a shock, but it was like all he cared about was getting bumped up to captain and getting that butt-ugly ring. Owwww, Mom! You're hurting me."

"Sorry." I released my death grip on her arm. "What ring?" I asked, hoping I sounded more casual than I felt.

"Just these ugly gold rings. Both the team captains had them. They hung them on chains around their necks and wore them under their shirts."

"Where'd they get them?"

"Dunno." Her forehead creased. "I guess I never thought about it. Cool maybe?"

That's what I'd been thinking.

"Anyway," she went on, "Troy's been acting really weird for a while, but as soon as he got his stupid ring, he really started acting like an ass."

"That just means he was an ass all along," I said. "You're better off without him, sweetie."

"I guess," she said. "But if that's true, why's it got to hurt so much?"

"If I could answer that, I'd have Oprah's job, and we'd be rich and well-adjusted." Another smile. "Come here," I said, holding out my arms. She came, and I held her tight, rocking a little as I remembered all our past crises and imagined all the ones to come. As far as crises involving demonic minions, though, I sincerely hoped that it would be the last.

My daughter's heart might be breaking, but I couldn't help but be a little joyous. There's no way she'd go to the exhibition tomorrow and risk seeing Troy, so that worry was off my head.

And now I knew about the rings. Cool—or, rather, Asmodeus—was using the surf captains.

For what exactly, I didn't know. But I was certain of one thing. Whatever it was, it wasn't good.

Eighteen

I left Allie to sleep off her depression, and met Stuart in the hall coming out of Timmy's room. "He's down for the count," Stuart said. "How's Allie?"

"She'll survive," I said. "Boys. It's never easy."

"Never," he said, with just a hint of apology in his voice.

"Oh no. Not you, too."

"I thought since dinner didn't happen that I'd run back to the office. I've got a stack of files on my desk a mile high, and if you want me home over Christmas, I really need to make a dent."

"Go ahead." Considering my own schedule, it wasn't much of a hardship to be magnanimous.

"You're sure?"

"Stuart, honey, don't ask permission twice. When your wife says yes, the smart thing is to take that yes and run with it."

"You're right. What was I thinking?" He caught me around the waist and planted a deep, long kiss on me. "That's just to keep you thinking about later," he said.

I stood there, a little weak in the knees, as he hurried down the stairs. I followed at a more reasonable pace and found Laura, Mindy, and Eddie staring up at me from the living room. "How's our girl?" Eddie asked, speaking for the group.

"She's okay. We had a long talk," I added, giving Eddie and Laura what I hoped was a meaningful glance.

"Why don't you go on up?" Laura asked Mindy, apparently realizing there was a story there, and wanting to hear it.

"Allie'd probably like the company," I confirmed. I figured the girls would get so caught up in their own deconstruction of the evening and general bitch session about Troy, that we'd be able to talk without interruption or fear of being overheard.

While Stuart gathered his various bits of office paraphernalia, I made a pot of coffee. Anything to distract myself until Stuart cleared out and I could talk freely.

Eddie and Laura relocated to the breakfast table, then kept shooting me meaningful looks, as if I could make Stuart move faster.

The chime of the doorbell echoed through the house. Eddie and Laura and I looked at each other. Was it Troy? If it was, he was going to regret coming by. Bad enough that he's in cahoots with a demon, but standing up my daughter? That's completely unacceptable.

I checked the peephole, and the wave of righteous indignation receded. Not Troy. *Father Ben.*

I tugged the door open, and he burst through, his hair wild and his features tight. He had a thick folder under one arm, and he pushed it into my hands. "We must talk," he whispered. "Is it safe to talk?"

Before I could tell him it wasn't, though, Stuart stepped into the entrance hall, and I swear Father Ben jumped three feet.

"Father Ben!" Stuart said. "Did I startle you?"

"No, no," Ben said. "I'm fine."

"What's up?"

Father Ben's eyes were wide, a deer caught in the head-lights.

I stepped away from the wall and lifted the folder. "More things from Delores to catalog," I said. I'd been doing a lot of volunteer work at the church, and one of the jobs was itemizing the various donations to the church that had been made over the year. The project had been interesting, to say the least. More important, Stuart knew I was doing it, so my fabrication was that much more plausible.

"Oh," he said. He looked at his watch.

"I apologize for the hour," Father Ben said. "Delores is going out of town and wanted you to have these, and I vol-unteered to bring them by. I tried to call, but I'm afraid I've been unable to get through."

Allie. She and Mindy were probably going over Troy's be-trayal with every one of their friends. We have call-waiting, of course, but my daughter was obviously ignoring it.

"Do you want to come in?" I asked, hoping I sounded ca-sual. "Stuart has to run to the office, but we have some great leftovers, and you could sit and talk for a while."

"I'd love a bite. Thanks so much for offering."

He followed me into the kitchen, where Laura had put out all the food, along with some Tupperware, foil, and Press'n Seal. Troy's absence had put a damper on dinner, and leftovers were the order of the day.

Not that the boy's faux pas had queered Eddie's appetite. He looked up from where he was digging into Laura's lasagna, gestured with his fork, and ordered Father Ben to "pull up a chair and start shovelin' it in."

Stuart stepped into the room, and we all looked at each other, making awkward small talk while we waited for my husband to gather his keys and wallet and head into the garage. Except that he didn't. Instead, he was looking thoughtfully around the room at us.

"Stuart?" I said, my voice wary. "What's up?"

"I'm being a lousy host," he said. He tossed his briefcase up in front of the microwave. "The least I can do is stay and chat with everyone for a while."

"Oh, no, no," I said, as the others joined in with similar protests. "You don't have to do that."

"It's really not necessary," Father Ben said.

"Get your tail to the office and earn your keep," Eddie added.

Stuart looked from Eddie to Father Ben and back to me. "If I didn't know better, I'd say you're trying to get rid of me." His eyes narrowed. "Are you trying to get rid of me?"

"Of course not," I said, standing up and steering him toward the garage. "But there's no reason to change your plans. You have work, right?"

"Sure, but—"

"And you have to go into the office to do it, right?"

"Kate . . ."

"Just hear me out, Stuart. If you're going to spend time at the office catching up, I'd much rather you do it now while Timmy's asleep. If you stay here with us, all it's going to mean is that you have to go in tomorrow when your little boy wants to play with you. And for what? So you can have some of Laura's cobbler? If that's what you want I'll put some in Tupperware for you."

I stepped back and took in a deep breath, a little exhausted by my speech. Stuart was still staring at me. "Father Ben won't mind," I added lamely. "Will you, Father?"

"On the contrary," the padre said. "I'm sure Timmy will be thrilled to have his daddy around in the morning."

"All right," Stuart said. "I can take a hint. I don't know what you're up to, but I'll go."

I smiled, then fell back, exhausted, against the closed door as soon as he stepped through it. We all waited in silence like conspirators, which in a way I guess we were. The sound of the engine faded as Stuart pulled out, then the garage door creaked its way down. As soon as we heard the *thump* when it hit the concrete, we all started talking at once.

Father Ben held up a hand. "Whatever you have to say can wait," he said.

I leaned forward, my mouth open, desperate to tell him about the rings. He tapped a finger on the table in front of me. "Trust me, Kate. It can wait."

With that kind of conviction, how could I argue? I nodded, sat down in a chair, and absently nibbled at a carrot stick.

"We were right," he said, looking to each of us in turn. "It's all about the two demons imprisoned in Tartarus." He slammed the folder onto the table, then opened it, revealing an assortment of papers covered with ornate writing—in Greek, as far as I could tell—and intricate line drawings depicting the torments of the damned.

"I spoke with Father Corletti at length this morning. He found these references within the Vatican library. His assistant scanned the images and e-mailed them to me."

I shot Eddie a significant look, which he, of course, ignored.

I rifled through the papers, realized I had no clue what any of it meant, and asked Father Ben to boil it down to the bottom line.

"Two imprisoned demons," he said. "Two demons on Earth in the service of the imprisoned. And two humans who have given assistance to the forces of evil."

"What kind of assistance?" Eddie asked.

"The act itself doesn't matter, but the evil taints the human. The ritual takes place when the sun is at its peak. At the conclusion, the humans will be sucked into Tartarus, taking the place of the imprisoned demons, lost forever in eternal torment."

"Someone pushed the janitor and made him a demon," I said, stepping back so I could look into the living room. "Did any of you hear that?"

"Hear what?" Laura asked.

"Maybe nothing. I just thought I heard a swishing sound."

"Swishing," Eddie repeated. "Probably your damn cat."

Actually, Kabit *was* camped out in the corner by the drapes, his tail going back and forth, every other swoosh or so hitting the drapes and making them shimmy. "I guess you're right."

I turned my attention back to the group in the kitchen. "Is something like killing the janitor what you meant? By assistance, I mean?"

"Absolutely," Father Ben said.

"Before he died, the janitor griped about kids. He was cursing them as if they'd bothered him in the past. So maybe the kids had been sneaking into his basement."

"And talking to demons," Father Ben finished. "Yes, I think that's likely. They found the book, read the pages, and learned what they had to do."

Dear God, the thought made me ill.

"Well the janitor's now one dead demon," Eddie said. "So he doesn't count. But Cool makes one."

"And Creasley's the other," I said.

"It's the assistants we should focus on," Father Ben said. "They are the key to the ritual. If we can find and stop them, perhaps we can forestall Asmodeus's plan."

"I think we've already found them," I said. I explained what Allie had told me, about the surf club captains and their rings.

"But what I don't understand is why these kids would do this," Laura said. "I mean, why would they want to get sucked into Hell?"

"Demons lie, remember?" I said.

Father Ben nodded. "Perhaps the Tartarus demons used the book to promise the boys wealth, power, immortality. Who knows? The point is the boys believed."

"And were willing to kill for the lie," I said with a shiver. To think my daughter actually fell for a boy like that. Not for the first time, I wished I could wrap her up in some sort of force field and just keep her safe forever.

Laura still looked confused. "So is that how the book fits in to all this?"

"I'm afraid not," Father Ben said. "The book is also essential to the ritual. The imprisoned demons will rise up through the pages of the book."

"That's good news, at least," I said. "We've got the book."

"There are other things that must fall into place, too," Father Ben said. "The ritual involves the rendering of a geometric symbol." He ran his hands through his hair, making it stick up even more. "I've tried to find a description or drawing, but haven't had any luck. Something, though. Lines and angles."

"A pentagram," Laura said.

"Cliché," Eddie said.

Laura shrugged. "Works in the movies."

"I don't think it matters what it looks like," I said. "They're going to be at the beach, right? They'll just draw the symbol in the sand."

"I'm afraid you're probably right," Father Ben said. "At

the same time, this *is* a complex plot. Foil any piece of it, and we may be able to prevent the whole."

We all stood quietly, thinking about that. And then I heard that swishing noise. "There it is again! Like a soft scraping sound. Don't you guys hear it?"

"I don't hear anything," Laura said, but I was already out of my chair and around the divider into the living room. *No one.*

No one, that is, except Kabit, who was sharpening his claws on Eddie's recliner.

Just to be certain, I tiptoed upstairs, tapped once, then opened Allie's door. The girls—plugged into their iPods— didn't even notice.

"Anything?" Laura asked when I returned.

"Nothing."

"You know," she said, "I'm wondering if all this may not be as bad as we think."

We all looked at her.

"Go on, girl," Eddie said. "If you've got good news, now's the time to share it."

"Well, I was thinking about the book. They need that, right? And they don't have it. So even if they do have two demons, they still can't do their ritual." She looked to Father Ben and then to me. "Right?"

I shrugged. "That's the padre's department."

"I think Laura has a good point. And probably an accurate one," he said. "But as far as we know, this ritual has never been performed before. We might have mistranslated the texts. Or the texts might be purposefully inaccurate, designed to deceive. We just don't know."

Laura's smile was thin. "So much for my theory."

I gave her a quick hug. "It's a sound theory. And no matter what, I know I feel better knowing that some freaky book that can speak for demons is safely hidden in the altar."

"Thanks," she said. "I just want this to be over."

"It will be," I said. "Somehow, it's ending tomorrow. Timmy's old enough to get the whole Christmas thing this year, and there is no way my baby's holiday is getting spoiled by some demon who decided to throw his own holiday bash."

I bit back a sigh. I meant my words even if I wasn't sure how to carry them out. But that was the nature of my life lately: question after question.

Would my current husband win the election? Was my first husband wandering San Diablo in the body of another man? Would I finish my Christmas shopping in time? Would we ever get around to buying a Christmas tree or hanging Christmas lights? Would my daughter survive her first heartbreak and at the hand of a demon-serving teenage thug? The usual stuff.

I could handle some uncertainty. I mean, that's life, right? But there was one question I intended to see answered only in the affirmative: Would we stop Asmodeus and prevent the release of the Tartarus demons? The answer had to be yes.

And the sooner the better.

Because Eddie and Father Ben plowed through so much of the food, we ended up needing only about half of the Tupperware that Laura had set out. Even after Ben left, Eddie was still working on the dessert (a truly yummy peach cobbler that Laura swore she could teach me how to make).

Laura and I ended up drinking coffee in the living room, trying to get our minds off the demon/Eric/Paul thing by watching *The Bishop's Wife.*

"I don't know," Laura said as the end credits rolled. "I just like Cary Grant so much better. David Niven's so clueless.

And Cary obviously loves her so much. And she loves him . . ."

"But Cary's an angel," I pointed out.

"The wedding would be a little unorthodox, sure . . ."

That reminded me of the nephalim. "Did I ever tell you why the demons were put into Tartarus in the first place?"

She made a face. "We're back on demons?"

I waved a hand. "This is interesting," I said. "In a sick and disgusting sort of way." I filled her in on what Father Ben had told me a few days before.

"So, these demons looked like humans? And then they slept with women to make them pregnant with these super nephalim babies?"

"Pretty much," I said. "Although, I guess technically they were still angels when they did it. That's why they got booted."

"Angels or demons," she said, "the whole thing is icky."

I laughed. "And on that note . . ." I stood up. "I'm exhausted. You want me to walk you back to your place?"

"I feel like a six-year-old, but yeah. I do."

I grabbed my purse and shoved an ice pick in my back pocket. Just in case. When we got to the back door, though, I stopped cold. The dead bolt already was turned.

What the hell?

I grabbed the doorknob and turned slowly. The latch gave, and I pushed the door open easily. The alarm didn't beep to signal a breech, and I paused, suddenly fearful. Then I checked the keypad, and relaxed. Stuart had disabled that feature earlier since we had so many people coming and going tonight. After Troy's no-show, he must have forgotten to reset.

"I probably forgot to lock the door behind me," Laura said, correctly reading my concern. "Or Mindy did."

"I want to check the house anyway. Stay here," I said. "I'll be right back."

I scoured the house thoroughly, but found nothing out of place. Not even our daughters, both of whom were fast asleep at the remarkably early hour of eleven.

I finished the upstairs, then made a run through the downstairs before meeting Laura back by the door. "Everything's fine. We probably did just leave it open."

"Sorry," Laura said. "It was probably my fault."

"Don't worry about it. We've been here all evening. So unless we had a very neat thief who decided to walk in very, very quietly while the house was full of people—"

I snapped my mouth shut and looked to Laura. Her hand had flown to her mouth, and I knew she'd realized, too. The unlocked door. The noises I'd heard in the house. They weren't made by the cat. They were made by invisible teenagers, subservient to a demon.

I got to the cathedral in record time, but the cops still got there first. I found Father Ben by the altar, the EMTs already working on him. "Is he okay?"

"He'll be fine," the tall one told me. "We'll take him to the hospital to make sure, but it looks like a mild concussion."

Father Ben reached up and tugged at my hand. "They got the book, Kate. I didn't even see them coming."

"You wouldn't have," I said. I tapped my ring finger and mouthed a single word. *Invisible.*

He closed his eyes and let his head fall back. "Of course," he whispered. "They coldcocked me. I was out for . . . I don't know how long. I checked the altar. Kate, it was gone."

"It's okay," I said. "It's okay. It's not your fault."

No, it wasn't his fault. It was mine. I'd heard them, right there in my house, and I hadn't done a damn thing except tell them exactly what they'd wanted to know.

*   *   *

"**No answer,**" **David said,** then he pounded on the door once again, just for good measure. "Mr. Myerson? Mrs. Myerson? Troy? Is anybody home?" He turned back to me. "Not there."

I nodded and flipped closed the phone that I'd had pressed to my ear. "No one's answering their home phone, either."

"Have you tried Troy's cell?"

"Twice."

"That's it then," he said, taking a seat on the Myersons' front stoop. "Both of the surf captains are missing tonight. I'm betting they stay missing until the exhibition tomorrow."

I sat down next to him and rested my elbows on my knees, then cradled my forehead in my hands. As soon as the ambulance had pulled out of the cathedral parking lot, I'd called Laura to check on the kids and give her an update. All was calm there, which was some good news, I supposed.

Right after that, I'd called David. We'd met at an all-night café on the Coast Highway and I'd brought him up to speed. Fortunately that hadn't taken too long. David's a bright man. He picked up on the high points pretty quickly, then hustled me into his car and we'd started driving the town, checking both of the surf captains' houses.

Nobody was home. Not a surfer, not a parent, not even a pet.

"Do you think the parents are involved?" I asked. "Worse, do you think they're dead?"

David shook his head. "No. I don't think they'd kill them. Our theory is the boys think they're getting something out of this, right? Immortality, money, something. For that, they'll steal, but I don't think they'll kill."

"Right," I said. "They think they'll be around when this is over. You can't spend millions if you're doing time for murder."

Made sense, I thought. And the demons would have tricked the parents to get them out of the way. Make them think they'd won a cruise or an all-expenses-paid vacation. For that matter, it didn't even need to be a trick. Considering the magnitude of Asmodeus's plan, I figured the local demon union would happily kick in for the cost of airfare and hotel.

"Let's patrol," I said. "Maybe we'll coax a demon out of hiding."

The plan made some sense, but it didn't work. We spent the rest of the night walking the beach, walking the boardwalk, walking up and down the streets that made up the touristy, beachfront part of San Diablo.

Nothing.

"Maybe the demons are at the Denny's on the 101," I said. "This town has thirty thousand people. We're patrolling a tiny fraction."

"Or maybe there are only two demons in town right now," David said. "Maybe they can't risk us taking one out."

"Because if they don't have two, the plan can't go forward. You may have a point." I yawned. "Of course, if we'd thought of that before three in the morning, I could have gotten a decent night's sleep." For that matter, I could have made it home before Stuart. I'd left him a voice mail telling him I was going to the hospital to sit with Father Ben, who'd been mugged. I crossed my fingers, hoping Stuart hadn't questioned my message. Or, worse, gone to the hospital to sit there with me.

David and I were all alone on the boardwalk now, and nowhere near the hospital. The lights in the shop windows had flickered out hours ago, and the only illumination now came from the odd streetlamp and the glow of the moon.

"Ready to head back?" he asked.

"Sure," I said. Then, "No. Wait."

"What?" His voice was sharp, alert. "You see something?"

"No, no. I just . . ."

I closed my eyes, feeling stupid.

"Kate?"

I knew I shouldn't open the gate, but I couldn't stop myself. And so I opened my eyes, stared at the ground, and whispered, "Tell me about Eric."

He looked sideways at me, then started walking again, the action so unexpected that I thought maybe he hadn't heard me.

"David?" I hurried to keep step with him. "Did you hear me?"

"Do you love your husband?"

"Stuart? Yes. Of course I do."

He stopped, then looked me up and down. "You didn't even hesitate."

"Well, no. Why would I? It's the truth."

"Then what's the point?"

"The point?" I repeated. And then I understood. My eyes welled, and a tear spilled out.

He brushed it away with his thumb, the intimate gesture making me shiver. "Kate?"

I shook my head, grappling for an explanation. I couldn't find one. "I don't know the point," I said. "I wish I did, but I don't."

He started walking again. This time, I didn't prod. After a while, he spoke again. "I will tell you one thing. He loved you, Kate. He loved you very much. And I think he'd be damn proud of your daughter."

This time, I couldn't stop the tears. I captured his words and held them close. They weren't everything. But for right then, they were enough.

Nineteen

The house was quiet and dark when I got back home, which really isn't that unusual for four-thirty. I crept upstairs and peeked in on the kids. Then I got into bed, this time without waking Stuart, who had left me a single rose and a note saying he'd gotten my message and he hoped Father Ben was doing okay.

The note had warmed me, and I scooted close, pressing against him until he shifted in his sleep and closed his arm around my waist. I fell asleep that way, letting all the confusion drift out of my head, and filling my senses with the scent and feel of my husband.

Morning came all too quickly, which tends to happen when you stay out until four, and I woke to Timmy's insistent "Pick me up, Momma! Pick me up!"

I peered bleary-eyed at my little boy in his Buzz Lightyear pajamas, his hands stretched out for me. "Hey, shortstuff," I whispered.

"Up! Up, up, up!"

"Psh fin yup," Stuart said, which I interpreted as an order to pick the kid up. I did, and Timmy started happily bouncing across the bed while singing the chorus of "Jingle Bells" at the top of his lungs.

Stuart moaned and sat up. He gave me a quick kiss. "How's Father Ben?"

"Doing okay," I said. "Thanks for the rose."

He brushed his finger along my nose. "You'd had a hard day."

"That I had."

Stuart propped himself on his elbow and regarded Timmy. "Hey, little man. You want to go with Daddy to the zoo today?"

That got my attention. "Sweetheart, I can't go to the zoo today."

"Well, that's convenient then. Because this is a man's outing."

"Oh really?" I crossed my arms over my chest as I studied him. "You look like my husband . . ."

"I'm the new and improved model."

"Yeah? I don't recall ordering an upgrade."

"Automatic installation," he said. "The software upgrades when there's a need."

"Is there a need?"

He hooked an arm around my shoulder and pulled me close. "I've been thinking about us. About the kids. And so, yeah. I think there's a need."

"And you're starting with a trip to the zoo. He'll like that," I said, nodding toward our spastic child who'd switched from "Jingle Bells" to the "A, B, C" song.

"We could go to the exhibition, but I thought he'd like this more. And I didn't think Allie would mind if I missed. After the Troy fiasco, I figure she's going to get in, do her cheerleader stuff, and head home."

"I'm sure she won't mind if you miss," I said, not bothering to correct him about the rest. Specifically, that there was no way my daughter was going anywhere near that exhibition.

I slid out of bed and held my arms out for Timmy. "Come on, big guy. Let's get you dressed for your day with Daddy!"

He jumped into my arms with a squeal, and I spun him around. An act which naturally spurred a request for me to spin him again. And again. And again. After the fourth spin, the room was spinning, too, and I sat on the edge of the bed, waiting for it to slow down.

Stuart came to my rescue, hoisting Timmy up onto his hip. "Come on, kiddo. Let's let Mommy collapse in peace."

He paused in the doorway. "I almost forgot. I thought we could get a sitter for tonight, or see if Allie and Mindy want to earn a few bucks."

"What for?"

"I thought we could go see a movie. Hold hands. Eat popcorn."

A little tingle of pleasure shot through me. "What movie?"

"Does it matter?"

His grin was wicked, and I matched it watt for watt. "No, I guess it doesn't."

"So it's a plan then?"

I thought about the plans I already had for the day. Stop Asmodeus. Save the world.

Surely I'd be done by dinnertime.

I looked up at my husband, who looked just as rumpled in his pajamas as my little boy. "Yeah," I said with a grin. "I think I can squeeze you in."

Allie was still asleep when my two guys left, and I didn't bother waking her. Instead, I relaxed in the living room, drinking coffee and reading the newspaper and enjoying the quiet of the near-empty house.

I figured I deserved the downtime. After all, in a few short hours, I'd be up to my neck in demons and minions, trying to keep the vilest demons in history locked tight in Hell where they belonged. I needed to relax and get ready. Not to mention pump myself up with caffeine.

I was on my second cup when Allie barreled down the stairs. "Mom! It's already nine o'clock! How could you let me sleep so long?"

"You seemed tired."

"I *was* tired. But now I'm incredibly late!"

A little finger of worry snaked up my back. "Late? For what?"

"Duh. The exhibition. I've only been working on it for like forever."

"You're going? But I thought . . ."

"What? Troy?" She lifted her chin. "I am so over him."

"Yes, but he's going to be there."

"I'm not a baby, Mom. And I'm not about to give him the satisfaction of not showing up."

"Yeah, Allie," I said. "You are."

She blinked at me. "What?"

"I don't want you going anywhere near that exhibition. Do you understand?"

"Do I understand? No! I don't understand. Mom, I *have* to go."

"No, young lady, you don't." I stood up, working to keep my voice calm and level. "I don't want you anywhere near that boy or near Cool. We talked about this once already."

"God, Mom! All I'm going to do is stand around serving food and perform a couple of cheers."

"No, you're not."

"That's so unfair! Everyone's going to think I'm a total slacker!"

"Then we'll get you a doctor's note. We'll tell them you have Ebola or something, but this is one argument you're not going to win."

She spun around, then stomped up the stairs and disappeared. A few seconds later, the house shook with the force of her slamming door.

Well.

Someday I'd explain how I'd kept her out of harm's way. In the meantime, I figured I'd earn some brownie points by renegotiating my stand on eyeshadow. But later. Right now I needed to get dressed and go to the exhibition that I'd just prohibited my daughter from visiting.

I took a quick shower, got dressed, then gathered my weapons and backpack-style purse. On my way out, I tapped on Allie's door. No answer. I debated, then decided to go on in. "Al?"

The lump on the bed moved.

"Are you still mad at me?"

No answer.

"So I'm getting the silent treatment?"

Still no answer, but the lump moved again.

"Fine. Sulk if you want, but I'm going to go run some errands. Stay home, keep the alarm set, and call Mrs. Dupont if you need anything. Okay?" Eddie was at the hospital with Father Ben, but I'd give him a call from the road and get him to go home and stay with Allie.

A hand emerged from under the blanket, flashing me a thumbs-up sign. I stifled the urge to roll my eyes, then gathered my things, strapping a utility belt on under my leather jacket, and arming myself as best I could without being too obvious.

I was checking the lock on the back door when I noticed two of the water pistols Allie had bought for Timmy.

I grinned, considering the possibilities. And then I opened the door, grabbed the things, and shoved them in my backpack.

I found David in the thick of things, giving directions to a cluster of parent volunteers. He caught my eye, then signaled for me. As soon as he was free, he came over and steered me to a quiet spot.

"Lots of people here," I said. "I'll do what I have to, but I hate having this thing go down in front of so many people."

"Is it too late to cancel?"

"I thought about that yesterday, but what if Asmodeus and the others scatter? At least now, we know where to find them." He frowned. "Or we thought we knew where to find them."

"What do you mean?"

"The surfers were supposed to have been here by now. I'm starting to wonder if we called this wrong."

I turned and looked out toward the sea. At least six kids dotted the horizon, riding the waves. "Aren't they here?"

"Not the captains," he said. "And not Cool."

"Well, hell," I said. "Maybe they're invisible?"

"I don't think so," David said. Honestly, I didn't believe it, either.

"They can't perform the ceremony until noon," I said. "Maybe they're waiting to come at the last minute."

"Or maybe they're somewhere else entirely," David said.

I frowned, but didn't say anything. He was right, of course. But where else would they be? Why plan out this whole thing and not use the beach? Not questions I could answer, and I fought a wave of helplessness. "No," I said. "There has to be a way to figure this out."

With David following in my wake, I headed down toward the surf, staying far enough back from the froth of the incoming waves to keep my shoes dry. One of the team members was climbing out of the water, a wide grin splitting his face. He held his arms out for a blond girl, who applauded and laughed. The blond, I realized, was Susan.

"Susan!" I called out for her, waving my arm over my head to get her attention.

She turned, then smiled broadly when she saw me. She grabbed the boy's hand and the two of them came over. "Hey, Mrs. Connor! Hey, Mr. Long! Did you see that? Wasn't it awesome?"

"Pretty nice," I said.

"Good job, Andy," David said, giving the boy a pat on the back. "I'm impressed."

The boy, who looked to be about Allie's age, blushed furiously. "Thanks. I've been practicing. Too late for today, you know, but I wanted to show Coach that I coulda been a team captain, too, you know?"

"He's *so* much better than Troy Myerson and Brent Underhill," Susan said loyally.

Andy ducked his head. "Nah, those guys are awesome. But I'm doing pretty good."

"You looked great," I said. "And believe me, there are a lot better things than being the team captain." Especially under the circumstances. But talking with Andy had proved one thing to me. The captains had been handpicked. Asmodeus had done his homework, selecting only boys he knew would be susceptible to his suggestions. Andy's sweet temper and modest nature may have kept him from being selected team captain, but it had also kept the eye of a demon off of him.

I would have liked to have told him that, but I didn't

quite know how to phrase it. Instead, I just asked where the team captains and Coach Cool were.

He shrugged and looked at Susan. "Dunno," he said. "They were here at ten. I saw Brent talking with JoAnn. And then the next time I looked for 'em, they were gone."

"Gone where?"

Andy shrugged. "Didn't say. They'll be back soon, though. I mean, we start in about half an hour."

"Why?" Susan added. "Are you looking for Allie?"

"No, Allie's not coming today."

"Sure she is. I saw her with Troy Myerson less than an hour ago."

The force of her words pushed me back, and I think I would have fallen had David not caught my elbow. "Could you say that again?" I asked.

Susan must have realized she'd broken some sort of carpool buddy's secret code, because she fidgeted, clearly uncomfortable. Andy, who I'd already decided was a stand-up guy, stepped up to the plate. "She was talking with Troy Myerson. Giving him a pretty nasty dressing down, actually." He flashed a wide grin. "She's got a mouth on her, Mrs. Connor."

David took a step up. "But you said she left with Troy. Did she look like she wanted to go with him?"

Susan shrugged. "I dunno. I guess so. I mean, she looked a little stiff, but I thought she was probably still just pissed off, you know? Or she's been working out too hard. Or something."

"Where did they go?" I asked, hearing the edge of hysteria in my voice.

"Honestly, I don't know."

I turned to David, who pressed a finger over my lips. "Thanks, guys," he said to the kids. Then he took my arm and led me away, his steps quick and defined. His hand on my arm was hot, and I could feel his panic seeping into my body to mix with my own. She snuck out! Allie had never once disobeyed me! So why did she have to pick today?

Honestly, as soon this was over, she was going to be so grounded.

"Kate?"

I fought back tears, desperately hoping I'd have the chance to ground her.

"I don't get it," I said. "They have the book. They have the human assistants. They have two demons. Why risk coming here? And why take the girls?"

"I don't know," he said, his voice tight.

But I did. All of a sudden, I knew for sure. "Nephalim," I said. "Oh, dear God, when the demons rise up they're going to . . . they want to . . ."

I clenched my fists, unable to give voice to the thought.

David took me by the shoulders and looked into my eyes. "It's not going to happen, Kate, because we're going to stop it."

I nodded. Right. He was right. Allie wasn't even old enough to date. There was no way she was going to end up the single mom of a superhuman demonic baby. No way in hell.

We were just about to climb into David's Jeep when Marissa Cartwright ran toward us. "Kate! Wait!"

"In a hurry, Marissa! I'll be right back." A lie, but she didn't need to know that.

"Wait! I'm trying to find JoAnn!"

I stopped, suddenly overwhelmed with compassion for this woman I didn't much like.

"I don't know where she is," I said honestly.

"The last I saw, she was with your daughter." There was accusation in her voice, and I stiffened against it. I didn't say anything, though. I'd been accusing myself just as harshly.

"I don't know where they are, Marissa. Maybe they're off practicing a cheer."

Her face tightened. "I'd hoped you kept better track of your daughter than you did of poor Mr. Sinclair."

That did it. I stepped forward, every muscle poised to pummel this woman. To tell her that she'd lost track of her daughter, too. And that if she wanted JoAnn safe she needed to get off my back and let me do my job.

I couldn't say any of it, though. I might consider Marissa the spawn of Satan, but I knew in my heart it wasn't literal. And right now she was just a mom who was concerned for her daughter.

I drew a breath and put a soft hand on her arm. "I'm sure JoAnn's fine," I said. "And when I see Allie, I'll be sure to tell her you're looking for her."

That didn't satisfy her, I could see that much in her eyes, but I'd spared as much time for Marissa as I intended.

"Can you take charge of the parent volunteers?" David asked her as I slid into the car. "I need to run a quick errand."

Marissa's face was still pinched, but she nodded. And then, full of newfound power, Marissa marched back toward the exhibition tables.

"Go," I said, but David already had the car started. He backed out of the parking lot and pulled onto PCH.

"Where?"

To that, unfortunately, I didn't have an answer.

While David drove as slowly as he could manage down the Coast Highway, I looked out toward the ocean. Maybe they'd simply gone down the beach, looking for a less crowded spot to perform the ceremony. I saw nothing, though. And, honestly, that didn't feel right.

"Think," I said to myself. "Where could they go to perform a ritual?"

I looked at the clock. Twenty to twelve.

Time was running out.

My cell phone rang, and I snatched it up. *Laura.*

"Allie's gone!" she said without preamble. Then rattled off a story about how she'd come to find Mindy and found her asleep in Allie's room—alone.

I kicked myself, realizing that the lump in Allie's bed had been Mindy. The possibility hadn't even occurred to me.

I cut Laura off, though, because none of that mattered. "She's with Cool," I said. "And we were wrong. The ceremony's not at the beach. We don't know where it is. Can you get online and find every article you can about Cool? Especially after the wipeout?"

"What am I looking for?" she asked.

"I have no idea."

I heard her tapping in the background. "Nothing so far. Just a mention of the exhibition. Involved in the community. Blah blah blah."

"Nothing else?"

"Still looking. Wait. Here's a picture of him and a woman. The caption says she's his girlfriend. Maybe they're at her house?"

"Does it say her name? Can you find an address?"

"Looking."

I fidgeted in my seat, wishing I was there looking over her shoulder. Wishing I was driving. Wishing I was pounding something sharp through that bastard demon Asmodeus's eye. *Anything* but sitting helpless in a car while my baby was in danger.

Allie. Dear God, Allie.

Beside me, David didn't look much better. His mouth was firm, his face hard, and his hands were so tight on the steering wheel his knuckles were pure white.

"Nothing," Laura said. "I can't find a reference to an address, a job or anything. Do you want me to—"

"Wait!" I turned to David. "The Danvers Museum. Head to the museum."

"Kate?" That from Laura.

"Allie said that Cool's girlfriend was a museum docent. That she was mousy, and so he must be a nice guy, because why else would he hang on to a mousy museum docent when he could have a *Baywatch* babe."

"For that matter," Laura said. "Why does a demon need a girlfriend at all?"

"Unless he *needs* her," I said. "The museum's closed until January. But if she can get inside, it would make sense for him to keep her around."

"Yeah," Laura said. "They're setting up for some Macedonian artifact exhibit."

"I saw that exhibit," I said. "One of the display cases was filled with stone tablets covered with geometric shapes."

I was looking at David when I said that. He'd already been flying through town, but now the car seemed to go even faster.

"Call Eddie," I said to Laura. "Tell him and Father Ben what's going on. And," I added, "tell them to pray."

Twenty

There were no cars in the museum parking lot when we arrived, and when we tugged on the front door, we discovered that it was locked.

"We could be wrong," David said.

I looked at my watch and fought a shiver. "No," I said. "We don't have time to be wrong."

I turned around, fighting panic as I looked for something large and heavy. "There," I said, pointing to a large clay planter.

I watched, numb, as David hoisted it, then slammed it against the glass doors.

Nothing. Not even a scratch.

"Goddamn it!" he screamed, as my body turned hot, then cold. I clenched and unclenched my fists against the alternating urge to pummel someone and to curl up into a ball and cry.

As David yanked the door handle and cursed, I looked around, trying to keep my focus and find another way in.

I'd spent half of my life learning to keep calm. To control my emotions. To rein in my fear and use it against my enemies. Those were good lessons, and I dug deep to find that same strength again. Because I couldn't lose control. Not now. Not when Allie needed me.

With sudden decision, I whipped around to David and held out my hand. "Give me your keys."

"What are you——?"

But I'd already taken the keys and was running down the stairs to the parking lot. I jumped into his Jeep, shifted into gear, and gunned the thing. It shot forward, rattling up the stairs just as easily as climbing over a pile of rocks.

On the marble patio, I paused just long enough to fasten my seat belt. David caught my eye, his nod quick and determined. I clutched, shifted, gunned it—then smashed through the front door of the Danvers Museum, sending shards of glass flying and exploding an airbag into my face.

I expected the shrill shriek of an alarm system to pierce the air, but there was nothing, just the oddly hollow sound of the airbag hitting my body and the crunch of glass under David's feet as he raced to me. He threw open the door and took my hand, pulling me out even as I unfastened the seat belt.

We raced into the heart of the museum, me leading the way to where I'd seen the Macedonian display. I hoped it was still there. More, I hoped Allie was.

The second we rounded the corner into the darkened special exhibits room, I saw her, and my heart flooded with relief even as I wanted to scream in terror. There she was, my beautiful daughter, on her knees in front of the open book, her hands tied behind her back. Troy Myerson stood behind her, his expression determined, her ponytail tight in his hand. And beside them both were JoAnn and Brent, similarly positioned as captor and captive.

David grabbed me by the collar and pulled me back to him, hiding both of us in the relative safety of the black drapes that still covered the walls. "Wait," he whispered.

I wanted to struggle, to burst out and rescue my girl, but I knew he was right. We were outnumbered here, and if we went rushing in without a plan, someone might get killed. Someone who wasn't a demon.

Cool loomed large, Creasley at attention beside him. Cool's skin shimmered, the rotting flesh of the demon Asmodeus revealing itself with each beat of his human heart.

He stood directly across from Allie and JoAnn. Both girls were shaking, silent tears streaming down their cheeks.

I wanted to strangle the bastard, to send him back to Hell with my bare hands. It took every ounce of willpower in my body to wait. David's hand closed on my shoulder, a silent reminder that I couldn't jump the gun here. I couldn't let my emotions rule my actions. Not if I wanted to win.

Asmodeus's arms were raised, a stone tablet tight in both hands. Across the room I saw the display case, now a jumble of metal and shattered glass.

The room was still done up in the black velvet drapes, black lights providing the dim illumination that made the whole scenario seem that much eerier and caused the patterns on the tablets to glow.

The demon closed his eyes and started muttering in Latin, words and phrases I didn't understand, but which clearly were working, because the pages on the book suddenly started to flip, as if stirred by a strong breeze.

"Out of time," I whispered. My stiletto was already snug at my wrist, but now I slid it out, engaged the blade, then carefully replaced it in the wrist holster. With the two knives on my belt, that made three. I just needed one more thing.

I slid the backpack from my shoulder, then tugged the drawstring silently open. I took out two pistols and handed

one to David, smiling despite the circumstances at the look
on his face when he saw the SpongeBob image stamped on
the grip.

"Shoot straight," I whispered. Then I burst into the room,
gun blazing, a stream of holy water hitting Cool in the face and
knocking him backwards. More important, it silenced him.

Beside me, David did the same, nailing Creasley with his
steady spray.

The stench of burning demon flesh filled the room, the
putrid odor of sulfur and filth almost overpowering.

I raced toward Allie, her cry of *"Mother!"* echoing around
me, the hysteria in her voice ripping at my heart.

"I'm coming, baby," I yelled. "Hang on."

JoAnn saw me and started screaming, crying out for me
and Mr. Long to save her.

As I watched, Troy jerked Allie's ponytail, pulling her to
her feet. At the same time, his free hand whipped around,
and I saw the flash of metal as he pressed the blade of a knife
against her throat. She looked at me, her eyes wide with fear.

"Stay back!" he yelled. "Hands up, or I swear I'll kill her."

"It's you who's going to die, Troy," I said, keeping my
hands up, my wrists toward me so that he couldn't see my
stiletto. "Whatever they promised you, they're lying. You're
not getting power or immortality or any of that. You're being sacrificed, Troy." I forced my voice to stay level and
calm. I kept my eyes on the boy, trusting David to take care
of everything else. "You're the sacrificial lamb, and you
don't even know it."

"Liar!" he screamed.

Off to my left, I heard Creasley scream in pain as David
got him with another stream of holy water. I saw a flash in
the queer purple light as Creasley pulled a knife of his own,
then rushed David. I stiffened, but I never took my eyes off
my daughter. "David?"

The breathless reply came back almost instantly. "Don't mind me."

I exhaled in relief. I had no intention of leaving Allie. As far as I was concerned, David needed to take care of himself.

JoAnn was screaming hysterically for me, and Troy was yelling for Cool to get up. To do something. To shut me up. Allie, bless her, stayed straight and silent, her chin high and her eyes focused. I'd never been more proud or more terrified. Or, for that matter, more impotent. Because Troy could slice her throat with one quick move, and I didn't have a clue how to keep that from happening.

So I stood there thinking as David battled Creasley and as Cool climbed to his feet. From within the chalk outline of a triangle I could now see on the floor, he seemed to loom over all of us. He looked at me, his piggy eyes blood red. "If she drops her hands," he said, his words like ice, "kill the girl."

Troy nodded shakily, and even from several yards away, I could hear his shallow breathing. "But she's lying, right? I'm mean, like, she's a total liar, isn't she?"

The demon's response was low and harsh. "You doubt my word?"

"No! I . . . I mean, I . . ."

"Silence!" And then the demon began the Latin chant again. I caught only a smattering of recognizable words— Hell, prison, a demand to come forth. I didn't need to hear the words to know what was happening, though. The tablet pulsated, the patterns glowing bright even as the book seemed to come alive. Once again, the pages flipped wildly, and the horrific cries of the damned escaped the pages to echo throughout the room.

Troy gasped, staring at the spectacle even as he tightened his grip on the knife. I could see Allie cringe as the blade pressed against her flesh, and I forced myself to remain still, afraid that even the slightest misstep would push the boy over the edge.

With me stuck like a statue, David stepped into the gap, emptying his pistol onto Asmodeus. But now the demon ignored the pain, barely even flinching when the water cut a path down the oozing red flesh.

A trancelike state had overcome the demon, and as he muttered the incantation, the book began to release the first Tartarus prisoner.

JoAnn saw it first, her high-pitched scream piercing the air. "A claw! Oh, God, *what is going on?*"

Sure enough, a grotesque hand formed of burned and oozing flesh, and with wolflike claws had emerged from the book and was grappling for purchase. Troy saw it, too, and as revulsion registered on his face, I saw his arm go slack.

We might not have a better chance. And we were damn sure running out of time. *"Now!"* I screamed to Allie, and she reacted like a pro, shooting her arm up and out, getting Troy at the wrist and forcing the knife away from her throat. She timed the move perfectly with a backwards head butt. Surprised, Troy spun backwards, but he recovered quickly, leading with his knife as he lunged back toward her.

My little girl had played it smart, though, and the instant she was free, she'd dropped and rolled. And that gave me the opportunity I needed. I shifted the gun to my left hand, then pulled the stiletto out with my right.

Then I sent it flying, hoping what little practice I'd gotten in over the last few months would suffice. The knife plunged into his thigh, and Troy flinched, screaming in pain as he dropped to the ground.

"Bitch!" he cried.

"Go!" I screamed to Allie.

She went, but instead of racing out of the room like I'd hoped, she tackled Brent, knocking the surf captain to the ground. JoAnn screamed and I raced that direction, but by the time I got there, it was all over. Allie had grabbed Brent's head and smashed it back hard against the stone floor. The boy was out.

So, for that matter, was JoAnn, having released one final ear-splitting scream and then dropping into a dead faint.

In front of us, the cause of her scream protruded from the book. A slime-covered head, like something emerging at birth, materialized from the pages, the two hands that had already been released grasping for purchase on the stone floor as the demon struggled for freedom.

"Go!" I said to Allie. I pointed to JoAnn. "Get her out of here, and *stay out!*"

"*What's happening?* What's going—"

"Dammit, Allie! Just *go!*"

She hesitated, the uncertainty on her face almost masking the terror. Then she went, dragging JoAnn by the underarms toward the exit as I emptied the water pistol on the emerging Tartarus demon. The flesh popped and sizzled, but didn't even slow the demon down.

Worse, my pistol was empty. I tossed the useless thing aside, pulled another knife from my belt, and rushed in to do battle with Cool.

He'd retreated into the far corner, and his incantations were louder and faster. If he finished—if he drew out the Tartarus demons—David and I would be dead meat. So, I figured, would most of San Diablo.

His legs were thick and powerful, like an animal's, and while he held the tablet aloft, he kicked at me, the powerful thrusts forcing me backwards toward the book and the Tartarus demons.

I lashed out with the knife, managing to inflict a deep wound, but paying the price when he kicked the knife out of my hand, then landed a solid kick to my ribs, sending me flying.

I landed a few feet from the book, near where Allie and JoAnn had been. Troy, I saw, was gone, having slipped through the far exit. I imagined he was out of the museum right now, running as fast as he could away from this place.

I forced myself not to go after him and punish him for the hell he'd put my daughter through. The threat was still here, and powerful. And if I didn't stop it, Allie would be living a far worse hell very soon.

A few feet away, the Tartarus demon continued to fight his way out. My entire body ached as I crawled toward it, then tried to slam the book shut. I couldn't make it budge.

The claw reached for me, and I jerked back. The demon was still partially in Hell. If he caught hold of me, could he suck me back in with him?

"Kate!"

David's sharp yell cut through the cacophony and had my blood running cold. I rolled over to see David on the floor. The marble tiles were slick with holy water, and as he tried to find purchase to push himself up, Creasley was coming at him, knife at the ready.

"Cane!"

I searched, found it beside me, then slid it across the floor toward David even as Creasley leaped for his attack.

He caught it just in time, running his hand down to knock off the rubber tap at the bottom to reveal a steel point. As Creasley's knife descended, David slammed the cane up, that lethal point sinking deep into Creasley's eye.

The demon escaped to the ether, and the body sagged to the ground. With only one demon left, only one Tartarus demon could escape. That, however, was one too many.

I didn't bother waiting for David; I clamored to my feet

and raced back toward Asmodeus. The Tartarus demon's shoulders were out of the book now, and a puddle of slime was forming on the floor around where he emerged. Soon, he'd be out. And the only foolproof way to stop him was to stop the incantation.

To do that, we needed to kill Asmodeus.

The demon loomed before us, having gained height and bulk as he shed his human form. Open sores oozed with greenish pus and the stench he emanated was almost unbearable. I told myself this was a good thing. A revealed demon is a vulnerable demon. Never mind that he's also a damn strong demon. So long as he stayed outside the human shell, he could be killed. And somehow, David and I were going to do just that.

I rushed in, knowing the move was risky, but needing to land a blow. More, needing the demon to shut up—to stop the incantation. I didn't bother with fancy moves. Instead, I just lunged, burying my last knife in his midsection.

He screamed in pain, one thick leg shooting out to knock me backwards, even as his arms continued to hold the tablets aloft. I landed near Brent's unconscious form, breathless, my knife still stuck in the demon's thick hide.

I'd stopped the incantation, though. For at least a few seconds, I'd slowed the release of Hell upon the earth.

David bought us a few more seconds, rushing into the fray even as I climbed to my feet. I'd lost all three of my knives, and now I looked around for something to use as a weapon. I saw my stiletto shining on the far side of the room, no longer buried in Troy's flesh. I started to dive for it, but stopped when I heard the familiar voice call my name.

"Yo! Katie-girl. Over here!"

I spun, handily catching the super-squirter water pistol that Eddie tossed to me. I hooked the strap over my shoulder, then held up my hand for the sheathed sword that came next.

Only then did I see that Eddie was armed with a squirter of his own. "Now get that son of a bitch."

He aimed and fired, rushing toward the demon with more speed than I would have thought him capable of. As the holy water fired by Eddie cut pus-filled paths on the demon, David and I attacked those vulnerable spots with our weapons.

"The tablet!" I yelled. "It's not the book, it's the tablet!"

But try as we might, we couldn't get to it.

We kept at it until both Eddie and I had emptied the pistols. The incantation had slowed, but the demon was far from defeated. He was huge, vile, and strong as hell. In a nutshell, we were screwed.

I honestly didn't think it could get any worse.

Of course, it did.

"I'll kill her!" Troy's voice filled the room, and I spun around to see my daughter standing terrified, a knife seemingly floating in space pressed tight against her throat. "You let him finish!" the invisible boy shouted. "This is mine! And you can't take it away from me!"

"Hold on there, boy," Eddie said, refilling his squirter from an opaque jug even as Asmodeus started back up with the incantation.

I kept my eyes on Allie, but took a tentative step toward the demon.

"Don't!" Troy called. "I'll do it, I will."

And I believed him. I'd heard that wild hysteria before. The maniacal timbre in the voice of a human who'd been promised wondrous, horrible things. I believed him, and I froze. And if that meant that a demon from Tartarus would be loosed upon the world, then so be it. But I wasn't going to risk my daughter's life just to keep them in Hell.

Beside me, David stood just as still, his face frozen in a mask of fear and determination.

He turned his head slowly, then mouthed a single word to me: *Listen.*

I frowned. Listen to what? The incantation? The boy?

"Finish!" Troy yelled to Asmodeus. "Finish and give me my reward!"

The demon ignored him, never breaking from his chant. And as he chanted, Troy started to reappear. His form fading in and out like poor television reception.

"It's happening, Troy," I said. "Listen to me. Believe me. You're becoming visible because he's abandoning you. That demon on the floor is going to take your place, and you're going to be sucked straight into Hell."

"You lie," he hissed, his revealed face now contorted in pain.

I looked to David to help me out here—to try to convince the boy—but he had his head down and was praying. "Hail Mary, full of grace. The Lord is with you . . ."

I stared. He was praying the Hail Mary? Did that mean—?

A keening wail rose behind me, and I turned to see the demon almost fully emerged from the book. He rocked back on his haunches, black shark eyes aimed toward the ceiling, and his mouth open to release the sounds of torment in Hell. Only a tail remained in the book, just a tiny bit of flesh restraining him from fully entering our world.

I caught Allie's eye, saw both bravery and fear.

"Let her go, you screwed up little pup of a boy." Eddie's voice rang out, filling the room. He held his super squirter at the ready.

"Eddie!" I screamed.

"Idiot!" howled Troy. "You think that holy water's going to do any good against me?"

"Why not?" Eddie said. "You're practically demonic."

And as Troy laughed, Eddie fired. And then, to my

complete amazement, Troy screamed out in pain. Allie didn't waste any time, breaking free from his hold even before I could scream her name.

"Ha!" I heard Eddie say as Allie started demonstrating some of Cutter's more brutal moves on Troy. "Hot sauce. Gets 'em every time."

I'd spun around, and was about to leap on Asmodeus. I had no weapon, but I also had no choice. I had to shut him up. Had to stop that damned incantation.

Before I could leap, though, David cried out for me. "Katie," he called, the tone and inflection of his voice so familiar it ripped my heart in two. "Now!"

I didn't think. I couldn't. I just heard his earlier Hail Mary prayer in my head and saw now that he was looking up toward the light fixture and the caged, fluorescent black light.

The Tartarus demon was almost free, and I ran toward David as if the devil himself were chasing me. In a way, I guess he was.

If I was wrong, we'd crash and burn and the demon would be free. If I was right, we might—*might*—have a chance.

I prayed I was right. And as David grabbed me by the waist and tossed me into the air, I knew my prayers had been answered.

I grabbed the cage and swung out, kicking my legs and praying. Praying *hard.*

Below me, David thrust his cane into the belly of the beast, distracting Asmodeus from what I was doing. And, thank God, it worked. Yes, the demon reared his head back and saw me. But by that time, it was too late. My foot connected with the tablet, and it went flying, landing on the hard marble floor and shattering on impact.

A column of fire shot up from the book, then spun like a whirlwind of fire and damnation before being sucked back down with a *whoosh* into the pages, taking the nearly released Tartarus demon back down with it.

Asmodeus howled in frustration and anger, his clawed hand finding my leg and yanking me free from my precarious grip on the light fixture.

While one hand held my leg, the other grasped my head, and I knew without a doubt that he was about to rip me in two.

I heard Allie scream for me, and below, I saw David swing the sword, and I knew he was aiming to throw it, aiming to cut off the demon's head.

I didn't even have time to pray before the blade was released, flying through the sky toward my captor's neck.

And then, suddenly, I was falling.

I landed with a thud on the ground, then rolled over quickly, expecting to see an oily stain of bile marking the demon's remains.

Instead, I saw Cool.

The demon had changed back at the last minute, transforming out of his vulnerable state. He was on the ground, as shocked and breathless as I. But not for long. I threw myself on him, and before he could gather the strength to toss me off, I grabbed one of the shards from the broken tablet, and jammed it right into his eye.

The demon left in a puff and I fell backwards onto the floor, with barely enough energy to call for my daughter.

She was at my side in an instant. "What's happening, what's happening?" She repeated the question, over and over, as I stroked her hair and told her, "It's okay. It's okay. It's over. It's okay."

We held each other like that, rocking and crying until we couldn't stand it anymore.

"Come on, kiddo," I finally said, pressing my hands to

her cheek and looking into her eyes. "Let's go. It's over. It's finally over."

Except it wasn't over. Not really. In fact, if anything, I think it was just the beginning.

Afterward, we stood in the flashing lights from a dozen police cars and told our story to the officers who were trying to make sense of what happened. Brent and Troy had been hauled away, arrested on charges of kidnapping, with more charges—related to the drug cult David and I had hinted at—sure to come.

JoAnn had been taken to the hospital, unable to remember anything past leaving the beach with the boys. The paramedics assured her and Marissa that her memory would return. I had to wonder, though. In my experience, when an encounter with a demon creates hysterical amnesia, the mind usually stays blank. Frankly, I think that's a good thing.

Marissa rode in the ambulance to the hospital, and I promised to drive her car back to my house. She'd nodded a quick thank-you, then wiped away the tears that had battled through her defenses. Then she'd reached over and hugged me. Tight.

I didn't ask, but I had a feeling that marker I owed her had been satisfied.

We'd had very little time to talk before the police arrived, but the story David and I had come up with was that we'd learned that the boys were involved in some weird cult rituals. When we learned they'd taken Allie and JoAnn, we'd gone after them. We probably should have called the police right away, but we weren't thinking clearly.

So far, at least, the police seemed to be buying it.

My daughter, though . . .

She'd seen enough to know that our story didn't quite match reality. So far, we hadn't had the chance to talk, and I still wasn't sure what I was going to tell her. About me, or about what happened in the museum. I wanted to protect her from the truth, but sometimes you have to take the blinders off and let your kids see reality.

I'd reached that point with Allie. It was time she knew the truth about my life. It was, after all, her life, too.

I looked over to where she was talking with David and shivered, wondering suddenly about my own definition of truth. The Hail Mary maneuver. The tone of his voice. His urgent cry of *Katie* in that oh, so familiar voice.

I brushed away a tear. I'd learned a few truths today, too. Of that, I was certain. But I wasn't at all certain what I was going to do about it.

And what, I wondered, was he talking about with Allie? I took a step that direction, my stomach tight as I thought about the things David could be telling her. But I was held back by the gentle press of a hand on my shoulder.

"Hold off there," Eddie said.

"But he might—"

"Won't do it," Eddie said. "Do you really believe he'll tell the girl anything you don't want her to know?"

I thought about that, relaxing a bit when I realized that Eddie was right. Whatever his name, the man she was talking to would never do an end run around me. For better or for worse, with regard to matters demonic, I was the only parent Allie had. And the decisions to be made were mine alone.

I squared my shoulders and joined them. Allie immediately sagged against me. David gave her a quick hug, then aimed a smile my direction. "I'll let you two talk," he said, then stepped away.

"Wait!"

He turned back, a question in his eyes. I didn't want to leave Allie's side, but I had to talk to him. "Allie, I need to—"

"I'm gonna sit," she said, then moved to the steps. I watched her for a second, then turned back to face David, not sure what I wanted to say, or what I wanted to hear.

"Kate?"

"That move," I blurted. "The Hail Mary. How did you know?"

He studied my face. "Eric told me," he finally said. He looked away, focusing on something over my shoulder. "I'd forgotten, but your crash landing at Cutter's reminded me."

"That's it?" I didn't believe him. Not for a minute.

He looked me in the eye. "Is there some other answer you'd prefer?"

My breath hitched in my throat as I thought about that. Thought about my life and my husband and my little boy. One word, and my family would change forever. That wasn't a decision I could make. Not right then. Maybe not ever.

"No," I said, my voice thick with tears. "Thank you."

His smile was warm, but his eyes were sad. "Anytime, Katie-kins."

He turned away then, leaving me shaky and not at all sure I'd done the right thing.

I took a deep breath to steady myself, then turned and walked to Allie. "I'm sorry I snuck out," she whispered. "Am I grounded?"

"We'll talk about it later," I said, baffled by the wonders of the teenage mind. Everything that had happened over the last few hours, and she was worried about being grounded?

She nodded, apparently satisfied, then tugged at a loose thread on the knee of her jeans. "So, where's Stuart?"

"They're sending a patrol car for him. He sounded too freaked out on the phone. I didn't want him driving." I'd also wanted to buy a few extra minutes, but I really had been worried. I could just see the pileup on the highway from Stuart breaking every traffic law to get to us.

"Oh." The thread came loose, and she wrapped it around her index finger, cutting off the circulation until the tip turned pink. "So he'll be a little while getting here?"

I looked at my watch. "Probably a few minutes more." I asked her why, but, honestly, I didn't really need to.

She lifted a shoulder. "I dunno. So, like, do you remember that conversation we had on the way to Los Angeles? The one about secrets?"

Even though I'd been expecting it, I stiffened. "Yeah, baby. I remember."

"I think you've got some secrets, too, Mom," she said, looking me in the eye for only an instant before dropping her gaze back down to her hands. "Do you?"

I drew in a breath, let it out. "Yes, Allie. I have a few."

She nodded slowly, as if considering that. And this time when she looked at me, her gaze didn't waver. "Well, then, Mom, I think it's time. I think it's time for you to tell me your secrets."

"Yeah," I said, feeling surprisingly giddy as I wrapped my arm around her shoulder and pulled her close. "It is."

AVAILABLE FROM BERKLEY

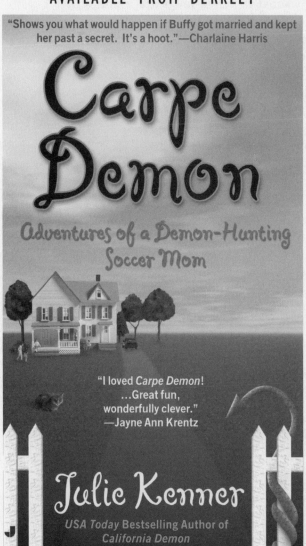

"Shows you what would happen if Buffy got married and kept her past a secret. It's a hoot."—Charlaine Harris

Carpe Demon

Adventures of a Demon-Hunting Soccer Mom

"I loved *Carpe Demon*! ...Great fun, wonderfully clever." —Jayne Ann Krentz

Julie Kenner

USA Today Bestselling Author of California Demon

0-425-20252-6